Mermaids Singing

Dilly Court grew up in North East London and began her career in television, writing scripts for commercials. She is married with two grown up children and three grandchildren, and now lives in Dorset on the beautiful Jurassic Coast with her husband and large, yellow Labrador called Archie. *Mermaids Singing* is her first novel.

Dilly Court

Mermaids Singing

arrow books

Published by Arrow Books in 2006

18

Copyright © Dilly Court 2005

Dilly Court has asserted her right under the Copyright, Designs and
Patents Act, 1988 to be identified as the author of this work

First published in the United Kingdom in 2005 by Century

Arrow Books

Addresses for companies within The Random House Group Limited
can be found at: www.randomhouse.co.uk/offices.htm

The Random House Group Limited Reg. No. 954009

www.randomhouse.co.uk

A CIP catalogue record for this book
is available from the British Library

Typeset by SX Composing DTP, Rayleigh, Essex

Penguin Random House is committed to a sustainable future for
our business, our readers and our planet. This book is made from
Forest Stewardship Council® certified paper.

Printed and bound in Great Britain by Clays Ltd, Elcograf S.p.A.

Dedicated to my mother,
Delysia Sylvia Cox 1919 – 1997.

Chapter One

A long shadow fell across the muddy foreshore, jolting Kitty out of her daydream. A vicious clout round her ear sent her tumbling off the empty orange crate where she had perched, dabbling her bare feet in a pool of water warmed by the setting sun. Her mind had been far away from the city stench, the flapping, russet sails of the Thames barges, the hoots and throbbing engines of the steam ships. The gnawing hunger growling away in her belly had deafened her to the shouts of the lightermen and stevedores. She hadn't heard the squelch of booted feet coming up behind her until it was too late, and she landed face down in the stinking mud, yelping with pain.

'Bloody idle little slut.'

Grabbed by her hair, Kitty was jerked to her feet and shaken until her teeth rattled.

'I weren't shirking, Sid,' Kitty cried, spitting out a mouthful of foul-tasting mud streaked with blood. Her eyes watered as he swung her by the hair, but she knew it was useless to struggle. Her brother-in-law's breath reeked of stale beer and tobacco; the smell of Billingsgate Fish Market clung to his clothes and hands.

'Give it me.' Sid shook her again like a terrier with a rat. 'Hand it over or you'll be sorry.'

'It's for Maggie and your nippers. Me sister'll skin us alive if I doesn't bring something home.'

'And I'll give you what for if you don't, so give it here!'

A fist bigger than a bunch of bananas, thrust in her face, was enough to convince Kitty and she fumbled in her skirt pocket.

Sid let her go and, prising her fingers apart, he tipped the coins into his palm. 'That all?'

Kitty backed away from him. She pointed to a small pile of artefacts that had taken a whole day of back-breaking work to dredge from the silt, leaving her fingers mottled and swollen like beef sausages and her feet corpse-white, wrinkled and tingling with chilblains.

Grunting and swearing, Sid kicked out at the stack of empty bottles, broken clay pipes and potsherds. 'Not worth tuppence, the lot.' Raising his arm, Sid fisted his hand for a punch that never landed. Air exploded from his lungs as a bullet-shaped head butted him in the ribs, pitching him backwards into a shallow pool.

'Run for it, Kitty.'

For a split second Kitty stared at Jem, open-mouthed with shock, but a furious bellow from Sid, flailing about on his back like an upturned beetle, brought her frozen limbs back to life. Bundling her skirts up around her thighs, she pelted after Jem, her bare feet skimming over the stones. Agile as an organ grinder's monkey, she raced up the slippery wooden steps that led to Sugar Quay. Reaching the top and glancing over her shoulder, she saw Sid, clasping his belly and gasping for breath.

'That'll learn him,' Jem said, chuckling.

'You'll be laughing on the other side of your face if he catches up with you, Jem Scully.' But Kitty couldn't help grinning now that she was out of Sid's reach, even though it made her lip bleed again.

'Get on home. Quick!' Jem jerked his head in the direction of Sugar Alley, giving Kitty a gentle shove.

Kitty hesitated, curiosity getting the better of her. 'What you doing here then? Why ain't you working on the lighters?'

'I've had enough of that lark. I'm off down the docks to find a ship's master what'll take me on.'

'That's daft. You're too young.'

'Nah! I can pass for sixteen, easy.'

Her ear was aching, but a new pain shot to her heart, and Kitty bit back tears. She had known Jem all her life; they had gone to the same school and he was her best friend. How could he talk about leaving and look so cheerful? 'You'll get drownded like your dad.'

'Not me! I'm going to be a master like me old man and I'm going to make enough money to pay the doctor's bills for our Polly. Then Ma won't have to take in commercial travellers no more and –' Jem stopped, turning to Kitty, his eyes shining with inspiration – 'and you can come and live with us.'

'Ta, but I couldn't leave Maggie and the nippers, not with Sid spending all his wages in the boozer.'

'And knocking you about when he's had a bellyful. You got to get away from Sugar Yard.'

'And I will,' Kitty said, lifting her chin. 'I've told you afore, Jem. I'm going to be a lady what works in a dress shop up West.'

'Not like that you ain't,' Jem said, pointing at her bare feet. 'Tell you what, though, Kitty. With me first pay packet I'll buy you a pair of shoes and maybe a frock too, then you can go up West with your head held high and get yourself that fancy job.'

For a happy moment, Kitty had forgotten all about Sid, but a loud roar from behind her made her spin around. Cursing and swearing, Sid heaved himself onto the quay wall.

Shoving Kitty behind him, Jem clenched his fists, dancing about on his toes like a boxer. 'Pick on someone your own size, you drunken old bastard.'

'Stop it,' Kitty cried, tugging at his arm. 'He'll murder you.'

Jem continued to prance about, shouting insults as Sid stumbled onto the cobbles. 'Get off home, Kitty. He won't catch me.'

One look at Sid's purple face was enough to convince Kitty; she turned and ran.

At the end of a narrow alley slit between blackened warehouse walls, Sugar Yard opened into a small square festooned with lines of washing that hung, like tattered flags, dripping a permanent mist of rain onto the cobbles.

Maggie and Sid Cable rented two rooms in the four-storey building. One privy in the back yard served the whole house, and sewage pooled after a rainstorm, or if there was an unusually high tide. The smell of boiled fish and cabbage hung in a damp cloud and cockroaches scuttled across the floorboards, disappearing into cracks and knotholes. Kitty was not scared of roaches, spiders or mice, but she did hate the big black rats that slunk past, glaring at her with bold, red eyes. She raced up the stairs and hurled herself against the door.

Maggie was kneeling by the fire, coaxing heat from a smouldering pile of coal dust. Her eyes widened as she took in Kitty's dishevelled condition. 'Look at the state of you. What happened?'

'I fell over.'

Maggie struggled to her feet, stepping over

three-month-old baby Harry, who was lying on the rag rug, kicking his bare legs in the air and gurgling. She took Kitty by the chin, staring suspiciously at her bruises. 'You fell onto someone's fist, by the looks of things. You haven't been cheeking Sid, have you?'

Kitty shook her head. 'No, honest I didn't. He's been on the booze.'

Maggie's face crumpled like a wizened apple. 'He promised, he swore he'd bring his pay packet home. Is he far gone?'

'He took the five pence I'd found.'

'Dear God!' Maggie cried, scooping Harry up in her arms, rocking him and rubbing her cheek against his downy head. 'It'll be the Sally Army soup kitchen for us next week. I'll not be able to hold me head up in Sugar Yard for the shame of it.'

'Don't get upset, Maggie,' Kitty said, patting her shoulder. 'I'll go down to the river first thing. Pickings should be good after a high tide. It'll be all right, you'll see.'

'It'll never be right,' Maggie said, settling Harry in the drawer that served as his cot. 'Once the drink gets a man there's no hope.'

'I'll get a job in the flourmill or the match factory. It pays better than the mudlark game.'

'And end up with ruined lungs or phossy jaw? Never, not while I've got a breath left in my body,' Maggie said, snapping upright. 'I promised our ma on her deathbed that I'd take care of you and I'll not go back on it for a few bob a week.'

'I'm fourteen now – maybe I could get a job in a dress shop up West. I'd give all me money to you afore Sid could get his maulers on it.'

Maggie cast her a pitying glance. 'D'you think they'd give a second look to a poor little cow in raggedy clothes, without a decent pair of shoes to her name?'

'I'll do it somehow, Maggie. One day I'll make you proud of me.'

'That's as maybe, but you'd best eat your bit of bread and scrape and be in bed before he comes home.' Maggie thumped her hand on the wall as muffled giggles echoed through the thin partition. 'And you kids better go to sleep right now or there'll be ructions.'

Kitty tiptoed into the room that she shared with the children, slipped off her top clothes and lay down on the straw-filled mattress, avoiding the damp patch where Frankie had wet the bed. Billy and Charlie, arranged top to toe as neat as sardines in a tin, snored softly, and two-year-old Violet snuggled up to Kitty like a warm puppy.

A jagged shaft of moonlight filtered through the cracked windowpane and, staring up into the night sky, Kitty imagined herself climbing that star-bright stairway to a heavenly place. Ma and Pa and her five baby brothers were already there, safe inside the Pearly Gates. She could barely remember what Ma and Pa looked like after all this time, but Ma had smelled nice, just the same as the violets sold on street corners up West. Pa had a husky voice and his moustache had tickled when he kissed her good night. Kitty closed her eyes with a sigh; up there, in the blue velvet sky, bedbugs didn't bite, bellies were always full, and you didn't get belted for nothing.

Next day Jem was waiting for her on the quay wall.

Kitty's heart fell as she saw his triumphant grin. 'You done it then?'

Jem tossed his cap up in the air and caught it with a whoop of glee. 'I done it, Kitty. And guess what? Me dad's old friend Captain Madison has agreed to take me on as a deck apprentice, and we're sailing on the tide for New Zealand.'

Kitty tried to smile even though a lump the size of an egg was sticking in her throat. 'New Zealand! That's on the other side of the world.'

'Don't I know it? I've got a berth on one of them new refrigerated steam ships, the *Mairangi*, bound for Auckland.' Jem hesitated, frowning. 'Don't look like that, Kitty. Ain't you happy for me?'

'What does your ma say?'

'She'll be pleased as punch,' Jem said, grabbing

Kitty's hand. 'Come with me now and see her face when I gives her the good news.'

Betty Scully covered her face with her apron, let out a low moan and sank down on the nearest kitchen chair.

'That's the ticket, Ma,' Jem said cheerfully. 'You'll soon get used to the idea.'

'You're not to go. D'you hear me, Jem? I won't allow it.'

Jem tweaked the material off her face and planted a kiss on her cheek. 'Now, now old girl, don't take on. You always knew I'd go sooner or later.'

'The sea took my Herbert away from me and now you're going too. I can't bear it.'

'Now see what you've done!' Kitty said, frowning. 'I don't call that breaking it gently.'

Jem's grin faded. 'Look, Ma. I'm a man now and I'll not stand by idle while you turn our home into a lodging house. You've fair worked yourself to a shadow, taking in commercial gents, not to mention spending your evenings sewing dresses and shirts until your fingers are red raw and your eyes pop out.'

'Jem, I done it all for you and Polly, just as your father would have wanted.'

'I know you have, but I've made up me mind. I'm going to sea with Captain Madison – you always said you liked him, Ma – and I've made

9

an allotment to you from me wages. I'll send home more if I can.'

'Oh, Jem!' Betty said, taking off her spectacles and wiping her eyes on the corner of her apron. 'You're a good boy. I don't know what I'll do without you.'

'I'll send you postcards and write you letters.'

Kitty shook her head at him. He might at least try to sound sorry he was leaving.

'I'll get my gear and be off,' Jem said, making for the door.

'You'll say goodbye to your sister first,' Betty said, rising unsteadily to her feet. 'You'll tell our Polly face to face. I'm not going to be the one to break her heart.'

'She'll understand.'

Exchanging anxious glances, Kitty and Betty followed Jem up the narrow staircase. A huge brass bedstead dominated the sitting room on the first floor. The walls and every available surface were covered with mementoes of Captain Scully's voyages and a watercolour of his ship, the *Belvedere*, hung over the bed. It made Kitty shudder to look at a painting of the ship that had gone down in the China Seas, taking the captain and the whole ship's complement to a watery grave. It was hard to imagine how Mrs Scully and Polly could fall asleep beneath such a grim reminder.

Polly lay on the sofa, her wasted limbs covered

by a crocheted blanket. She opened her eyes as Jem sat down beside her.

'I've got to go away for a bit, Poll,' Jem said, stroking her hair back from her forehead.

Polly made a guttural noise in her throat and rolled her eyes.

'I knowed you'd understand, Poll,' Jem said, planting a smacking kiss on her cheek. 'I'll be back soon and I'll bring you lots of presents.'

'Poll is going to miss him ever so much,' Betty said, clutching Kitty's arm. 'You will come and visit often, won't you, ducks? You'll help to keep her mind off things.'

Kitty swallowed hard and nodded. If she stayed much longer she was going to bawl her eyes out. 'I'll come when I can, but I got to go now or Maggie will be after me.' Awkwardly, she laid her hand on Jem's shoulder. 'Bye Jem,' she said, choking on a sob. 'Come home safe.'

Kitty didn't stop running until she skidded on the wet cobbles of Sugar Yard. Mrs Harman, who lived on the ground floor, and the Widow Blacker, who had one room for herself and her six children in the attic, sat on upturned beer crates, smoking roll-ups and chatting. Maggie's boys and the Blacker kids were rolling on the ground, play-fighting, snapping, snarling and yelping just, Kitty thought, as Mr Rudyard Kipling had described the lion cubs in *The Jungle*

11

Book, a story that Miss Draper had read out loud to the class at school. Maybe it was stories of India and far-off places that had given Jem the wanderlust; sighing, Kitty crept past Mrs Harman and the Widow Blacker. They were too busy gossiping to notice her and Kitty was glad of that; her heart was too full of sadness to want to speak to anyone.

'Where've you been?' demanded Maggie. 'I got to go to the corner shop for some tea and sugar. Violet's gone down with a bit of a fever and I need you to keep an eye on baby.'

Kitty was suddenly nervous. 'You won't be long?'

'I'll be as long as it takes. What's the matter with you?'

'Nothing,' Kitty said, looking away. If she told Maggie that she didn't want to be here alone when Sid got back from work it would only make her angry.

'Good, then I'll be off,' Maggie said, wrapping her shawl around her shoulders. 'If Violet wakes up, give her a drink of water.' She went out, slamming the door behind her.

As soon as the door shut, Harry began to howl and Kitty picked him up, walking him up and down until he fell asleep against her shoulder. She laid him gently in his bed and was about to check on Violet when she heard the creaking protest of the bottom stair tread. Feeling her hackles rise in fear, she held her breath, her ears pricked like a hunted animal, listening for the telltale clumping sound of booted feet and the thud of a drunken body lurching from wall to wall. Frozen to the spot, her heart racing, Kitty stood poised for flight but it was too late; the door burst open, screaming on its hinges, and Sid staggered in.

'Where's Maggie?'

'Gone to the shop,' Kitty said, swallowing convulsively. He'd been drinking – she could smell it from here – but how much? It was hard to tell, as he never seemed completely sober these days. 'She'll be back in a tick.'

'I want me dinner.'

'I'll do it.' Kitty reached into the bread crock, taking out the stale crust of yesterday's loaf. She could feel Sid watching her as she sliced the bread, scraping on dripping with a shaking hand. Just lately, even when he was comparatively sober, Sid had been looking at her funny, and last week he'd made her sit on his knee. She'd been too scared to refuse, even when he put his hand under her skirt, running his fingers up the inside of her leg. Maggie had come into the room just then and Sid had pitched Kitty onto the floor, saying it was just a game. Kitty knew it wasn't a game and she had desperately wanted to tell Maggie, but somehow she couldn't. What he'd done was wrong, she knew that, but her shame was mixed with terrible guilt.

13

Sensing that Sid was looking at her, Kitty glanced up nervously. His gaze was fixed on her chest at the exact spot where the top button was missing off her blouse. Her hand flew to her neck, clutching the material together, as she gave him his supper.

Dashing the tin plate from her hand, Sid caught her by the wrist, dragging her towards him. 'You're a good girl really, Kitty,' he said in a strange, thick voice. 'And you're growing up fast.'

Finding strength in desperation, Kitty wrenched herself free. 'You'll be wanting a cup of tea,' she said, backing towards the door. 'I'll go and see if Mrs Harman has got a drop of hot water to make a brew.'

'Come here and don't be a silly little girl,' Sid said, baring his teeth in a smile that didn't reach his eyes. 'I'll not hurt you, Kitty.'

Kitty made a dive for the door but Sid was too quick for her and, pinning her against the wooden panels, he caught her by the throat. 'You be nice to me, Kitty, or you'll be sorry.'

'Let go of me.' Kitty's voice shook and she was trembling, but she raised her chin, glaring at him.

'Didn't know you had it in you, girl,' Sid said, with a feral snarl. 'I like a bit of spirit.'

Kitty spat in his face.

'Bitch.' Sid slapped her cheek, snapping her head back against the door panel. Kitty opened her mouth to scream but Sid shoved his shoulder against her face, pinning her to the door as he ripped her blouse open to the waist. His work-roughened hand groped beneath her skirt, raking his fingers up her thigh, probing into the soft, secret place between her legs with savage thrusts that sent daggers of pain shooting through her body.

Kicking and struggling, Kitty gasped for air. 'Get off me.'

'Shut up, whore. You know you want it.' Sid struck her across the mouth.

Tasting blood, Kitty thought for a moment that she was going to faint but Sid was forcing her legs apart. She could feel him fumbling with the buttons on his trousers; the bristles on his chin scraped down her neck and his tongue rasped the soft flesh of her breasts. Rage and revulsion replaced terror and, acting purely on instinct, she drew up her knee and caught him hard between his legs. Sid let out a howl of agony and doubled up on the floor, groaning. Harry was bawling but Kitty was too panic-stricken to go to him and, wrenching the door open, she fled down the stairs.

Stumbling blindly out of the building, Kitty was grabbed by the scruff of the neck. Sobbing and clutching the torn shreds of her blouse in a feeble attempt to cover her naked breasts, Kitty found herself looking into Mrs Harman's pale, coffee-coloured eyes. Mrs Harman barked an order at the eldest boy to keep an eye on the younger ones and half dragged, half carried Kitty into her own living room.

'I could see it coming,' Mrs Harman said, slapping a wet rag over Kitty's blackened eye. 'I tried to warn Maggie but she wouldn't have none of it.'

Shivering uncontrollably, Kitty couldn't stop crying; couldn't speak for pain and shame.

Mrs Harman cocked her head on one side, listening. 'Let's hope that's your sister coming. I got a few words to say to her.' She marched to the door and wrenched it open. 'Maggie! Come in here!'

'What's up?'

Mrs Harman stood aside, jerking her head in Kitty's direction. 'See for yourself.'

'Kitty! My Gawd, who done this to you?' Maggie cried, dropping her packages on the floor as she ran to Kitty, falling on her knees beside her.

'Don't be a fool, Maggie Cable,' Mrs Harman said, closing the door with a bang. 'You know very well who done it.'

Maggie turned on her. 'I dunno what you mean.'

'Only one man went up them stairs and it weren't the tallyman. Your Sid half killed the girl, by the looks of her.'

'My Sid's got a weakness for the drink but he'd never lay a finger on Kitty or the nippers.'

'And I suppose she done that to herself, did she?'

Maggie caught hold of Kitty by the shoulders. 'Tell me who done this to you. It weren't Sid. You tell her, Kitty.'

'He done it,' Kitty said, and began to retch.

'She don't know what she's saying,' Maggie said, jumping to her feet. 'You tell me the truth now, you wicked girl.'

'Hey, there,' Mrs Harman said, grabbing Maggie's arm. 'Leave her alone. Can't you see she's telling the truth? Why are you standing up for him, Maggie, when you know he's a drunken sot?'

'I ain't got no choice.' Maggie broke away from her, trembling visibly as she snatched up the brown paper packets. 'If they put Sid in the clink, me and the nippers will end up in the work-house.'

'Maggie!' Kitty struggled to her feet, but a wave of dizziness swept them from beneath her, and she slumped back on the stool, holding her head in her hands. 'I never did nothing wrong, I swear it.'

'You was the youngest,' Maggie cried, tears welling in her eyes. 'You don't remember, but I seen our five little brothers taken off by want and sickness afore they was out of petticoats. They're

17

lying in the churchyard, buried alongside our mum and dad, with not even a headstone to mark their graves. I'll not let that happen to my babies.'

'It won't,' cried Kitty. 'I'll help. Don't send me away.'

Maggie backed towards the door, clutching the packets to her chest. 'You can't never come home, Kitty. I done my best by you but you're almost growed up now and you got to make your own way.'

'I thought better of you, Maggie,' Mrs Harman said, hooking her arm around Kitty's quivering shoulders. 'What's to become of the poor little cow if you throw her out on the street?'

'I c-can't help it. I can't risk having her under my roof a moment longer. I'm sorry, Kitty.' Maggie ran from the room and her footsteps echoed up the staircase, followed by the thud of the door slamming behind her.

The sound echoed in Kitty's head, every bone in her body ached, and the room was spinning around her. If Maggie had stuck a knife into her heart it couldn't have hurt more. This couldn't be happening, it was a nightmare, and any moment she would wake up on the crowded mattress with the children snuggled up beside her.

'Kitty, d'you hear me?'

Mrs Harman was shaking her, heaving her up

off the stool and wrapping something warm and tickly around her shoulders.

'You can't stay here, ducks, and you can't go home.'

Kitty opened one eye but the other remained stubbornly closed. There was someone moving about the room and she was in a strange bed. Jack-knifing into a sitting position, Kitty opened her mouth to scream as the terrifying events of the previous evening came back to punch her in the belly.

'Hush now, you're all right, ducks.'

Wrapped in a motherly hug, Kitty was vaguely aware of the comforting scent of Sunlight soap, tea and hot buttered toast. 'Betty?'

'Yes, it's me,' Betty said, perching on the edge of the bed. 'You're safe here in my house. I won't let no one hurt you.'

'He'll come and get me,' Kitty whispered.

'He won't dare. You got to put it all out of your head now.'

'It weren't my fault, but Maggie said it was.'

'Maggie knows what's what, she just don't want to admit it.' Betty stood up, dropping a kiss on Kitty's forehead. 'Don't cry, love, you'll waken Polly.'

For the first time, Kitty realised that she was sharing the bed with Polly, who lay on her back, snoring gently. 'You give up your bed for me?'

Pouring water from a jug into a flower-patterned bowl on the washstand, Betty smiled. 'You was in such a sorry state, I thought you'd sleep best in the big bed. Now you get yourself cleaned up and don't disturb Poll, or I'll never finish getting my commercial gentlemen off to business.'

Kitty nodded, her lips were still swollen and her jaw ached, making it almost impossible to speak, but somehow she managed to slither off the bed and hobble to the washstand.

'You'll need something to wear,' Betty said, bustling over to a chest and opening a drawer. 'I had to burn those rags you came in. They was alive, God bless you.'

'I don't want to be no trouble.'

'Lord love you, ducks. I'm only doing what any right-minded person would do.' Betty riffled through the neatly folded garments and, taking out a faded cotton frock, she laid it on the bed. 'This is one of Polly's and it might be a bit short on you but it'll have to do for the moment. D'you think you can manage to dress yourself?'

Kitty nodded, too choked by tears to answer. Betty's motherly kindness was almost over-whelming, but it couldn't erase the memory of the nightmare events of yesterday.

Betty gave her a hug. 'Don't take on so, Kitty.'

'S-sorry,' Kitty said, wiping her eyes on her

sleeve. 'I c-can't stop c-crying and y-you've been so k-kind to me.'

'Stuff and nonsense, ducks! I love you like one of my own.' Betty fumbled in the pocket of her apron and brought out a clean cotton hankie, handing it to Kitty. 'Dry your eyes and you get yourself dressed while I go downstairs and make the breakfasts for my gentlemen.'

For the first few days, Kitty jumped at the slightest sound, hiding under the bed every time someone knocked at the front door in case it was Sid, come to get her. She kept well away from Betty's commercial gentlemen; the mere sound of a male voice was enough to make her tremble from head to foot. Her cut lips made eating difficult but she had little or no appetite and Maggie's furious, frightened face haunted her dreams. Above all, Kitty missed the children and somehow she couldn't stop blaming herself for what had happened. Maggie had said it was her fault and she was lost in a pea-souper of guilt and shame. Betty had promised she would sort everything out but Kitty couldn't see how things were ever going to come right again. She had lost her home and her family. Her sister might have a sharp tongue and a quick fist, but Maggie had brought her up like a mother, and now she must hate her. The future was a terrifying place, full of shadows and loneliness. Although Kitty's bruises had begun to fade and her body was healing, no amount of kindness from Betty, or unspoken sympathy from Polly, could take the pain from her heart. Added to all this, her inability to contribute any money to the household made Kitty feel that she was a financial burden on Betty.

Fear of Sid kept Kitty housebound. Working as a mudlark was out of the question, but she tried to repay Betty by helping with the household chores. In the evenings, she struggled by candlelight, learning to sew a straight seam. Betty's true trade was that of seamstress but, without the money to purchase a sewing machine, and with hands gnarled with rheumatics, she could barely make enough from dressmaking to feed herself and Polly, let alone pay the doctor's bills. Taking in commercial travellers helped to keep food on the table, but with Kitty now sleeping in the attic room, Betty had only two letting rooms. Even allowing for Jem's allotment from the New Zealand Shipping Company, money was tight. It hurt Kitty to know this, and her heart ached to see Betty sitting at the kitchen table night after night, straining her tired eyes, as she attempted to balance her household accounts. Life in Tanner's Passage was hard enough, but far removed from the grinding poverty of Sugar Yard. Kitty knew that she could not live off Betty's charity for much longer. She would have to find work, even if it meant selling matches or bootlaces in the street.

Curled up on the window seat, Kitty snipped the thread as she finished sewing buttons on an afternoon dress for one of Betty's clients, the wife of a prosperous silversmith who lived in Shoreditch. The sensual feel of the grey tussore beneath her fingers sent thrills of pleasure rippling through her veins. It was the most beautiful garment that Kitty had ever seen and she rubbed it against her cheek. One day she would work in a dress shop up West, even if she had to sleep beneath the counter at night and spend the day picking up pins and bits of cotton thread. Up West, bright lights twinkled like boiled sweets; everyone wore shoes or boots, and ladies smelt of perfume and powder. Up West, people didn't scratch all day from fleas and lice; rats kept to the sewers below the streets and you didn't stumble across stiffs frozen to death in back alleys and shop doorways.

Glancing at Polly, just to make sure she was still sleeping peacefully on the sofa, Kitty allowed her gaze to wander down below to the bustling crowds in Tanner's Passage; sailors, stevedores, costermongers, beggars and street urchins jostled each other as they went about their business. It was almost dusk, too early for the drunks and street women, but high time that Betty returned home. She had gone out earlier on one of her mysterious errands and, with a sigh of relief, Kitty spotted her familiar figure scurrying home.

Minutes later Betty breezed into the sitting room, tossing her bonnet and shawl onto a chair and smiling. 'Kitty, love, you'll never guess where I've been. I've got something to tell you.'

'You've been to see Maggie and she wants me to go home?' Kitty held her breath.

Shaking her head, Betty came to sit beside her. 'You can't never go back there, ducks.'

'She still blames me?'

'No, she don't. Maggie would have you back in a shot, if it weren't for him, but she admits that Sid is a bad lot and you got to be kept well away from him.'

Kitty's heart jolted as though she'd missed a step on the stairs. 'You're sending me away too?'

'You've always got a home here with me, but we got to be practical. Now Maggie and me got our heads together, and we think it's best if you're out of the way for a bit. Don't cry, love. Just hear me out . . .'

Leaving Polly in the capable hands of a neighbour from across the street who owed Betty several cups of sugar, not to mention half a loaf of bread, Kitty and Betty set out early next morning. In one of Betty's old skirts, cut down so that it almost fitted, and a white cotton blouse, taken in a few inches, Kitty knew that she was not exactly dressed in the height of fashion, but at least she was clean and tidy. A knitted shawl and gloves finished off her outfit and Betty had given her a red ribbon with which to tie back her long, curly hair. The ribbon was so beautiful, soft and shiny, that Kitty had to keep putting up her hand and touching it, just to make sure it was still there.

For economy's sake, they walked most of the way, and took a hackney carriage from Temple Bar. Kitty was horrified at such extravagance, but Betty said it was a question of keeping up appearances. She wasn't going to arrive at her old employer's home looking like a pauper. The cabbie drove them to Mayfair, setting them down in Dover Street.

'We've got ten minutes to spare,' Betty said, shaking out the creases of her Sunday best black bombazine dress. 'We'll have to go in through the servants' entrance at the back, but I wanted you to see what a fine house you'll be working in.'

Kitty stared around her in awe; Mayfair was so grand that it took her breath away. She had seen several big, shiny, horseless carriages weaving in and out between the horse-drawn vehicles that jostled chaotically in the busy streets around

Piccadilly Circus. The people strolling along the pavements in St James's were plump as partridges, and wore such fine clothes that she could hardly believe her eyes. The reality of being up West was better than the wildest of her dreams. In her excitement she had almost forgotten that her feet were pinched and sore in a borrowed pair of Betty's high-buttoned boots. Her heart was fluttering inside her ribcage and her stomach felt as though it had tied itself in a knot. She felt elated to be here in the world of her dreams, but she also felt out of place amongst the rich and beautiful people; she was bubbling with excitement and yet trembling with nerves. Her relief at being far away from Sugar Yard was being eaten up by the aching sadness of leaving Maggie, who really did love her, and the children, who must be missing her just as much as she missed them.

Betty stopped suddenly, pointing to a double-fronted, five-storey Georgian mansion on the far side of the street. 'That's Sir Desmond Mableton's house where me and your dear mother worked as housemaids, years ago. Ain't it fine?'

Lost for words, Kitty could only stare at the imposing building. A carriage drawn by two, finely matched chestnut horses had drawn up outside. A liveried footman ran down the steps to open the door, while a man in a black tailcoat waited under the portico.

'That's Mr Warner, the butler,' Betty whispered. 'He runs the household below stairs and it was him what arranged your interview with the housekeeper, Mrs Brewster. Look, Kitty, that's Sir Desmond himself getting out of the carriage.'

Sir Desmond, Kitty thought, looked very old and very grand in his frock coat and top hat, but he was totally eclipsed by the elegant young lady alighting from the carriage, aided by the footman.

'She's beautiful,' Kitty said, breathless with admiration. 'Is that his daughter?'

Betty's mouth formed a tight little circle as if she had just sucked a lemon. 'Keep your voice down or they'll hear you, and don't stare. That's Lady Arabella Mableton, Sir Desmond's second wife. She's no better than an actress.'

'An actress?'

'Worse!' Betty said, with a disapproving sniff. 'She performed in the music halls.'

'What's wrong with that?'

'Most gentlemen of his station would have set her up in a nice suburban villa, but Sir Desmond went and married her.' Betty grabbed Kitty's hand. 'Come on or we'll be late.'

Kitty didn't move; she couldn't take her eyes off the lady with her golden hair piled high beneath a wide-brimmed hat, her ruffled, ivory silk gown nipped at a tiny waist, a long-handled parasol clutched in her gloved hand. Sir

Desmond was already at the top of the steps but, as Lady Mableton went to follow him, she appeared to stumble, dropping her parasol. Sprinting forward, dodging between a gentleman on horseback and a hansom cab, Kitty crossed the street and snatched up the parasol.

Lady Mableton's startled expression was replaced by a charming smile that lit her blue eyes and dimpled her cheeks. 'Thank you, my dear! How kind of you.'

If an angel had suddenly come down to earth and spoken to her, Kitty couldn't have felt more tongue-tied. She bobbed a curtsey.

Betty appeared at her elbow, breathless and red in the face. 'Come away, Kitty.'

'Kitty, that's a pretty name. I'm indebted to you, Kitty, er . . .'

'Kitty Cox, Ma'am. I come to be a scullery maid in your house.'

Lady Mableton's eyes clouded with concern. 'Oh, you poor child.' She turned to Betty, laying a gloved hand on her arm. 'Madam, if you love your daughter, don't make her do this. Take her home with you now, I beg you.'

Chapter Two

Kitty sat on the edge of her chair in the house-keeper's office, gazing in amazement at the splendour of her surroundings. She had never seen anything so fine as the mantelshelf swathed in crimson velvet, trimmed with dangling gold tassels that reflected the flames from a coal fire, blazing up the chimney. They must be rich as kings, she thought, to afford such a luxury in September, when the weather had turned a bit nippy, but was nowhere near cold.

Before she had time to study the details of the fancy wallpaper and the gas mantles with smoked-glass shades, the door opened and Mrs Brewster sailed into the room. She looked every bit as imposing as the picture of Queen Victoria that had hung on the classroom wall in Kitty's school, where skinny, little Miss Draper, with squint eyes and a flat bosom, had taken a personal interest in Kitty's natural ability to draw. Miss Draper had brought magazines into the classrooms so that the children could cut out pictures and paste them into scrapbooks. Amongst these Kitty had been quick to pounce upon copies of *Milliner, Dress-maker and Draper*, the *Lady's Pictorial* and *Queen, the Ladies' Newspaper*, all of which had been bought and discarded by the rich widow to whom Miss Draper's sister was lady's maid. And this house, Kitty thought, was much more grand than anything she had seen in the periodicals, and Mrs Brewster did look like the Queen. Dragging herself back to the present, Kitty stared at the housekeeper, wondering if she ought to curtsey. Casting a nervous glance at Betty, Kitty followed her example and stood up.

Mrs Brewster went to sit behind a large, oak desk. 'You may sit down.' Hooking a pair of steel-rimmed spectacles over her ears, that were half hidden by swathes of iron-grey hair dragged back into a knot at the nape of her neck, Mrs Brewster shot Kitty a cursory glance. She turned to Betty. 'So, Mrs Scully, you were formerly employed here as a housemaid?'

Betty sat bolt upright, clearing her throat. 'Yes, Mrs Brewster, more than twenty years ago. Me and Kitty's mother worked under Mr Warner in those days.'

'Before my time, of course,' Mrs Brewster said, glaring over the top of her spectacles as if she expected Betty to argue.

She didn't.

'And you think this girl would suit our strict requirements?'

Betty nodded her head. 'Like I told Mr Warner when I wrote him, Kitty is a good girl, clean and tidy.'

Mrs Brewster turned her steely gaze on Kitty. 'Are you willing to work hard, Kitty?'

'Yes'm.' Kitty felt herself blushing and she wriggled nervously on the hard wooden seat of the chair.

'Yes, Mrs Brewster! And don't fidget, girl.'

'Yes, Mrs Brewster.' Kitty sat on her hands.

Mrs Brewster turned back to Betty, as if Kitty weren't capable of answering for herself. 'She looks undersized for her age, and peaky.'

'She may be small, Mrs Brewster, but she's wiry and she's used to hard work. Aren't you, Kitty?'

Before Kitty could answer, Mrs Brewster came in on the attack. 'I don't put up with shirking, Kitty Cox. Are you a shirker?'

'No, Mrs Brewster.'

'Are you an honest, God-fearing girl?'

'Yes, Mrs Brewster.'

Mrs Brewster stared at Kitty for what seemed like an hour with cold eyes that reminded Kitty of the fish heads that Sid brought home from the market. 'You might do,' she said at last. 'All right, Mrs Scully, I'm prepared to take the girl on for a trial period of one month. But if she doesn't come up to scratch she'll be sent back to you without a character, is that clear?'

'Yes, Mrs Brewster, Ma'am. Thank you.'

'She'll be paid ten pounds a year, all found. Have you anything to say, Kitty?'

Kitty shook her head, tempted to tell this hard-faced old crow what she could do with her rotten job, but ten pounds a year was a fortune and, anyway, she couldn't have spoken a word, not without bursting into tears.

'I didn't hear your answer,' snapped Mrs Brewster, leaning across the desk. 'Cat got your tongue, Kitty Cox?'

The housemaid, summoned by Mrs Brewster to take Kitty down to the servants' hall, bobbed a curtsey, shot Kitty a scornful glance and strode off. Following her through the maze of narrow passages, painted dark green at the bottom and a yellowed cream at the top, Kitty had to run to keep up. The housemaid barged through a baize door that led into the kitchen, letting it swing back, almost knocking Kitty off her feet.

'Who's this then, Dora?' demanded the cook, wiping her floury hands on her apron.

'It's the new scullery maid,' Dora said, giving Kitty a spiteful nudge in the ribs. 'Tell Mrs Dixon your name, girl, if you've got a tongue in your head.'

Kitty drew herself up to her full height, but even then she was only up to Dora's shoulder. Everyone was staring at her and she wanted desperately to run back to Betty and beg her to take her home to Tanner's Passage. Stifling the impulse, she took a deep breath. 'Me name is Kitty Cox.'

A housemaid with a sly, feline face, giggled behind her hand. 'Don't they know how to talk proper where you come from, Kitty Cox?'

'That'll do, Olive.' Mrs Dixon shook a finger at her, frowning. 'I hope you're stronger than you look, Kitty, or you won't last a day in my kitchen.'

'Yes'm.'

'I've seen bigger rats in the yard,' Olive muttered, winking at Dora.

'Get on with your work, all of you,' Mrs Dixon said. 'Kitty, you go with Florrie and she'll show you what to do.'

Dora and Olive went off giggling and Kitty followed Florrie into the scullery. A mountain of greasy pots and pans cluttered the wooden draining board. The clay sink looked big enough to bathe all Maggie's little ones at one go.

'That's your job,' Florrie said, handing Kitty a dishcloth. 'That's what you'll do, day in and day out, until your hands are red raw. When you've finished that you come to me and I'll tell you what to do next.'

Wallowing all morning in a sea of greasy water, Kitty scrubbed pots and pans until her hands were more wrinkled than if she'd been sifting through the mud on the foreshore; her feet ached and the pain in her back was worse than toothache. She would have been left behind when the dinner gong sounded, if it hadn't been for a boy, who struggled in from the yard, carrying a hod full of coal. Setting it down on the quarry tiles, he angled his head, staring at her. Kitty stared back.

'Hello there, half-pint,' he said, wiping his forehead on his shirtsleeve. 'So you're the new scullery maid.'

'Me name's Kitty, not half-pint.'

'Ho there, spunky little thing, aren't you?'

Too tired to retaliate, Kitty shrugged her shoulders.

'I'm George, the hall boy,' he said, with a superior smile. 'I'm above you and you have to do as I say.'

'If you say so.'

'Here, are you all right?' George peered anxiously into her face. 'You've gone a funny colour.'

The faint feeling was passing and Kitty managed a brief nod. 'I'm fine.'

'Lucky it's dinner time 'cos you look like you could do with a good feed,' George said, tossing her a glass cloth. 'Tidy yourself up a bit and come with me. Do as I tell you and you'll soon learn what's what.'

'I'll not be here for long,' Kitty said, wiping her hands. 'I'm going to work in a dress shop.'

'I'd keep quiet about that if I was you,' George said, grinning. 'Them tabby cats have got it in for you, so you'd better watch your step. Come on, or they'll have gobbled up the lot.'

Following George to the servants' hall, Kitty found that they were expected to sit, on their own, at a table beneath the window that looked out onto the area and a blank brick wall. The rest of the servants sat in order of precedence at the big table, males on one side and females on the other, eating in silence unless spoken to by Mr Warner. Kitty couldn't help peeking at him, as he presided over the table; with his black suit, stooped shoulders and hooded eyes, he reminded her of the ravens that she had once seen, on a rare excursion to the Tower of London.

Although they were the last to be served, the best pieces of meat had been taken and the food was only just lukewarm, Kitty had never had such a good meal in her whole life. She ate everything on her plate and was about to pick it up and lick off the gravy when George kicked her shins, shaking his head. It was a crying shame to waste good gravy, but everyone else had placed their knives and forks neatly, side by side. Reluctantly, Kitty did the same. Mr Warner rose from the table and led the upper servants from the room which, George told Kitty in a whisper, was so that they could have their dessert in the butler's parlour, away from us riffraff. As soon as the door closed on them, everyone began to talk at once.

Florrie brought a steaming rice pudding from the kitchen and began spooning it into bowls. Following George's example, Kitty stood in line to receive her portion and, if he hadn't given her the nudge, she would have missed out on the dollop of Mrs Dixon's homemade plum jam. Savouring every mouthful, Kitty felt as though her stomach was going to burst. When she thought no one was looking, she ran her finger round the inside of the bowl, again and again, until she had licked it clean. George eyed her severely; then, grinning, he did the same.

A full belly made up for a lot, but before the day was out, Kitty realised that George had been right about one thing: the housemaids, Dora, Olive and Jane had it in for her. They reminded Kitty of witches from a storybook that Miss Draper had once read to the class and she had shown them the pictures too; one of them looked exactly like Dora. Spotting the likeness did nothing to make Kitty's torment easier. The housemaids poked fun at the way she talked, her hand-me-down dress, her shabby, oversized boots and her curly, chestnut hair that simply refused to stay inside the mobcap that Mrs Dixon insisted she must wear. Worst of all, Olive had pinched her beautiful red satin ribbon and would not give it back. No matter how much she tried to avoid them, they seemed to pop up from nowhere to tug at her hair, administer a spiteful pinch or say something nasty. Florrie was not so cruel, but she seemed a bit scared of the other girls and didn't say much at all. Every time Kitty finished one pile of pots and pans, Florrie found some more for her to wash. Stoking the fires was also part of her job and, although George fetched the coal, the iron hod had to be hefted in order to feed the insatiable mouth of the range.

Although the kitchen and parlour maids were supposed to have time off between two thirty and four, things didn't seem to work out that way. Luncheon in the dining room above stairs went on well into the afternoon and that entailed more washing up. When that was done, Kitty had to mop and scrub the kitchen and scullery floors. Then it was time to stoke the fires, ready for Mrs Dixon to begin preparing dinner, and the gruelling cycle of washing up began all over again. The tasks were endless and by eleven o'clock, when the final dish had been dried and put away, Kitty was so exhausted that she barely had the energy left to follow Florrie up the servants' staircase to the top of the house. By now everything about her felt numb, from her brain to her feet. Her mind and heart were detached from her body. All emotion and feeling seemed to have been drained, leaving her dazed and confused.

The attic rooms led off a windowless passage. Following the flickering light of Florrie's candle, Kitty stumbled along in the dark; her feet were so swollen that she was barely able to put one in front of the other. Florrie opened a door at the far end.

'Get a move on. I haven't got all night and I'm dead on my feet.'

Kitty hesitated, peering into the gloomy space beneath the eaves that was just big enough for an iron bedstead and a chest of drawers.

'See that alarm clock on the chest? It's set for six sharp. Up you get and make sure that the range is stoked up before Mrs Dixon gets down to do the breakfasts, otherwise she'll skin you alive.' Florrie walked away without waiting for an answer.

Left alone in the dark, Kitty felt her way to the bed and sank down, tugging at the buttons on her boots. Kicking them off, she lay down. As her eyes grew accustomed to the gloom, she could see a single star shining like a candle through the black rectangle of the skylight. Keeping her eyes focused on its friendly, twinkling light she tried not to listen to the soft scurrying sounds in the rafters. It was probably mice but, hopefully, not rats. No doubt there were spiders as big as sparrows lurking up there too, but Kitty tried not to think about that. She had never slept on her own in her whole life, but she was too exhausted to feel scared. She missed the warmth of Violet's little body snuggling up to her in the dark, and the comforting sound of the boys' rhythmic breathing. That bright star, she thought, must be shining on Maggie and the children, on Betty and Polly, and maybe on Jem too, wherever he was at this moment. Things were bad, very bad, but she was not going to let them get her down. She had survived her first day and, no matter how they bullied or tormented her below stairs, she would not let them see that she was hurt and frightened. Jem would have told her to keep her chin up; he wasn't afraid of anything or anyone. Gradually, Kitty felt her eyelids becoming too heavy to keep them open and she tried to imagine the lumpy flock mattress was a soft, pink cloud floating in a summer blue sky.

Having been awakened by the shrill ringing of the alarm clock, and still half asleep, Kitty felt her way down the staircase as the first grey shards of dawn filtered through the skylight. She must have taken a wrong turn at the foot of the stairs as, stumbling in the darkness, she walked into something hard, barking her shins. She fell onto something warm and soft that let out a yell and snapped upright, catapulting her onto the tiled floor.

'Gawd's strewth, Kitty!' George said, pulling the blanket up to his chin. 'What d'you think you're doing?'

'Sorry,' Kitty gasped, scrambling to her feet. 'I thought this was the way to the scullery.'

'It's that way,' George said, pointing down the corridor. 'Better make a dash for it. You'll be in real trouble if you're caught in the men's quarters.'

Kitty ran. After taking another wrong turn and ending up in the boot room, she managed to find her way to the kitchen. She was struggling to get the range going, when Dora appeared, stopping in the middle of a yawn as she caught sight of Kitty.

'Well, if it ain't the guttersnipe.'

'I ain't no guttersnipe. I was a mudlark. That's a respectable trade, I'll have you know.'

'Ho! A mudlark was you? Up to your waist in mud and stinking sewage – that sounds about right.'

'And now I'm trying to get this here fire going, so I'll thank you to leave me alone,' Kitty said, riddling the coal and coughing as a backdraught blew soot and smoke into her face.

'Here, let me help you then, mudlark,' Dora said, baring her teeth in a smile.

Kitty tried to sidestep her, but Dora was too quick. Still smiling, Dora ran her hand round the rim of the coal hod and, grabbing Kitty by the ear, she wiped the soot all over her face and down the front of her blouse.

'That'll teach you to cheek your betters,' Dora

said, tipping the contents of the ash pan onto the floor. 'You'd better learn your place or you'll suffer for it, and that's a promise.'

'I ain't afraid of you.' Fisting her hands, Kitty squared up to Dora.

'Want to fight, do you, half-pint?' Dodging sideways, Dora put out her foot. 'Have a nice trip, ducks.'

Kitty only just saved herself from falling by making a grab for the table.

Crowing with laughter, Dora took off in the direction of the broom cupboard where the housemaids kept their cleaning materials. Biting her lip to hold back tears, Kitty threw herself down on her hands and knees in a frantic effort to brush the soot and grit into a dustpan, but it was too late, Florrie had come into the kitchen.

'Gawd's strewth, what's going on?' Staring in horror at the mess on the floor and noting Kitty's filthy appearance, Florrie threw up her hands. 'What will Mrs Dixon say?'

Kitty pushed a lock of hair back from her forehead with a sooty hand. The temptation to snitch on Dora almost got the better of her, but she fought against it. 'I'm doing me best.'

'The fire isn't hot enough to boil a kettle, let alone cook the breakfasts. You've got soot everywhere and you look like a chimney sweep,' Florrie said, grabbing Kitty by the scruff of her neck and dragging her to her feet. 'You'll be for it if Mrs Dixon sees you looking like that.'

Just then Mrs Dixon entered the kitchen. One look at her crumpled features and sour expression was enough to convince Kitty that Mrs Dixon was not in her best mood first thing in the morning.

'What's all this?' Arms akimbo, Mrs Dixon glared at Kitty.

Kitty lowered her head and said nothing.

'I've just come down and found her like this, Mrs Dixon,' Florrie said, hastily.

'I'll not have anyone working in my kitchen that can't keep themselves clean and tidy, and I won't stand for sloppy work.' Mrs Dixon bustled over to the range and let out a snort of annoyance. 'The range is barely warm. You'd better learn quickly, my girl, or you'll not last the week. Fetch George and get him to show you how it's done. And tidy yourself up. Change your blouse and put your cap on properly.'

Feeling a hot flush of shame spreading up her neck to her cheeks, Kitty had to speak out. 'Please, Mrs Dixon. I ain't got no more clothes.'

Mrs Dixon threw up her hands. 'What was Mrs Brewster thinking of, taking on a child from the slums? Well, it's up to her to sort this out. As soon as the breakfasts upstairs are done, you'll report to Mrs Brewster's office.'

*

'So, you're in trouble on your first full day of work. That's not a very good start, is it?' Mrs Brewster stared at Kitty over the top of her spectacles.

'I couldn't help it,' Kitty protested, stung by the huge unfairness of it all. 'I ain't got no more clothes and this rig-out was one of Betty's, what I cut down to fit me and stitched up again.'

'Did you now?' Mrs Brewster chewed the tip of her pencil, frowning thoughtfully. 'I don't usually give out dresses until I'm satisfied with a new girl, but we can't have Mrs Dixon upset. You'd better come with me to the linen room and we'll see if we can find something to fit you.'

Minutes later, dressed in a print frock at least two sizes too large and belted in at the waist with an equally large, white apron, Kitty went back to the kitchen.

'Look at her,' Olive said, pointing a finger at Kitty. 'What a scarecrow.'

'Don't be unkind, Olive,' Florrie said, looking up from the scrubbed pine table where she was peeling onions. 'She's only a kid, after all.'

'You've changed your tune a bit,' snapped Olive.

'She's trying hard. It's not fair to go on at her all the time.' Florrie wiped her eyes with the back of her hand and sniffed. 'Bloody onions.'

'I won't have foul language in my kitchen,' Mrs Dixon said, pummelling the bread dough as if it were her worst enemy. 'And you get on with your work, Olive. You're supposed to be dusting above stairs.'

'Yes, Mrs Dixon.' Olive snatched up her box of polish and dusters, pulling a face at Kitty behind Mrs Dixon's back.

'Don't get on the wrong side of her,' Florrie told Kitty, when they were alone in the scullery. 'Olive can be spiteful when she has a mind to.'

Kitty shrugged her shoulders. She doubted if Olive had a right side to get onto, or if she had, then she kept it well hidden.

After a few weeks, Kitty had come to realise that there were two completely different, but co-dependent, worlds in the grand house in Dover Street. Her place was firmly below stairs, confined to the scullery and kitchen, ignored by the upper servants and tormented by those lower down the pecking order. The only time she was allowed beyond the green baize door, into the fairy-tale land above stairs, was each morning for prayers, when the servants gathered in the entrance hall. They lined up in order of precedence, waiting in respectful silence until the family, led by Sir Desmond and Lady Mableton, emerged from the dining room.

The one bright spot in Kitty's day was to steal covert glances at Lady Mableton's lovely face and silently worship her. From the bottom of the heap, Kitty could only gaze upwards and idolise her ladyship. She was, Kitty thought, just how she would have imagined an angel from heaven, and the cloud of perfume that lingered about her was sweeter than the scent of all the flowers in Covent Garden. Her elegant gowns, in sweet pea colours, trimmed with waterfalls of lace or tiny pleated frills, were so beautiful that they made Kitty want to cry. Sir Desmond read the daily lesson in a well-modulated voice, but Kitty never listened to his words; she daydreamed of being allowed to wait on Lady Mableton, just like the formidable Miss Lane, her personal maid. What a job that would be, even better than working in a dress shop.

After prayers, the family drifted away and the servants waited, heads respectfully bowed, until their betters were out of sight. Kitty knew she was risking a clip round the ear from Mrs Dixon if she was caught peeping, but she just had to catch the last glimpse of Lady Mableton gliding up the staircase, her hand resting lightly on Sir Desmond's arm. Miss Iris, Sir Desmond's daughter by his first wife, followed behind them, her thin face sour as vinegar and, by all accounts, her nature was just the same.

George had taken it upon himself to instruct Kitty in everything, from lessons in manners and improving her speech, to passing on servants' gossip about the family. Miss Iris had an elder brother, Captain Edward, who was away fighting the Dervishes in the Sudan with Lord Kitchener. George had never met Captain Edward but he had heard all about him and, he said, Captain Edward was as handsome and charming as his sister was plain and grumpy. According to reports from the above-stairs servants, Miss Iris hated her stepmother, who was not only much more beautiful, but also several years her junior. Miss Iris took every opportunity to make unfavourable comments about Lady Mableton's past career on the stage but, in George's opinion – and Kitty had quickly learnt that George had an opinion on everything – Miss Iris was simply jealous. She might pretend to be fond of her spoilt little half-sister, two-year-old Miss Leonie, but, George said, everyone below stairs knew that she thoroughly disliked the poor mite.

Kitty had not seen much of Miss Leonie, who was looked after by Nanny in the nursery suite, but she had heard enough of her tantrums, which echoed throughout the house, to form her own opinion that someone needed a good spanking. Little Violet was the same age and she wouldn't get away with such bad behaviour! In Sugar Yard small children soon learned to know their place and, if they didn't behave, they got a clip round the ear from their mother and, when they grew bigger, they got a taste of their father's leather belt across their backsides.

Suddenly everyone was on the move; Miss Lane broke away from the servants' ranks and followed the family upstairs. Kitty was a bit in awe of Miss Lane; she was always neat as a pin in her severe grey dress, but she had bold, gypsy-black eyes set in a handsome face and, no matter how strictly she confined her raven hair in a bun, some of it always escaped, curling in tendrils round her forehead. Miss Lane, who had apparently been Lady Mableton's dresser in the old days, gave as good as she got below stairs and Kitty sensed that the housemaids were actually a bit scared of her.

Least important and therefore last in line, Kitty shuffled behind George, glad that Olive and Dora went on ahead so that they didn't have a chance to pinch or prod her. Returning to the scullery and the endless pile of washing-up, her head was still full of the glories of life above stairs. When living in Sugar Yard, she could never have imagined that there were people who lived in such unashamed luxury.

At the end of the first month, Mrs Brewster called Kitty to her office, told her that she would be kept on and handed her a cotton purse that jingled with coins.

'Normally you'll be paid quarterly, but Sir Desmond is a generous employer and he allows the lower servants an advance at the end of the first month. You'll get the balance at the end of the quarter. You're allowed one half-day off a month,' said Mrs Brewster, locking away the tin cash box. 'Mrs Dixon says she can spare you tomorrow afternoon, but you must be back by six o'clock sharp.'

'Thank you, Mrs Brewster.' Kitty left the office with the purse tucked into the pocket of her skirt. She had never had any money that was hers alone and, as she skipped along the flagged passage, the jingling of the coins was sweet music to her ears. But her joy was short-lived when Olive jumped out of the broom cupboard, seizing Kitty by the upper arm and pinching her soft flesh between bony fingers.

'So you've been paid, have you, half-pint?'

Kitty tried to wriggle free. 'Let me go.'

Olive only pinched her all the harder. 'Not until you've paid me back the money you owe me.'

'I never had any money off you.'

'Are you calling me a liar?' Olive twisted Kitty's arm behind her back.

'No, Olive.'

'Then pay up, you little bitch. Two shillings or I'll tell Mrs Brewster you stole it off me.'

'What's going on then?' Bob, the first footman, who had never bothered to speak to Kitty before, stepped out of the silver store, locking it behind him.

'Mind your own business,' snapped Olive.

'It is my business,' Bob said, barring Olive's way as she tried to push past him, using Kitty as a shield. 'What's she done?'

'I ain't done nothing,' Kitty said, kicking out at Olive's shins.

'She owes me money and I want it back.' Olive twisted Kitty's arm, making her yelp with pain.

With a swift movement, Bob separated them, sending Kitty stumbling against the wall. 'Leave her be, Olive. That's an old trick and it won't wash with me. Best get on with your work before Mr Warner catches you.'

Olive looked as though she would like to retaliate, but thought better of it, and went off grumbling under her breath.

'You'd better get back to the scullery,' Bob said, not unkindly. 'And I'd put that purse some-where safe if I was you, half-pint.'

Kitty mumbled a thank you and scurried back to the kitchen, rubbing her bruised arm. There would be yet another purple mark to add to the mass of bruises and scratches that disfigured her pale skin when she undressed at night. Dora and Olive gave her sly looks, but they hurried away without saying anything when Mrs Dixon stamped in from the cold larder, waving a knife and demanding to know why the pheasants hadn't been plucked. Red-faced and sweating, Florrie stuck her head round the scullery door and called for Kitty to come and help her quick smart as the pheasants, four brace of them, had to be plucked and drawn, ready for a dinner party that evening.

The washing-up took Kitty until well after midnight and she crawled up the ninety-seven stairs to the attics on her hands and knees. She undressed in the dark and fell into bed, sliding her bare feet under the coverlet. A scream of horror was torn from her throat as her feet touched something cold, clammy and spiked with bristles. She fell onto the floor with a thump. The door opened and a thin stream of candlelight dazzled her eyes.

'Had a bad dream?' Dora said, giggling.

'Got out of bed the wrong side?' Olive poked Kitty with her bare foot.

Kitty scrambled to her feet and, pulling back the coverlet, she saw that the offending object was a raw pig's trotter.

Helpless with laughter, Olive and Dora stuffed their hands in their mouths and ran off down the corridor to their own room. Trembling with shock and rage, Kitty was about to close her door when she heard Mrs Brewster's angry voice scolding them for larking around. Serve them right, she thought, grabbing the trotter and hurling it across the room.

*

Next day, when the family luncheon dishes were washed and put away, and with Mrs Dixon's permission, Kitty wrapped Betty's old shawl around her shoulders and set off for Tanner's Passage with the purse clutched firmly in her hand. No one had mentioned the pig's trotter incident, although Olive had given her some black looks and George had been grinning all over his face.

Kitty walked as far as Trafalgar Square, enjoying the golden October sunlight that bathed the grey Portland stones of the buildings in a soft light. The sound of the coins jingling in her purse made her heart leap with pride; she had earned every penny of the money and now she would be able to repay some of Betty's kindness, and send some home to Maggie and the nippers, who were never far from her thoughts. Stopping at a sweetshop, she purchased two ounces of bulls-eyes for Betty and two ounces of cream fudge for Polly, who might choke on anything harder. Kitty couldn't resist sampling one of each herself, rolling the sweets around her mouth and making them last until she caught the horse-drawn omnibus that would take her down the Strand, Fleet Street and into the City. She walked the last mile or so to save her pennies and, as she neared Billingsgate, the familiar smell of fish, engine oil, naphtha, soot and sewage told her she was almost home.

Entering the narrow canyon of Tanner's Passage, Kitty was startled to see everything through different eyes, and having just left the elegance of Dover Street and the West End, the contrast in lifestyles was appalling. She had always thought that Tanner's Passage was so much better than Sugar Yard, but the reality was quite shocking. Mean dwellings were squashed between gaunt warehouses, broken windows stuffed with rags and newspaper; snotty-nosed, ragged children playing in the gutter next to the corpse of a long-dead cat. The foul smell of overflowing privies made her want to retch. Pressing a penny into the blue fingers of a half-clad child who sat on a doorstep, staring at her big-eyed, with painful-looking scabs of impetigo marring her pretty face, Kitty put her head down and hurried along the street to number seven.

Betty opened the door and her face split into a grin that was so reminiscent of Jem that Kitty almost cried. As the door closed on the depressing poverty outside, Kitty was aware only of the love and human warmth within, and was instantly ashamed of comparing Tanner's Passage unfavourably with Dover Street. Betty hugged her until she was breathless, and then sent Kitty upstairs to see Polly, who chortled with delight at the sight of her.

'You look splendid, dear,' Betty said, when she

brought up a tray of tea and a plate of biscuits. 'Don't she look just the ticket, Poll?'

With her mouth full of cream fudge and a little dribble sliding down her chin, Polly smiled her lop-sided smile and nodded.

'I can't stay long,' Kitty said, glancing at the lantern clock on the bureau. 'I've got to be back in Dover Street afore six or I'll be mincemeat.'

'I hope they're treating you right,' Betty said, pouring the tea and frowning. 'I asked Mrs Brewster to keep a special eye on you.'

'It's fine,' Kitty lied. 'I got me own bedroom and three meals a day, what more could I want?'

'Well, now, that's lovely.' Betty handed her a cup of tea. 'And I swear you've grown an inch since you left here.'

'Have you seen Maggie?' Kitty's hand shook a little as she took the teacup. 'And the nippers – have you seen them?'

Betty shook her head. 'No, dear, I thought it best to keep away from Sugar Yard for a while in case I bumped into you-know-who. But I have had a letter from Jem.' Taking a scrap of paper from her pocket, Betty handed it to Kitty, smiling proudly. 'He's doing ever so well, although he's not a great one for letter writing.'

In Jem's typical style, the letter was short, to the point, and ended saying that he was having a fine time, had seen sights that would make their eyes pop out and was getting the hang of things.

He missed them all and hoped to be home in the spring.

'I'm ashamed that I haven't written to him,' Kitty admitted, handing the letter back to Betty. 'I couldn't bring meself to write after what happened, but now I'm settled in me new position I will write to him.'

The clock ticked on relentlessly and, all too soon for Kitty, it was time to go. She kissed Polly and hugged Betty. Then delving into her pocket, Kitty brought out her purse and tipped a couple of coins into her hand, holding them out to Betty.

'What's this then, Kitty?'

'It's not much, just a couple of shillings, but I want you to see that Maggie gets it.'

Betty's eyes widened and she shook her head. 'After what she did to you?'

'It's for the nippers,' Kitty said, trying not to shame herself by crying. 'I think about 'em all the time. Just tell our Maggie it's for the nippers.'

'You're a good girl. I don't know many as would be so forgiving when they was treated so bad,' Betty sniffed, fumbling inside her sleeve for her hankie.

Next morning, after the breakfast things were cleared away, Kitty was stoking the range when Olive and Dora stalked into the kitchen. Mrs Dixon was with her ladyship, discussing the menus for the day and Florrie was in the larder, checking the stores. George was chopping sticks in the yard. Kitty knew that she was alone and at their mercy. She slid the iron lid back in place, turning to face them, bracing her shoulders. Maggie had always told her to stand up to bullies; she wouldn't let them see that she was dead scared.

They came towards her; two she cats stalking their prey. Kitty thrust her chin up and held her ground as they circled her, tweaking at her cap and pulling her hair.

'What a dirty little bitch we have here,' Olive said, prodding Kitty in the stomach.

'Leave us alone or I'll bop you one,' Kitty said, balling her hands into fists.

'You and whose army?' sneered Dora, tugging off Kitty's mobcap so that her hair tumbled down over her shoulders.

'Leave me be,' Kitty cried, making a grab for her cap.

'Look at this dirty girl's hair.' Olive grabbed Kitty by the hair. 'I bet she's brought a head full of nits back with her from the slums.'

'I can see them all hopping about,' Dora cried in mock horror. 'You know what you've got to do, Olive.'

'Indeed I do,' Olive said, taking a pair of scissors from her pocket. 'Hold her still, Dora.'

Kitty fought and struggled but Dora was taller

and much the stronger; every time Kitty wriggled or kicked, Olive tugged mercilessly at her hair, nicking Kitty's scalp with the sharp points of the scissors. Snip after snip, Kitty's curls fell to the floor. Olive cut the last lock and gave Kitty a shove that sent her spinning across the flagstones, crashing into a chair. Unable to save herself, Kitty fell to the floor. Doubled up with laughter, they pointed at her, shrieking for her to find a mirror.

'You missed a bit,' Dora said, making snipping movements with the scissors and lunging at Kitty.

Scrambling to her feet, Kitty fled from the kitchen, up the stairs, barging through the baize door and racing down the passage that led to the main entrance hall. Too late, she realised that Sir Desmond and Lady Mableton were standing in the middle of the hall talking to Mr Warner. Kitty skidded to a halt, sliding across the polished marble floor and cannoning into Mr Warner's stomach.

Chapter Three

Deadly silence. Mr Warner's fingers dug into Kitty's shoulders, his eyes narrowed to slits and his lips tightened into a straight line. Sir Desmond made a sound between a choke and a cough. Closing her eyes, Kitty waited for the inevitable blow that must fall and strike her to the ground. She covered her head with her hands and the clumps of stubble, left by Olive's vicious application of the scissors, felt like coconut matting interspersed with bald patches, sticky with blood, where the blades had nipped her skin.

'How absolutely shocking!' Lady Mableton's voice broke the silence. 'I'm appalled.'

'My lady, I can't apologise enough,' said Mr Warner, giving Kitty a good shake.

'Who is this little animal?' demanded Sir Desmond.

'Desmond, have pity. She's just a child and she's hurt.'

Kitty opened her eyes to stare up at Lady Mableton and saw to her astonishment that, although her lips curved in a tender smile, her cornflower blue eyes were bright with tears. 'You poor girl, who did this to you?'

'Allow Warner to deal with this, Bella,' Sir Desmond said, taking his hat, cane and gloves from Bob. 'We're going to be late.'

'Then we'll be late. I want to find out exactly what has been going on below stairs and who has allowed this dreadful thing to happen in our home.'

Mr Warner cleared his throat. 'My lady, I'm sorry that this extraordinary event has come to your notice, but it really would be best dealt with by myself and Mrs Brewster.'

'Come along, Bella. Leave it to Warner,' Sir Desmond said, thrusting his hands into his gloves. 'This is a ridiculous fuss over something that doesn't concern us.'

'Desmond, please.' Lady Mableton's voice was cream laced with honey. 'Let me have a moment.'

Kitty felt the pressure of Mr Warner's fingers tighten until it seemed as though her bones would snap.

Sir Desmond's moustache quivered as he hesitated, frowning. 'Have it your own way, my dear. I'll wait for you in the carriage. But don't be long.'

All smiles, Lady Mableton kissed his cheek and then spun round to glare at Mr Warner. 'You may go, Warner. My maid, Lane, will see to the girl.' She held her hand out to Kitty. 'Come with me, Kitty.'

Kitty hesitated, glancing anxiously up at Mr Warner, whose well-schooled features had turned to stone. He released her with a slight inclination of his head and took a step backwards. Kitty could see that he was not best pleased.

Lady Mableton ascended the staircase, seeming to float rather than to walk, her long skirts trailing behind her, giving the impression that she moved on a cushion of air rather than on human feet. Kitty scuttled past Mr Warner, following her ladyship up the stairs. Her feet sank into the thick pile of the carpet and, as she came to the first landing, her eyes almost popped out of her head. The ornately papered walls were hung with oil paintings in gilded frames. Rosewood side tables were scattered with porcelain bowls exuding the scent of pot pourri, and tall vases filled with exotic flowers; the air was heavy with their mingled fragrance. Entering Lady's Mableton's boudoir was like finding herself inside a pearly pink seashell, and Kitty stared around in sheer wonderment; she would never have believed that anything like this existed in the whole world.

Miss Lane came in from an adjoining room, stopping short when she saw Kitty. 'Good God, what's this?'

'Maria, this is Kitty Cox.'

'I know that,' Maria said, with a sniff. 'I make it my business to know everything that goes on in this house. She should be where she belongs, in the scullery.'

'Don't talk nonsense! I know very well what sort of thing goes on below stairs and I won't be party to bullying and torturing a child of this age.' Lady Mableton put her arm around Kitty's shoulders. 'See what you can do with her hair and put some salve on the cuts.'

Maria folded her arms across her chest, shaking her head. 'You know you shouldn't interfere, Bella. They'll only take it out on her later. It's up to Warner to deal with the servants.'

Kitty stared from one to the other, hardly able to believe her ears. No servant would dare talk back like that to Mr Warner or Mrs Brewster, and yet this fiery little woman was daring to talk to her ladyship like an equal.

'I've never liked Warner and I don't trust him. That's exactly why I want you to keep her up here until I get home,' Lady Mableton said, patting Kitty's shoulder. 'I have to go now, Kitty. Maria will look after you.' She was gone in a flurry of ostrich feathers, leaving a trail of French perfume in her wake.

Kitty stood with her hands knotted behind her back, waiting for Miss Lane to pounce on her, which she did; a cold-eyed swooping bird of prey, gripping Kitty in her talon-like fingers. She steered her through the bedroom, past a four-poster bed draped in white lace, and on into Lady Mableton's private bathroom. The walls and floor were tiled in pink marble; the cast iron bath stood on brass claw feet and had taps that looked like real gold. Momentarily, Kitty forgot her pain and humiliation. She stood dumbly, dazzled by the gaslight flickering and reflecting off shelves ranged with cut glass bottles filled with sparkling crystals and coloured potions. Catching sight of herself in a tall mirror, Kitty gulped and raised her hand to her bleeding scalp. Her reflection stared back at her, horribly out of place in this glittering palace.

'Right,' said Maria, putting the plug in the bath and turning the taps full on. 'Don't stand there gawking. It's the bathtub for you, my girl.'

Wrapped in the softest pink towel imaginable, Kitty sat on the stool in front of Lady Mableton's dressing table, while Maria took the scissors to what was left of her hair. She worked in silence, her full lips drawn into a tight line of concentration. Kitty could see her reflected in the triple mirrors, and she could only admire the way Maria's capable fingers worked to tidy up the mess that Olive had created. The cuts had been bathed and treated with salve and, somehow,

Maria had managed to persuade Kitty's hair to cover most of the bald patches.

'You look more like a lad than a girl, but it's the best I can do,' Maria said, whipping the towel away from Kitty's shoulders and giving it a shake.

Naked except for the towel wrapped around her waist, Kitty folded her arms across her chest, shivering and feeling her cheeks flush with embarrassment.

'You haven't got anything I haven't seen before,' Maria said, wrinkling her nose as she wiped the comb on a towel. 'Put your clothes on before you catch your death of cold. We don't want to upset her ladyship, seeing as how she's taken a fancy to you, though God alone knows why.'

Kitty scampered into the bathroom and dragged her dress over her head.

Maria bustled into the room and threw a cloth at her. 'It's your dirt, you clean the bath, wipe down the walls and make sure there's no water left on the floor. I'm not waiting on the likes of you.'

When Kitty was certain that the marble walls were shining and the bath was spotlessly clean, she went back to the boudoir and found Maria, sitting at a table, mending a lace frill on one of Lady Mableton's evening gowns.

'If you've missed a bit I'll make you do the

whole bathroom again,' Maria said, snipping a thread.

'I ain't missed nothing,' Kitty said, stung into answering back. 'I didn't ask to be brought up here. I'll be in for it when I goes back below stairs.'

'Yes, I daresay you will.' Maria smiled grimly as she put the needle back in its case, closing the sewing box with a snap, and getting to her feet. 'Right then, I'm going below stairs for my dinner. What am I going to do with you?'

'I dunno,' Kitty said, staring down at the flower pattern on the carpet.

'I'm not leaving you here in my lady's room and that's final.'

Kitty looked up and saw that Maria was staring at her with an exasperated look on her face. She said nothing; it seemed safer that way. Maria grabbed her by the arm and propelled her towards the door. At first, Kitty thought she was going to be taken back to the servants' quarters, but Maria led her along the landing and up the next flight of stairs to the nursery. Kitty had only seen Nanny Smith briefly, when she came down to the kitchen to collect her tray of food to take back to the nursery. The housemaids and Florrie always made fun of Nanny, but only behind her back. It seemed to Kitty that they resented her because she was treated like the upper servants. Nanny Smith slept in a small room next to the nursery, had her own bathroom, and didn't mix with them below stairs. Olive said she was a stuck-up snob.

Nanny Smith looked up from spoon-feeding Leonie. 'What's this, Miss Lane?'

Maria gave Kitty a shove, sending her into the middle of the room. 'There's been some trouble below stairs. My lady wants us to keep the girl out of the way until she gets back.'

Leonie waved her small fists, knocking the spoon from Nanny's hand, and began to howl.

'All right, she can stay for a bit but you go away, Miss Lane. Miss Leonie always plays up when you come into the nursery.'

Maria looked as though she would like to say something, but seemed to think better of it and, turning on her heel, she stalked out of the room and slammed the door behind her. Kitty stood, clasping her hands behind her back, uncertain what she was expected to do next. Leonie's howls rose as she worked herself into a tantrum and Nanny Smith picked her up. She began to pace the floor, patting Leonie's back, and crooning to her, but this only seemed to make things worse.

'She doesn't like strangers,' Nanny said, pausing for a moment. 'Better go and sit in the night nursery until I quieten her down, or she'll go on like this until she turns blue in the face.'

Kitty hesitated; she'd seen Violet try the same

trick a dozen times in the past and Leonie must be about the same age. 'Let me have a go.'

'Are you mad?'

Kitty shook her head. 'We got a two-year-old at home. I know how to deal with her sort.'

Nanny Smith glanced longingly at the covered dish on the tray set with her midday meal. 'I suppose it won't hurt, just the once.' She handed Leonie over to Kitty.

Leonie yelled even louder and struggled in Kitty's arms. Kitty hoisted her up on her shoulder and began to dance around the room, ignoring the howls and singing "Ring-a-ring o' roses, a pocketful of posies". When she reached the "Atishoo, atishoo, we all fall down" bit, she threw herself down on her knees. Leonie caught her breath on a sob and stopped crying. Kitty jumped up and repeated the process all over again and when she collapsed to the ground, Leonie began to chuckle.

'Well, I never did!' exclaimed Nanny, with her mouth full of roast potato. 'If I hadn't seen it with my own two eyes, I'd never have believed it possible.'

Nanny Smith had impaled a slice of bread on a toasting fork and was holding it in front of the fire in preparation for Leonie's tea, while Kitty sat on the floor, encouraging Leonie to play with a set of brightly coloured wooden building blocks.

Lady Mableton came into the nursery, sweeping Leonie up in her arms and kissing her chubby cheek. 'And how is my little angel this afternoon?'

Leonie's rosebud mouth drooped at the corners and she let out a howl of rage, struggling, kicking and demanding to be put down. Kitty scrambled to her feet and, following Nanny Smith's example, bobbed a curtsey.

'Has naughty Mama spoilt your game,' crooned Lady Mableton, setting the screaming Leonie back on the floor. She subsided onto her knees in a swirl of lavender silk and lace, but Leonie pushed her mother away and began to drum her feet on the carpet. 'Bad girl to kick poor Mama.'

'If you please, my lady, I think perhaps Miss Leonie is hungry.' Nanny Smith hurried forward and bent down to pick Leonie up, receiving a kick in the face for her trouble. She staggered backwards holding her nose, her eyes watering.

'Naughty, naughty baby,' Lady Mableton cried, getting hastily to her feet. 'What shall Mama do with you?'

Wondering how two grown women could let a little tyrant boss them about like this, Kitty lunged at Leonie and swept her up in her arms. 'You say sorry to your poor ma, Miss Leonie. It ain't nice to behave like this.'

Leonie struggled a bit, but she had stopped

crying, and her eyes widened in astonishment as she stared into Kitty's unsmiling face.

'That's more like it,' Kitty said, nodding in approval. 'Now you say you're sorry.'

Leonie plugged her thumb in her mouth and shook her head.

'I ain't waiting all day,' Kitty told her, frowning.

Leonie unplugged her thumb. 'I sorry, Mama.'

'Bless my soul,' cried Nanny Smith.

Leonie held her fat little arms out to her mother and Lady Mableton seized her in a fond embrace. 'My precious baby.' She smiled at Kitty over Leonie's curly blonde head. 'Now I know what I'll do with you, Kitty. You will help Nanny Smith look after Miss Leonie. What do you think about that Nanny?'

Nanny Smith bobbed a curtsey. 'I'd be very pleased to have some help, my lady.'

'That's settled then.' Lady Mableton handed Leonie back to Kitty. 'You take your orders from Nanny now or directly from me. I'll speak to Warner about it immediately.'

Kitty was dazed by the sudden turn of events. Her life seemed to have changed in the space of a few hours. She was allowed to move her few possessions from the garret room to the night nursery, where a truckle bed was placed against the wall opposite Leonie's cot. It was directly underneath the window, and at night she could lie in bed looking up at the sky and imagine that Jem was on his ship sailing homewards, guided by the same stars that twinkled above her. As long as she did exactly what Nanny Smith said, life in the nursery was much easier and more peaceful than it had ever been in the scullery. She was given one of Nanny's old uniforms to cut down and alter to fit herself, and a navy serge coat and felt hat that had belonged to the previous Nanny, which fitted perfectly.

Kitty soon found out that Nanny Smith was sweet on Bob, the first footman, although romance between the servants was strictly forbidden. If Mr Warner or Mrs Brewster had the slightest suspicion that there was anything going on between them, Nanny would be discharged without a character and Bob would be given a stern talking-to. Kitty knew that Nanny's evening strolls in Green Park were not unaccompanied. She had watched from the window in the night nursery as Nanny set off along Dover Street towards Piccadilly and, a few moments later, she had seen Bob strolling along in the same direction. If Maria came into the nursery looking for Nanny Smith, Kitty had a string of alibis ready to trip off her tongue. She had no particular liking for Nanny, who seemed determined to keep her firmly in her place, and clearly resented the fact that Lady Mableton favoured her. But Nanny was not spiteful like Olive and Dora, nor was she cockney-smart like Maria, who had a mouth on her that reminded Kitty of Maggie when she was riled.

Conversations between Kitty and Nanny Smith were usually one-sided, with Nanny giving instructions and Kitty carrying them out to the best of her ability. Occasionally, in the evening after supper, when Miss Leonie was safely tucked in her cot and the nursery was clean and tidy, they would sit by the fire drinking tea and Nanny Smith would tell Kitty about her childhood on a farm in rural Essex. Life on a small farm didn't sound much easier than the back-breaking hours Kitty had spent scavenging in the stinking detritus, washed up by the Thames, but Nanny's brown eyes misted with tears when she spoke of her younger brothers and sisters. This was something that Kitty understood only too well.

She missed Maggie and the little ones more than she would have thought possible but, even though the memory of Sid's assault was fading into the realms of a bad dream, Kitty knew she could never return to Sugar Yard. Sometimes, when she awakened in the cold, dark hours before dawn, Kitty lay in bed worrying how Maggie would be coping without her. There would be no one to cuddle little Violet when she woke up, scared by a bad dream. If Maggie was busy feeding baby Harry, who would put arnica on Billy's eye when he'd come off worst, fighting the Blacker boys? If Maggie had another baby, an event that happened regular as clockwork every year, there would be no one to help wean Harry onto sops of bread and milk. Kitty had worked out in her mind that it was not Maggie's fault that she had sent her away. Maggie had done it for her own good, because Maggie loved her in spite of everything. It was Sid who was to blame for all the bad things that had happened to her; he had shamed, hurt and humiliated her and, for the first time in her life, Kitty knew what it was like to really hate someone.

'You look peaky today, Kitty. Are you feeling quite well?' Lady Mableton studied Kitty's face with a frown puckering her smooth forehead.

Kitty bobbed a curtsey. 'Yes, my lady, thank you.' Leonie was tugging at her hand, demanding to be released but Kitty held on, knowing that she would make straight for the box of chocolates that lay open on the drum table, beside a bowl full of jewel-bright chrysanthemums.

'It's all right, Kitty. Leonie won't be happy until she's found the violet creams, will you, Angel?' Lady Mableton went to the table and picked up the satin-covered box, laughing as

Leonie scampered towards her and plunged her chubby fingers into the chocolates.

Kitty shifted from one foot to the other as she waited to be dismissed. Miss Leonie was all dressed up in her outdoor clothes, ready for the promised carriage drive to Hyde Park. Maria had laid her mistress's fashionable Persian lamb jacket and matching muff on the back of the chaise longue and she stood silently, with her arms folded across her chest, waiting and tapping her toe. Watching Maria out of the corner of her eye, Kitty wondered for the ump-teenth time how she managed to get away with such behaviour. But Lady Mableton didn't seem to care, or even notice, and she allowed Leonie to stuff several chocolates into her mouth before she put the box out of reach.

'You spoil that child,' Maria said, snatching up the fur coat.

'I want her to grow up knowing that she's loved. I want her to have everything that I didn't.'

'So you keep saying,' Maria said, turning away, sniffing.

Leonie dribbled chocolate and, realising that the trickle would soon become a stream and flood down the front of Leonie's sky-blue velvet coat, Kitty leapt forward to wipe her mouth on a clean hankie.

'Greedy baby!' Lady Mableton said, laughing.

'But I do hope she won't be sick in the carriage. You must come with us, Kitty. The fresh air will bring the roses back to your cheeks.'

Kitty glanced nervously at Maria. 'It's not my place, my lady. Shall I fetch Nanny Smith?'

'Certainly not! I want you to accompany us today. I decide what is right and proper in my own household,' Lady Mableton said, tossing her head. 'And I saw that look, Maria. Don't browbeat the girl. I'll take her with me if I want, never mind what Nanny Smith says, and you may have the morning off to do your Christmas shopping or whatever you wish.'

'Have it your own way,' Maria said, shrugging.

'Get your coat and hat, Kitty,' Lady Mableton said, picking up her muff. 'It's cold and frosty out of doors and maybe the Serpentine will be frozen over.'

Downstairs in the hall, Miss Iris seemed to be arguing with Warner and, as they approached, she shot a withering look at her stepmother. 'I wanted the carriage this morning, Arabella, but Warner says that you are going out.'

'I'm taking Leonie for a drive in the park,' said Lady Mableton, smiling sweetly. 'We'll be back in time for luncheon and you may have the carriage all afternoon, if you wish.'

'That is so unfair,' Iris said, stamping her foot.

'I have an invitation to luncheon at Brown's Hotel.'

'For goodness' sake, Iris! It's just down the street, you could walk there in two minutes.'

Iris's eyes sparked, making her look like an angry cat and, Kitty thought, if she had fur it would be sticking up all over.

'Arrive on foot like a common shop girl? What would my friends think of that?'

'They would probably admire your spirit of independence,' Lady Mableton said, taking Leonie by the hand. 'Come along, darling. You too, Kitty.'

Warner stood aside, his expression rigidly controlled but, as Kitty hurried past him, she noticed a small muscle twitching at the corner of his mouth. Bob sprang to open the front door.

'Surely you're not taking the nursery maid with you?' demanded Iris, her voice shaking with outrage.

'Goodbye, Iris,' Lady Mableton said, over her shoulder.

'I'll tell Father,' Iris called after her. 'You'll have everyone talking about us and laughing.'

But Lady Mableton seemed not to have heard this last remark, or if she had, she chose to ignore Iris's outburst.

Bob handed her into the carriage and lifted Leonie in after her. He gave Kitty a conspiratorial wink as she climbed in after them. She answered, with the briefest of nods, to confirm that she would cover for Nanny Smith that afternoon and evening. Nanny had been all twitchy and excited for days, confiding in Kitty that her half-day and Bob's had coincided and they planned to spend it together. As the carriage door closed, Kitty tucked herself into the corner, leaning back against the padded leather squabs, and lifted Leonie onto her knee.

Lady Mableton glanced out of the window at Iris, who was standing on the top step with a martyred look on her face and shivering exaggeratedly. Bob gave the coachman the signal to move forward and Lady Mableton turned to Kitty with a rueful smile. 'My stepdaughter disapproves of me.'

'No, my lady, that's not possible. I think you're lovely.'

Lady Mableton laughed, but it was not a happy sound. 'You'll learn as you grow older, Kitty, that sometimes having a pretty face is a curse rather than a blessing.'

'I don't understand, my lady.'

'I think you do. I saw it in your eyes when you first came to Dover Street, that sad look of lost innocence. I knew then that we had much in common. One day you'll grow into a beauty, my dear, and you'll discover that men fall in love with their eyes.' Lady Mableton sighed and turned her head to gaze out of the window.

Kitty tried to puzzle this out as the carriage sped smartly along Piccadilly in the direction of Hyde Park. The suggestion that she had anything in common with such a goddess was startling, shocking and totally inexplicable. How could anyone as beautiful, kind and rich as Lady Mableton not be happy?

Leonie, who up to this moment had been sitting quietly on Kitty's lap, began to wriggle and tug at her bonnet strings. It took all Kitty's patience and ingenuity to keep her amused until they reached the gates of the park, giving her little time to enjoy the sheer luxury of travelling in a private carriage. But she filed the experience away in her mind, intending to put it all in the letter to Jem that she had been writing, just a line or two each night before she went to sleep.

The carriage came to a halt by the bandstand and, almost before it had stopped, the groom had leapt off the dickey seat, opened the door and let down the steps. Getting out last, Kitty looked around in awed delight. The pale winter sun reflected off the glassy surface of the Serpentine and the wine-cold air had a smoky smell. This was the first time she had ever been to Hyde Park and Kitty had never seen so many trees or so much grass in her whole life. It was, she thought, just like being in the country.

Lady Mableton instructed the coachman to walk the horses and they set off on foot. The park was filled with nannies pushing their charges in perambulators or sitting on benches, chatting and keeping an eye on the older children as they raced around or played ball on the frosty grass. Leonie trotted after her mama with Kitty following close behind them, but she could not help noticing that their presence was causing something of a stir amongst the nannies. Heads turned to stare at Lady Mableton, which did not surprise Kitty, seeing that her mistress was the most elegant figure in the park, but she was uncomfortably aware that there was an undercurrent of whispers and giggling. She walked past them with her head held high, balling her hands into fists at her sides and resisting the temptation to slap their silly faces. Lady Mableton, however, appeared not to notice. She walked ahead at a brisk pace, taking the path that curved around the end of the lake, leading to the rose garden where the last of the frostbitten blooms sparkled like drops of blood amongst the thorns. When they reached Rotten Row, where the rich and powerful exercised their fine horses, Lady Mableton stopped and waited for Kitty and Leonie to catch up with her.

'You'd better hold Leonie's hand, Kitty. I don't want her to run in front of the horses.'

Kitty obeyed instantly, despite Leonie's loud protests.

'It's too cold to walk much further,' Lady

Mableton said, tucking her hands deeper into her muff. 'We'll walk back to the Serpentine Road and meet the carriage there.'

They had barely gone more than a few paces when two gentlemen approaching them on horseback drew their mounts to a halt beside them. Instantly on her guard, Kitty didn't like the way the younger man, with flashing, dark eyes, was smiling at her ladyship, as if he wanted to gobble her up in great big mouthfuls.

'My dear Bella,' he said, doffing his top hat, 'what a wonderful surprise.'

Lady Mableton backed away from the prancing stallion, the colour draining from her cheeks, and a look of alarm on her face. Kitty knew instantly that her distress could not be simply due to fear of the flailing hooves. She felt a stab of pride as her ladyship drew herself proudly upright.

'I don't know you, Sir.'

'Come now, my dear. You know that's not true.'

'I'd say her ladyship has a conveniently short memory, Rackham,' said his companion, urging his horse to circle around them.

'I heard that you'd snared a baronet,' said Rackham, his blackberry-dark eyes twinkling. 'You've deprived us all of your talents, Bella. That wasn't fair and we're most upset.'

'You've had your joke at my expense, Sir. Now

please let us pass.' Lady Mableton's voice shook, but she gave him back stare for stare, raising her chin with a defiant toss of her head.

Rackham leaned towards her, caressing Lady Mableton's face with the tip of his finger, outlining her cheek and the angle of her jaw, his smile fading, his voice sounding almost sad. 'You're even more beautiful than you were three years ago; I wouldn't have thought it possible.'

'Leave her alone, Giles,' his companion said in a bored voice. 'Can't you see she don't want to play? Let's get on with our ride.'

'Let me pass,' Lady Mableton said, her voice rising shrilly as Leonie began to cry.

'Running away again, Bella?'

Whether by chance, or urged on by his rider, Rackham's horse moved sideways, pushing Lady Mableton so that she staggered against Kitty. Anxiety bubbled into rage and, scooping Leonie off the ground, Kitty thrust her into her mother's arms.

'Leave her alone, you bloody bullies,' Kitty screamed, throwing herself between the horses, slapping each of them on the rump.

The startled animals reared on their hind legs, whinnying and lunging, almost unseating their riders. Kitty would have gone down beneath their flailing hooves if Lady Mableton had not grabbed her by the scruff of the neck and dragged her to safety.

'That was brave but foolish, Kitty,' Lady Mableton said, peering anxiously into her face. 'Are you all right?'

Kitty nodded; her teeth were chattering too much to allow her to speak.

'Come then,' Lady Mableton said, hoisting Leonie onto her hip and taking Kitty by the hand. 'Leave them to their own stupidity.'

The carriage was waiting in the Serpentine Road. It was not until they were all safely inside, and on their way back to Dover Street, that Kitty was able to speak.

'Who was them men, my lady?'

Lady Mableton's lovely mouth drooped at the corners. 'Part of my past, Kitty, another life best forgotten.'

'You're late,' Nanny Smith snapped, casting a meaningful look at the clock on the nursery wall. 'You knew it's my half-day off and I should have been gone an hour since.'

'It couldn't be helped,' Kitty said, undoing the buttons on Leonie's velvet coat.

'Just because you're the favourite today,' Nanny said, ramming her bonnet on her head. 'Sucking up to her ladyship and pushing me out. You'd better watch your step, young Kitty, or I'll see that you go back to the scullery and let Olive and Dora sort you out.'

'Sorry, Nanny.'

'I should think so.' Nanny yanked at the ribbons on her bonnet, making an unsuccessful attempt to tie a bow. 'Bother the thing! My fingers are all thumbs and it's your fault, Kitty.'

Sitting Leonie in her chair at the nursery table, Kitty offered to tie the bow and, somewhat grudgingly, Nanny allowed her to help.

'Don't tie it too tight,' Nanny said, frowning. 'And I may be a bit late back seeing as how you've kept me waiting.'

'That's all right,' Kitty said, giving the bow a final tweak. 'I got it all worked out if Miss Lane comes nosing round.'

'Right then,' Nanny said, studying her reflection in the mirror above the mantelpiece. 'You owe me that. Now I'm off to meet my young man and if you don't do everything just right, I'll not be responsible for my actions when I get back. Do you understand me?'

'Yes, Nanny.'

'And you see to it that Miss Leonie gets her tea and supper on time.'

Dora and Olive were off duty when Kitty went down to collect the nursery tea tray. The only person in the kitchen was the new scullery maid, a skinny little thing, all elbows and knees, who could not have been a day over twelve. She didn't answer when Kitty spoke to her, just stared with saucer-like eyes and ran into the scullery, closing the door behind her. It wasn't hard to imagine that this was the housemaids' new object of spite. When she came down later to collect her own supper tray, she caught Olive and Dora tormenting the poor girl and Kitty's temper flared.

'Ain't you lot got nothing better to do than pick on them what can't fight back?'

Dora spun around, her mouth twisted as if she had just sucked a lemon. 'Well, look here, Olive. Her high-and-mightiness speaks to us now.'

'You may think you're better than us now you've sucked up to her ladyship,' Olive said, sneering, 'but you're still the same turd that floated in on the tide.'

'I don't care what you say,' Kitty retorted, sticking her chin out. 'You leave that poor girl alone or I'll . . .'

'You'll what?' Dora pushed Kitty with the flat of her hands. 'You'll sneak to Madam?'

'I ain't scared of you, Dora.'

With a swift movement, Dora had Kitty's arm pinned behind her back. She jerked it upwards until Kitty yelped with pain. 'Are you scared of me now?'

Kitty shook her head, even when another savage tug threatened to snap her bones.

'Say it.' Dora spat the words in Kitty's ear, hissing like a snake.

'N-never.'

Olive clawed at Dora's arm. 'Careful, Dora, if you break her arm you'll be in trouble.'

With a hefty push, Dora sent Kitty sprawling onto the tiled floor. 'Get out of my sight, you bag of piss.'

Rubbing her grazed knees, Kitty scrambled to her feet. Holding her head high, she picked up her supper tray, ignoring the pain from her arm, leaving the kitchen to catcalls and hoots of laughter from Dora and Olive.

Upstairs in the nursery, having settled Leonie for the night, Kitty sat down to eat her supper. Taking the cover off the dish, she stifled a scream, jumping to her feet with her hand clamped over her mouth. Lying on the plate was a large, dead rat.

Chapter Four

'What's the matter with your arm, Kitty?' Bella said, noticing that the girl was pale, with dark shadows beneath her eyes and holding her arm limply at her side. 'Have you hurt yourself?'

Kitty bobbed a curtsey. 'I slipped in the bathroom and twisted it a bit, that's all.'

Bella could spot a lie a mile off, she had told them often enough in the past. 'Are they treating you well below stairs? You would tell me if they weren't, wouldn't you?'

'It was an accident, my lady. Shall I take Miss Leonie back to the nursery for her bath?'

Scooping Leonie up in her arms, Bella kissed her rosy cheek, inhaling the sweet scent of Pears soap and the sugary smell of the sweet that Leonie had dribbled all down her chin. 'Night, night, baby. Mama will see you in the morning.'

'Kitty.' Jerking away from her mother, Leonie held her chubby arms out to Kitty.

'She loves you.' Suffering a pinprick of jealousy, Bella passed Leonie into Kitty's arms and was immediately ashamed of herself as she saw Kitty flinch with pain. 'If your arm isn't better by tomorrow, I shall insist that you see my doctor.'

Bobbing a curtsey, Kitty carried Leonie out of the room.

'You spoil that girl.'

Bella spun around to see Maria standing in the doorway that led off her boudoir to her bedroom. 'I know that the poor child is being bullied by the lower servants but she won't admit it.'

'She's a kid from the slums, she's tough and she'll get over it.'

'Some things you never get over,' Bella said, sinking down on the padded velvet stool in front of her dressing table.

'The past is past and you've done all right for yourself,' Maria said, yanking steel pins out of Bella's elaborately coiffed hair. 'Don't meddle with what goes on below stairs.'

'Ouch, that hurt,' Bella said, wincing as Maria dragged the comb through a stubborn knot. 'Be more careful.'

'You've got a face as long as a fiddle!' Maria eyed her reflection in the mirror with a suspicious gleam in her eyes. 'What's up with you tonight?'

'Sometimes I wish I'd stayed single, plain Bella La Rue, singer and dancer, working the music halls. I'm only twenty-three; I'm still young and yet I feel my life is over.'

'You don't mean that.'

'Yes, I do. I mean it with all my heart. I'm tired of pretending to be something I'm not. At least when I'd done my act on the stage I could go back to being myself.'

'Don't talk daft, Bella. This life is a bed of roses compared to flogging yourself to death in cheap music halls, lodging in flea-ridden rooms with damp beds and never knowing where the next penny was coming from.'

'But at least I was free then,' Bella said, sighing. 'People took me for what I was and didn't sneer at me behind my back.'

Maria's harsh expression softened just a little. 'They're just jealous. Now sit still and let me get you ready. You know Sir Desmond hates being kept waiting and you don't want to turn up late at Lord Swafford's dinner party.'

'I don't want to go at all.'

Maria picked up a silver-backed hairbrush and began brushing Bella's hair in long, sweeping strokes. 'What happened today that upset you so much?'

'Nothing.'

'Such a fuss about nothing?'

'Well, Iris was being difficult as usual – and then I met Giles Rackham and his hateful friend in the park.'

Maria's slanting black eyebrows snapped together. 'Rackham! I thought that bastard had gone abroad for good.'

'So did I, but he's back and if he chooses to speak out, I'll be ruined.'

'I doubt he'll do that. He's got too much pride to want the world to know that you ran away from him.'

'I thought he'd abandoned me in Dover. You said he wouldn't come back.'

'And he didn't, not for three whole years, so don't you forget that, my girl. You keep away from him, Bella. He's trouble.'

'I hate him,' Bella said, snatching the hairbrush from Maria's hand and throwing it across the room. 'I hate, loathe and detest him. He's an unprincipled seducer of young girls, a gambler and a liar.'

'Just you remember that when he turns on the charm then,' Maria said, shaking her head. 'Sir Desmond is no fool and a scandal could lose him his seat in the House of Commons. You keep your head, my girl, and think of little Leonie.'

An hour later, dressed in a shimmering gown of ivory satin, trimmed with Brussels lace, Bella glided down the marble staircase to the entrance hall. Sir Desmond and Iris were already there, wrapped in their outdoor clothes, waiting for her.

'You're late, Bella,' Sir Desmond said, making a show of consulting his gold pocket watch. 'You might at least make an effort to be ready on time.'

'I'm sorry, Desmond,' Bella said, as Maria slipped her sable cape over her shoulders. 'It won't happen again.'

'I managed to be ready on time,' Iris said, shooting a resentful glance at Maria. 'And I don't have the luxury of a personal maid. I have to make do with Jane.'

'That will do, Iris,' Sir Desmond said, striding towards the door. 'I don't want to listen to two women bickering all the way to Belgrave Square.'

Iris's mouth turned down at the corners and she tossed her head, but she refrained from answering. Bella could feel her eyes boring into the back of her head as she followed Desmond down the stone steps, and a shiver went down her spine. If Iris were to discover her past relationship with Rackham . . . The mere thought of it made her feel sick with dread.

Lord Swafford's mansion in Belgrave Square was filled with politicians and their wives, eminent writers, artists and intellectuals. Acting out her role as a dutiful wife, there to enhance her husband's reputation and to be decorative rather than to contribute anything to the evening, Bella smiled a lot and said very little. Desmond's contemporaries seemed to appreciate her reticence, and she overheard one of the ladies saying that, in spite of her background, Sir

Desmond's young wife seemed a charming, well-mannered young lady. From the looks that Iris was giving her, Bella knew that she didn't agree. She turned away, determined not to let Iris see that her constant sniping bothered her, and came face to face with Giles Rackham.

'My dear Lady Mableton,' Rackham said, with a small bow. 'How delightful to meet you twice in the same day.'

Bella felt her heart pounding against the cage of her tightly laced corsets and prayed silently that she wouldn't faint. She couldn't keep up the pretence of not knowing him and risk drawing attention to herself. Inclining her head, she forced her lips into a smile. 'Good evening, Mr Rackham.'

Rackham grinned, his teeth startlingly white against his olive skin. 'So you remember me now.'

'I do,' Bella said, unfurling her fan and fluttering it in front of her face. 'And I'm surprised they allowed a libertine like you to enter this house.'

'I'm devastated, my dear Bella,' Rackham said, holding his hand over his heart, his eyes gleaming with amusement. 'You seem to have lost your good opinion of me, but I remember a time when it wasn't so.'

'And I'd rather forget it,' Bella said, in a low voice. 'I don't know how you managed to worm your way into this party but, if you have even the slightest vestige of regard left for me, you'll leave now, before anyone notices you.'

'You know that I would do anything to oblige you, my darling. But it might prove be a bit difficult since our illustrious host, Lord Swafford, is my uncle.'

Glancing over his shoulder, Bella saw Iris watching them with a frankly curious expression on her face. To make matters worse, Desmond had just come into the room, chatting with Lady Swafford, and they were heading this way.

'Just leave me alone, Giles,' Bella said. 'For God's sake, leave me be.'

Rackham took her hand and brushed it with his lips. 'I will. For now, at least.' And he strolled off.

Rackham was seated on the opposite side of the table from Bella at dinner, a few places down and too far away for conversation, but close enough for him to catch her eye every time she turned her head in his direction. Every mouthful of food seemed to choke her and, by the time Lady Swafford rose to her feet, requesting the ladies to join her in the drawing room, leaving the gentlemen to their port and cigars, Bella had developed a pounding headache.

In the drawing room, Lady Swafford, a large

lady with a deep bosom that seemed to droop beneath the weight of her diamond and ruby necklace, sailed up to Bella and laid her hand on her arm. 'You look a little pale, my dear. Are you not feeling quite the thing?'

'Just a headache,' Bella said, glancing over Lady Swafford's ample shoulders to make sure that Iris was not within earshot. Mercifully, she was seated at a card table on the far side of the room. 'It will pass in a moment or two.'

'I understand,' Lady Swafford said, with a knowing smile. 'I was like that every time I was in an interesting condition.'

'No, no,' protested Bella, feeling the colour flood to her cheeks. 'It's not that.'

'No? But of course you already have a little daughter, have you not?'

'Leonie, yes, she is just two.'

'And Sir Desmond already has a son and heir,' Lady Swafford said, her gaze shifting as her interest appeared to wane.

'Yes, Edward, but I have yet to meet him.'

A spark of curiosity lighting her eyes, Lady Swafford put her head on one side. 'I believe that the gallant captain is in the Sudan fighting the Dervishes.'

'We all hope he will return safely before too long.'

'Yes, of course, we hope that for all our brave men, and no doubt the gentlemen are still mourning the death of poor General Gordon at Khartoum, and celebrating our glorious victory at Omdurman. You'll excuse me, my dear.'

Lady Swafford patted Bella's hand, moving on to speak to an elderly dowager, who was clutching a hearing trumpet to her ear and shouting at her companion, a thin, pale-faced young woman who looked as though she would rather be anywhere but here.

Bella could sympathise wholeheartedly with that feeling, but she was thankful that Lady Swafford's interrogation had ended so quickly, although she could sense the covert stares of some of the older matrons. Once again, she had the uncomfortable feeling that she was the main topic of conversation. Her head ached miserably and her stomach muscles felt as though they were tied in a knot; she dreaded the moment when the gentlemen joined them and a further, inevitable encounter with Rackham. Iris appeared to be deeply engrossed in her card game or else she was deliberately ignoring her. Either way, Bella thought this infinitely preferable to direct confrontation. She took a turn around the room and found a quiet corner where she sat down on a love seat, watching the door. When the gentlemen joined them, she would seek out Desmond, plead her headache and ask him to send for the carriage.

*

Iris had not spoken a word on the short carriage ride home, but Bella was well aware that she was furious with her for spoiling the evening. Inscrutable as ever, Warner had taken their outer garments and sent the second footman to the kitchen with Iris's demand for a tray of hot chocolate to be sent to the drawing room.

'And send the hall boy with coal for the fire,' Iris said, casting a sidelong glance at Bella. 'It's far too early to retire to bed.'

Desmond tucked Bella's hand in the crook of his arm and led her to the foot of the staircase. 'You look very pale, my dear.'

'It's just the headache, Desmond.'

He slipped his arm around her waist and placed his lips close to her ear. 'Have you something to tell me, Bella?'

Bella stifled a sigh. Why did everyone assume that her only purpose in life was to produce children like a brood mare? Desmond's breath was hot on her cheek, smelling of brandy and cigars, but she resisted the urge to pull away from him. 'No, it really is just a headache.'

'We'll have to see what we can do about that,' Desmond said, running his finger over the curve of her breast. 'Send Lane away as soon as possible, my dear, I'll join you in a little while.'

Bella forced a smile as she slid from his grasp. She could feel him watching her as she mounted the stairs and she suppressed a shudder. Instead of going directly to her room, she climbed the next flight of stairs to the nursery suite. The day nursery was in darkness and the fire had burned to white ash. Thinking that Nanny was probably asleep in her room, Bella tiptoed into the night nursery. Leonie lay, sleeping soundly in her cot, her cheeks round and rosy in the flickering glow of the nightlight. Leaning over to lay the lightest of butterfly kisses on Leonie's golden curls, Bella tucked the fluffy blanket beneath her chin. Her heart swelled with love and her throat constricted with emotion as she gazed at her adored child. Leonie was so innocent, so perfect and so utterly beautiful. Nothing else mattered in the world other than providing her with the love and security that had been so painfully missing in her own childhood.

Wiping a tear from her cheek, Bella turned to look at Kitty. She lay in her truckle bed with the curtain pulled back, as though she had been gazing up at the night sky, before she had fallen into a deep sleep. Her feet were poking out from beneath the serviceable cotton quilt and, as Bella went to cover them up, she hesitated for a moment. Taking a closer look at the callused soles of Kitty's feet, Bella recognised the results of going barefoot, even in winter. There were crimson patches over her toes where badly fitting boots had rubbed her skin into blisters: these had burst, festered and formed weeping sores.

Snatching up Kitty's boots, Bella shook her head, stifling an exclamation of disgust at their worn state. The heels were worn down; the soles holed and padded with brown paper. Replacing them on the floor beside the bed, Bella reached out to stroke the uneven regrowth of hair on Kitty's head. Poor kid, she thought sadly, you could be me just a few years ago and I know exactly the kind of hell you've been through. Creeping out of the room, Bella closed the door quietly behind her. She could do nothing to wipe out Kitty's past, and she could not be seen to favour her too much, but at least she could do something about the boots. She would give Nanny Smith instructions to take Kitty to Harrods first thing tomorrow, and ensure that she was fitted out with a new pair of properly-fitted, leather boots.

Seeing a glimmer of light beneath the door to Nanny's room, Bella opened it just far enough to peep inside. The gaslight on the wall made popping sounds but the room was empty and the bed neatly made up. Bella gave an exasperated sigh; Nanny Smith should have been close at hand in case Leonie needed her. She would have something to say to that stupid country girl in the morning, but that would have to wait. Her headache was getting worse by the minute and now she was feeling sick. Bella made her way slowly down the stairs. She hoped desperately that Desmond would forget his promise to come to her bed and that he would lose himself in the brandy bottle. Try as she might to put it out of her head, Rackham's darkly handsome face kept appearing in her mind's eye, sending icy shivers down her spine at the thought of what he might say or do. Desmond would not tolerate a scandal.

As Bella entered her room, Maria emerged from the bathroom, followed by a cloud of scented steam.

'You don't have to tell me,' Maria said, undoing the tiny buttons at the back of Bella's evening gown. 'I can tell by your face that it's your curtain call tonight.'

'I can't do it, Maria. I've got a splitting headache and you know what he's like when he's been drinking.'

'Not as bad as your father was, that's for sure. At least Sir Desmond don't come at you with the buckle end of his belt,' Maria said, deftly slipping the satin gown off Bella's shoulders and allowing it fall to the floor. She began to loosen the laces of Bella's corset. 'Get yourself into the bath and I'll mix you a few drops of laudanum in some brandy. You'll get through it, Bella. You always do.'

Next morning, Bella had her breakfast brought to her room. She could not venture downstairs until Maria had skilfully covered the bruises around her mouth with her own special mixture of cold cream and fuller's earth. When that was done to her satisfaction, she tinted Bella's ashen cheeks and lips with a touch of Roger & Gallet's pink salve. A silk blouse with a high neck covered the purple fingermarks on her throat and Maria deftly combed a lock of hair over the bruise on her temple.

'You'll do, but I still say you should have stayed in bed,' Maria said, standing back to gaze critically at her handiwork.

Getting stiffly to her feet, Bella winced with pain as her corsets pressed on her sore ribs. 'And give Iris the satisfaction of thinking that I'm a pathetic, sickly creature like her poor mama?'

'I don't wonder that the first Lady Mableton took to her bed and died young,' observed Maria, folding her arms across her chest. 'If this is what you get for nothing, I'd hate to see what you'd get for something.'

'Please, I don't want to talk about it,' Bella said, walking stiffly towards the doorway. 'As you said, it's nothing to the beatings my own father gave me. The bruises will fade and he'll be so sorry this morning that he'll go out and spend a small fortune in Asprey. I'll get yet another expensive bauble for my pains.'

'If that's all you get, you'll be lucky,' Maria said, scooping up the telltale pots of cream and powder.

'At least he'll let me be if I'm with child. He seems convinced that Edward will be killed in action and quite happy to replace him with another son. I don't believe the Mabletons know the meaning of the word love.' Bella left the room before Maria had a chance to say anything more on the subject, and made her way painfully up to the nursery.

Nanny Smith dropped a curtsey but not before Bella had seen a look of alarm cross her face.

'Where were you last night, Nanny?'

'My lady?'

'I came to the nursery quite late but you weren't here, nor were you in your room. You know that you're not supposed to leave Miss Leonie unattended.'

Nanny Smith blushed and her eyes started from her head. 'I'm sorry, my lady. I was . . .'

'Nanny went downstairs to get me a boiled onion for my earache,' Kitty said, spooning bread and milk into Leonie's pink mouth. 'I had earache something terrible.'

She's lying, Bella thought, but I mustn't seem to favour her. 'You were sleeping soundly enough when I came to look at baby. You looked very peaceful to me.'

'That's right, my lady,' Nanny said, hastily. 'I did go to the kitchen but I had to wait for the water to boil. I came back as quick as I could. It won't happen again, I promise you.'

'Make very sure it doesn't, or I might consider replacing you.' Bella had the satisfaction of wiping the smile off Nanny's face. She had never particularly liked the woman, but then she had had no say in selecting her for the position. When Desmond had brought her home, after their hastily arranged marriage in Caxton Hall, Iris had already organised the setting-up of the nursery and that had included the hiring of Nanny Smith.

'It won't happen again, my lady. I'm truly sorry.'

'Then we'll say no more.' Bella grasped the back of a chair as a wave of dizziness swept over her. Maria had been right; she should have stayed in bed. 'Nanny, I want you to take Kitty to Harrods this morning and buy a pair of serviceable boots that fit her properly. Charge them to my account.'

'Yes, my lady. Are you all right, Ma'am?'

'Just a dizzy spell. Kitty, let me lean on your shoulder.'

Dropping the spoon, Kitty leapt to her feet.

'Help me back to my room,' Bella said, as the room began to swim crazily around her.

Collapsing onto the chaise longue in her boudoir, Bella caught her breath, coughing and spluttering, as Maria wafted sal volatile beneath her nose.

'You would have it your own way,' Maria said,

closing the lid on the silver vinaigrette with a snap. 'I'll turn back your bed and you're to lie down until I say you're fit to get up again.'

Through half-closed eyes, Bella could see Kitty staring at her with a disturbingly adult look of understanding and sympathy in those remarkable topaz eyes. 'Thank you, Kitty,' she whispered. 'I feel much better now.'

'Can I get you anything, my lady?'

Shaking her head, Bella managed to smile. 'You're a good girl, Kitty. Tell me, are you happy here?'

'Yes, my lady, but . . .'

Forgetting her own troubles for a moment, Bella raised herself to a sitting position. 'But what? You must tell me if anything is wrong.'

'No, Ma'am, you've been kindness itself to me. It's just that once, when I was young, I had a silly dream. It's nothing.'

Resisting the temptation to smile, Bella nodded seriously. 'We all dream when we are young. Tell me, how old are you, Kitty?'

'Fifteen, my lady.'

'And your dream, tell me about it.'

'I wanted to work in a dress shop up West but now I think I'd rather stay with you.'

'I'd hate to lose you, my dear, and Leonie would be heartbroken if you were to leave. You'd best go back to the nursery and make sure that she's all right.'

'Yes, my lady.' Kitty bobbed a curtsey and left the room.

Bella lay back against the buttoned velvet of the chaise longue and closed her eyes. In less than a week it would be Christmas Day and the house would be full of guests; there would be luncheons and evening parties leading up to New Year's Eve. She felt a tear slide down her cheek as she thought of the start of yet another New Year tied to a husband that she did not love. Would it be a new beginning or just the continuation of the life that she had made for herself? She adored Leonie with all her heart and soul, but the thought of a new pregnancy terrified her; it would be just another link in the chain that bound her to Desmond, and from which there was no escape. That was, unless Rackham chose to denounce her, and then there would be the inevitable scandal, disgrace, divorce and a headlong tumble back into poverty.

When she was up and about again, Bella discovered, to her utter dismay, that Rackham had wheedled his way into Sir Desmond's good books by paying marked attention to Iris. And Iris seemed to have metamorphosed overnight from a sharp-tongued spinster, officially on the shelf, to a simpering débutante hanging on Rackham's arm. Bella had no alternative but to watch Rackham expertly using his charm, flattering and cajoling Iris until she was soft and malleable as melted wax. What his intentions were, Bella could only guess, but she prayed that he was looking for a rich wife. Iris was independently wealthy, having inherited a substantial sum of money from her maternal grandfather's estate. Bella was certain that, if Rackham knew this, he would be willing to marry Iris, if only to get his hands on her fortune. She wondered if Iris knew that Rackham frequented gambling clubs, bet heavily at the races and was spectacularly unlucky at both. The thought of having Rackham as a stepson-in-law was so appalling that it made her feel physically sick, but at least it meant he would leave her alone. Even Rackham would stop short of trying to seduce his stepmother-in-law. Wouldn't he?

The New Year celebrations were overshadowed by the news that Captain Edward had been one of the officers wounded at Omdurman and had been confined to a military hospital, although there were few details as to the degree of his injuries. Desmond was in daily contact with the War Office, but did not seem unduly worried; Bella had grown used to this callous show of indifference. Instead of being proud that his son was fighting for his country, Desmond seemed aggrieved that Edward had not stayed at home to run the country estate in Essex and to oversee the London properties owned by the Mableton family. You couldn't trust damned land agents, Desmond often said, or bloody solicitors if it came to that. They would either cream off some of the rents or be too soft on recalcitrant tenants. Bella had already decided that if Edward was like his father or Iris, then she would really rather not make his acquaintance.

On the night of the opera, just four weeks into the new year, Bella had pleaded a headache in order to escape the inevitable meeting with Rackham, who was now well and truly ensconced as Iris's suitor. But Desmond had not been in a sympathetic mood and had told her abruptly to pull herself together; she must accompany them to the opera or people would draw the wrong conclusions.

In the first interval, Desmond had gone to the bar and Iris had spotted a friend in the next box. Failing to persuade Rackham to accompany her, she had pouted and flounced off alone.

'So, Bella,' Rackham said, moving swiftly onto the gilded chair beside Bella, 'I have you all to myself for once.'

Fanning herself vigorously, Bella kept her gaze fixed on the audience below them. 'You have Iris besotted with you, can't you be satisfied with that?'

Rackham moved a little closer, running his

fingers down her arm and taking her hand in his. 'You know that I want you, Bella. I've no interest in a skinny old maid.'

Bella snatched her hand away, rounding on him angrily. 'Leave me alone or I'll tell Desmond that you're annoying me and you won't have a chance to win Iris's hand and fortune.'

Rackham leaned back in his seat, smiling lazily. 'Iris is desperate for a husband and she'll believe me rather than you any day. As for Sir Desmond, I can tell him intimate little details about you that only a husband would know. How do you think he would react to that?'

Bella's heart gave an uncomfortable thud and her pulse began to race, but she raised her chin and looked Rackham in the eye. 'I hear your gambling debts are threatening to bankrupt you. You would lose a rich wife and have nothing to gain.'

Rackham's eyes sparkled appreciatively. 'I love it when you fight back. I can't stand mealy-mouthed, timid little women. I'm a gambler, my dear; I'll risk it all for you. Doesn't that excite and flatter you, Bella?'

'It revolts me, if you must know.'

Rackham slid his arm around her waist and put his lips close to her ear. 'It excites you, admit it.'

Wriggling out of his grasp, Bella rapped him across the knuckles with her fan. 'I hate you.'

'I may be a fool but I can't get you out of my mind.' Rackham leaned back in his chair, his eyes clouded with desire. 'I'll not rest until I have you again, Bella.'

'Never,' Bella said, feeling a bubble of hysteria rise to her throat. 'They're coming back – I can hear them. For pity's sake, Giles, stop this now.'.

'Never!' Rackham said, mimicking the inflection in her voice, his eyes dancing mischievously. 'You'll agree to come to me in my rooms in Half Moon Street or I'll kiss you now, in front of the entire audience of the Royal Opera House.'

As he leaned across her, Bella caught the once so familiar scent of his body – lemons, sandalwood, Macassar oil and musk. The smell was so evocative that it made her feel weak and dazed, but also furious. She pushed him away just as Iris opened the door and entered, bristling with annoyance.

Apparently unruffled, Rackham leapt to his feet and held out a chair. 'My dear, Iris, how was your friend?'

Iris glared suspiciously at Bella and sat down, fanning herself. 'Eustacia is very well and she wants to meet you, Giles. In fact she couldn't understand why you didn't accompany me to her box.'

Rackham sat down beside her, taking her hand in his. 'It wouldn't have been proper to leave

Lady Mableton all on her own, now would it, my love?'

Behind Iris's rigid back, Rackham cast Bella a mocking glance. Conscious of the colour rushing to her cheeks, Bella turned her head away.

Sir Desmond staggered back to the box just as the curtain went up on the second act, and he slumped down onto the chair next to Bella. A fine tracery of scarlet veins flushed his face and he smelt strongly of brandy. 'I'm not in the mood for these damned warblers bellowing away in a foreign language,' he complained in a loud voice. 'I've sent for the carriage. We're going home.'

Bella's heart sank as she recognised the hot look in his eyes. 'We can't leave in the middle of the opera.'

'Can't we, though?' Desmond got to his feet rather unsteadily and jerked Bella from her seat. 'Giles will bring Iris home, won't you, my boy?'

The next day, after a season of excessive indulgence, Sir Desmond was confined to his room by a severe attack of gout, giving Bella a legitimate excuse to cancel dinner parties at the house and refuse the invitations that arrived in the post. The doctor visited daily. He shook his head over Sir Desmond's chronic condition, warning him that if he continued to drink port and brandy, and did not follow the strict eating regime of plain food washed down with weak tea or water, then he could not be held responsible for Sir Desmond's failure to recover. Needless to say, his advice was ignored and Bella gave up trying to persuade Desmond to moderate his habits.

Freed from his nocturnal visits, she found it easier to be in his company, spending each morning helping him go through his constituency papers and writing letters that he dictated. Every afternoon she spent with Leonie and Kitty, driving in the carriage if the weather was bad and walking in the park when it was fine. In this way, she made certain that she was out of the house when Rackham paid his daily calls on Iris.

The grip of the bitter winter weather gradually eased into a mild and balmy spring and, after months of waiting, a telegram arrived for Desmond bearing the news that Edward was almost fully recovered and on his way home. Desmond seemed moderately pleased that his son was safe but Bella's heart sank at the prospect of Edward's imminent return. She dreaded meeting yet another Mableton; he was bound to be like his father or, worse still, like Iris.

Three weeks later, and with no definite news of Edward's impending arrival, Bella had seized the opportunity to escape from the house in Dover Street for an hour or two by taking Leonie and

Kitty to St James's Park. She sat on a bench by the lake, watching Leonie and Kitty feeding the ducks. Kitty had gained at least an inch in height since she had been put to work in the nursery, and her hair had grown back into a mass of short curls with the sheen of a conker. There was almost no comparison now with the scrawny little waif who had come to work as a scullery maid. With a little kindness and care, Kitty had blossomed into a confident, happy girl who would soon be sixteen and Leonie adored her. Bella smiled as she listened to Leonie's squeals of delight as Kitty threw crumbs to the ducks. Kitty would be an excellent replacement for Nanny Smith who was, for some unknown reason, becoming increasingly unreliable and overemotional.

Relaxing in the dappled shade beneath the canopy of fresh green leaves, Bella was startled as a shadow fell across the path in front of her. Shading her eyes against the sun, she looked up to find a tall, thin man dressed in the uniform of an army officer, standing in front of her.

'Would you mind awfully if I sat down on your bench?' he asked in a deep, slightly gruff, but pleasant voice.

Bella saw that he was leaning heavily on an ebony cane and she moved up a little, making a space. 'No, of course not.'

He sat down, staring absently at the water, and Bella couldn't help stealing a glance at him. He was deeply suntanned and what she could see of his hair beneath his military cap was light brown, streaked almost white at the tips by exposure to the sun. As if he sensed that she was staring, he turned his head and Bella found herself looking into smiling eyes that were an incredible shade of hazel, flecked with gold.

'I – I'm sorry,' Bella said hastily. 'I didn't mean to stare. I was just wondering if you had come home from the war in the Sudan. It's really none of my business.'

'Don't apologise. It's a natural assumption and you're quite right. I've just arrived.'

'And you're going home. How wonderful for you and your family.'

His smile faded and he stared into the distance. 'I doubt if I'll get much of a welcome, but yes, I am going home although I'm putting off the moment for as long as possible.'

Bella swallowed an inexplicable lump in her throat as her heart went out to him. She wanted to reach out and take him by the hand but she stopped herself just in time. 'That's so sad, but I know exactly what you mean.'

He turned his head, his eyes bright with interest and surprise. 'You do?'

Bella felt herself blushing. 'Yes, I do.'

'I can't believe that anyone as beautiful as you wouldn't be totally adored and cherished by her family.'

His words might have sounded like blatant flattery coming from someone like Rackham, but this man had an honest, open face and candid eyes that convinced Bella of his sincerity. She was conscious of a huge surge of physical attraction that thrilled and scared her. And he felt it too, she was certain of it. This was mad, dangerous and it had to stop right now. 'That's my daughter,' Bella said, pointing to Leonie who was attempting to hand-feed a wary pigeon.

'You're married?'

Bella's breath caught in her throat as she heard a note of disappointment creep into his voice. 'I am.'

Getting to his feet with the aid of his stick, he took off his hat and his hair shone in the sun like a halo; he stood to attention, bowing from the waist. 'May I introduce myself, Ma'am? Edward Mableton, at your service.'

Chapter Five

Hearing her mistress's cry of surprise, Kitty spun around to see Lady Mableton jump to her feet, clutching her hand to her breast. The tall army officer seemed to be just as taken aback and, for a moment they stood, mutely staring at each other. The gentleman appeared to recover first and his taut features relaxed into a charming smile that, although it was not directed at her, went straight to Kitty's heart. It seemed to have the same effect on Lady Mableton, who hesitated for a moment, and then tucked her hand in the crook of his arm. Slowly, they began to walk, their heads inclined towards each other, so rapt in each other's company that they seemed to have forgotten that anyone but themselves existed.

Kitty picked up Leonie and put her in her favourite toy of the moment, a galloping gig with two wooden horses that pranced when the chair was pushed along. Leonie gave a token protest and called for her mama, but quietened immediately when Kitty put the reins in her chubby little hands. Following them at a discreet distance, Kitty could see that they seemed to have a lot to talk about. He must, she thought, be a very old friend.

When they reached the house in Dover Street, Kitty was astonished to see that, instead of taking his leave and walking away, the officer rang the doorbell. Even more astounding, when Warner opened the door, his eyes widened with surprise and then, strangest of all, he actually smiled. Following them into the vestibule, Kitty lifted Leonie from the gig and, as Bob came to wheel it away, she caught him by the sleeve.

'What's going on?'

'Don't you know?' Bob grinned at her, jerking his head in the direction of the officer. 'That's Captain Edward, Sir Desmond's son, come home from the war in the Sudan where he'd been wounded in battle. He's a hero.'

Bursting with the news, Kitty took Leonie by the hand, leading her up the three flights of stairs to the nursery. No wonder her ladyship had looked surprised and pleased at the safe return of her stepson. He was a handsome young man and he didn't seem to be anything at all like his sister, Miss Iris, and bore no resemblance at all to Sir Desmond. He must, she thought, take after his poor dead mother, while Miss Iris was definitely very much like her father. Kitty had learned to be very careful when it came to Miss Iris. You never quite knew what sort of mood she would be in;

she could be happy and smiling one minute, especially if Mr Rackham was there, but she could turn in a moment, sour as yesterday's milk.

Leonie's chubby legs made climbing the stairs a slow process and, growing impatient, Kitty carried her the rest of the way. Kicking and screaming, Leonie made it clear that she did not appreciate this indignity and Kitty was relieved to set her down on the nursery floor. She was about to pass on the news that Captain Edward had come home safe and sound, but she stopped short. Nanny Smith was hunched in her rocking chair by the empty hearth, with her hands covering her face and great sobs shaking her whole body.

'You must not cry,' Leonie said, toddling over to Nanny and tugging at her apron string. 'Stop it, I say.'

Scooping Leonie up in her arms, Kitty sat her at the nursery table, where afternoon tea was laid out ready. 'Nanny's not well, Miss Leonie. You eat up your tea like a good girl and then I'll read you a story.'

Leonie snatched a slice of bread and butter and crammed it into her mouth.

'Good girl,' Kitty said, filling her beaker with milk. 'You eat up while I look after poor Nanny.' Making sure that Leonie had enough food to keep her busy for a while, Kitty went over to Nanny. 'What's wrong?'

Nanny Smith rocked backwards and forwards shaking her head. 'I'm ruined, ruined.'

'Keep your voice down,' Kitty said, taking her by the shoulders. 'You're frightening Miss Leonie.'

Hiccuping and sniffing, Nanny wiped her eyes on her apron. 'It'll be the workhouse for me now. My dad won't take me in and I'll be dismissed without a character.'

Kitty stared at Nanny's swelling belly and wondered how she could have missed the signs; she had seen them often enough with Maggie. 'You're in the family way?'

'Yes, are you satisfied? Now you'll get my job and I'll be out on the streets.'

'But Bob will marry you, won't he?'

Nanny shook her head. 'I dunno, I haven't told him yet. He'll have to leave service if we get married, then what will we do?'

'You'll manage,' Kitty said, trying to sound positive. 'My sister, Maggie, has five nippers. It's hard but they get by somehow.'

'You don't know anything about anything,' stormed Nanny, glaring at her, red-eyed. 'You're the mistress's pet now, but you just wait until you fall for what some bloke tells you and you let him have his way. You're no better than me, so shut up.'

Kitty shuddered inwardly at the thought of being intimate with any man. Sid's probing fingers and mask-like expression as he tore at her clothes flashed before her eyes. She had not been near Sugar Yard since that day and, even in the relative safety of Tanner's Passage, Kitty always walked warily, jumping at shadows.

Looking into Nanny's woebegone face, swollen and ugly from her bout of crying, Kitty felt nothing but pity. Even though it had been grudgingly given, Nanny had helped her a lot during the past few months. She had been assiduous in teaching her manners and correcting her speech, although Kitty knew quite well that this had been done more out of irritation than a conscious attempt to educate her. Even so, Kitty was grateful and had been eager to learn. If she could improve herself it would help her get work in a dress shop or, her latest and most burning ambition, to be Lady Mableton's personal maid. After all, Miss Lane was getting on a bit; she must be fifty, if she was a day, and that was very old. Perhaps, one day soon, she'd retire to a cottage on Sir Desmond's country estate in Essex.

'You must speak to Bob,' Kitty said earnestly. 'Tell him the truth and find out if he means to stand by you.'

Nanny shot her a suspicious look. 'Why would you care what happens to me?'

'It could happen to anyone,' Kitty said, suppressing a shudder. 'Us women have got to stand together, like them in that Women's Suffrage movement.'

In the days that followed, there seemed to be uproar both above and below stairs. Captain Mableton's unannounced arrival had caused panic in the servants' quarters. Mrs Brewster sent the housemaids scurrying up to get his room ready and Mrs Dixon set about making his favourite meals. Kitty overheard Olive, Dora and Jane chatting excitedly about the captain's dashing good looks and lovely manners. They nudged each other and suppressed coy giggles when they were supposed to be saying morning prayers. Kitty thought they had all gone quite mad; as if someone like the captain would look twice at a serving maid! But at least Nanny was a lot happier now that Bob had agreed to stand by her. They had both given their notice in at the same time, leaving Mr Warner and Mrs Brewster just a month to find suitable replacements, and that only added to the feverish atmosphere below stairs. James, the second footman, was tipped by the lower servants to get Bob's job, but nothing was yet settled and Mr Warner went about looking harassed.

Above stairs, Sir Desmond had become even more demanding than before, raging at the painful condition that kept him chairbound, and was not resolving as quickly as the doctors had predicted. His shouting and roaring could be heard from the nursery suite. But if Sir Desmond was not too happy, then her ladyship was positively blooming, and Kitty knew instinctively that this was entirely due to Captain Edward. The whole household had fallen under his spell; he had charmed them all with his easygoing ways and abundant good nature. Unlike Mr Rackham, whose brooding presence sent shivers down Kitty's spine and seemed to cast a dark shadow over Lady Mableton. Miss Iris, on the other hand, changed completely and became all giggly and skittish when Mr Rackham was present. She had taken to wearing daringly low-cut dresses and Jane was required to spend at least an hour each evening helping her to dress and put up her hair. Kitty heard all this from George, her one ally below stairs, but she could see for herself that Miss Iris was a clinging ivy and Mr Rackham the tree trunk. Kitty had also seen the look in Mr Rackham's eyes when they rested on Lady Mableton, and she sensed danger.

Quarter day, when the servants were paid, coincided with Kitty's half-day off and she set out once again to visit Betty and Polly in Tanner's Passage. She carried a small wicker basket packed with a pot of Miss Lane's rose and glycerine hand salve, a present for Betty, and a paper poke with two ounces of pink and white coconut ice for Polly. In her pocket a purse jingled with coins that she had set aside for Maggie and the children. Although Kitty longed to see them, she realised with a heavy heart that to visit Sugar Yard would be asking for trouble. She would, she had decided, leave the purse with Betty and ask her to make sure that Maggie got it when Sid was at work in the fish market.

Kitty walked a good part of the way, stepping out in her new boots that made walking a pleasure, and she caught the horse-drawn omnibus in the Strand. She could smell the city stench even before she stepped onto the pavement. The heat reflected off the paving stones, unrelieved by even the slightest breeze. Kitty could feel the sweat trickling down between her shoulder blades as she walked briskly towards the river and Tanner's Passage. The door to number seven was open – probably, she thought as she stepped inside, to let a bit of air into the stuffy house. She could hear voices coming from the kitchen; unmistakably there was Betty's high-pitched chatter and the deeper tones of a man. Thinking it must be one of Betty's gentlemen lodgers, Kitty entered the room, blinking as her eyes adjusted to the gloom.

'Kitty,' cried Betty. 'What a lovely surprise and what good luck you came today of all days. Look who's here.'

'Kitty! I don't believe it.'

'Jem?' Dropping her basket on the table, Kitty gasped in amazement, but the breath was knocked from her body as Jem leapt forward and, wrapping his arms around her, gave her a hug that lifted her clean off her feet.

'Little Kitty, you've grown up.' Jem held her at arm's length, his lean, deeply tanned face split into the familiar grin.

'What about you?' Kitty gasped, looking him up and down in amazement. 'You must be at least a foot taller. I hardly recognised you. I can't believe you're really here.'

'I'm here, right enough, safe and sound and glad to be home.' Jem hooked one arm around Kitty's shoulders and the other around his mother.

'He walked in that door as large as life and twice as cocky,' Betty said, wiping her eyes on her apron. 'Gave me quite a turn. I might have fainted if I'd been the fainting sort.'

'And how is my Polly?' demanded Jem. 'How has she been, Ma?'

'Same as ever, love. Poll never complains, poor little soul.'

'I must see her,' Jem said, heading for the door.

'Take it gently, Jem,' Betty cried, hurrying after him. 'I don't want her getting a shock.'

But Jem had bounded on ahead, taking the stairs two at a time. Betty clambered up after him, puffing and panting with the effort, with Kitty following close behind. By the time they reached the sitting room, Jem was seated on the sofa and cradling Polly in his arms.

He looked up with a watery grin. 'I missed you all so much, but I'm home now for a bit of leave and I want to hear everything that's been going on since I went away. But first,' Jem gave Polly another hug and laid her back against the cushions as he got to his feet, 'but first I've got presents for each one of you.' He dashed from the room and they heard his feet pounding down the stairs. He returned more slowly, hefting his wooden sea chest. Setting it on the floor he threw himself down on his knees to open it. 'There's a fine woollen shawl for you, Ma.'

Betty draped the soft grey shawl proudly around her shoulders, even though the temperature in the room resembled that of an oven on baking day. 'It's wonderful, Jem,' she said, with a wobbly smile. 'Just beautiful.'

'And for you, Poll, a dolly all the way from New Zealand.' Jem brought out a rag doll with yellow woollen hair and an embroidered smile.

Polly hugged it to her, making crooning noises.

Jem laughed and patted her cheek. 'Good girl, that's the ticket.' He sat back on his haunches and regarded Kitty with a wry grin. 'Now for you, Kitty. I didn't forget my promise to bring you some boots, but I see that you're well fitted out there now. So it's just as well I didn't know your shoe size and bought you these fancy silk slippers instead.' With a flourish, Jem handed Kitty a pair of scarlet satin slippers, embroidered in silk with dragons and oriental flowers that sparkled with glass beads.

Betty let out a gasp of admiration and Kitty took them in her hands, staring at them wide-eyed. 'Jem, I don't know what to say. I never seen anything so beautiful in my whole life.'

'That's a girl,' Jem said, flushing beneath his tan. 'Well then, Ma, how about a nice cup of tea? And then you can both tell me what's been going on. I can see that things have changed in your quarter, Kitty. I'm not sure about your hair – I liked it best when it hung down your back in curls – but you still look pretty as a peach. Things must be better nowadays in Sugar Yard.'

'I nearly forgot,' Kitty said, jumping to her feet. 'I brought you a present too, Betty, and some sweeties for Poll.'

Jem glanced from Kitty to his mother, frowning. 'Is there something you ain't telling me?'

'I'll get the tea,' Betty said, casting an anxious glance at Kitty. 'You'd best tell all, ducks. If you don't, then I will.'

By the time Kitty had finished telling Jem everything that had happened since the day that

Sid tried to rape her, his expression had darkened to one of disgust and fury.

'If I'd been here I'd have killed him,' Jem said, jumping to his feet and going to stand by the window, staring down into Tanner's Passage. 'Say the word, Kitty, and I'll go round there this minute.'

'No, don't,' Kitty cried, clasping Polly's hand as she began to cry. 'Don't speak of it again. You're upsetting Poll, and anyway, it was a long time ago now. I'm settled in a good position in Dover Street. I ain't complaining.'

'A good position,' Jem said, turning his head to stare at her hair. 'And they did that to you? I thought life at sea was tough when I first joined up but I can see it's a lot harder on land.'

'Things is better now, Jem. I'm a nursery maid, not a skivvy.' Touching her hair, Kitty felt the colour rush to her cheeks. Her curls had grown back but her hair was still unfashionably short.

'I liked your hair the way it was.' Jem's jaw stuck out in a stubborn line and it might have ended in an argument if Betty had not returned at that precise moment.

'Well now, Jem,' Betty said, setting the tray down on the fruitwood table. 'Let's have a cup of tea and you can tell us all about your voyage.'

Jem looked as though he would argue, but seeing that Polly was doing her best to attract his attention, he went to sit by her, taking hold of her hand and stroking it. 'I'll tell you some tales, Poll. I've seen sights that would make your eyes pop out of your head.'

Polly gurgled appreciatively.

'I've seen whales bigger than a London omnibus,' Jem continued, giving her a cuddle, 'and fish that fly in the air. I've seen mountains taller than St Paul's and I've heard mermaids singing.'

'Don't go filling her head with a lot of nonsense, Jem,' Betty said, handing him a cup of tea. 'She mustn't get overexcited.'

'You're set on the life at sea then?' Kitty put in quickly as Jem opened his mouth to protest. 'You think you'll stick at it?'

'I'm a deck apprentice now,' Jem replied, puffing himself up proudly. 'Captain Madison is putting me in for my third mate's ticket next year.'

'Jasper Madison was a good friend to your dear father,' Betty said, glancing up at the picture of the *Belvedere*. 'But I could wish you'd chosen a different profession, son.'

'There's no danger these days, Ma. Not on a steam ship with powerful engines like the *Mairangi*. I'll be first mate before I'm twenty and I'll take care of you and Polly – Kitty too.'

'Thanks, Jem,' Kitty said, a bit annoyed at his assumption that she needed looking after. 'But there's no need for you to worry about me. I can take care of myself. I'm a nanny now and I'm doing very nicely, thank you.'

'Well!' Jem said, his sun-bleached eyebrows knotting over the top of his nose. 'I don't know about that.'

'I do,' Kitty said, with a stubborn lift of her chin. 'I got my own life all planned.'

'I always thought that one day you and me would be a pair, Kitty.'

Betty clapped her hands. 'I can't think of anything that would make me happier than to see you two married.'

'I'm only just fifteen,' Kitty said, shaking her head. 'And even if I was older, I wouldn't be thinking of getting married, not to anyone. I've seen how it works out and I can't say I'm keen on the idea.'

Jem's frown darkened into a scowl, but his irrepressible sense of humour bubbled to the surface, and he shrugged his shoulders, grinning. 'We'll talk about it another time. Right now, I'm just glad to be home and I'm starving hungry.'

'Oh Lord, and I've nothing in the house to eat,' cried Betty, throwing up her hands.

'Not to worry, Ma,' Jem said, jingling the coins in his pocket. 'I'm going to treat us all to pie and mash or jellied eels, whichever you prefer. And then I'll take Kitty back to Dover Street in style, in a hansom cab.'

As the cab drew to a halt, Jem leapt out to help Kitty down. 'Wait here, cabby,' he said. 'I'll need you for the return trip.'

'Don't walk me to the door, Jem,' Kitty said, taking a quick look down the area steps, half expecting to see Olive or Dora peering up at her through the window of the servants' hall.

'I'll see you safely inside. Young girls like you shouldn't be out at night in London, not even up West.'

'We're not allowed followers, you'd best get back in the cab quick before they see you.' Seeing that Jem's mouth had set in a determined line, and his jaw was sticking out in a way that meant an argument would follow for certain, Kitty reached up and kissed his cheek. 'I expect you'll have gone back to sea before I get my next half-day off, so ta for the lovely slippers, and I'll write to you often.'

Kitty made a move towards the doorway but Jem sidestepped, blocking her way. 'Hold on a bit, Kitty. I've three weeks ashore and I don't mean to waste them. We're still friends, ain't we?'

'Of course, but—'

'Then tell me when you take the nipper out walking, and I might just happen to be strolling along the street at that particular time of day. They can't object to that.'

'I ain't got all day, young sir,' called the cabby.
'Just coming, mate. Well, Kitty?'

The door below them opened and Dora poked her head outside, her face alive with curiosity.

'We leave the house each afternoon at three, now go away for pity's sake,' Kitty said, running down the steps and brushing past Dora.

Dora was apparently not in the mood to be ignored. 'I'll tell Mrs Brewster that you've got a fella and that'll put paid to your airs and graces, Nanny Cox.'

Turning on her, Kitty saw Dora's face contorted into a spiteful sneer. She tossed her head. 'And you'll look pretty daft when I tell her it was my brother what saw me home.'

Grabbing Kitty by the wrist, Dora's fingers knotted into a claw. 'You think you're better than us now, but you ain't. I'll get you one day.'

Drawing herself up to her full height, Kitty looked Dora in the eye. 'I'm not a scared kid any more. You don't frighten me.'

'Brother, my eye.' Dora spat the words at her.

Grinning to herself, Kitty ran up the back stairs to the nursery. Well, it was partly true, she thought. Jem might have dreamed silly dreams about love and romance in the long months at sea, but they were more like brother and sister than a lot of folk who were true blood kin. All the same, it was a cheering thought that she might see him again before he sailed away to the other side of the world. Jem had certainly changed a lot during his year away, and any girl would be proud to step out with such a fine-looking fellow. Safe in her room, Kitty took a last, loving look at the satin slippers and sighed, knowing that she would never be able to wear them while she lived in this house. Unless she wanted to find them cut to ribbons, she would have to hide them carefully under the mattress, away from the prying eyes of Dora and Olive.

Sir Desmond's condition had become chronic and his doctor advised a trip to Bath to take the waters. Kitty gleaned her knowledge from snippets of conversation that she overheard between her ladyship and Miss Lane, and the rest from George. Lady Mableton had almost fainted when it was suggested that she should accompany her husband to Bath.

Kitty might not have believed this, but she had brought Leonie to her mama, all dressed up for a walk to the park, and she had found Miss Lane administering smelling salts and a few sharp words to Lady Mableton. Once again, Kitty had been shocked by the familiar tone that Miss Lane used when talking to her mistress. She couldn't help wondering why her ladyship didn't give Miss Lane a good talking to instead of taking her scolding to heart and looking as though she might burst into tears at any given moment.

Kitty had been within an ace of telling Miss Lane to leave out speaking to her ladyship like she was her equal. It wasn't right and it wasn't fair.

For several days, Kitty could feel the tense atmosphere above stairs and Miss Leonie was at her most fractious and demanding. Lady Mableton kept to her rooms and Captain Edward went daily to the Officers' Club. When Kitty went down to the kitchen to collect the meals for the nursery, George told her in whispers that James and Jane had reported fierce rows amongst the family above stairs. Then all of a sudden it seemed that Sir Desmond had changed his mind and he left early one morning, accompanied only by Mr Warner.

Immediately the atmosphere in the house seemed to change. Lady Mableton's fragile beauty that had faded like a wilting rose under the strain of Sir Desmond's tempestuous outbursts, bloomed once again with an almost incandescent radiance. Captain Edward curtailed his visits to his club, staying at home and, it seemed to Kitty, that he was always with Lady Mableton. Their high spirits seemed to affect everyone living in the house; even Miss Iris appeared less vinegary and more pleasant. The only person who did not seem relaxed and happy was Mr Rackham. Whenever Kitty happened to see him, she felt an inexplicable shiver of apprehension run down her spine.

Their afternoon walk to Green Park became an established routine, with Lady Mableton and Captain Edward walking on ahead, and Kitty pushing Miss Leonie in her galloping gig, just a little way behind. She did not have to turn her head to know that Jem, who had been lounging casually in a doorway a bit further along the street, was now strolling along behind them. Once they were in the park, Lady Mableton and Captain Edward walked beneath the trees, too deeply absorbed in each other to notice what was going on around them.

Jem and Kitty played ball with Leonie, fed the ducks or sat on a park bench, keeping an eye on her while she picked daisies or chased butterflies. An hour would slip by and then two, and still Lady Mableton and Captain Edward continued to walk and talk. Keeping a careful eye on them, in case they should suddenly return, Kitty observed that they had taken to holding hands. On one occasion, as she listened to Jem telling her of yet another of his thrilling adventures at sea, Kitty saw Captain Edward draw her ladyship into the shade of a willow tree. He kissed her hand and then, with a swift movement, he drew her closer and kissed her on the lips. They pulled apart almost immediately, casting anxious glances around, and then, apparently satisfied that no one had seen them, they clasped hands, gazing at each other and smiling. Kitty turned her head away, her stomach muscles knotted in alarm. How stupid had she been not to realise that my lady and Captain Edward had been slowly and inexorably falling in love? And what terrible consequences would come from such a passion?

'You haven't heard a word that I've been saying,' complained Jem. 'What's the matter, Kitty? You look like you've lost a shilling and found threepence.'

Kitty shook her head. She couldn't even tell Jem; it was my lady's secret and she would guard it with her life. 'I heard you all right.'

'No you didn't. You was miles away.'

Kitty jumped up to catch hold of Leonie's petticoats as she started to run towards her mother. 'Not yet, Miss Leonie. Wait here for your mama.'

'There's something rum going on there,' Jem said, following her gaze. 'Ain't they related in some way?'

'That's none of your business, Jem Scully,' Kitty said, brushing bits of grass off her skirt. 'And you'd better get going before they come back and catch us together.'

Jumping to his feet, Jem caught Kitty around the waist. 'Never mind them, Kitty. You know this is my last day ashore. I'll be sailing on the evening tide.'

'I didn't know that. I mean, surely not so soon?'

'So you will miss me a bit then?'

Jem's blue eyes were laughing but there was an eager look in them that made Kitty catch her breath. 'Of course I'll miss you. You're my best friend, Jem, and always will be.'

'More than a friend, Kitty. You and me belong together.'

'Please don't start all that again.'

Jem dropped his hands to his sides and his smile faded. 'I'm not giving up that easily, Kitty. One day I hope you'll change your mind about us, but I can wait.'

Kitty caught a movement out of the corner of her eye and, turning her head, saw that Lady Mableton and Captain Edward were coming towards them. 'You'd better go quick.'

'Not unless you promise to come and see me off at the docks.'

'You know I can't.'

Leonie broke free from Kitty's restraining hand and ran towards her mother. Lady Mableton bent down and lifted her up, kissing Leonie's rosy cheek. 'Bad girl to run away from Nanny.'

'I'm sorry, my lady,' murmured Kitty, glancing nervously from Lady Mableton's flushed face to Captain Edward's. She was relieved to see they were both smiling.

'It's all right, Kitty. No harm was done,' Lady Mableton said, casting a curious glance at Jem. 'Is this young man a friend of yours?'

'I'm sorry, my lady,' Kitty said, before Jem had

a chance to speak. 'I know it ain't allowed, but Jem is an old friend.'

'And a seafarer by the looks of things,' said Captain Edward, eyeing Jem's reefer jacket and shiny brass buttons. 'What ship do you sail on, young man?'

Tugging off his cap, Jem snapped to attention. 'The *Mairangi*, Sir. We set sail on the evening tide, bound for New Zealand.'

'How splendid!' cried Lady Mableton, her eyes shining as she set Leonie down on the ground. 'How romantic to sail to such a faraway place.'

'I don't know about that, Ma'am, but I would sail away far happier if Kitty could come and see me off.'

Appalled by Jem's boldness, Kitty nudged him in the ribs. 'Jem, you shouldn't speak so to Lady Mableton.'

'I admire a bold fellow,' Lady Mableton said, laughing and casting a sidelong glance at Captain Edward. 'Of course you must go and see him off, Kitty.'

Despite Kitty's protests, Lady Mableton insisted that she must have the evening off, and Captain Edward wished Jem *bon voyage*, handing him some coins with instructions to send Kitty home in a hansom cab.

When they arrived back at Tanner's Passage they found that Polly had suffered one of her funny turns, and had been put to bed with a draught of laudanum to quieten her down. Betty cried and hugged Jem. She blessed Kitty for coming to see him off, as she could hardly leave poor Poll in this sad state. Jem went upstairs to say his own goodbyes to Polly and came down again, blowing his nose and rubbing his eyes, pretending that he had a speck of dust in them. Kitty knew he was blinking away tears and she wanted to hug him, but she stopped herself in time; Jem would take it all wrong and she mustn't give him false hope.

'Goodbye, Ma,' Jem said gruffly. He wrapped his arms around his mother and hugged her. 'Take care of yourself, old girl.'

'Let me go, you big stupid,' Betty said, pushing him away. 'You get going or you'll miss your ship.' She managed a brave smile, but Kitty could see her mouth working as though she wanted to cry.

'I'll be back afore you know it,' Jem said, hefting his sea chest onto his shoulder. He headed for the door, knocking a chair over on his way.

Kitty righted it, turning to Betty with a wobbly attempt at a smile. 'He'll be all right. You mustn't worry.'

The dock was crowded with horse-drawn wagons, carts and people milling about in a seemingly disorganised fashion. A constant stream of men poured up and down the gang-planks of the steam ship *Mairangi*, loading the provisions for its long journey. The air was filled with noise, and Kitty almost lost Jem in the midst of the hustle and bustle. She heard him calling her name and then, craning her neck, she spotted him standing on his sea chest, waving his cap.

Edging her way through the crowd, Kitty was hot and flustered by the time she reached him. 'I thought I'd lost you.'

'No chance of that,' Jem said, grinning. 'You're stuck to me like glue, Kitty.'

'We're much too young to even think about courting.'

'Maybe, but I'm a faithful sort of chap and I'll not change.'

'We'll always be friends.'

Jem stared at her for a moment, pushing his cap to the back of his head. 'I wish I was good at words. It's all here in my head but when I start talking it all comes out wrong.'

'I care about you, very much. Can't we leave it like that?'

Shoving his hand in his pocket, Jem brought out some coins. Selecting a golden guinea he held it up in front of her face. 'D'you know how many days I got to work to earn this much money?'

Kitty shook her head. 'I don't.'

'A lot of days.' Jem took a knife from his belt.

'This coin is like you and me. You're the one side and I'm the other.'

'What are you doing?' Kitty watched in horror as Jem knelt on the cobbles and hacked the coin in half. 'Have you gone mad? It takes me over a month to earn a guinea.'

Scrambling to his feet, Jem pressed one half of the coin into her hand, closing her fingers around it. 'That's my pledge to you, Kitty. No matter what happens, you hang on to that and I'll keep mine. One day I hope you'll look at me different, but I'll not press you.'

'I'll always love you like a brother, Jem. I can't promise nothing more.'

'That's all I ask, for now at least,' Jem said, kissing her on the tip of her nose. Taking her hand, he pressed two half-crowns into her palm, closing her fingers over the coins. 'I told that cabby over there to wait and take you back to Dover Street. It ain't safe for you to walk these streets on your own.'

Eyeing the coins, Kitty shook her head. 'It's an awful waste of money, Jem. This would feed a family for a week.'

'Promise me you'll take the cab.'

'I promise, but I still think—'

Twisting one of her short curls around his finger, Jem looked deeply into her eyes. 'I love you, Kitty.'

Before she could answer, he had picked up his

sea chest and was off up the gangplank. As he boarded the ship, Jem turned and blew her a kiss. With a last cheery wave, he disappeared from view.

Kitty stood on the quay wall, watching while the crew went about their duties and the great engines purred into life. Steam belched from the funnels and the gangplanks were hauled up. The mooring ropes were released and the great ship began to move. Kitty thought she saw Jem briefly on deck before the *Mairangi* slid away from its moorings. She waved anyway, hoping he might be able to see her. She stood on the dockside until the ship was out of sight and then made her way slowly along the quay wall, heading towards the cabstand. She had not expected to feel anything but a slight sadness that Jem had gone away but, as the sun plummeted behind the buildings, drowning the City in dusky purple, Kitty suffered an almost overwhelming feeling of loss. Her best friend was sailing away to foreign lands; she would miss Jem more than she could have imagined possible.

Realising that she still clutched the piece of gold coin in her hand, she glanced nervously over her shoulder to make sure no one was looking, and then tucked it safely away inside her corset so that it nestled between her breasts. It was a daft thing for Jem to have done but it had touched her deeply. The knowledge that someone cared that much about her made her feel all warm and squashy inside; it was strange but sweet, to be treasured and stored away like the fragment of gold coin. She smiled to herself as she made her way to where the cab had been waiting, but it seemed the cabby had got tired of waiting or had picked up another fare. Shrugging her shoulders, Kitty set off to catch the omnibus and, still thinking about Jem and not considering where she was going, she followed the familiar route that would take her past Sugar Yard.

Realising her mistake, she broke into a run, but as she reached the pub where Sid drank away his wages, Kitty couldn't help glancing through the open door. The smell of stale beer and tobacco smoke made her wrinkle her nose; her heart missed a beat when she saw Sid leaning against the bar. Instinct told her to run but she froze with terror at the sight of him and her limbs wouldn't respond. Forcing them to move, Kitty felt as though she were wading in deep water, her breathing was ragged and the sound of her own blood drumming in her ears deafened her. She broke into a run but a pair of strong hands caught her, pinning her arms to her sides. Kicking and screaming, she was dragged inside the pub door.

'Look what I found lurking outside, Sid. Does this belong to you?'

Kitty saw Sid's fist coming towards her but she

couldn't dodge the blow . . .

She regained consciousness to find herself being dragged into a dark alleyway between two warehouses.

'Thought you'd got away with it, did you?' Sid muttered through clenched teeth. He threw her down on the cold, hard ground. 'Well, now I'll give you what for, my lady. Put you in your place right and proper.'

Kitty kicked and fought but another clout round the head stunned her. Sid came at her like a maddened bull, forcing her legs wide apart. His raddled face hovered above hers like a hideous incubus, his eyes darkened with lust and his breath foul with stale drink and tobacco. His weight pinned her to the cobblestones, making struggling futile, and his knuckles grazed her flesh as he ripped his trousers open, sending buttons pinging onto the cobbles. She opened her mouth to scream, but he clamped his free hand over her face.

The searing pain of his first thrust into her almost tore her apart. Writhing with agony, she bit at his hand but he was crushing her, squeezing the breath of life from her lungs. Again and again he thrust into her, tearing her bodice and exposing her breasts, kneading them like putty and sucking savagely at her nipples. She was suffocating, she couldn't breathe. The sour stench of his breath made her want to vomit. This couldn't be happening; it wasn't real. It was a terrible dream: a terrifying nightmare. But the pain was real; the terror was real and so was the disgust and utter humiliation. After what seemed like an eternity he collapsed on top of her, panting and laughing, but it seemed that he was far from finished. He ran his tongue down her cheek, nipping at her neck and sinking his teeth into the soft flesh of her breasts, biting her nipples, until the pain became unbearable and Kitty sank into the black pit of oblivion.

Chapter Six

'Bella, there's been an accident.' Maria burst into the bathroom where Bella lay relaxing in a hot, scented bath. 'The police have brought Kitty back in a terrible state.'

Bella jerked herself upright, sending a wave of fragrant water onto the marble-tiled floor. 'Oh my God!' She leapt out of the bath, snatching the towel from Maria. 'I'll come at once.'

'Best get dressed first.'

Ignoring Maria's protests, Bella rushed into her bedroom and dragged a blue silk robe over her naked body. Stuffing her feet into swansdown slippers and wrapping a shawl around her shoulders, she hurried from the room with Maria close on her heels.

In the servants' hall, Bella found Mrs Brewster bending over Kitty's inert body. She lay on the sofa, apparently unconscious, with Florrie waving burnt feathers under her nose in an attempt to revive her. Olive and Dora huddled together in the doorway and Jane clutched at James's arm, her eyes wide with shock. Two burly police officers stood to attention behind the sofa.

'What happened?' demanded Bella. 'Is she badly hurt?'

The older and more senior officer took off his helmet and tucked it under his arm. 'Begging your pardon, Ma'am,' he said, bowing stiffly from the waist, 'but this isn't a subject fit for a lady's ears. If I might have a word with Sir Desmond . . .?'

Bella drew herself up to her full height. 'My husband is away from home, Officer. You may speak quite openly to me. I am not easily shocked.'

The sergeant gave a delicate little cough, casting a wary glance at Maria, who stood close by Bella with her arms folded across her chest and a warning scowl on her face.

'It was an assault, my lady. The young person was found unconscious in an alleyway near Billingsgate Market. She had been attacked most brutally.'

Bella leaned over Kitty, shuddering at the sight of the ugly bruises on her face and the parts of her body left exposed by her torn, bloodstained clothing. Taking off her shawl, Bella covered Kitty's traumatised limbs. 'Has anyone sent for the doctor?'

'If you please, Ma'am,' Mrs Brewster said, bobbing a curtsey, 'I took the liberty of sending George for the doctor as soon as Kitty was brought home.'

Kitty stirred and coughed as the acrid smell of the burnt feathers began to work. Her eyelids fluttered, opened for a moment, and then closed again.

'You're safe now, Kitty,' Bella said, patting her hand.

Florrie dropped the feathers on the floor and began to snivel, burying her face in her apron. 'Poor Kitty – who would have done such a dreadful thing?'

'And what was she doing out all alone in a place like that, I'd like to know?' Olive said, in a loud whisper to Dora. 'Especially when it wasn't even her night off.'

'Now, now, Olive,' Mrs Brewster said, glancing anxiously at Bella, 'that's no way to talk. Kitty had my lady's special permission to visit a friend.'

'Some people get what they deserve.' Dora's face twisted into a malicious grin. 'I knew that fella wasn't her brother. This is what you get for acting like an alley cat.'

'Silence! I won't tolerate this dreadful behaviour.' Casting a fierce look in Dora's direction, Bella turned to the sergeant. 'Have you any idea who would do such a dreadful thing, Officer?'

He shook his head. 'Ma'am, if we might have a word in private . . .?'

'Of course.' Bella drew Maria aside, speaking in a low voice. 'Stay with Kitty. I want to be informed immediately the doctor has seen her. I'll be in the drawing room with the police officers.'

Bella was halfway up the steps when Edward came hurrying through the baize door.

'I heard the commotion. What on earth is going on?'

'In the drawing room, please, Edward,' Bella said. 'There's been some trouble.'

Upstairs in the drawing room, the two police officers stood grimly to attention.

Edward sat down on the sofa beside Bella and his hand sought hers, giving her fingers a gentle squeeze. 'Have you any idea who did this terrible thing?' Edward directed his question at the sergeant.

'No, Sir. The young person was unconscious when we arrived on the scene, alerted by a constable on patrol. She come round just long enough to tell us her name and give us this address.'

'I hope you catch him,' Bella said, curling her fingers around Edward's hand. 'The brute who did this to her should be hanged.'

'Quite so, my lady,' the sergeant said, running his finger round the inside of his uniform collar. 'A dreadful act indeed! We'll need to speak to Miss Cox when she recovers sufficiently. But, in the meantime, if you could let us have some personal details of the unfortunate victim, then we won't bother you any longer tonight.'

Bella shook her head. She knew nothing about Kitty's past or, if it came to that, she knew nothing about any of the servants in her household. How far she had come from her roots in the East End now that she was a titled lady. Seeing Kitty lying on the sofa, battered and brutalised by a horrific rape, had brought the past flooding back. The poor girl, not yet grown to womanhood, could have been herself at a similar age; only then it was not a cruel stranger who had raped her, but someone much closer to home. She closed her eyes, pressing her hand to her temples in an attempt to banish the appalling memories.

Edward's arm went about her and she could hear his voice, but it sounded far away. 'Lady Mableton is naturally distressed, Officer. I'm sure that Mrs Brewster has the details you need.'

'Of course, Sir. We'll find our own way out.'

Edward's arms tightened round Bella as the door closed behind the police officers. 'Darling, Bella. Are you all right?'

She leaned her head against his shoulder. 'I'm sorry, I just felt a bit faint.'

'You should have stayed in your room and let me deal with this terrible situation,' Edward said, his voice filled with tenderness. 'I'm here to look after you now, my darling.'

Bella wanted to laugh hysterically and to cry at the same time. 'Oh, my dear, if only it was as easy as that.'

Edward held her closer and, for a wonderful, dangerous and self-indulgent moment, Bella slid her arms around his neck. She could feel the heat of Edward's muscular body through his starched cotton shirtfront, searing her flesh as if the thin layer of her silk robe had melted away. She caught her breath as his lips caressed the hollow at the base of her throat, moving upwards in light, teasing kisses. His mouth claimed hers with a fierce hunger that matched and inflamed her desperate need for him.

Edward pulled away first, his eyes clouded with desire as he dropped butterfly kisses on Bella's forehead, nose and lips. 'My God, Bella. I love you so much.'

Trembling and dizzy, Bella laid a finger against his lips. 'And I love you, Edward.'

'Say it again. Let me hear you say it again, my darling.'

'Edward, there's so much you don't know about me.'

'There's nothing you could say or do that would make me love you any the less,' Edward said, clasping her hands in his. 'I want you so much, my love, that it's tearing my heart out being so close to you and yet so far away.'

'We have so little time together, Edward,' Bella

said, her voice catching on a sob. 'Don't spoil it.'

Edward's eyes darkened and he dropped his gaze, staring down at their intertwined hands. 'You are my father's wife and I have no right to love you, Bella.'

'We can't help how we feel about each other.'

'I fell in love with you the first moment I saw you sitting on that bench in St James's Park,' Edward said, slowly raising his head.

Bella felt her heart give an erratic leap as she saw the tortured expression in his eyes, but she forced herself to sit quietly, resisting the almost overwhelming temptation to admit that she didn't care a jot about honour or loyalty.

Edward got slowly to his feet. 'If I'd been an honourable man I would have gone away again without ever setting foot in this house, but I couldn't let you go, not when I'd just found you. That was my mistake and now we're both paying for my selfish stupidity.'

Bella stared up at him, unable to move as the pain of his words shafted through her heart. The tears that she had been struggling to hold back began to flow unchecked.

'Don't say that, Edward. Please don't say that.'

'Oh, my darling, don't cry.' Edward lifted her to her feet, holding her to him and stroking her hair. 'I can't bear to see you hurt and upset, that's why I have to go away.'

'Go away? You can't go away.'

'And I can't stay here under my father's roof, seeing you every day, knowing that you love me as I love you, but never being able to do anything about it.'

'You can't leave me. You mustn't leave me. I'll die if you go away.'

Smiling gently, Edward kissed her on the forehead. 'Part of me will die too, my love, but I'm a professional solder and my wounds are healed. I have to rejoin my regiment and it's better if I go sooner rather than later, before it's too late and we do something that we'll both live to regret.'

Bella wrenched herself free, anger burning away sorrow. 'So you're running away, back to battlefront where you can be a hero and leave me here to suffer the consequences.'

Edward's face contorted with pain and he dropped his arms to his sides. 'My father loves you, I'm certain of that. How could he not? And you have Leonie to consider.'

Bella stuffed her clenched fist into her mouth to prevent herself from screaming out that his father was a sadistic brute, a cruel bully, who beat her in the name of love in order to satisfy his perverted sexual appetite; but she couldn't bring herself to tell Edward anything so dreadful about his own father.

Edward's strong features crumpled with distress and he took her by the shoulders, looking deeply into her eyes. 'I don't know if it's cowardice or bravery, but I do know that if I stay in this house one night longer I'll forget you're a married lady and that I'm supposed to be an honourable gentleman.'

But I'm not a lady, Bella thought miserably. If you knew the sordid details of my past, my beloved Edward, then you might not be so damned honourable. But, there again, you might walk out on me in disgust. Exhausted by a flood of conflicting emotions, Bella laid her head against his shoulder, unable to speak. She could feel Edward's heart beating against her breast and his blood drummed to the same beat as her own.

A sharp rapping on the drawing room door barely registered in her consciousness, she only knew that Edward had pushed her gently away, bidding the person to enter. Looking up, Bella saw that it was Maria.

Casting an anxious glance at Bella, Edward rose to his feet. 'What is it, Miss Lane?'

'Lady Mableton asked to be informed as to Nanny Cox's condition, Sir.'

'I'm coming,' Bella said, getting to her feet and walking towards the door. She dared not look back at Edward. If she wavered for a moment, she knew that her resolve would crumble and she would never be able to leave him.

Maria marched on ahead up the stairs to the nursery suite with Bella following close behind.

Silently she opened the door to the nanny's bedroom, where Kitty lay beneath the sheets on the narrow iron bed. Her face was deathly pale with livid blue-black bruises on her temple, around her eyes and mouth, with lips swollen and split.

Bella's stomach gave a sickening lurch as she saw teeth marks on the slender column of Kitty's neck. 'Poor child! Poor little girl.'

'The doctor gave her a strong dose of laudanum,' Maria said, straightening the bed-clothes. 'She should sleep for a good few hours.'

'I'll stay with her,' Bella said, pulling up a chair. 'You'd best sleep in Leonie's room.'

Maria folded her arms across her chest, frowning. 'I hope you're not planning to go to him tonight.'

Bella sank down onto the hard wooden seat; it was impossible to conceal anything from Maria and she was too exhausted to be angry. 'That's all over. He's leaving in the morning and returning to his regiment.'

'Thank God for that,' Maria said. 'You've had a lucky escape, my girl.'

Bella sat up all night, watching over Kitty. Maria came in early next morning and sent her off to bed, insisting that she needed her sleep. It was midday when Bella awakened with a start. In the long, dark hours while she had been sitting at

Kitty's bedside, she had been rehearsing what she would say to Edward to stop him leaving: now it could be too late; he would probably have left the house hours ago. Bella sat up, swinging her legs over the side of her bed, reaching for the bell pull. Her hand closed on the tassel and she hesitated. If she summoned Maria to help her dress, she would have to admit that she was going out alone. Cold unthinking panic seized her. She had to see Edward one last time. If she couldn't make him change his mind, at least she could say goodbye. If she hurried, she might catch him at the Officers' Club.

With Warner away in Bath, the servants had become a bit lax and, as Bella came down the stairs, she breathed a sigh of relief to find that the vestibule was deserted, with not a sign of a footman or hall boy. Her heart pounded erratically against the whalebone cage of her corsets as she opened the front door and slipped outside, very nearly colliding with Giles Rackham.

'Well, good afternoon, Lady Mableton,' Rackham said, doffing his hat. 'This is a delightful surprise.'

'I'm afraid the pleasure is not mutual,' Bella said, sidestepping him.

'Don't tell me that Lady Mableton is going out unaccompanied even by the trusty Maria,' Rackham said, following her down the steps.

'What would Sir Desmond say if he got to hear about it?'

'Mind your own business, Rackham,' Bella said, waving her parasol as a hansom cab turned the corner of Grafton Street. To her annoyance, it clattered past.

'But my dear Bella, it is my business. As your prospective son-in-law I feel a certain amount of responsibility towards you.'

Bella turned on him in a fury. 'Don't play games with me, Giles. I know you too well.'

Rackham threw back his head and laughed. 'What an admission! Shall we tell Sir Desmond about our past, illicit relationship? Now that would be interesting.'

'You're bluffing. If you tell my husband that I was your mistress, do you think he'd let you marry Iris? He'd kill you, even if he believed you.' Bella walked on quickly, heading towards Piccadilly, and to her chagrin Rackham fell into step beside her.

'And what would the honourable Captain Edward Mableton think if he knew the truth about you, my pet?'

'Go away.'

'I've hit a nerve, I see. You wouldn't be heading for a secret assignation with the gallant wounded soldier, would you, Bella?'

Bella stopped and faced him. 'Don't talk rubbish.'

'I've seen the way he looks at you and I've seen the way you look at him. I'm not a fool like your husband. I know there's something going on between you. Why else would you be out alone, risking censure and gossip?'

Bella struggled to keep her composure but she felt faint and sick all at the same time. Giles was too clever by half, and he was a dangerous man to cross. She forced a smile. 'If you must know, I'm going to my modiste to buy a new and very expensive gown, and then on to my milliner to purchase a frivolous and very, very expensive hat, or even two.'

'While your poor sick husband is out of town, that's very deceitful, Bella my dear, and I wholeheartedly approve.'

'Goodbye then, Giles. You can go and court Iris with a massively guilty conscience.'

'Oh, no, my pet. I wouldn't miss this for the world. I'm coming with you. I'll willingly help you to spend your husband's money, and give you my invaluable advice on choosing your gown and hat. You know I have exquisite taste.'

With her heart sinking, but unable to think of a plausible excuse, Bella had no choice but to allow Rackham to accompany her to Madame Jolie's establishment. She painted a smile on her face, but inside she felt as if she were dying slowly and painfully, inch by inch. If she could not contact Edward before he rejoined his regiment, he would be lost to her forever; it took all her skill as an actress to conceal the creeping misery that etched itself into her soul.

Madame Jolie greeted them with a slick smile and, if she was surprised to see young Lady Mableton arriving accompanied, not by her personal maid but by a gentleman who was most certainly not her husband, she was too much of a professional to show it.

Bella went through the motions of looking through fashion plates and swatches of dress material, praying inwardly that Rackham would be so bored that he would get up and go, but to her dismay, he appeared to be enjoying himself. She had tried so hard to blot out the memory of their years together that she had forgotten his impeccable taste. Not only did Giles have knowledge of women's clothing that Bella was sure most women would have considered shocking in an unmarried man, but he also knew exactly what styles and colours suited her best.

After Rackham had virtually chosen two new outfits for her and had been applauded for his good taste by Madame Jolie, no doubt revelling silently at the thought of the enormous bill that she would be sending to Sir Desmond, Bella was becoming more and more frustrated. Her chances of catching Edward before he left his club receded by the minute.

In a last desperate attempt to rid herself of his company, Bella suggested that Rackham ought to return to Dover Street, where Iris would be waiting for him, probably seething with rage because he was so late. Rackham merely laughed and said it would do Iris good. She was too accustomed to getting her own way, and he was damned if he'd allow Bella to choose hats without his guidance.

Two hours later they returned to Dover Street and were met in the vestibule by Iris pacing the floor. She marched past Rackham, ignoring James and George, who were standing stiffly to attention, their expressions carefully controlled. She came to a halt in front of Bella, her face pinched and pale with rage. 'I might have guessed that this was your doing.'

'I don't know what you're talking about, Iris.'

'There's a name for women like you.' Iris screamed, clawing her hands in front of Bella's face, as if she would like to scratch her eyes out.

With a swift movement, Rackham's arm deflected the blow. He caught Iris's wrists in one hand, holding them in an iron grip that brought her wheeling round to glare into his face.

'I think you forget yourself, Madam. This isn't the sort of behaviour I would expect from a lady to whom I am unofficially affianced.'

The angry expression wiped from her face, Iris stared at him pale and wide-eyed. 'Engaged?

Giles, you take me by surprise. You've never mentioned marriage.'

'I haven't spoken to your papa as yet, but now I'm not certain if I wish to do so,' Rackham said, releasing her with a scornful shrug of his shoulders.

If Rackham had slapped Iris across the face she could not have looked more shocked and, for a moment only, Bella almost felt sorry for her.

'Giles, don't be angry with me,' Iris pleaded, running after him as he made to leave. 'I didn't mean it. I was upset, and rightly so, that you had broken your promise to take tea with me.'

Rackham stopped and turned his head to look down at her with raised eyebrows. 'I think you owe Lady Mableton an apology.'

'Never!' Iris cried, tossing her head. 'You can ask anything of me, Giles, but I'll never apologise to that woman. She's cast her spell on you as she did first to my papa and then my brother. If she had not turned his head with her simpering smiles and obvious charms, Edward would never have made the decision to leave the house so suddenly, let alone return to his regiment before he was completely well. Now who knows what dangers he might face and it's all her fault.'

Horrified, Bella stared at Rackham; this was his chance to denounce her to Iris and bring her whole world crashing down about her ears. He would no doubt take malicious pleasure in seeing her humiliated and thrown out onto the street. She clutched at the curved balustrade, with one foot on the bottom stair tread, ready for flight.

Rackham hesitated, staring thoughtfully into Iris's spiteful countenance. Then, raising his eyes to Bella's, holding her gaze for a long moment, a slow smile spread across his hawkish features. 'So the gallant captain has run away, has he? My dear Bella, you have the most abominable luck with men.'

Bella lifted her chin defiantly. She would not let them see that her heart was cracking into shards inside her breast. But it was true and the truth hurt: Edward had run away from the intensity of their feelings for each other. Wouldn't a real man have stayed and fought for the woman that he loved?

'Goodbye, Giles,' she said, surprising herself with the calmness of her tone. 'Thank you for escorting me to my modiste this afternoon. I know I can always rely on you to be present at the wrong time and the wrong place.'

'What does she mean?' cried Iris. 'There is something going on between you, I knew it. I shall tell Papa directly he comes home.'

Rackham tipped his hat in Bella's direction and she saw a gleam of respect in his dark eyes before he turned an impassive face to Iris. 'If you wish to see me ever again, Iris, I suggest you moderate your tone and put an end to these wild imaginings.'

'You can't speak to me like that. I won't have it.'

James sprang to open the door, staring straight ahead as Rackham strode out of the house.

Iris let out a scream of rage and spun around, pointing her finger at Bella. 'You harlot! You can't be satisfied with one man, can you? You have to have them all. Wait till I tell Papa what's been going on in his absence. Just wait.'

'Do what you like, Iris. I'm past caring,' Bella said, slowly mounting the staircase.

Even before she opened the door to the nursery suite, Bella could hear Leonie's high-pitched voice demanding attention and Maria's low-voiced, grumbling reply.

'What's the matter with my baby?' cried Bella, bending down to pick up Leonie as she catapulted towards her, sobbing.

'She's been a little devil this afternoon,' Maria said, throwing up her hands. 'You've spoilt that child and no mistake.'

'Mama, Mama,' sobbed Leonie into Bella's shoulder. 'Bad, bad Maria.'

'There, there, poppet,' crooned Bella. 'Don't cry. Mama is here now.'

'It's no use, Bella. I can't look after a sick girl and Leonie as well as yourself. Best send Kitty below stairs and let Mrs Brewster see to her.'

Bella sat down holding Leonie on her lap, trying to ignore the fact that she had smeared jam all over the bosom of her ivory tussore afternoon gown. 'How is Kitty?'

'Not too good. The police were here again today but she couldn't or wouldn't tell them who did it. It's my guess that she knew the beggar but is too afraid to say.'

Bella cuddled Leonie to her and shuddered. 'She must be cared for. I'll speak to Mrs Brewster and see what can be arranged, but I'll not let any of the lower servants look after Leonie. We'll manage between us.'

'Humph,' said Maria, gazing pointedly at the spreading stain on Bella's dress. 'Better change your dress before you send for Brewster. And don't expect me to help you – I've got my hands full here.'

Bella had already decided that Kitty would not be well looked after below stairs, even before she interviewed Mrs Brewster on the subject. To her surprise, Mrs Brewster was in total agreement with her and suggested that Kitty would benefit from a week or two in the care of Betty Scully. George was sent off in a cab to Tanner's Passage and returned an hour later with a written note from Betty, saying that she would be happy to look after Kitty for as long as her ladyship wanted. Next morning, ignoring Maria's protests that it was not seemly for her to go gallivanting around town in a hired cab, Bella accompanied Kitty to Tanner's Passage.

'Heaven help us. What did that brute do to you?' cried Betty, flinging her arms around Kitty. 'Come upstairs and we'll make you comfy on the sofa with Poll. She'll be so pleased to see you.'

Following them up the narrow staircase, Bella waited until Betty had fussed about settling Kitty on the sofa and wrapping her in a crocheted blanket despite her protests. While Kitty was occupied calming Polly's excited babbling, Bella drew Betty aside.

'Do you know who did this terrible thing to her?'

'I got a good idea but Kitty won't split on him.'

'Then you must, Mrs Scully. You must tell the police.'

'It's Betty, your ladyship.'

'And it's Bella, Betty.'

'Come downstairs and have a cup of tea. I'll tell you everything, but only if you promise to keep it to yourself.'

Sitting in Betty's kitchen, Bella sipped her tea, listening in silence while Betty told her enough about Kitty's past life to bring her to tears. The story was so painfully familiar to her own that she was even more determined to protect Kitty. Finally, after saying goodbye to Kitty and promising to bring her home as soon as she was fully recovered, Bella handed Betty a purse full of money to pay for Kitty's keep.

'Don't worry about our Kitty,' Betty called out as Bella climbed into the waiting cab. 'I'll take good care of her.'

Bella leaned towards Betty, lowering her voice so that the driver could not hear. 'I won't repeat anything you've told me, but I seriously think you ought to tell the police.'

'It would be her word against his, Bella. I know his sort – he'll say she led him on and the law officers are all men; they'll want to believe him.'

'A crime like that must not go unpunished.'

'Don't worry, once the word gets round I don't fancy Sid's chances.'

'Keep her safe, Betty.'

Betty bobbed a curtsey but her answer was lost as the horse sprang forward and the cab pulled away.

Bella leaned back against the worn leather squabs. She was tempted to break her word and inform on Sid, but she had been bred in the East End and she knew that the tight-knit community would close in on itself where one of their own was concerned. There would be justice in the end but it would be meted out by his peers, in whatever way they thought fit, without the involvement of the police. Kitty would be well cared for and safe with Betty Scully. Now there were more urgent matters to contend with. Bella tapped the top of the hood with her parasol.

'Knightsbridge Barracks, please, cabbie.'

It was a vain hope, and Bella knew it, but she had spent half the night working out what to say when she arrived at the barrack gates. With her veil covering her face she stepped out of the cab, ordering the cabby to wait for her. She approached the guardhouse with her head held high even though her heart was pounding a tattoo and her palms were clammy. She knew how it must look and the sceptical expression on the face of the sergeant confirmed her worst fears. He listened politely enough, but it was clear that he had her labelled as a lovesick young woman and, as she gave her maiden name instead of her title, she was barely surprised when he politely but firmly sent her on her way.

Feeling a hot blush flood to her cheeks, Bella was thankful that her veil hid most of her face as she went back to the cab, instructing the driver to return to Dover Street.

The musty smell of the squabs was making her feel sick, and tears of frustration ran unchecked down her cheeks. She was gazing out of the window, barely noticing the cool green expanse of Hyde Park as the cab rattled along the South Carriage Drive, when she saw an army officer on foot, walking with a slight limp. Calling to the cabby to stop, Bella leaned out of the window, calling Edward's name regardless of the curious stares of passers-by. Barely waiting for the cab to draw to a halt, she flung the door open and, catching the heel of her shoe in the lace of her petticoat she would have fallen to the ground if Edward had not rushed forward to catch her.

'Edward, my darling,' Bella cried, flinging her arms around his neck. 'I've been searching for you. How could you leave without telling me?' She lifted her face with her lips parted, longing for his kiss, but he caught her hands in his and drew them gently down to her sides, looking nervously over his shoulder, a dull flush rising from his neck to his thin cheeks.

'Bella, not here, in public.'

Snatching her hands free, Bella stared at him, desperately trying to read the expression in his eyes. 'Aren't you pleased to see me?'

With an abrupt command to the cabby to follow them, Edward tucked her hand in the crook of his arm and began to walk slowly towards Hyde Park Corner. 'Of course I'm pleased to see you, my love, but I'm in uniform.'

There was a coolness in his tone that sent an icy shiver down her spine. Bella stopped in the middle of the pavement. 'You're ashamed to be seen with me?'

Edward ran his finger around the inside of his uniform collar, glancing about, as if expecting to see his commanding officer hiding behind the nearest tree. 'We can't be seen together now. You're my stepmother, for God's sake, Bella. Don't you understand that is why I had to leave without seeing you? Do you think it was easy for me? It nearly tore my heart out, but I knew that I was doing the right thing.'

'So you ran away and left me without so much as a goodbye. That was cowardly, Edward.'

Edward shook his head, a dull flush suffusing his handsome face. 'I was terribly wrong. I should never have let my feelings get out of control. Please forgive me, Bella.'

'How can you stand there and ask me to forgive you when you've broken my heart?' Bella cried, grasping him by the hand. 'I love you and I'd give up everything to be with you.'

Refusing to meet her eyes, Edward turned his head away. 'Don't make this more difficult than it is.'

'Look at me, Edward; don't look away. Tell me you don't love me and I'll go home and never speak of it again. But just say one word and I'll follow you to whatever place the British Army is fighting. Whether it's the Dervishes or the Boers, I'll be there by your side, no matter what happens.'

'You are such a child, Bella,' Edward said, raising his eyes at last, with a reluctant smile. 'It wouldn't work that way. I'd have to resign my commission and we would have to quit the country and live abroad. The scandal would ruin us all and destroy the family. I can't do that to them or to you.' He raised her hand to his lips and kissed it. 'This has to be goodbye. You must understand that.'

'You are weak and you are cruel,' sobbed Bella, beyond caring whether anyone saw or heard. 'Go back to your hateful war and play at being a hero.'

Edward's expression hardened. 'Goodbye, Bella.' With a small bow, he turned on his heel and walked away.

'Oh, Edward, I didn't mean it. Don't go. Please don't go.'

Without turning his head, Edward quickened his pace and walked on.

The cabbie drew his horse to a halt and leapt off his seat, his wizened face crinkled with concern as he peered into Bella's ravaged face. 'Don't take on so, Ma'am. Shall I take you home?'

Chapter Seven

'Wake up, sleepy head! The doctor says you can get up today.'

Kitty opened her eyes and blinked as the sun filtered through the sooty panes of the attic window. 'I don't think I can.'

Betty stood with her arms akimbo, shaking her head. 'Stuff and nonsense! If the doctor says you are well enough to be up and about, then up and about you shall be, and I won't take no for an answer. So drink your tea, put on your wrap and I expect to see you in the sitting room in five minutes.'

'I really don't feel well.'

'Poll's been asking for you and you don't want to disappoint her, do you? Five minutes,' Betty said, wagging her finger to emphasise the point. She left the room, closing the door firmly behind her.

Raising herself on her elbow, Kitty sipped the hot, sweet tea. Betty was right, of course, she must make an effort to get back to normality or Sid would have won. He would have broken her spirit, just as he had done to poor Maggie. Slowly and stiffly, Kitty raised herself from the bed. Her clothes had been washed, neatly mended and laid out on a chair by the bed. Kitty let her nightgown fall to the floor and slipped her shift over her head. She felt dizzy even with such a simple effort. After a moment's rest, she tried to lace her corsets, but the pain from her bruised ribs was too great, and she had to give up the attempt.

It was then that she remembered Jem's half-sovereign and she began to rummage through her things. It wasn't there. She slumped down on the bed, her throat constricting with tears. After everything he had done to her, Sid must have taken the one possession that mattered the most to her in the entire world. Anger, hatred and disgust made her retch and she leaned over the china washbowl, dashing her face with cold water until the nauseous feeling passed.

After a bit of a struggle with laces and buttons, she managed to dress herself and, with a superhuman effort, she made her way down the narrow, twisting staircase to the living room.

Polly looked up with a chortle of delight and flapped her hands excitedly.

Kitty went to sit beside her and stroked her hair. 'There, there, Poll. I'm all better now, as you see.'

Polly managed a nod and a crooked grin.

Kitty reached for a dog-eared book of fairy

stories that was Polly's favourite. 'Would you like me to read you a story?'

'Well, then,' Betty said, bustling into the room carrying a tray of food, 'that's what I wanted to see, Kitty. You're well on the way to mending now.'

'I'm sorry to have been such a burden on you,' Kitty said, taking a bowl of bread and milk and beginning to spoon it into Polly's mouth. 'I should go back to work very soon.'

'I don't know about that,' Betty said. 'But there's a young lad downstairs who says he has a message for you from Dover Street.'

'Is it George? Perhaps Lady Mableton has sent for me.'

'If George has got ginger hair and freckles, then that's who it is,' Betty said, smiling. 'Do you feel up to seeing him?'

'I feel as though I want to crawl into a hole and die, but if I give in to my feelings then that brute has won. I won't let him ruin my life.'

'Then I'll send the young man up?'

'Yes, I'll see him.'

A minute or two later Kitty heard footsteps bounding up the stairs and George burst into the room and then stopped, dragging his cap off his head and going rather pink in the face. 'She said you was well enough for a visitor.'

'I'm much better now.'

'You look a sight better now than you did a

couple of weeks ago.' George stared nervously at Polly as she began to howl. 'Is she all right?'

Kitty patted Polly's hand. 'Sit down, George. You're scaring her. She's not used to strangers.'

George perched on the edge of the window seat, sitting quietly with his hands on his knees while Kitty fed Polly the last of her bread and milk.

'There,' Kitty said, wiping Polly's mouth with a bit of rag. 'See now, Poll. George is all right. He's just come for a visit. No need to be scared.'

'I should say not,' George said primly. 'I'm a respectable bloke. I don't frighten little girls.'

'Why have you come? Has Lady Mableton sent for me?'

George leaned forward, keeping a wary eye on Polly, but obviously bursting with news. 'There's been a right to-do at Dover Street. Miss Iris sent for the master and he cut short his visit to Bath and come storming back. We could hear him shouting at her ladyship, even though the drawing room doors was tight shut. Next thing we knew she was packed off on her own to the country house, and who knows when she's going to be allowed home?'

Kitty stared at him, shaking her head. None of this made any sense. 'What for? What had she done?'

'No one knows exactly, but it seems that Miss Iris thought her gentleman friend, that Mr Rackham, had a fancy for her ladyship.'

'But that's daft. She can't stand the sight of him.'

'Well, I can't say as I blame the chap,' George said judicially. 'But the master ain't taking no chances.'

'What about Miss Lane and Miss Leonie?' In between soothing Polly and taking in this alarming bit of news, Kitty could only stare at George. Surely he must have got it all wrong.

'The master wouldn't let them go with her. Said she wasn't a fit mother.'

'She is too,' Kitty cried. 'She's an angel and little Leonie will be heartbroken.'

'I dunno about that,' George said, shrugging. 'But Miss Iris is hopping mad because Mr Rackham don't come to the house no more.'

'Serve her right, but it can't be because of him. The mistress hates Mr Rackham, I've heard her say so and –' Kitty broke off mid-sentence. She had almost let it out that her ladyship and Mr Edward were sweet on each other, and had just stopped herself in time. 'And she wouldn't want him if he was the last man on earth.'

George tapped the side of his nose. 'That's when a woman really likes a fellow, or so Olive says. You can't blame him for preferring the mistress – she's a corker, there's no denying that. Anyway, here's the rest of it and you'll never believe this, Kitty . . .'

Kitty closed her eyes. 'But you're going to tell me anyway.'

'Mr Edward went off sudden like and Miss Iris accused the mistress of flirting with him. Not that anyone believes her. She's a spiteful cat and no mistake.'

Kitty's head was buzzing as if a whole hive of bees was flying around inside it and she rubbed her hand across her eyes. 'Am I to come back and look after Miss Leonie then?'

George pulled a crumpled note from his pocket and handed it to her. 'Miss Lane sent this. That's why I'm here and I'm supposed to hurry back or I'll be in trouble.'

With one arm still tucked around Polly, who was rocking herself and sucking her thumb, Kitty smoothed the sheet of paper, staring at the spidery writing in Lady Mableton's hand, but obviously written in a state of great distress.

> Mableton House,
> Dover Street
> 25 August 1899
>
> Dear Kitty,
> I have to go away for a while. Do not return to Dover Street unless Miss Lane sends for you. I will see to it that you receive your wages and, when I return from the country, I will send for you.
> Bella Mableton

'But where has she gone, George? Where is Sir Desmond's country house?'

'Dunno exactly, but I heard Mrs Dixon saying it was somewhere out in the wilds of Essex. A gloomy place on the edge of the salt marshes that should have been pulled down years ago, according to her.' George leapt to his feet and his grin faded into a concerned expression. 'You look fagged out, Kitty. I didn't mean to upset you, not after what you've been through.'

Settling Polly back in the corner of the sofa, Kitty got shakily to her feet. 'I'll be fine, George. I'm just worried about the mistress. She was good to me.'

'You get yourself fit and well and come back to Dover Street soon. It ain't the same without you.'

George's visit, together with the disturbing news that he had brought with him, acted like a catalyst in Kitty's recovery. The more she thought about her poor, mistreated mistress sent away in disgrace, denied access to her beloved child, the angrier Kitty became. The thought of her lady-ship abandoned in some gloomy house, in the middle of nowhere, made Kitty shudder. How would she cope without Maria to care for her? She must be so lonely and so sad. Kitty's heart ached for her. Sir Desmond was a brute, almost as bad as Sid; Kitty felt sick at the thought of what he must have put her poor lady through.

Despite her worries about Lady Mableton, Kitty realised that there was nothing she could do, except sit tight and wait.

After many weeks of loving care from Betty, Kitty began to feel more like her old self and, with the appearance of her first monthly since the assault, Kitty cried with relief. Her knowledge of how babies were conceived had been gained mostly by what she had heard through the thin partition wall in Sugar Yard. Betty had warned her gently that a baby could have been the outcome of that savage attack in the alley. Now that she was released from that particular worry, Kitty felt freer than she had for a long time. Her hatred and loathing for Sid had crystallised into a hard nugget somewhere deep inside her soul but, as she grew stronger, Kitty vowed that she was not going to let him ruin her life. She would not hide away, afraid to go out alone and terrified of shadows; she would put it all behind her, but she would never forget, and she would never forgive him.

The weeks had turned into months and now it was winter. Venturing out on her own for the first time since the attack, Kitty insisted on walking to the shop in the next street to buy the hot, crusty bread straight from the baker's oven. Having successfully made it that far, she ventured to the corner shop, where she bought sugar, tea and a brown paper bag full of broken biscuits, so that

Poll had something to dunk in her tea. By the time she had filled the shopping basket, Kitty's heart had stopped racing and the tight, breathless feeling in her chest was forgotten as she walked back towards Tanner's Passage. The primrose-pale November sun struggled to penetrate the haze of smoke and industrial pollution that belched from the factory chimneys alongside the tea-coloured waters of the Thames. A chill east wind whipped up the river from the marshes, bringing with it the stench of the glue works and the sulphurous fumes from the match factory, and yet Kitty couldn't help smiling to herself, as she breathed in the noxious cocktail of smells; she had conquered her fear and she was not afraid to walk the familiar, dirty streets of the East End, which, after all, was her home. She would, she thought, never be afraid of anything again.

'So there you are, ducks,' Betty said, as Kitty walked into the kitchen with her basket of groceries. 'I thought you'd gone and got lost.'

'No, I walked back past Sugar Yard and along the quay wall past the place where it happened.'

Betty's face crinkled with concern. 'You shouldn't have done that, love.'

'Well, it's done and I'm glad I did it. I'm not going to let Sid Cable frighten me ever again.'

The sound of the doorbell jangling urgently, followed by someone hammering on the door knocker, made them both jump. Kitty hurried to answer it before the noise awakened Polly from her morning nap. 'Maggie!'

'Let me in, Kitty, quick!' Glancing anxiously up and down the street, Maggie scuttled into the narrow entrance hall. She leaned against the wall, holding her hand to her chest as she fought to catch her breath.

Joy turned to fear as Kitty stared into Maggie's ashen face. 'What's up? Has something happened to one of the nippers?'

Maggie shook her head. 'Let me sit down for a bit and catch me breath.'

Kitty hooked her arm around Maggie's thin shoulders and guided her to the kitchen.

Betty dropped the potato that she was peeling. 'Gawd above, Maggie Cable! What brings you here?'

Maggie dropped down onto the nearest chair, her breath coming in ragged gasps. 'I see'd you walking past Sugar Yard, Kitty, and it weren't just me. Ned Harman saw you too and he'll tell Sid. You shouldn't have come back. It ain't safe.'

'That's a fine way to talk to your own sister,' Betty said, waving the paring knife at Maggie. 'You should be ashamed of yourself and that vile creature you married. I don't know how you got the brass nerve to come here.'

'Leave her be,' Kitty said, flying to Maggie's defence. 'It ain't Maggie's fault. Can't you see she's done in?'

Betty stabbed the knife into a potato, glaring pointedly at Maggie. 'Where were you when Kitty needed you, I like to know? And how can you live with that man after what he did?' With an angry toss of her head, Betty marched towards the doorway. 'I'm going to check on Polly. You'd best be gone by the time I come back, Maggie, or I won't be responsible for my actions.' Betty stomped out of the kitchen, slamming the door behind her.

Taking the brown teapot from the top of the range, Kitty filled a mug with the strong brew, adding a generous amount of sugar and a dash of fresh milk. Silently she handed it to Maggie and watched her drink. It was alarming to see Maggie looking so pale and drawn; she was even thinner now than she had been when Kitty last saw her and her eyes were sunken into her head, underlined with bruise-like shadows. Her hands trembled as she grasped the mug of tea and she seemed to have difficulty in swallowing.

'Why did you come, Maggie?' Kitty asked. 'I never seen you in such a state.'

'I know who done it,' Maggie whispered, staring into the mug of tea. 'I heard what happened to you and I know it was Sid what done it. You got to get away, girl, afore he comes looking for you.'

'He wouldn't dare. The police would get him for sure.'

'That's what he's afraid of. He thinks you'll split on him.' Maggie grabbed Kitty's hands. 'Get back to Dover Street, for all our sakes.'

'I didn't tell the police nothing and I won't neither,' Kitty said, gently easing her hands free. 'But you've got to leave him, Maggie, before he hurts you or the little 'uns.'

'And end up in the workhouse?' Maggie shook her head. 'He don't bother me that way now. I think he's too ashamed of what he done. He gives me just enough money to pay the rent and the tallyman. He drinks away the rest, but at least he's quiet when he falls unconscious from the booze.'

'But you have to eat,' Kitty said, frowning.

'Your money keeps us going for some of the time. Then there's the Sally Army soup kitchen, and I does a bit of ironing for Mrs Harman. I can manage, Kitty, but if Sid was sent to jail it would be the end of us all.'

'So that's the real reason you came here today.' Kitty shivered as a new pain stabbed her heart. 'Not for my sake, but to make sure I didn't tell the police that it was that bugger you married.'

Maggie's head snapped backwards as though Kitty had slapped her face. She struggled to her feet. 'I don't say as I blame you for thinking that, but it ain't so. Not a day goes by but I don't blame meself for taking Sid's side against you when I knew you was telling the truth.'

'Oh! Maggie!' Kitty cried, holding out her arms.

'I got to go.' Shaking her head, Maggie backed towards the door.

'Wait a moment,' Kitty said, going to the mantelshelf, standing on tiptoe and reaching for the cocoa tin where she kept what was left of her wages. Counting the coins, Kitty took out three silver crowns and pressed them into Maggie's hand. 'Take this and spend it on food and coal. I'll give you more when I can.'

Maggie stared at the coins and tears gushed from her eyes. 'You're a good girl.'

'You shouldn't have to put up with that vicious brute,' Kitty said angrily. 'I'll get you and the nippers away from Sugar Yard, if it's the last thing I ever do.'

Maggie wiped her eyes on her sleeve. 'Don't you set foot near Sugar Yard again. I'm more than grateful for your help but you got to keep away and forget about us.'

'Never!'

Maggie wrenched the kitchen door open and ran into the hallway, stopping at the front door and delving her hand into her pocket. 'I nearly forgot. Is this yours?'

Kitty stared in disbelief at the gold half-sovereign that glinted on Maggie's outstretched palm. 'I thought it was lost,' she said, picking it up with trembling fingers. 'Jem gave me this before he went back to sea.'

'It was in Sid's pocket. I thought he'd just stolen

it. If I'd known the truth then I think I'd have stabbed him while he lay a drunken sot sleeping off the booze. Then, when I heard what had happened to you, it wasn't hard to put two and two together.' Maggie grabbed Kitty by the shoulders and shook her. 'You got to get away from here, Kitty. Go now, afore it's too late.' Maggie wrenched the door open and ran out into the street.

'She's right, Kitty,' Betty said, coming slowly down the stairs. 'Maggie's right. Now you're up and about, it's not safe for you to stay here.'

'I'm not frightened of Sid. I'll not let him drive me away and I can't go back to Dover Street until I hear from the mistress.'

'Kitty, I love you like a daughter, but we're poor people,' Betty said, smiling ruefully. 'Her ladyship hasn't sent you any more wages and I'm losing money on the rent of your room.'

'I'll help you with sewing the dresses for your rich ladies. I can make the breakfasts for your gentlemen lodgers.'

Betty shook her head. 'I know you'd try and help, ducks, but the winter is here and Polly will sicken again for sure, and then there'll be the doctor's bills to pay. I hate to say it but, for all our sakes, you'll have to go back to Dover Street and ask Mrs Brewster for your job back.'

Large feathery flakes of snow were falling from a pewter sky as Kitty made her way, sliding and slipping down the area steps to the servants' entrance. Olive opened the door and would have slammed it in Kitty's face had she not put her booted foot over the sill. Kitty was cold, tired after her long walk, and in no mood to wrangle with Olive. She found Florrie in the scullery, up to her elbows in the stone sink, scouring out saucepans and, ignoring her open-mouthed gasp of astonishment and Olive's protests, Kitty strode through the kitchen. George almost dropped the hod of coal he was hefting into the fiery throat of the kitchen range, but he gave her a friendly wink. Mrs Dixon uttered an outraged cry as Kitty walked straight past, heading for the housekeeper's office.

Mrs Brewster's expression was hardly welcoming and she shook her head when Kitty told her that she had returned to work.

'You're not needed here now,' Mrs Brewster said, eyeing Kitty over the steel rims of her spectacles. 'Miss Lane looks after the child.'

'Lady Mableton said I should come back when I was recovered,' Kitty said, with a defiant lift of her chin.

Mrs Brewster leaned across her desk, frowning. 'Lady Mableton is still unwell and living in the country. You will have to find alternative employment.'

'Lady Mableton would want me to stay.'

'Don't you defy me, Kitty Cox,' Mrs Brewster

said, her voice rising in anger. 'I'll not have you answering me back.'

Kitty backed towards the door as Mrs Brewster rose to her feet and moved swiftly around the desk. She came at Kitty with her hand raised, but a sharp rapping on the door stopped her in her tracks.

Maria marched into the room. 'I could hear you shouting all the way down the passage, Mrs Brewster. Everyone could hear you.'

'This is my business, Miss Lane. Not yours.'

Maria folded her arms across her chest and Kitty watched in awe as the two women squared up to each other. Prizefighters in the boxing ring could not have eyed each other in a more threatening manner.

'I need help in the nursery, Mrs Brewster. I'm a lady's maid, not a nanny. Lady Mableton left instructions that Kitty was to come back as soon as her health had improved.'

'Lady Mableton isn't here, Miss Lane. I'm in charge of the female servants and don't you forget your place.'

'I'll go to Sir Desmond then, and see what he has to say.'

Mrs Brewster's face flushed to deep purple and her bosom heaved. 'There's no need to do that. Sir Desmond doesn't want to be bothered with household trivia.'

'Then do as I say and take the girl on.'

Kitty looked from one to the other; she could almost see the sparks flashing between their locked gazes. Maria folded her arms across her chest and Kitty could hear the toe of her boot tapping on the linoleum.

Mrs Brewster was the first to look away. 'Kitty can come back as scullery maid,' she muttered, between clenched teeth. 'If and when her ladyship returns, I'll review the situation.'

Maria slowly nodded her head. 'Very well, but I shall be keeping an eye on her, Mrs Brewster. If there's any sign of bullying I will take the matter straight to Mr Warner.' She swept out of the office, leaving Mrs Brewster making gobbling noises.

Eyeing her warily, Kitty was reminded of the Christmas turkeys in Smithfield Market.

'Well, girl, what are you standing there for, gaping like an idiot? Get back to the scullery, give Mrs Dixon my compliments and ask her if she can spare me a moment or two.'

At least Florrie and George were pleased to see Kitty back in her old job as scullery maid; Florrie confiding that the last girl only stuck it for a week and then took off without a by-your-leave.

George was only too eager to fill Kitty in on all the events that had occurred in her absence. It seemed that after Lady Mableton's departure, Sir Desmond had become morose and bad-tempered, complaining about everything to Mr Warner, who took out his frustrations on the servants below stairs. Miss Iris had lost her gentleman admirer and was, according to George, a wasp buzzing around and stinging anyone who got in her way. Mr Rackham hadn't been seen in Dover Street since her ladyship went away and that, George said, tapping the side of his nose, was proof that something had been going on, or he was a Dutchman.

Miss Leonie cried a lot, but then she was little more than a baby, and it was natural for her to want her mama. Miss Lane went about with a face like thunder, snapping at anyone who dared speak to her. A big, horrible black cloud had settled over the house in Dover Street and there didn't seem to be much chance of Lady Mableton being allowed home, not while Sir Desmond was in this sort of humour.

At first Olive and Dora kept their distance, keeping a watchful eye on Mrs Dixon, who was nifty with the rolling pin or soup ladle when annoyed. But after a couple of days of uneasy truce, Olive came into the scullery followed by Dora and they stood watching Kitty as she worked.

'Not so hoity-toity now, are we?' Olive said, sniggering. 'You've sunk back to your proper place in the gutter.'

'Yes,' Dora added, grinning, 'they say water

finds its own level. You're sewer water, Kitty Cox.'

Ignoring them, Kitty continued scrubbing the copper saucepan.

Dora nipped forward and tugged at the strings of Kitty's apron, untying them. Shaking the water off her hands, Kitty tied the apron and returned to her work without saying a word.

This time it was Olive who stepped forward and, scooping a handful of fat from a dirty pan, tossed it into the clean pan that Kitty had just set aside to dry. 'Oh dear, you'll have to do that one all over again.'

Kitty turned on them, her temper at snapping point. They had been deliberately tormenting her since early morning and she had had enough. She advanced on them with her chin stuck out and her hands balled into fists. She had the satisfaction of seeing them back away in surprise, their smiles fading.

'That's it,' Kitty said, waving her fists in front of their faces. 'I ain't a kid now. I'm as big as you two and I ain't afraid of you neither. So who's going to take me on then?'

Olive and Dora backed towards the door.

'Can't you take a joke?' Olive said, glancing over her shoulder into the kitchen. 'Mrs Dixon will be back in a moment and she'll sort you out.'

'You're cowards, the pair of you,' stormed Kitty. 'I wouldn't waste my time giving you the slapping you deserve. But come near me again and I might change my mind.'

'You showed 'em.' George stood in the doorway with an empty coal bucket in each hand. He put them down on the flagstones, chuckling at the sight of Olive and Dora scuttling back into the kitchen.

'I'm fed up with them,' Kitty said, tucking a wayward curl back under her cap.

'You got lovely hair, Kitty.' Shuffling his feet, a flush rose from George's throat, disappearing into his hairline.

'Don't talk rot, George.'

The freckles on his nose stood out in brown clumps. 'Well, you have and you're pretty too.'

'Kitty, come here.' Mrs Dixon's voice echoed round the steamy scullery.

George pulled a face. 'I bet they told on you, miserable bitches.'

Kitty hurried into the main kitchen, ready for another fight. But Olive and Dora were nowhere in sight and the bell from the nursery suite was jangling on its spring. Mrs Dixon waved a floury hand at Kitty.

'There's no one left to take the nursery tray upstairs. You'll have to do it, Kitty. Look smart.'

Carrying the heavy tray up four flights of stairs left Kitty panting and breathless and she rapped on the nursery door. It was wrenched open and Maria dragged her into the room.

'Thank God it's you, Kitty.'

'What's wrong, Miss Lane?'

Maria seized the tray, dumping it on the table. 'It's Leonie, she's took sick. The doctor has just been and he says it's the measles.'

'We all had it at home,' Kitty said, shuddering at the memory. 'Our Violet nearly died of the fever.'

'I'll need you to help me look after her. But most of all, the child needs her mother. She keeps calling for her again and again. It's driving me mad.'

Kitty could hear Leonie's muffled sobs coming from the night nursery. 'Shall I go to her then, Miss Lane?'

'Yes. No, first we must get a message to Bella and tell her she must come home. Can I trust you, Kitty?'

'I'd do anything for her ladyship and Miss Leonie.'

'Sir Desmond won't have it, but we've got to bring Bella home before it's too late.' Wringing her hands, Maria began pacing the floor; her voice trembling with suppressed emotion. 'This is a judgement on me, a dreadful judgement on the way I've lived, and Bella will never forgive me if anything happens to Leonie. I've done terrible things in my life but I can't stand by and see the poor child suffer.'

'What can I do?' Kitty asked, watching helplessly.

Stopping in her tracks, Maria gripped Kitty by the shoulders, her eyes blazing. 'I've always said I'd like to see him go to hell, but there's only one person I know who would dare go against Sir Desmond. I want you to slip out of the house without anyone seeing you and take a message to Mr Rackham.'

Clutching the hastily scrawled note in her hand, Kitty crept through the entrance hall. James was busy polishing the brass door furniture and her heart sank; there was no way she could get past him without being seen. Hearing the patter of footsteps running down the main staircase, Kitty dodged behind a marble column.

'James!' Jane leaned over the banisters. 'Miss Iris wants the carriage brought round right away.'

Passing within a few feet of Kitty, James sauntered over to speak to Jane. Peeping round the column, Kitty saw them head to head and, thanking her lucky stars that James was sweet on Jane, she slipped out of the house unseen.

It was raining and Kitty had come out as she was, without even a shawl to protect her from the weather. Barely noticing the chill of the rain soaking through her clothes, Kitty ran all the way to Rackham's lodging, only to be told by his landlady that he was not at home. Refusing to be fobbed off, Kitty stood her ground until the woman grudgingly admitted that she might find him at his club in Pall Mall.

Soaked to the skin by the time she reached Rackham's club, Kitty argued fiercely with the doorman, who refused to let her in or even to take a message to Mr Rackham. Driven by desperation and the memory of Leonie's pitiful, feverish cries for her mother, Kitty butted him in the stomach and barged into the cloistered quiet of the vestibule. Leapt upon by a couple of footmen, Kitty opened her mouth and screamed Rackham's name over and over again, biting, kicking and scratching as they tried to eject her from the premises. They had got her as far as the double doors when she saw Rackham coming towards them.

Breaking free, Kitty ran to him. 'Mr Rackham, you got to help.'

'Do you know this young person, Sir?' The affronted doorman grabbed Kitty by the scruff of the neck.

'It's all right, Hobson. I'll deal with this.' Rackham hooked his arm around Kitty's shoulders and guided her out of the building. 'Now then, young Kitty. What's wrong?'

Kitty thrust the note from Maria into his hand. 'You got to come, Sir. Miss Leonie's mortal sick with measles and my lady's been sent off to the country.'

Rackham's black brows drew together in a frown. 'She didn't go willingly?'

'Sir Desmond forced her to go and he wouldn't let her take Miss Leonie. Now the poor little mite is off her head with fever and calling for her mummy.' Shivering violently and barely able to control her chattering teeth, Kitty grabbed him by the hand. 'We got to bring her ladyship back to London afore it's too late. Are you going to help, Sir, or are you going to stand there asking bleeding silly questions?'

Chapter Eight

Bella shivered, huddling closer to the fire in the inglenook. It was, she thought dismally, large enough to roast a whole ox, but the flames curling around the damp logs sent most of their heat up the chimney, barely taking the chill off the oak-panelled room. Her feet were numbed with cold; chilblains made her legs itch and burn at the same time. Sleet was hurling itself against the leaded panes of the windows and a handful of ice came down the chimney, sputtering in the flames and sending a cloud of smoke into the room. Coughing and jumping to her feet, Bella paced the floor, wrapping her arms around herself in a futile effort to keep warm. Pausing by the window, she gazed out through the hailstorm to the mist-shrouded salt marshes, disappearing into the sea. Dusk was beginning to gobble up the land and sea alike, adding to the sense of isolation and the inescapable prison of her circumstances.

Bella longed to draw the curtains, shutting out the dismal scene, but that would plunge the room into almost complete darkness. She would have to wait until Mrs Quelch, the cook-general, came to light the paraffin lamps.

Perching on the window seat for a moment, Bella tried to work out how long she had been at Mableton Manor. It must be two or, maybe, three months since that fateful night when Desmond had accused her of having an affair with Rackham. She was certain that Iris was partly to blame, but it must have been Rackham who had sewn the seeds of doubt in Desmond's jealous mind. He had been hell-bent on engineering her downfall from the start and he had used Iris as a pawn in his foul game.

Bella shuddered, remembering Desmond's uncontrolled fury that had been both terrible and terrifying. He had ranted and raged at her, calling her all the filthy names that he could think of, until she had collapsed on the floor of her bedroom with her hands over her ears. Then he had beaten her, viciously and unmercifully until she had lost consciousness. Next morning, when Bella had summoned up the strength to ring for Maria, it was Iris who came to her room. Even now, she could remember the vicious look, and cruel words, that Iris had used to tear her character to shreds. Bella had tried to defend herself, but it had been like dealing with a mad woman. She shuddered at the memory.

'Pack your bags,' Iris had said finally, with a triumphant curl of her thin lips. 'My father has seen sense at last and he's packing you off to our country estate in the wilds of Essex. I hope you rot there, you cunning bitch.'

With that, Iris had swept from the room, locking the door behind her. Bella remembered struggling with the laces on her corsets and the pain of her bruised ribs. She could almost laugh at it now; how foolish she had been to worry about dressing herself nicely when her whole world was about to be torn apart. After what had seemed like an hour, the door had opened and Jane had sidled in, carrying a breakfast tray. She had kept her gaze firmly fixed on the floor, answering Bella's demands to have Maria sent to her by shaking her head and running from the room.

Bella had thrown the plate of toast at the door, watching a dribble of butter run down the cream paintwork with childish satisfaction. She remembered picking up the coffeepot, tempted to toss it as well, but she had been thirsty and she had drunk two cupfuls before she began to feel drowsy and light-headed. The next thing she knew, she was slumped against the leather squabs of the carriage, her head was aching and her mouth dry. She had realised, as the fog in her brain cleared, that Desmond must have drugged the coffee. She had tried to make the coachman stop but he had kept the horses going at a spanking pace. The landscape outside the carriage windows had been unfamiliar. The awful truth had slowly come upon her that Desmond was sending her away, without Maria and, to her horror, without Leonie.

Bella choked back a sob, thinking about Leonie, her baby, her beautiful child. At three years old she was too young to understand what was going on around her. All she would know was that Mama had gone away. Mama had left her. Bella braced her shoulders and wiped her eyes on her sleeve. She must not give way to morbid thoughts. At least Maria was with Leonie; surely Desmond would not have been so cruel as to put someone else in charge of the nursery? She shivered and began pacing the floor again. Desmond, when angered, was capable of anything.

Without much hope of it being answered, she tugged at the bell pull. Quelch and his wife, the only living-in servants, were a surly, ignorant pair, who had obviously been instructed to treat their mistress more like a prisoner than the respected wife of their employer.

Taking a turn around the room, Bella stared with distaste at her surroundings. How she hated this awful house, this oubliette to which Desmond had condemned her without trial and without pity. Built in the seventeenth century, it might have been beautiful then but now it was a neglected old hag. The ill-fitting windows let in the damp salt air and, when the wind was in a certain direction, the chimneys smoked dismally. There was no gas and no electricity. The musty smell of damp rot permeated Bella's clothes and every morning her shoes bloomed with grey mould. In her mind, the whole house reeked of neglect and despair, mirroring her own depression.

She must do something; inactivity was killing her. Making up her mind, Bella went to the desk beneath the sombre oil painting of one of Desmond's ancestors, and sat down. Taking a sheet of headed paper, she dipped a pen in the inkwell, and sat chewing the tip. How would she begin it this time? She racked her brains, trying to think of yet another beginning to a letter to Desmond, begging him to let her come home. Not that he would reply; he had not replied to any of the letters, sometimes two or three a week, that she had sent. Heaving a sigh, she felt as though she was beginning to lose her mind, stuck here in the country with no one but the morose caretakers for company. There were a couple of women who came in daily from the village to do the cleaning, but they were simple souls with little conversation. In fact, they must have been instructed to avoid her, since they scuttled off whenever she approached them.

Bella was still trying to think of something that would move Desmond to end her enforced exile, when the door opened and Mrs Quelch ambled in carrying a tray of food.

'It's a long walk from the kitchen and my bunions are playing up in this cold weather,' Mrs Quelch grumbled, slamming the tray down on the table by the fire. 'Better eat up quick, before it gets cold.'

'Please light the lamps before you go, Mrs Quelch,' Bella said, rising to her feet. 'And the log basket is nearly empty.'

Ignoring Mrs Quelch's mumbling retort, Bella went to the table and sat down, willing herself to lift the cover on the dish, but at the same time, dreading what she would find. She was starving, but Mrs Quelch was not an inspired cook. The mutton stew that was served almost daily might have been almost palatable when hot, but when cold, congealing with globules of grey fat floating on the surface, it was barely fit to feed to a dog. Bella had lost so much weight that her dresses were all too big for her and she had no need for corsets to nip in her waist.

Shuffling her feet, Mrs Quelch lit the lamps and left the room, still grumbling beneath her breath. Lifting the cover on the dish, Bella replaced it quickly. Perhaps Desmond intended to starve her to death in this dreadful place. She broke the hunk of bread into small pieces and crammed them into her mouth, washing them down with a glass of water. She was still hungry but nauseated at the thought of eating yet another of Mrs Quelch's vile meals. She shivered, hugging her shawl closer around her shoulders. How long would Desmond keep up this dreadful punishment? Being a virtual prisoner in this miserable place was bad enough, but being separated from Leonie was unbearable. If only she could get word to Edward, Bella was certain that he would not stand for her being treated in this cruel way.

Plans for escaping and getting back to London had been formulating in her mind for weeks, and then discarded because of their impracticality. Mableton Manor was too isolated for Bella to make a getaway on foot. The narrow country lanes networked alongside the salt marshes, and to take a wrong turn would be a fatal mistake. The only horse in the stables was an ageing carthorse that Quelch harnessed to the dog cart for his monthly trip to Maldon which, as far as Bella could gather, was seven or eight miles away. If she had calculated correctly, tomorrow would be the day that he set off to do whatever business he had in the town.

The log basket was empty and the fire was burning away to white ash. Quelch had not yet brought in the firewood and Bella was about to tug at the bell pull when, without knocking, he came shambling into the room carrying a wicker basket full of green, moss-covered logs. He tossed a couple on the fire and they hissed and steamed, spitting out sparks and belching smoke.

'Quelch,' Bella said, adopting a firm manner, despite the fact that she was inwardly quaking, 'I will be accompanying you when you go into Maldon tomorrow.'

Quelch tipped the rest of the logs into the basket and turned his head to stare at her, his weathered face an expressionless map of lines and furrows. 'Not possible.'

Bella took a deep breath and summoned up all her acting skill. 'Of course it's possible. You will do as I bid or I will tell my husband.'

'The master gave orders that you weren't to go nowhere,' Quelch said, scowling. 'I take orders from Sir Desmond.'

'And in his absence you take orders from your mistress. Have the dog cart at the front door at eight o'clock sharp unless, of course, you want me to report your behaviour to my husband.'

Having left London at the end of the summer, with no time to pack more than a few necessities, Bella had no winter clothes to combat the bitter wind that blew across the saltings straight from the Urals. It was snowing quite heavily by the time they reached the outskirts of the town. She was so cold that she had lost all feeling in her extremities and, although Mrs Quelch had been prevailed upon to find an old umbrella, Bella's thin jacket was wet through and her skirts were crusted with snow, clinging damply around her legs, as she climbed down from the cart outside the Blue Boar Inn.

Quelch handed the reins to an ostler. 'I'll be out directly,' he said, jerking his head to Bella to follow him.

Unable to feel her feet, Bella hobbled into the warm interior of the inn. She hesitated in the doorway as the smell of hot coffee, mingled with delicious aromas from the kitchen, assailed her nostrils. Faint with cold and hunger, she swayed dizzily.

'Are you all right, Ma'am?'

With difficulty, Bella focused her eyes on the landlord's anxious face. 'If I may sit down for a while . . .'

'The lady will wait here in your parlour,' Quelch said, drawing the landlord aside.

Bella could not hear what was said, but the landlord nodded and Quelch strode outside into the stable yard without so much as a glance in her direction.

'You look perished, Ma'am,' the landlord said, opening the door to a small parlour just off the main bar room. 'There's a fire in here and I'll send the girl in with some coffee.'

As the door closed on him, Bella realised that she was just as much a prisoner now as she had been in Mableton Manor. What Quelch had told the innkeeper she could only imagine, but at this moment she felt so weak from lack of food, and chilled to the bone, that she doubted if she could walk as far as the stable yard. She took off her wet jacket and went to sit by the fire, spreading out her skirts and watching the steam rise from them. A few minutes later a maid bustled in carrying a tray with a pot of coffee and a plate of freshly baked scones, oozing with melted butter. She set it down on a small table by Bella's chair, smiled, curtsied and left the room without saying a word.

Cramming the crumbly scones into her mouth Bella closed her eyes, savouring each delicious mouthful. Washed down with hot, sweet coffee, the food began to have its effect and she started to feel better almost immediately. Having finished everything on the tray, and licked the butter off the plate into the bargain, Bella got to her feet and went to the door. Opening it a little, she peered up and down in the narrow corridor that separated the parlour from the bar room. A chambermaid scuttled past her carrying a sweeping brush and a dustpan and two men sat by the fire in the bar, chatting and drinking ale.

'Can I help you, Ma'am?'

Bella jumped and spun round to see the landlord standing at her elbow. 'No, I mean yes. I have business in the town. Did my man tell you what time he would be back?'

'He was concerned that you should stay here in the dry, Ma'am. It's not fit for man nor beast out there and we'll have more snow by nightfall. Best wait in the parlour.'

His bulk blocked the passageway and Bella had no alternative but to retreat to the parlour. She was not dressed for walking, nor had she any money to hire a horse or pay for a carriage to take her to the nearest station. In her desperation she had planned to try to exchange her gold earrings, the only item of jewellery that she had been able to bring from Dover Street, for a train ticket to London. If all else failed, then perhaps, when the inn filled with travellers and tradesmen, she could find someone who would post the letters to Desmond and also to Edward that she had finished writing before she retired to bed the previous evening.

Running to the window, Bella peered out into the swirling snow, drumming her fingers on the windowsill and then, unable to sit still, she got up and went to stand by the fire. The ticking of the timepiece on the mantelshelf seemed to grow louder as she stared at the ivory clock face, watching the hands move almost imperceptibly, and wondering how long it would be before Quelch returned from his errands.

Unable to settle, Bella hurried to the window every time she heard footsteps or horses' hooves on the cobbled yard, peering through the frosted panes in the hope of seeing a likely traveller. An hour went by and then two, as she paced the floor, making fresh plans and discarding them almost immediately as being unworkable.

She had just sunk down on the chair by the fire when she heard the unmistakable sound of a motor car pulling up in the stable yard. Leaping to her feet, she ran to the window. The snow had all but obliterated the view and she could only make out dim shapes. She hurried to the door and opened it just wide enough to peep into the passage. The arrival of a traveller in a horseless carriage must be something of an event, Bella thought, as the innkeeper rushed past her, followed by chattering chambermaids and the potman. Her stomach knotted with nervous tension. Her knuckles whitened as she gripped the door handle so tightly that her nails dug into the flesh of her palm. This could be her one chance to escape; it didn't matter where the traveller was going, or who it was; she had to get away before Quelch returned. As she stepped into the passage, Bella heard the landlord barking orders at his staff and she pressed herself against the wall as they scurried past her. She could hear the innkeeper's voice speaking in unctuous tones to the new arrival.

'Come this way, Sir. There's a fire in my best private parlour and I can offer you excellent accommodation and good, wholesome food.'

The reply was lost in the general hubbub. Bella

edged along the narrow passageway, intent on discovering the identity of the traveller.

'But surely, Sir,' the landlord said, 'a glass of hot punch would keep out the cold. And perhaps the young woman would appreciate some coffee.'

'Thank you, no. What I need urgently is the direction to Mableton Manor.'

The familiar voice made Bella start forward, pushing past the potman. 'Rackham!'

Surprise, relief and a flicker of a smile crossed Rackham's taut features in quick succession only to fade into a bland, shuttered expression as Bella flew at him.

'You utter wretch, Giles. I might have known you were at the back of all this.'

Rackham caught her by the wrists. 'My dear Bella, what a pleasant surprise.'

'You are unspeakable,' Bella cried, struggling. 'Let me go.'

The landlord gave a polite cough. 'If you'll excuse me, Sir . . .'

'Sisterly love!' Rackham said, grinning. 'It's the very devil.'

'Ah, yes, precisely so, Sir. Maybe you would prefer the privacy of my best parlour.'

'I'm sure I would,' Rackham said agreeably. 'Come, my dear, we have so much to talk about.'

The maidservant set the tray down on the table,

bobbed a curtsey and scuttled out of the parlour.

'You bastard!' Bella cried, wrenching her hands free from Rackham's iron grip. 'If you've come to gloat over my situation, then get it over and done with.'

Rackham shrugged off his greatcoat, dropping it carelessly on the nearest chair. 'Don't be so melodramatic, Bella.'

Kitty, who up until this moment had kept silently in the background, sprang forward to lead Bella to the settle. 'You don't understand, my lady. Please sit down and let Mr Rackham explain.'

'I'm sorry to see you in such company, Kitty,' Bella said, glaring at Rackham, who was pouring coffee as though nothing untoward had happened. 'I thought you were loyal to me. I thought we were friends.'

'I am your friend, I am truly,' Kitty cried, grasping Bella's hands. 'You don't understand.'

'I understand that you've been duped by a rogue and a liar who uses his charm to get his own way.'

Rackham sipped his coffee. 'And I thought you might actually be pleased to see me, Bella, considering I came hotfoot to rescue you.'

'You told Desmond about us. I'll never forgive you, Giles. Never!'

'No, I wouldn't do that to you,' Rackham said, his flippant smile fading. 'As a matter of fact I haven't been near Dover Street since I left the country for Paris over three months ago.'

'I don't understand.'

'Iris was demanding an engagement ring and, quite simply, I thought it best to put some distance between her and myself, not to mention my creditors. When I returned to London I heard that you'd gone to the country for your health. I could only assume that, after the gallant son and heir decided he would rather face the Boers than stand by the woman he professed to love, you were rusticating to mend your poor broken heart.'

'What do you mean, face the Boers? That war was over years ago.'

'I forgot you'd been out of touch for so long. The war is very much on again and no doubt, as we speak, the valiant captain is being heroic in besieged Ladysmith or Mafeking.'

'Don't speak of him like that, Giles. Edward is a brave man and he loves me. He did the honourable thing.'

Rackham's generous mouth set in a hard line and his eyes flashed. 'Honourable? He made love to his father's wife and then left you to take the consequences of his own weakness and cowardice.'

'Mr Rackham.' Kitty caught him by the sleeve. 'Please don't, Sir. Remember why we come.'

Bella leapt to her feet. 'Why did you come then, if it wasn't to gloat over my sad condition and to report back to Desmond?'

'We've come to take you home and Desmond knows nothing about it,' Rackham said, in a gentler tone. 'I've borrowed Swafford's motor and he'll be mad as hell when he finds out.'

Bella met his eyes and felt a trickle of cold fear run down her spine. 'There's something you're not telling me.' She turned to Kitty. 'What is it? What has happened?'

Kitty shot an anxious glance at Rackham. 'I'm not supposed to say, Ma'am.'

'We didn't want to alarm you, Bella,' Rackham said. 'But Leonie is unwell.'

Bella's hands flew to her cheeks. 'Oh my God!'

'Miss Lane is looking after her. We both done what we could,' Kitty said, her bottom lip quivering. 'But Miss Leonie has been crying for you something terrible and the doctor said it was the measles.'

'Measles? Oh, no! Why didn't you tell me that in the first place? We must leave at once.'

Rackham took her by the shoulders, giving her a gentle shake. 'Keep calm, Bella! As long as the weather doesn't worsen, we should be able to reach London before nightfall.'

Picking up Bella's jacket, Kitty ran her hand over it, frowning. 'This is soaking wet. Where's your coat, Ma'am?'

'That's all I have. My winter clothes are all in Dover Street.'

'You'll catch your death of cold if you put this

back on,' Kitty said, shrugging off her own coat. 'You must wear mine.'

Smiling through her tears, Bella threw her arms around Kitty and hugged her. 'I've missed you, Kitty, you are such a good girl, but I can't take your coat.'

'Never mind all that,' Rackham said, snatching up his own coat and throwing it around Bella's shoulders. 'There are mackintoshes and fur travel rugs in the motor. Luckily for us, Swafford is always prepared for the vagaries of the English weather. We'd best get going.'

The journey back to London was a nightmare of skidding and sliding on snow-covered roads, with visibility at times down to just a few yards. However, by the time they reached Romford, the snow had turned to sleet and then to rain.

It was early evening when they reached Dover Street, and Bella was feverish with anxiety. Rackham offered to escort her into the house but she refused, saying it would only make matters worse. He left, somewhat reluctantly, saying he had better return the motor to Lord Swafford, before the chauffeur reported it stolen. It was not until he had gone that Bella realised she had not thanked him. Shrugging off the feeling of guilt, she started up the front steps but Kitty stopped her, suggesting that it might be better to go in unnoticed, using the servants' entrance.

Florrie opened the door, staring wide-eyed at Bella and bobbing a curtsey.

'I'll explain later,' Kitty said, in a low voice. 'We have to get to the nursery without being seen.'

Florrie hesitated, glancing nervously over her shoulder. 'I'll be in dead trouble if they know it was me that let you in.'

'No one will know if you're careful,' Kitty said, giving her a push towards the main kitchen. 'You keep Mrs Dixon talking while we take the back stairs.'

On seeing Bella, Maria threw up her hands with a cry of relief. 'Thank God you've come.'

'How is Leonie? For heaven's sake tell me the truth.'

'The doctor left just a few minutes ago. There's nothing can be done until the fever breaks.'

Throwing off her jacket, Bella ran into the night nursery and scooped Leonie's hot little body up in her arms. 'Leonie, my poor baby. Mama is here.'

Leonie moved restlessly in her mother's arms, moaning and muttering feverishly.

'She's been like this for hours,' Maria said dully. 'I've done the best I could.'

'I know you have,' Bella said, gently cradling Leonie. 'You look exhausted. You should get some rest.'

Maria ran a weary hand across her forehead. 'I can't sleep until I know the crisis is over.'

'What can I do?' Kitty hovered anxiously in the doorway. 'There must be something.'

'Make us some tea,' Maria said. 'I'm sure we could all do with some.'

Kitty went into the day nursery and Maria sat down on a chair, closing her eyes. Within minutes her head lolled forward as she fell into an exhausted sleep and Leonie's feverish cries were calmed as Bella rocked her in her arms, singing a lullaby. But the peace was shattered by the sound of the door to the day nursery being thrown open, followed by Desmond's harsh voice demanding to know if the doctor had called.

'Miss Leonie is sleeping, Sir Desmond,' Kitty replied, her voice rising anxiously. 'Please don't wake her.'

'Keep your place, girl, and don't you dare to tell me what to do.'

Striding into the room, with Kitty close on his heels, Desmond came to a sudden halt. 'Bella! How in hell did you get here?'

'I'm sorry, my lady,' Kitty cried, her eyes wide with alarm. 'I did try to stop him.'

Desmond turned on her, his face twisted with contempt. 'Get out of my house, you little slut.'

Groggy with sleep, Maria staggered to her feet. 'No need for that sort of talk,' she said. 'There's a sick child in the room.'

'Be silent,' Desmond roared. 'I won't have a servant speaking to me in that insolent manner.'

'Keep your voice down, Desmond,' Bella said, laying Leonie gently in her cot.

Clenching his fists at his sides, Desmond's face turned an alarming shade of purple. 'It was Rackham who brought you here, wasn't it? Your damned lover brought you to my house.'

Rising slowly to her feet, Bella met his furious gaze calmly and, to her surprise, unafraid. He had hurt her physically and tried to destroy her mentally. There was nothing more he could do to her; all she cared about now was her ailing child. 'It's your sick mind that makes every man into my lover. But think what you like, Desmond, you'll not part me from Leonie ever again.'

Gripping her by the shoulders, Desmond forced Bella down onto her knees. 'You whore! Do you think I would allow my daughter to be brought up by you and that rake?'

The harsh tone of his voice must have reached Leonie even in her feverish state and she started whimpering and thrashing about.

'Leave her alone,' Kitty cried, tugging at Desmond's sleeve. 'Let her be.'

'Pick on someone your own size. You're nothing but a bully.' Maria tugged at his other arm.

Shaking them off, Desmond pointed a shaking finger at Bella, who had hastily scrambled to her feet. 'I want you out of this house now and I don't ever want to see you again.'

Drawing herself up to her full height, Bella found she was trembling uncontrollably but it was with cold, hard anger and not fear. 'I'm staying with Leonie until she's well again and you can't make me leave. Do you want to kill your own child?'

Desmond glanced down at Leonie and for a moment his face softened. 'No, of course not. Leonie is the only good thing to come out of my misalliance with you, but you'll leave the moment she is out of danger. I want nothing more to do with you and don't think you'll get a penny from me. The law takes a poor view of an unfaithful wife and I'm no longer responsible for you.'

'You're well rid of him, Bella,' Maria said, as the door to the day nursery slammed behind him.

'Nothing matters except making Leonie well again,' Bella said, sinking down onto a chair by the cot. 'But if she recovers, I swear to God, I'll never be parted from her again.'

All that night and well after daybreak, Bella sat by Leonie's bed, cooling her fever with wet flannels and singing nursery rhymes and lullabies until she lost her voice. Kitty and Maria took turns at sleeping on the truckle bed, making tea and running to and fro with bowls of cold water to refresh the flannels.

'Mama, Mama. Wake up.'

Bella jerked upright, realising that she had fallen asleep where she sat. Had Leonie spoken to her, or had it been part of her dream? A small hand flapped feebly on the counterpane and her heart swelled with joy as she saw Leonie smiling up at her. The feverish flush had vanished and she looked pale, with dark smudges underlining her blue eyes but they were clear and focused. Bella gave a shout of joy and scooped her up in her arms. 'My baby, my baby.' Tears ran unchecked down her cheeks but she was laughing and crying all at the same time. 'Kitty, the crisis is past. Leonie is going to get well again.'

Leaping up from the truckle bed, Kitty flung her arms around Bella. 'Thank God. Oh, thank God!'

The doctor confirmed Bella's hope that Leonie was out of danger. He recommended rest, quiet and nourishing food and advised Bella to get some sleep now that the crisis was past. Leaving Kitty and Maria watching over Leonie and, no doubt, pandering to her every whim, Bella went to her room and ran her own bath. She lay, wallowing in the almost forgotten luxury of hot water and scented bath salts. After a long, refreshing soak, she dried herself on thick Egyptian cotton towels.

Wrapped in her lace *peignoir*, Bella was about to lie down on the bed when Desmond walked unceremoniously into the room. Clutching her wrap to her throat, Bella faced him defiantly. She recognised the gleam of lust in his eyes as they raked across her body, that was barely concealed by a thin layer of Brussels lace but, although she shook inwardly, she was determined that he would not lay a finger on her ever again.

The hot look vanished from his eyes, replaced by a scornful sneer. 'Don't worry, my dear. I don't want tarnished goods. First you seduce my son and then you make a play for your stepdaughter's fiancé. You're a bitch on heat and the only fit place for you is back on the streets where I found you.'

'I'd rather live on the streets than with a brute like you, Desmond, but I won't leave without my child.'

'The doctor has convinced me that you should stay here until Leonie is completely recovered. He seems to think that you're a good mother and that she will be in danger of a relapse if you leave too soon.'

'I am a good mother. It was you who sent me away. Leonie might not have been so desperately ill if you had let us remain together.'

Desmond shrugged his shoulders. 'No matter!

But let me be plain with you, Bella. I want you out of this house as soon as Leonie is well again. You'll leave as you came, with just the clothes you stand up in. While you're here you will confine yourself to these rooms and the nursery suite. And I'd advise you to keep away from Iris. She knows exactly whom to blame for her fiancé jilting her.'

Leonie grew stronger hour by hour, and in a week she was almost completely well, although Bella fretted over the fact that she tired easily and her normally rosy cheeks were pale.

'It's nothing that a bit of fresh air won't cure,' Maria said, spooning bread and milk into Leonie's mouth. 'Speak to Sir Desmond, Bella. Tell him that Leonie should go to the park for the sake of her health.'

Bella pushed her plate away, the cold chicken and salad barely touched. 'He made it perfectly clear that we're not to leave the house, or at least, that when I do it will be for the last time. He's determined to keep Leonie and nothing will change his mind.'

'And you're going to put up with that, are you?' demanded Maria, wiping Leonie's mouth.

'Of course not! What do you take me for? We're getting away from here as soon as I can think of a means, even if I have to sing on street corners.'

'I never thought I'd say it, but Rackham helped you once and I dare say he'd do it again if you only asked.'

'Rackham?' Bella sprang to her feet. 'I'd die first.'

Despite her brave words, Bella was deeply worried. She was well aware that the servants had been told to watch her every movement, and to report to Desmond if she so much as put a foot on the front doorstep. Time was running out, now that Leonie was well again. At night, when she couldn't sleep, she paced the floor of her room, making plan after plan and then discarding each one as impossible.

Edward had not replied to her last desperate letter entreating him to persuade Desmond to give her custody of Leonie, and there was no way of knowing whether or not he had even received it. The pain of their parting still stabbed Bella's heart every time she thought of it, and her body ached with longing. She yearned to feel Edward's arms around her and his lips, tantalising, teasing and exciting her desire until it was almost impossible to resist. But now he was far away in a foreign land, fighting for his country, and she could not even mention his name in this house, let alone beg for news of him. She had never felt so alone.

In the end Bella came to the painful conclusion

that, without outside help, there was no hope of escape and there was only one person whom she could ask. Despise him as she might, Rackham was neither afraid of Desmond nor of public censure. She knew that she had only to swallow her pride and, providing her escape did not interfere with an important card game or a trip to the races, he would be happy to oblige. She had no doubt that Rackham would almost certainly expect her to repay him by becoming his mistress once again, but even that was preferable to the life she had led in the gilded prison of her marriage. If that was the price to pay for escaping with Leonie, then so be it.

Early in the evening on the seventh day after her return from Essex, Bella had just sat down at her escritoire to write a brief note to Rackham when, without knocking, Desmond entered the room. He was dressed for an evening at the opera and he stood for a moment, eyeing her coldly.

'What do you want?' demanded Bella, covering the note with her hand.

'I want you out of this house first thing in the morning,' Desmond said, tapping his hand with his ebony cane. 'You will leave quietly and without Leonie.'

'Never!' Bella said, leaping to her feet. 'I'll never leave my child again.'

Desmond took a roll of notes from his breast

pocket and tossed it on the floor at Bella's feet. 'That's the last money that you'll ever get from me. My lawyers are drawing up the divorce papers and I want you out of my life.'

Bella stared at the crisp, white five-pound notes spilling out onto the thick pile of the Chinese carpet. 'I don't want your money, Desmond. I just want my child.'

'You should have thought about that before you took Rackham as your lover. Leonie is mine and she'll be brought up to think that her mother is dead. You are dead to me, Bella. You died the moment you attempted to seduce my son.'

'Your son is worth a million of you, Desmond. I love Edward and he loves me.'

With a howl of rage, Desmond lifted the cane above his head. 'I'll kill you for that.'

Chapter Nine

Hearing Bella scream, Kitty burst into the bedroom just in time to see Sir Desmond standing over her with his cane raised above his head.

'Kill me then,' Bella cried. 'For I'll not leave this house without Leonie.'

'No!' Kitty lunged at him but Desmond held her off with one hand, raising the cane higher, his eyes blazing with a wild light that made him look insane.

'Run, Bella,' Kitty shouted, struggling to free herself.

Bella stood her ground. 'I'll not run away. Strike me down, if you dare, Desmond.'

Shrugging his shoulders, Desmond hurled the cane across the room. 'You're not worth hanging for.' Turning on his heel, he strode from the room.

Kitty ran to help Bella, who was swaying dizzily. 'Sit quietly and I'll fetch you a glass of water.'

'I'm all right, Kitty. I've got to think what to do.'

'He's a mad brute, my lady,' Kitty said, chafing

Bella's cold hands. 'I seen that look in a man's eyes once and I don't never want to see it again.'

'I know what you must have gone through and I know how hard your life has been.'

Angling her head, Kitty looked into Bella's eyes and recognised genuine sympathy. 'How could a lady like you know what life is like in Billingsgate?'

'Believe me, I do. One day I'll tell you all about it, but for the moment I've got to think how to get us all out of here. I have to get Leonie to safety and away from my mad husband.'

'I know where he lives, my lady. The man who would help.'

'He will want so much in return.'

'Have you got a better idea?'

'You're right, Kitty.' Jumping to her feet, Bella went over to her escritoire and sat down, taking up a piece of headed writing paper and a pen. 'This isn't the time to be squeamish. I want you to take this to Mr Rackham and beg him on your knees if necessary.'

In less than an hour, Kitty and Rackham arrived back in Dover Street in a hackney carriage. Outside the air was green as pea soup and the fog clogged her nostrils, filling her mouth with the taste of soot and sulphur. Rackham waited in the cab while Kitty slipped in through the servants' entrance, making her way to the nursery where Bella and Maria were waiting, their faces white and strained with anxiety.

'I found him,' Kitty said, breathless but exultant. 'Mr Rackham is waiting outside in a hackney carriage but he says, make haste. It's a blooming pea-souper out there, and it's getting thicker by the minute.'

Waking Leonie from her sleep, Bella soothed her crying and dressed her in warm clothes, making pretence that it was all a game; they were going for a carriage ride in the dark, but they must be quiet as little mice. Bella led the way down the main staircase and Maria followed with Leonie in her arms, leaving Kitty to bring the baggage. The entrance hall was deserted, James was having supper in the servants' hall and there would be little likelihood of visitors arriving uninvited at this time of the night. Having reached the front door safely, Kitty could have cried with relief.

The choking, evil-smelling fog enveloped them as they stepped outside. Kitty could barely make out the shape of a cab on the far side of the street, although she could hear the horse snorting and moving uneasily between the shafts. Confused by the muffled sound of horses' hooves and the rumble of carriage wheels coming towards them, Kitty hesitated, peering into the smoky haze, uncertain as to which was Rackham's cab. She called his name and he answered, but the oncoming carriage loomed from the fog, coming to a halt outside the house. Close behind Kitty, Bella gave a cry of alarm as the door opened and Desmond leapt out onto the pavement.

'Take the child indoors,' Desmond barked at Maria, who was holding Leonie by the hand.

With her eyes wide with fright, Leonie began to cry and Maria snatched her up in her arms.

'Giles, help!' cried Bella, as he leapt from the cab and ran towards them.

'And you, Madam, can leave with your lover,' Desmond said, turning on her with an expression of pure hatred. 'I'll take great pleasure in naming Rackham as co-respondent in our divorce case.'

'I'm leaving, Desmond, but not without Leonie. You can't take my child from me.'

'I can and I will. The law is on my side. You are an unfit mother and a wanton. Now get out of my sight.'

'You can't do that, old boy,' Rackham said, stepping between them. 'Mother and child belong together. You can't separate them.'

'And have my daughter's morals corrupted by a scoundrel like you and her whore of a mother?'

'You've said your piece, Mableton,' Rackham said. 'Get Leonie into the cab, Bella.'

'You can go to hell, Rackham,' Desmond said, putting himself between Maria and Bella. 'Lane and the child stay with me.'

Kitty lunged at Desmond as Maria struggled to

free herself, but he brushed her off and, stumbling, she would have fallen if Rackham had not reached out and caught her. Lifting her bodily, he tossed her into the hackney carriage.

'Leave them alone,' Bella screamed. 'Give me my baby, Desmond.'

'Lane will stay here and look after Leonie as she did while you were away in the country. You left your child then. You can do it now.'

Screaming hysterically, Leonie beat her small fists against Maria's shoulder.

'You forced me to live apart from Leonie,' Bella sobbed, flying at Desmond and raking her fingernails down his cheek.

Grabbing Bella around the waist, Rackham swung her off her feet, setting her down behind him. 'Let Maria and the child go, Mableton, or I'll have great pleasure in flooring you.'

'Warner, fetch the constable,' Desmond roared, as Warner came running down the steps.

'Desmond, I'm begging you,' cried Bella. 'Let Maria go and give me back my child. I'll never ask you for anything ever again, I swear it.'

Leonie continued to scream, despite Maria's frantic attempts to pacify her.

'Keep the child quiet, Lane. Take her into the house and put her to bed.' Desmond barred Bella's way as she made a grab for Leonie.

'You can't order Maria about,' Bella screamed, tears running down her cheeks. 'She isn't your servant, Desmond. She has nothing to do with you.'

'Shut up, Bella,' Maria said, seizing the opportunity to slip past Desmond. 'Don't give him the satisfaction.'

'Pass her to me,' Kitty called, leaning out of the carriage.

'I'll have you arrested for kidnapping.' Desmond made a move to follow Maria, but Rackham barred his way.

'You're very brave when it comes to bullying women,' Rackham said, squaring up to Desmond. 'Let's see how you shape up against a man.'

'I'll see to it that Lane never gets another place in service,' Desmond said, backing away. 'And you, Bella, will be dealt with.'

'There's nothing more you can do to me, Desmond,' Bella said, struggling to regain her composure. 'And for your information, Maria is not a servant. She is my mother.'

'And your mother-in-law, God help me.' Maria leaned out of the carriage window. 'That will look good in the society columns, won't it, Desmond my boy? The Right Honourable Sir Desmond Mableton, Baronet, married to a gypsy's daughter.'

Desmond turned to Bella with a vicious snarl. 'You tricked me, you common little whore.'

'I may be common but at least I'm not a sadistic bully.'

'Do you want me to knock him down, Bella?' Rackham demanded. 'I'd be more than happy to oblige.'

'No,' Bella said, climbing into the cab. 'He's not worth it.'

'You won't get away with this,' Desmond shouted, as Rackham leapt in after her. 'I'll have the law on you.'

Rackham unlocked the door to his rooms and went inside to light the gas lamps, which shed an instant warm glow on the sparsely furnished room. Leonie had fallen asleep during the short cab ride to Half Moon Street and Kitty laid her gently on the sofa. It was hard to believe that they had managed to escape so easily. She had been sure that Sir Desmond would follow them, or send the constable to accuse Bella of kidnapping her own daughter. Perhaps the fog had served its purpose, making even the shortest journey hazardous.

Rackham went to the fireplace and poked the dying embers into flames, throwing on a shovelful of coal that sent sparks flying up the chimney. 'You'll be safe here tonight, but it won't take long for Desmond to discover my address.'

'We should get as far away from Dover Street as possible,' Maria said. 'But for now what we all need is sleep.'

Crossing the room, Rackham opened a door

that led to a bedroom. 'If you and Kitty don't mind sharing a bed, this should do for one night.'

'We'll manage,' Maria said, nodding. 'Leonie can sleep with us.'

Lifting Leonie so gently that she barely stirred, Rackham carried her into the room and laid her on the bed.

'Let me help you undress, my lady,' Kitty said, alarmed by Bella's pallor. 'You should get some rest.'

Glancing nervously at Rackham, Bella shook her head. 'I – I'm not sure where I'll be sleeping.'

Rackham went to the chiffonier, picked up a cut glass decanter and poured two generous measures of brandy into crystal glasses, handing one to Bella. 'Drink this and you'll feel better.'

Kitty waited, aware that Rackham and Bella had forgotten her existence. She could feel the tension buzzing between them as Bella sipped the brandy, eyeing Rackham over the rim of the glass. There was only one other door leading off the sitting room, Kitty reasoned, and that had to be his bedroom.

'I'd like another one,' Bella said, handing Rackham the empty glass.

'It's not very flattering, my dear.'

Blushing, Bella seemed unable to meet his gaze. 'I don't know what you mean.'

'I've never had to get a woman drunk to persuade her to sleep with me, Bella. And I'm not

222

starting now.' Taking her by the hand, Rackham led her into his bedroom.

Hovering in the doorway, Kitty waited for instructions; she had no intention of leaving Bella until she was certain that she would be all right.

'It's all yours,' Rackham said, with a wry smile. 'I'll take the sofa and tomorrow morning, first thing, I'll go out and find you somewhere safer and more suitable to your needs.'

Bella stared at him for a moment and then she smiled reluctantly. 'You know, if you're not careful, Giles, you might turn into a gentleman.'

'Don't be fooled by my apparent gallantry, Bella. I'm no gentleman but I don't take advantage of helpless women.' Rackham lifted her chin and kissed her lightly on the lips.

Kitty's fingers closed around the handle of the valise containing Bella's things. If Bella needed protecting she was quite prepared to take a swing at Rackham and knock him down.

'You weren't so scrupulous when I was an innocent fourteen-year-old,' Bella said, breathlessly.

Kitty gave a little cough to make them aware of her presence, but they did not seem to hear. Rackham caressed Bella's cheek with his fingertip and his lips smiled but there was a hint of something akin to sadness in his eyes. 'You were innocent then, in spite of what that brute of a father put you through. And you would have been sold again and again if I hadn't come along and rescued you.'

'And taken me as your mistress when I was little more than a child.'

'We had a wonderful few years together – admit it, Bella.'

'You abandoned me. You left me on my own in that hotel in Dover.'

Rackham threw back his head and laughed. 'As I remember it, Bella, I left you with virtually all the money I had in the world, which was enough to set you up for quite a long time. Would you rather that I'd dragged you around the gaming hells and race courses of France until I'd built up my stake?'

'You have an answer for everything, haven't you?'

'Get some sleep, my pet. I'll respect your virtue tonight, but one day you'll come to me willingly, I'll bet my life on it.'

'Never.'

Kitty jumped clear as Bella slammed the door and the key grated in the lock.

Noticing Kitty as if for the first time, Rackham smiled and shrugged his shoulders. 'Are you a betting woman, Kitty?'

'No, Sir.'

'Never mind. Best get some sleep. I've a feeling that tomorrow is going to be a difficult day.'

Rackham walked over to the chiffonier and poured himself another drink.

Kitty crept into the bedroom and, taking off her top clothes, she slid into the bed beside Leonie, taking care not to wake her.

Lying very still but wide awake, Kitty tried desperately to come to terms with what she had just seen and heard. It did not seem possible that Maria, sleeping in the chair and snoring, could be Bella's mother. It was equally hard to believe that someone like Bella, who was a lady through and through, could have come from a background similar to her own. Bella had not denied any of the shocking things that Mr Rackham had said and yet, if they were all true, perhaps that explained why Bella had always been so sympathetic and understanding. Kitty saw her bright angel falling from the stars and, with a shock, she realised that they were not so very different after all.

Next morning Kitty was awakened by such a commotion coming from the passage outside the sitting room that she leapt out of bed. Wrapping the counterpane around her shoulders, she found Maria standing by the door with her ear pressed to the keyhole. Leonie stood in the middle of the room sucking her thumb, a baby habit that she had long since outgrown, but her eyes were round with alarm and she looked as though she was about to yell. Snatching her up, Kitty sat on the sofa, jiggling Leonie on her knee and singing 'Ride a Cock Horse to Banbury Cross'. Someone outside was shouting and thumping their fist on the door.

'Mr Rackham, Sir,' cried a female voice, 'there's a constable at the front door who wants a word with you.'

Hurrying out of Rackham's bedroom, Bella raised a warning finger to her lips, as Maria shot her an anxious look.

'Mr Rackham, answer the door, Sir. The constable says he won't go away until he's spoken to you.'

More bangs and thuds on the door and then the woman appeared to give up. Her grumbling and her footsteps grew quieter as she stomped down the stairs.

'Where is Rackham?' Bella demanded, lifting Leonie from Kitty's lap and giving her a cuddle.

Maria angled her head and raised her eyebrows. 'I thought he was with you.'

'Certainly not. He slept on the sofa.'

'He did,' Kitty said stoutly. 'I'll vouch for that.'

'Well, he wasn't here when I got up to use the water closet,' Maria said, shrugging. 'Looks like he's cleared off again. He knew that Sir Desmond would have the law on us.'

Kitty shot a worried look at Bella. 'What shall we do, my lady?'

'We must keep quiet,' Bella said, going to the window and peeping out from behind the lace curtain. 'I think the constable is going away. Yes, he is. I can see the top of his helmet as he walks off down the street.'

'Then let's get out of here before he comes back.' Maria rushed into the bedroom and began flinging things in the suitcase. 'We can't trust Rackham. He's probably sloped off, the stinking coward.'

'You're forgetting that we haven't anywhere to go,' Bella said, setting Leonie down on the floor.

'Hungry,' complained Leonie, running over to Kitty. 'Want breakfast, Kitty.'

'A mouse would die of starvation in this place,' Maria said. 'I've been through the cupboards and there's nothing, not even a crust of bread. We can't stay here, Bella.'

'Rackham said he would find us somewhere safe and I think we've got to trust him.'

'You've changed your tune,' Maria said, shivering. 'But we've got to do something. It's bloody freezing and we're all hungry.'

Stepping in between them, Kitty held up her hands. 'Arguing between ourselves isn't going to get us anywhere. We could go to Tanner's Passage. I know that Betty would take us in.'

'That's the first sensible suggestion I've heard today,' Maria said, hefting the suitcase from the bedroom. 'Let's get out of here.'

Bella turned back to stare out of the window. 'It's raining! We'll never find a cab.'

'Then we'll walk,' Maria said, picking up an armful of coats from the chair. 'We daren't stay any longer, Bella. My guess is that the copper went straight round to Dover Street to report to Sir Desmond. He'll be back with reinforcements any minute.'

'There's a hackney cab just pulled up outside,' Bella cried, pressing her nose to the window-pane. 'It's Giles. You were wrong, he hasn't deserted us.'

Kitty ran to the door and unlocked it, wrenching it open as footsteps pounded up the narrow staircase. Rackham came up the stairs, closely followed by his irate landlady.

'This is a respectable lodging house, I'll have you know, Mr Rackham. My reputation will be in ruins if word gets around that I'm harbouring runaways and criminals.'

Rackham stopped and pressed something into her outstretched hand. 'There you are, Mrs Hennessy. Perhaps that will recompense you for your trouble.' He bounded up the remaining steps, two at a time. 'I saw Desmond's carriage turning into Piccadilly. We must hurry.'

Mrs Hennessy stood in the doorway of her apartment, glaring at them as they left the house. There was a mad scramble to get everyone into the cab, but just as Rackham set his foot on the step, a hand fell on his shoulder.

'Is this the person, Sir Desmond?'

'Yes, Officer,' Desmond said, dragging Bella from the cab and snatching Leonie from her arms. 'And this is my daughter, who was abducted from my house last night.'

'No, it's not true,' Bella cried, desperately trying to wrest Leonie from his grasp.

'Did you think I'd let you steal my daughter?'

'Officer, there's been a mistake,' Rackham said, keeping a tight hold on Bella as she fought and struggled to get to Leonie, who was sobbing pitifully. 'This woman is the child's mother. That isn't abduction.'

The constable turned to Desmond. 'Sir Desmond?'

'My daughter was taken from my house without my permission. I think my good friend the Lord Chief Justice would agree with me that this is a case of abduction.' Desmond handed Leonie to Warner, who stood behind him, grim-faced as usual.

'You can't do this, Desmond,' Bella sobbed. 'Give me back my child and I'll come home. I'll do anything you ask.'

'Think yourself lucky that I'm not proffering criminal charges against you, Madam. I've plenty of witnesses to prove that you left the marital home to spend the night with your lover.

There isn't a court in the land that wouldn't grant me a divorce and custody of our child.'

'You're a wicked man,' Kitty cried, balling her hands into fists. 'That's a pack of lies.'

'You're a bully and a wife beater,' Maria screamed, leaping out of the cab onto the pavement. 'How would you like that bandied about in court, Sir Desmond?'

Desmond drew back, his face contorted with fury. 'If I'd known that you were the mother of that whore I would never have married her. If you or she ever come near my house again, I'll have you arrested and thrown in jail, so don't threaten me, woman.'

Thrusting Bella aside, Rackham sprang forward and, grabbing Desmond by the throat, he landed a left hook squarely on his jaw.

Desmond crumpled to his knees clutching his face. 'Arrest that man, Officer.'

'What's the matter, Mableton?' Rackham said, grinning. 'Can't you fight your own battles?'

'You'll go to prison for this,' Desmond said, getting stiffly to his feet. 'And I'll make sure they throw away the key.'

Approaching Rackham with a degree of caution, the constable unclipped a pair of handcuffs from his belt. 'I'd advise you to come quietly, Sir.'

With a careless shrug, Rackham held up his wrists. 'We've been here before, I think, Constable.'

Distracted by screams from Leonie, who was struggling in Warner's arms, kicking out with her feet and crying for her mother, Desmond turned his back on Rackham. 'Get the child into the carriage, Warner. We're taking Miss Leonie home.'

Bella threw herself down on her knees in front of Desmond, clutching at his coat. 'Desmond, I'm begging you, give Leonie to me. She needs her mother.'

Desmond jerked his coat free, looking down on her with a contemptuous curl of his lips. 'Leonie will be brought up to be a lady and you will never see her again. From this day on she has no mother. You will be as dead to her as if you'd thrown yourself off Waterloo Bridge into the Thames.'

Screaming obscenities, Maria flung herself at Desmond, only to be pulled back by another constable, who had come running in answer to his colleague's frantic blasts on his whistle. Losing his temper, Rackham struggled to break free, but was dragged off down the street and bundled into a horse-drawn police wagon. Kitty threw her arms around Bella, helping her to her feet, and they clung together sobbing.

'If you ever come near my house again, you'll join your lover in jail,' Desmond said, climbing into his carriage.

Leonie's sobs and screams could be heard even when the door slammed shut.

'Call yourself a gentleman,' Maria shouted, spitting at the coat of arms on the carriage door. 'You're a bigger bastard than Rackham.'

'That's enough of that,' said the constable. 'Make yourselves scarce, or I'll arrest the lot of you for breach of the peace.'

Maria spat on the pavement at his feet and wiped her mouth on the back of her hand. 'So much for the law.'

Bella drew herself upright, stifling a sob. 'It's all right, Officer. We're leaving.'

'Look, ladies, this is all very fine and I ain't seen a better show since *Maria Marten and the Red Barn*, but some of us got a living to make.' The cabbie, who had been watching everything from the safety of his driving seat, leaned down and tapped Maria on the shoulder. 'If you don't want me then I'd respectfully ask you to cough up the necessary.'

'Oh God, what shall we do?' Bella leaned against Maria, looking perilously close to fainting.

Thinking quickly, Kitty made the decision for them. 'Tanner's Passage, if you please, cabbie.'

White-faced, Bella fell back against the squabs of the hackney carriage and closed her eyes.

'Don't worry, my lady.' Kitty leaned over to pat Bella's clawed hands. 'We'll get Miss Leonie back. We'll find a way.'

'Don't give her false hopes,' Maria said, grimly. 'Mableton's got the law on his side and the money to back him up. The likes of us don't stand a chance.'

'I won't believe that,' Kitty cried, vehemently. 'We'll find a way even if we have to break into the house and really kidnap her.'

'You're just a kid. You don't know what you're talking about.'

'I know you can't just give up when things are bad. I know little Leonie belongs with her mother.'

The cab rumbled to a halt and Kitty leapt out, barely waiting for it to stop, leaving Bella to pay the driver. Rapping on the door knocker she listened and waited, stepping backwards and staring up at the sitting room window, knocking again when no one came, a cold shiver of alarm running down her spine.

Eventually Betty opened the door, staring dazedly at Kitty for a moment. She burst into tears. 'Kitty, Kitty, thank God you've come.'

'What's wrong?' Kitty cried, flinging her arms around her. 'Has something dreadful happened to Jem?'

Betty shook her head and, seeing Bella, she wiped her eyes on her apron. 'You'll have to excuse me, Ma'am, only I'm not quite myself today.'

'Perhaps we should leave,' Bella said. 'It seems we've come at a bad time.'

'Nonsense!' Maria said, pushing past her and dumping the bags on the flagstone floor. 'We haven't met, Mrs Scully, but I'm Maria Lane, Bella's mother. Whatever the trouble, I'm sure that we can help you.'

Betty stared at the luggage, shaking her head. 'If it's rooms you want, I'm afraid I can't help you. I have a very sick child to care for.'

'Polly!' Kitty clutched Betty's hand. 'What's the matter with her?'

'It's the measles. She's got it really bad. I have to sit with her day and night. Oh, Kitty, I'm sorry, ducks, but I can't let out rooms at present.'

'Mrs Scully – Betty – I'm so sorry,' Bella said, laying a hand on her shoulder. 'I do so understand. My own little girl has recently been sick with the measles and I do know what you must be going through.'

Sniffing, Betty rummaged in her pocket for a hanky. 'You'll understand then, my lady.'

'I thought we'd agreed, it's just Bella now, and this is Maria, my – mother.' Bella hooked her arm around Betty's shoulders. 'We are in urgent need of accommodation, just for a short while, and we will do everything we can to help.'

Polly was desperately ill. That fact became apparent to Kitty the moment she was allowed into the sickroom. Her heart went out to Betty, who steadfastly believed that Polly could make a recovery from the disease, even though it was obvious to everyone else that the poor child was clinging to life by the thinnest of threads. After a day or two, there was no question of them leaving the house in Tanner's Passage. Maria took over the household duties, cooking and cleaning and going out to buy food. Bella and Kitty took turns at Polly's bedside, allowing Betty to snatch a few hours much-needed sleep on the sofa.

Although she gave herself up entirely to helping care for Polly, Kitty knew that Bella never lost sight for a moment of her main aim, which was to get Leonie back from her father. They shared the night duties between them and, one evening when she came to relieve Bella, Kitty found her slumped in the chair sound asleep. In her hand was a letter that she must have been in the middle of writing to Edward. Ashamed of herself, but unable to resist the temptation, Kitty scanned the tear-stained, ink-blotted page where Bella begged Edward to intercede on her behalf with Desmond. If he had any feeling left for her, she had written, then he would understand her mother's heart and make Sir Desmond restore her child to her.

Folding the crumpled paper, Kitty tucked it into the pocket of Bella's apron and gently awakened her, insisting that she went to her bed.

Sitting beside Polly in the long night hours,

holding her hand, quieting her when she raved in fever and bathing her with cool water, Kitty felt her heart heavy with sadness – both for Bella, who had had her child taken from her, and for Betty, who would almost certainly soon lose her daughter. Kitty had seen enough of sickness and disease in Sugar Yard to know when life was ebbing away like the tide. Despite all the loving care lavished upon her, Polly grew weaker by the day; her enfeebled body unable to fight off the lung infection that threatened her fragile life.

Polly's funeral took place on a cold December morning. The graveyard sparkled with hoar frost and a savage wind blew from the Essex marshes, stinging the mourners' eyes. Even Maria, who normally never displayed any signs of emotion, wiped the tears away, complaining that it was the east wind that made her eyes water. After the pathetically small casket was lowered into the grave and the final words were spoken by the vicar, Betty broke down and sobbed. She had been so brave up until that final moment when the handfuls of earth fell upon the wooden coffin, but now she gave way entirely to her grief.

Between them, they got her home and Kitty put her to bed with a stone hot-water bottle and a dose of laudanum. Maria, practical as usual, began peeling vegetables to put in the pot with a beef bone to make a stew for their supper, but Bella appeared restless, saying that she wanted to go for a walk to clear her head. Afraid that Polly's funeral had aggravated Bella's own grief at the loss of her child, Kitty insisted that she went with her. Asking no questions, Kitty followed Bella onto the omnibus and was unsurprised when they alighted in Piccadilly. She knew then that they were heading for Dover Street, but she did not try to stop her.

Frost particles glinted on the Portland stone pavements and her breath curled around her face like smoke as Kitty kept up step for step with Bella. After an hour of walking up and down outside the house, all the feeling had gone from her feet and hands.

'Bella,' Kitty said, laying her hand on Bella's sleeve. 'I know you want to catch sight of Leonie, but it's not going to happen today. Let's go home.'

'I can't just give up. I kept thinking as they lowered poor little Polly into the cold black hole that it could have been my Leonie, and I would never see her again.' Tears flowed freely down Bella's cheeks.

'I understand, I really do, but we're getting funny looks,' Kitty said, hooking Bella's hand into the crook of her arm. 'Let's go. We can always come back another day.'

'I must have news of her, Kitty. Can't you see

that? I must know what's going on behind those closed doors or I'll go mad.'

Kitty stared at her helplessly for a moment. It seemed a lifetime ago that she had stood on this spot, a terrified scullery maid, worshipping the beautiful, angelic lady of the house. Bella had protected her then, saving her from the savage bullying below stairs but now they were more like sisters, the awful secrets of their past lives putting them on equal footing. Beautiful Bella, raised like herself in the East End, the daughter of an innkeeper and a gypsy, ravished by her own father and sold to the highest bidder, Rackham. Gazing at Bella's tragic face, Kitty remembered the conversation that had passed between Bella and Rackham that night in his lodgings. Whatever Bella said about him, Kitty sensed that deep down she still harboured feelings for the man who had been her first love.

'We aren't doing any good here,' Kitty said, dragging Bella along the street. 'Mr Rackham knows what's going on in society, what with him having a lord as a cousin. He owes you a few favours if you ask me – that's if he ain't in prison for bopping Sir Desmond on the nose.'

Mrs Hennessy opened the door and squinted at them short-sightedly. 'Yes?'

'Is Mr Rackham at home?' Bella demanded.

Mrs Hennessy's suspicious expression turned

into a full-blown scowl. 'No he ain't and I don't want the likes of you a-knocking at my door. This is a respectable lodging house, so go away.'

'How dare you speak to me in that tone,' Bella said, trembling with anger. 'Do you know who I am?'

'I know who you are, all right. You was here that night the coppers come banging on me door. I've read the newspapers and you should be ashamed of yourself, carrying on behind your poor husband's back. Get off my doorstep and don't come back.'

'I haven't read the newspapers, but whatever they say I'm sure that none of it's true. I must see Mr Rackham. If he isn't here at least tell me where I can find him.'

'He's gone abroad, so I heard, and good riddance to bad rubbish.' Mrs Hennessy slammed the door in their faces.

Chapter Ten

The house in Tanner's Passage was shrouded in a pall of sadness. Kitty felt as though her heart would break as she witnessed Betty's suffering; she tried to comfort her, but nothing she said or did seemed to have the slightest effect. Sometimes Betty stayed in bed all day, staring blankly into space, as if her mind was far away from her tired body. At other times, if she could be persuaded to get up, she would sit, huddled on the sofa, cuddling Polly's rag doll. If only Jem would come home, Kitty thought miserably. He had always been able to make his mother smile, but it would be several months before his ship was due to return to London. She had wanted to write to him and break the sad news gently, but Betty had been adamant that it must wait until she could tell him face to face. In her mind's eye, Kitty could see Jem's cheerful grin as he walked through the door on his homecoming, and his inevitable heartbreak when he learnt that his beloved Polly was dead. Out of loyalty to Betty, she was forced to abide by her wishes, but she grieved inwardly, anticipating Jem's pain.

Then there was Bella, who went about pale and silent as a ghost, saying nothing but quite obviously suffering torments at the loss of her child. Kitty sensed that missing Captain Edward was adding to Bella's deep sadness; but that was a question far too personal to ask, even though they had abandoned all the formalities that had constrained them in Dover Street. At first, it had been difficult dropping the 'my lady' and using Bella's given name, and even more so when it came to Miss Lane. The name Maria did not trip easily off Kitty's tongue, but Bella had insisted that they were just one family and it was foolish to stand on ceremony.

Maria seemed to be the least touched by the overwhelming emotions that raged in the grief-stricken household. If anything, Kitty thought, Maria was simply angry. She was angry with Sir Desmond for behaving so brutally, angry with Rackham for getting them so far and then apparently abandoning them. And most of all she was angry at their sudden dive into poverty. She made it plain that she hated the house, she hated Tanner's Passage and, sometimes Kitty thought, she seemed to hate everyone, even Bella.

The most pressing problem now was money, or the lack of it. With three extra people living in her house and with only three letting bedrooms, Betty was unable to supplement her income by taking in commercial travellers. In any case, Kitty thought wearily, even if they found alternative accommodation, Betty was in no state to be left on her own. She had not touched her sewing since Polly's death and, after several irate ladies had sent their servants to complain that their new dresses were long overdue, Maria and Kitty had worked hard to finish them. Their efforts had brought in little money, but at least it was enough to feed them for several days.

In the unhappy house, Kitty did her best to keep up their spirits, saying nothing about her own problems. She desperately wanted to go and see Maggie and the children, if only to check that they were in good health, but she was terrified of bumping into Sid. Christmas came and passed, almost unnoticed. Bella's money had run out and things were getting desperate.

At the beginning of the New Year, and when everyone else in the country seemed to be celebrating the dawn of a new century, Kitty was busy scanning the Situations Vacant columns of old newspapers in the pie and eel shop. She went knocking on doors in answer to advertisements for scullery maids in Islington, Bloomsbury and Kensington. She wore her boots out with trudging long distances on hard pavements, but it seemed that her character reference from Lady Mableton went against her, as much as having no reference at all. No one wanted to employ her.

Bella had tried every theatre manager in the West End and been turned down by all of them.

'It's so unfair,' Kitty cried, one morning at breakfast. 'Why does everyone take Sir Desmond's side?'

'Because men always have the upper hand,' Maria said, paring thin slices from a loaf of stale bread. 'I've a good mind to join that there Women's Suffrage Society we keep hearing about.'

'We need money,' Bella said, pushing her teacup aside. 'It's no use railing against Desmond and men in general. We have to help ourselves, for no one else is going to.'

'Oh, yes! And how do we do that when we're close to starvation?' demanded Maria. 'You've tried every theatre in London and been shown the door. Doesn't that make you hate bloody Mableton?'

'Hating Desmond won't put food on the table. I can still sing and act. There must be some theatre manager who will give me a chance.'

'That's the last of the bread and the marg,' Maria said, scraping a tiny amount of margarine onto a slice of bread. 'Take it up to Betty with a cup of tea, there's a good girl, Kitty.'

'I'll go back to my old patch on the foreshore,' Kitty said. 'Even if it's only a few pennies a day, at least it will help.'

'And they'll be fishing your dead body out of

the Thames if that bugger Sid should come across you,' Maria said, punctuating her words by stabbing actions with the bread knife.

'There's no need for Kitty to put herself in danger,' Bella said, jumping to her feet. 'If they won't give me a job up West, I'll go back to the East End, where I started.'

Maria dropped the knife with an exclamation of disgust. 'You're still Lady Mableton. You've risen above that sort of life.'

'No, Ma,' Bella said, slowly. 'I'm still the same person. Marrying Desmond didn't make me a lady.'

'No, Madam, but it gave you money, position and respectability.'

'And look where that got me. Anyway, I'd never have married Desmond if you hadn't kept on and on at me.'

'You'd have wasted your life waiting for Rackham to come back,' Maria said, with a sarcastic curl of her lip. 'We had comfort and security while you were married to Mableton. You'd never have had that with Rackham.'

'I hate Rackham,' Bella cried passionately. 'And I loathe Desmond. My life with him was a living hell. The only good thing that came of it was Leonie and now he's taken her away from me.'

'You, you, you!' Maria said, her eyes glinting angrily. 'I sacrificed my own identity to make you look good. Mableton wouldn't have looked at you twice if he'd known that your mother was half gypsy and your father kept a pub in the Commercial Road.'

'That was your idea,' Bella said, snatching up her hat and cape. 'I never asked you to do that. I never wanted to live a lie.'

Maria stared at her for a moment and her anger seemed to evaporate. She shrugged her shoulders. 'Perhaps it was, but don't think it was easy for me to act the servant in my own daughter's house.'

'I know it wasn't, Ma,' Bella said, her expression softening. 'I know you did it for the best.'

'And you can't go roaming round the East End on your own,' Maria said, untying her apron strings. 'I'll come with you.'

'I don't need a chaperone, thanks all the same.'

'Let me come with you, Bella,' pleaded Kitty.

Pausing in the doorway, Bella smiled. 'Thank you, Kitty dear, but I really can look after myself.'

Snatching up Betty's breakfast tray, Kitty followed Bella to the front door. 'Take care.'

'Don't worry,' Bella said, as she closed the door. 'I'll be fine.'

She is so beautiful, Kitty thought, as she trudged up the stairs. Bella is so kind and so brave. If only some nice theatre manager would give her a fresh start. How could anyone refuse to help someone who was so sweet and lovely and sang like a nightingale?

She went into the sitting room where Betty was still in bed with the covers pulled up to her chin. Kitty shivered. The room was freezing and her breath curled out in front of her like puffs of steam from a kettle. For weeks, there had been no money to buy coal for the fire, and damp patches had spread in great blots on the walls.

'Here's your breakfast, Betty. How do you feel today?'

'I'm not very hungry, Kitty love. You eat my breakfast or Maria will tell me off.'

Kitty put the tray down on the pine chest of drawers. 'You must keep your strength up,' she said, perching on the edge of the bed. 'What would Jem say if he could see you like this?'

Betty closed her eyes and her pale lashes stood out against the bruise-like shadows beneath them. 'Jem is far, far away. Anything can happen at sea. He might never come home again.'

Kitty seized her by the shoulders and shook her hard. 'Don't you dare say things like that. I won't hear of it. Jem is safe and well. I'd know it in my bones if there was anything wrong.' Kitty plunged her hand down inside her blouse and pulled out the half-sovereign that she had pierced and threaded on a piece of ribbon. 'We're like this, Jem and me, two halves of the same coin, like brother and sister. He'll be home in a few months' time and he'll expect you to be the ma he remembers, not some pale skeleton what's lost the will to live.'

'Oh, Kitty, don't you shout at me,' sobbed Betty. 'I know what you say is true but I haven't got the strength to drag my body from this bed.'

Clutching the piece of gold, Kitty felt tears burn the back of her eyelids. The thought of parting with her half of the coin was as painful as losing an arm or leg, but she couldn't stand by and see Jem's mother fading away through lack of food and warmth. She knew exactly what she must do.

Old Sparks, the pawnbroker, peered at her over the top of his steel-rimmed specs as he held the piece of coin between his thumb and forefinger. When he opened his mouth to bite the gold, Kitty caught a waft of foul breath from blackened and broken teeth. 'I'll give you a florin, young Kitty,' he said. 'Not a penny more.'

'But it's worth more than that.'

'Not to me it ain't. Cutting coins of the realm in half is against the law, don't you know that? I'll give you two shillings for scrap and that's my last word.'

Reluctantly Kitty held out her hand.

'I wouldn't let Sid Cable know you've got money,' Sparks said as he dropped the coins onto her palm. 'You been home yet, young 'un?'

Kitty shook her head, closing her fingers over the metal, and feeling a cold shiver run down her spine. 'No, why?'

'Word gets round,' Sparks said, tapping the side of his nose with a grimy finger poking out of a black mitten, 'and it ain't good.'

Icy fingers of fear clutched at Kitty's heart as she left the pawnshop. Bowing her head in the face of the nagging east wind, she hurried along the quay wall. The tea-coloured water of the Thames was pockmarked with sleet and it rattled off the decks of boats moored alongside. Passing Tanner's Passage Kitty broke into a run, her anxiety for Maggie and the children overcoming her terror of coming face to face with Sid. Her footsteps echoed eerily in the dark passage that opened out into Sugar Yard, but there was no one about and she entered the building unseen. She raced up the stairs, her feet crunching on the carapaces of scuttling cockroaches. She stopped outside the door, pressing her ear against the keyhole, listening for the sound of voices. Satisfied that if Maggie was there, she was alone, Kitty turned the handle and went inside.

Stuffing her hand in her mouth to stifle a cry of horror, Kitty threw herself down on her knees beside Maggie, who lay on the box bed, like a broken doll. Her face was so bruised, bloody and swollen that she was almost unrecognisable. For a terrible moment Kitty thought she was dead.

'Maggie, Maggie, speak to me,' Kitty cried, chafing her lifeless hands. 'Oh, Maggie, please don't be dead.'

Maggie's eyelids fluttered and a small sigh escaped from her swollen lips; a trickle of blood oozed from the corner of her mouth.

'Thank God,' Kitty cried, leaping to her feet. She grabbed a pitcher of water from the table and poured some into a tin cup. Kneeling at Maggie's side, she lifted her head and held the cup to her lips.

Maggie gulped thirstily, spilling more water than she managed to swallow. 'Kitty?'

'I'm here, Maggie,' Kitty said, hugging Maggie and rocking her like a baby. 'Poor Maggie, what has that wicked sod done to you?'

Maggie struggled to sit upright, staring around the room, wide-eyed and trembling. 'Where is Harry?'

Muffled sobs from the children's room made Kitty leap to her feet. Flinging the door open, she found Harry sitting in the middle of the mattress, clutching a piece of rag to his mouth. He had wet himself in his fright and he stared at her with big, scared eyes, like some small wild animal.

Sweeping him up in her arms, Kitty cuddled him, ignoring his sodden, smelly baby dress. 'Harry, it's me, Kitty.'

He had stopped crying but dry sobs wracked his small body. 'There, there,' Kitty said, carrying him back into the living room. 'Kitty's here now. Everything will be all right.' She picked her way through the debris of smashed crockery and the splintered remains of a wooden chair. 'Where are the nippers, Maggie?'

'Sid hadn't come home last night. I'd just sent them off to school when he came in roaring drunk. He wanted money but there weren't none. I don't remember much else.'

Kitty was silent for a moment, staring around her and wondering how she ever lived in such disgusting conditions. The air was stale and thick with the smell of mildew and mice droppings; she could hear rats scuttling around behind the skirting boards. She turned back to Maggie, who lay on the straw mattress looking more like a skeleton than a woman not yet twenty-five. Fear turned to white-hot rage, boiling inside her. 'I'm taking you away from this dreadful place and from him forever, Maggie.'

'It's no good, Kitty,' Maggie said, closing her eyes. 'He'd seek us out and he'd kill me.'

'He's killing you now,' Kitty said, rubbing her cheek on Harry's downy head. 'I'll not leave you again. You're coming with me to Betty's house and I'll fetch the kids from school.'

'He'll find us for sure.'

'If Sid comes near the place, I'll go to the police and tell them it was him that raped me. I'll see him in jail before I'll let you spend another minute in this midden.'

'I daren't, Kitty,' Maggie said, struggling to a sitting position. 'How will you feed and clothe us all? We'll end up in the workhouse.'

'Never,' Kitty said, shaking her head. 'You're coming with me.'

With Kitty's help, Maggie managed to walk as far as Betty's house before she collapsed in the hallway. With Harry sucking his thumb and perched on her hip, Kitty went to the kitchen to break the news to Maria, whose initial angry reaction dissolved into one of shock when she saw Maggie.

'Good God above,' Maria said, hooking Maggie's arm around her shoulder. 'What a state you're in!' She hoisted Maggie to her feet. 'Come into the kitchen and let's have a look at those cuts and bruises. Kitty, you'd better go upstairs and speak to Betty. It's her house, when all's said and done.'

Taking Harry with her, Kitty went up to Betty's room. She appeared to be sleeping but, on hearing Kitty's footsteps, she opened her eyes. Kitty explained briefly what had happened.

'Them poor little mites,' Betty said, snapping upright in her bed. 'Living with an evil brute like Sid Cable. Put Maggie to bed in the boxroom, Kitty. I'll get dressed and fetch the children from school.'

Untangling Harry's stubby fingers from her hair, Kitty stared anxiously at Betty. 'You haven't eaten a proper meal for weeks. Are you sure you can walk that far?'

'Yes, and further still if it means bringing the little ones to safety,' Betty said, two bright dots of colour flaming her cheeks as she swung her legs over the side of the bed. 'Just let Sid Cable come knocking on my door and he'll be sorry, that's all I can say.'

Bella came home that evening looking pale and exhausted. She was almost bowled over by seven-year-old Frankie, who had just tumbled down the stairs. Kitty came out of the kitchen, gave him a playful cuff round the ear, and told him to go and play in the back yard with the others.

Maria and Betty were in the middle of cooking supper, having spent Kitty's florin on groceries at the corner shop. Revived by a cup of hot, sweet tea, Bella sat at the table and listened, wide-eyed with horror, as they told her of Maggie's plight.

'Of course we must look after them,' Bella said, reaching out and clasping Kitty's hand. 'That man is a beast and it's up to us to keep Maggie and the children safe.'

'I agree,' Maria said, stirring a pan of soup. 'But Gawd knows how we're going to live.'

'Well, there's my good news,' Bella said,

smiling. 'I've got bottom billing at the Aldgate Palace of Varieties.'

Kitty jumped up to hug her and Betty clapped her hands.

Maria frowned. 'Bottom of the bill? You were top of the bill before.'

'It's a start,' Bella said calmly. 'The only problem is, I need a costume.'

Maria slammed the lid on the saucepan. 'When do you start?'

'Tomorrow night! I need a costume by tomorrow night.'

'That's impossible,' Maria said. 'We've nothing left to pawn and not a decent gown between us.'

'You could make a dress for Bella,' Kitty said, looking hopefully at Betty.

'The rheumatics have made me clumsy,' Betty said, looking down at her swollen fingers. 'I don't think I can hold a needle any more. But perhaps I could cut a pattern, if we had some material.'

'And Maria and I can sew the seams,' Kitty said, eagerly. 'You've got a box full of scraps of ribbon and lace, Betty.'

Betty's eyes brightened for a moment and then she sighed, shaking her head. 'We need more than scraps, Kitty.'

'I've nothing left of value,' Bella said, staring down at her bare fingers. 'My wedding ring went before Christmas and my gold earrings.'

Betty tugged at the band of gold on her left hand, sucking her finger and grimacing with pain as she wrenched it over her swollen knuckle. She laid the ring on the table. 'You've been good to me since our Poll passed away, and it's time I did something for you. We should get a few shillings for this and that should be enough to get a bolt of taffeta from the market. I can cut, if all of you can help with the stitching, and we'll send Bella off in style.'

Maria glanced at the clock on the mantelshelf. 'Leave it to me. I know what colours suit Bella the best. If I hurry I can just catch the market before they pack up for the night.'

'We'll feed the nippers and then put them straight to bed,' Betty said, rolling up her sleeves in a businesslike manner. 'Heaven knows, they all need a bath and clean clothes, but I think they've had enough upset for today. But tomorrow, Kitty, we'll put the tin bath in front of the fire and give them a good scrub.'

Nodding her head, Kitty's heart swelled with love and pride as she struggled to find the words to thank Betty for her generosity and to praise her courage, but she realised then that sometimes words were simply not enough, and she gave Betty a hug.

The kitchen table disappeared beneath yards of pink taffeta. Betty cut the material with a skilful hand, and Maria, Bella and Kitty sat up all night, tacking and sewing seams until their eyes watered and their fingers were sore. By early morning they had fitted, altered and stitched the basic shape of a dress that clung to Bella's shapely body, emphasising her tiny waist and accentuating her breasts, with the aid of a few ruffles sewn into the lining. Bella was sent upstairs to bed so that she would be fresh for the evening performance, while Kitty and Maria put the finishing touches to the gown. When Bella came downstairs, refreshed after her nap, Kitty was thrilled to see a bit of the old sparkle as Bella tried on the rustling pink gown. Showing it off, she did a succession of twirls and Kitty sensed that the real Bella would go out on stage and charm the audience just as she had in the past.

In the late afternoon, Bella and Maria set off for Aldgate with the dress stowed into a bolster case. Kitty stood in the doorway, watching them striding purposefully along the street. A thick fog was swirling in on the tide, gobbling them up even before they reached the corner. They were gone, Kitty thought, like two small soldiers, gallant fighters, marching to war in the battle for survival.

Closing the door against the chilling, smoke-laden fog, Kitty could hear the children's protests as Betty carried out her threat to bath them before she allowed them to sleep one more night in her clean beds. The howls and screams rose to an ear-splitting crescendo as Kitty opened the kitchen door. Naked and shivering, Frankie and Charlie were huddled in the tin bath in front of the range, protesting loudly as Betty sluiced them down with jugs of fast-cooling water. The room was cloudy with steam, laced with the odour of carbolic soap.

'Don't be a baby, Frankie Cable,' Betty said, as Frankie screamed that there was soap in his eyes. She scooped another jug of water from the pan on the range and tipped it over his head. 'Give me a hand, Kitty, and rub soap into young Charlie's hair.'

Chuckling and ignoring Frankie's pleas for help, Kitty set to work scrubbing Charlie while Betty dragged a fine-tooth comb through Frankie's hair. Having already undergone the torture, Billy, Violet and Harry huddled together on a chair. Wrapped in towels, they watched wide-eyed as their brothers suffered the indignity of being bathed and deloused. Violet's long hair had been shorn and it stuck up in spikes giving her the appearance of a baby hedgehog. She sat sucking her thumb and hugging a doll.

'You gave Polly's doll to our Violet?' Kitty said, tipping the last of the warm water over Charlie's head.

Betty jumped backwards as Frankie leapt from the bath, shaking himself and sending spray everywhere. Laughing, she tossed a towel at him. 'Yes, it was Poll's but I know she would want Violet to have it.'

'I wants me clothes,' Frankie said, sticking out his chin. 'You got no right to pinch 'em, lady.'

Kitty took him by the shoulders, gave him a shake, and then kissed him on the cheek, laughing as he pulled away, making a face. 'Where's your manners? It's Mrs Scully to you.'

'Your clothes are in the washhouse and tomorrow they'll be boiled in the copper,' Betty said, picking a pile of shirts from the dresser. 'These belonged to my son Jem who is a sailor now, just like his pa. Put these on and maybe I'll tell you some of the sea stories that my Herbert used to tell Jem.'

Violet unplugged her thumb from her mouth. 'Did he see mermaids?'

'Don't talk soft,' Frankie said. 'That's girls' stuff.'

Betty hooked a shirt over his head and ruffled his damp hair. 'I expect pirates and sea monsters are more your cup of tea then, Frankie.'

'I expects they might be,' Frankie said, shrugging his shoulders.

'Then I might just have a story that would suit you all,' Betty said, taking Violet on her knee and slipping a cotton nightie over her head.

Kitty guessed that the nightdress had belonged to Polly, but she kept her own counsel as she dragged a shirt over Billy's wet head.

'It ain't bedtime,' Frankie said, folding his arms across his chest. 'We don't go to bed until our mam does.'

'Frankie, be quiet.' Kitty said, frowning. 'Maggie is sick in bed and you've got to be a good boy.'

'Is our mam going to die?' asked Charlie, his bottom lip quivering.

'Of course not,' Betty said, setting Violet down on the floor. 'But she needs rest and quiet. If you all creep upstairs like little mice, you can sleep in the big bed in my best bedroom and I'll tell you a story about mermaids, sea monsters and pirates too.' Taking Harry and Violet by the hand, Betty winked at Kitty as she led the children out of the kitchen.

'Be good for Mrs Scully,' Kitty called, as she heard their scampering steps on the stairs and muffled laughter. After what they had been through it seemed almost miraculous that they could still laugh and play about like ordinary children. At least now they were safe under one roof, she thought, as she began to tidy up the kitchen.

With five more mouths to feed she would have to find employment, even if it meant working long hours for low pay, in the match or glue factory. Her dream of working up West in a dress shop seemed to be slipping further and further away. Kitty sighed, as she emptied the tin bath, jug by jug, pouring the dirty water speckled with dead fleas and lice into the clay sink, she would achieve her ambition one day; it would just take a bit longer, that was all.

The sound of someone crashing on the iron door-knocker made her drop the enamel jug into the tin bath, splashing water all over her skirt. Kitty's hand flew to her throat as she recognised Sid's voice, shouting for Maggie. She ran into the hall and stood by the door, trembling violently as each vicious clout from Sid's fists shook the timbers.

'Open up! I know she's in there. I'll not budge without Maggie and the kids.'

'Get away from here,' Kitty screamed. 'Go away before I call for a copper.'

The door shuddered as if Sid had put his shoulder to the wood. 'I might have guessed you was to blame for this, bitch.'

'You'll never see Maggie or the nippers again,' Kitty cried, backing towards the stairs.

'Just wait till I gets me hands on you,' Sid roared, kicking the door.

Kitty watched the timbers shiver and shake, screaming as the toe of Sid's boot broke through a rotting door panel. Her throat constricted with terror at the thought of what he would do if he managed to get into the house. She had to get help before it was too late, but that meant leaving the house and finding a bobby on the beat. Sid was kicking the door in and there was no time to think of her own safety. Praying that Betty, Maggie and the children would not hear the racket and be terrified, Kitty ran through the kitchen, out of the back door and into the yard. Yanking at the rusty bolt on the back gate, she ran into the alley that divided the back-to-back buildings.

It led into Tanner's Passage, just a few doors away from Betty's house. As she reached the street Kitty paused, gasping for breath. She peeped around the corner and saw Sid slamming his fist against the door of number seven. Curtains twitched at windows in the street, doors opened but were quickly closed again. No one came out to find out who was shouting and roaring like a madman. Almost as if he sensed her presence, Sid looked round just as she decided to make a run for it and, with a guttural snarl, he gave chase. She could hear his boots pounding on the cobbles, getting closer and closer, as she hurtled along the passage.

Reaching the main street, she turned instinctively towards the part of the river that she knew best, running until her heart and lungs felt as though they were about to burst. Was the pounding in her head the muffled sound of Sid's footsteps or the laboured drumming of her heartbeat? Even though Kitty knew every inch of the wharf and the fish dock, she was lost and disorientated by the fog that muffled all sound, dimming lights and making it impossible to see the edge of the quay wall. She didn't spot the bollard until it was too late and, leaping aside to miss it, Kitty caught her foot in a coiled rope and sprawled headlong on the ground. Winded and gasping to catch her breath, she tried to raise herself, clutching at nothing. Immediately below her, the black water of the Thames, veiled in swirling fog, sucked greedily at the stanchions.

With a triumphant roar, Sid threw himself down, catching hold of her ankles, his hands sliding up her bare legs and his fingers digging into her cold flesh. Kitty kicked out with all her strength. Freeing one foot, she lashed out and felt it connect with something so hard that she heard a bone crack. Sid howled with pain and let her go, giving her just enough time to scramble to her feet. She screamed for help but her voice was lost in the thick pea-souper. Dodging Sid's outstretched hand, she did an about-face and tore off along the quay wall in the direction of home. She could hear Sid's footsteps coming up behind her; he was gaining on her. Kitty sobbed with pain as her muscles cramped and went into spasm, and the fog filled her nose and mouth, suffocating her with its noxious fumes. She stumbled, falling to her knees. Curling herself into a ball, she waited for the inevitable blows from Sid's fist, but he cannoned into her, knocking her flat on her face. She heard him grunt as he fell, followed by a splash, then total silence, broken only by the muted moan of a foghorn downriver and the lapping and sucking sounds of the river as it swallowed everything that fell into its greedy maw.

Dragging herself to the edge of the quay wall, Kitty peered down into the dark, roiling water; the tide had begun to ebb, carrying the flotsam and jetsam down to the sea.

Chapter Eleven

Placing advertisements in shop windows had been Maria's idea. Handwritten cards inscribed with Betty's name and 'Dressmaker to ladies of fashion' with the address clearly printed and a recommendation from 'A Lady, wife of a prominent Member of Parliament', seemed to do the trick and a flood of orders for gowns poured in from wealthy merchants' wives who hitherto had only ordered the odd blouse or skirt. Betty did the cutting and Maria and Maggie sat up night after night, sewing seams until their fingers bled and their eyes were red-rimmed and sore. A sewing machine would make life easier but it was going to take months to save up enough money to purchase one. Sewing by hand was slow work and the merchants' wives often kept them waiting for their money; in the meantime, they had to rely on Bella's wages from the music hall.

After a successful first week, Bert, the manager, a leery old cove, with wandering hands and a partiality for blondes, had been pleased enough to keep Bella on. So far she had managed to hold off his amorous advances by playing up to him. She suffered a bit of cuddling and pawing, just enough to keep him happy, with the unspoken promise of further favours that she had no intention of fulfilling. It made Bella physically sick to encourage the old goat, but they were relying on her at home, and if she lost her job they would all go hungry.

In order to help with the household bills, Kitty had found herself work in the blacking factory, leaving at crack of dawn and coming home late, stinking of boot polish and covered from head to foot in sticky black dust. Bella had grown to love Kitty like a sister and she had tried to talk her out of factory work, but Kitty was as stubborn as she was loyal. She had ignored Bella's warnings about the people driven mad by working with phosphorus in the match factory, their faces deformed by phossy jaw, or flour packers coughing up blood, their lungs destroyed by the dust. There was little to choose between labouring in a laundry and suffering chronic bronchitis, or slaving in the sweatshops on scandalously low wages.

Singing and dancing in the Palace of Varieties paid comparatively well and Bella had learned at an early age how to hold an audience. There was the buzz of excitement and a flutter of stage fright before each performance, and the intoxicating thrill of hearing the applause and cheers as she took her final bow. Rackham had often told her that greasepaint was in her blood and she had hotly denied it, but at least here, in the East End, she had nothing to prove except her talent as an entertainer. She was not on trial every minute of the day as she had been as Desmond's wife, his embarrassing misalliance, with society watching and waiting for her to make a *faux pas* in speech or manners.

'Miss Lane, five minutes, please.' The call boy rapped on her dressing room door.

Bella dropped her powder puff and scrambled to her feet, smoothing down the creases in her pink taffeta gown, dragging herself back to reality. Checking her appearance in the mirror, she added a dash of rouge to her cheeks and curved her lips into a smile. Snatching up her parasol, she left the dressing room and made her way to the wings, waiting for her cue. She was second from bottom of the bill now, and in her tenth week at the Palace of Varieties. She could see Bert leering at her from the wings on the far side of the stage. As the orchestra struck up the opening bars of her intro, she blew him a kiss and danced out on the stage.

It was Friday night and she could feel the goodwill of the audience rising up on a waft of cigarette smoke and alcohol fumes. They were out for a good time and had responded noisily to the quips of the master of ceremonies. They had roared their approval of the tumblers, who had just come off stage after their energetic first act. Elated by the fizz of excitement skittering through her veins, Bella sashayed to the middle of the stage, blowing kisses in answer to the whistles and cheers. She went straight into a comedy song that soon had them tapping their feet in time to the music and laughing appreciatively at the risqué, cockney humour. She went through her lively dance routine, swaying seductively and then slowing down as the music changed from major to minor. Now she had them in the palm of her hand, ready for the sad ballad that would wring the hearts of the hardest and most cynical members of the audience. Coming to a dramatic halt centre stage, clasping her hands together against the exposed curves of her bosom, Bella raised her eyes to the gallery. With a tremulous smile, she swept her glance across the dress circle to the boxes on either side. She faltered as she saw him sitting there, nonchalantly leaning over the gilded parapet of the box. Rackham!

Bella missed her cue and, rapping his baton on the music stand, the conductor signalled the orchestra to repeat her intro. Somehow Bella managed to come in on the right note. The break in her voice, as she sang the heart-rending words, was so genuine that it held the audience rapt, until she finished on a sob of emotion. There was a moment of utter silence and then the whole theatre erupted in tumultuous applause. Bella took her bow with tears streaming down her cheeks to sympathetic murmurs and cheers, but they were tears of anger, and she was shaking with rage as she fled to her dressing room.

Almost immediately, the door was flung open and Bert erupted into the room, wrapping his arms around her and breathing stale beer in her face.

'My little canary! What a performance!'

There was no room to manoeuvre or to escape his groping, pork-sausage hands, but Bella was too furious to play along with him this time. She slapped his hand away.

'Leave me be.'

Bert's jaw dropped and he began to gobble like a turkey. 'Hold on, that's not nice, girlie. You'd best remember who pays your wages. Songbirds like you are ten a penny so don't get all hoity-toity with me.'

'Is this man annoying you, my dear?' Rackham demanded, leaning lazily against the doorjamb.

Bert's face turned puce and he rounded on Rackham, stopping short at the sight of a gentleman, whose clothes and manner belonged so obviously to the gentry. 'I'm the manager of this establishment, Sir.'

'Then kindly go off and manage something,' Rackham said, flicking an imaginary speck of dust off Bert's lapel with his white kid gloves. 'Miss Lane and I are good friends.'

Bert deflated like a pricked balloon, backing out of the dressing room, mumbling an apology.

'No we're not,' Bella spat at him as the door closed. 'You can get out of here too.'

'My pet, that's not very nice.'

'Nice? Nice?' Bella curled her fingers around her hand mirror, tempted to hit his smug face and rearrange his smile. 'You bastard! You watched them take my baby away from me and then you disappeared. How dare you turn up as though nothing has happened.'

Rackham's smile faded. 'I'm sorry about Leonie. I truly am sorry.'

'Don't give me that,' Bella snapped, dropping the mirror in disgust. 'You went away again and left me. What was it this time? Fleeing your creditors or a wager that you couldn't refuse?'

Rackham's hand shot out, gripping Bella's wrist so tightly that she yelped with pain. 'Look at me, damn you. Do you really think I'm that much of a cad, Bella?'

His molten stare burned into Bella's eyes and she found she couldn't look away, but she lifted her chin defiantly. 'Yes, that's just what I think. Where have you been all these months?'

Uncurling his fingers, Rackham released her

with a casual shrug of his shoulders and a cynical smile. 'I was detained at Her Majesty's pleasure, if you must know.'

'You were in jail? But your landlady told me you'd gone abroad.' Rubbing her wrist, Bella stared at him in disbelief.

'Your beloved husband pressed charges and the judge, in his wisdom, sent me down for six months. A bit of a harsh sentence for bopping Sir Desmond on the nose, don't you think?'

'That's awful. I – I knew the police had arrested you, but that woman said you'd gone away and I believed her.' Bella reached out and grasped his hand. 'I am so sorry I misjudged you, Giles.'

He was silent for a moment, staring at their intertwined fingers. 'No, you didn't misjudge me, my pet,' he said with a harsh laugh. 'You know me only too well. I'm a scoundrel and a blackguard, but on this occasion I really didn't mean to let you down.'

'How did you find me?'

'I knew you didn't have any money and that the great and good Sir Desmond Mableton would rather see you starve in the gutter than to help you. I guessed that you'd be forced back to the old way of life, and I've spent the past couple of weeks touring the East End music halls. It's as simple as that.'

'Why would you care what happens to me, Giles?'

'Maybe I have a sentimental streak, my love.'

'Or perhaps that fat trollop who runs the gaming house isn't so free with her favours these days?'

'I've told you before, Bella, Sal Slater is a good friend with a big heart.'

'And she hides it in an enormous chest,' Bella said, snatching her hand away. 'If you're feeling lonely I suggest you go and seek refuge in her arms. I'm not for sale now or ever again.'

With a rueful smile, Rackham lifted her chin with his forefinger and brushed her lips with a kiss. 'I don't suppose you would believe that my motives for seeking you out were purely unselfish?'

'Not in a million years! Go away, Rackham, I can manage well enough without you.'

'I'm going,' Rackham hesitated in the doorway, turning his head to give her a penetrating look. 'Are you still in love with him, Bella?'

She didn't pretend to misunderstand. 'Edward will come back to me as soon as the war in South Africa is over. By that time I'm sure that Desmond will have divorced me and there'll be nothing to stand in our way.'

'I hope the gallant captain doesn't let you down, my dear.'

'Please leave, Giles. I'm on again after the intermission and I need to rest.'

'At least allow me to see you safely home after the show.'

'If you insist; just go now.'

Rackham handed Bella out of the cab in Tanner's Passage. 'My God, Bella,' he said, frowning. 'This is no place for you.'

'It suits me fine,' Bella said, pushing past him and rapping on the front door.

'We'd have been living in the gutter if it hadn't been for Betty Scully's kindness.'

'Even so, this is a dangerous place to live.' Rackham caught her by the arm. 'Come to Half Moon Street, and share my lodgings, until I can find somewhere that's more suitable for you.'

Bella shook off his hand with a scornful laugh. 'Thank you, but I feel safer with the sewer rats than with you.'

Maria opened the door, scowling when she saw Rackham. 'So you've turned up again. You're a bloody bad penny if ever there was one.'

'And if you took me in, Giles dear,' Bella said, chuckling, 'you'd have to take my mother, Kitty and her sister, plus five small children. Goodnight, and thank you for the cab ride home.'

Early next morning, Bella set off for Dover Street in the pouring rain. Picking her way around the deep puddles, she could feel the damp soaking through the cardboard that she had used to pack the holes in her boots. The feathers on her hat clung damply round her face, sending trickles of water running down her neck. What had begun as an April shower had turned into a deluge and she could feel the rainwater running down her neck, soaking her to the skin. She quickened her pace, clutching the parcel wrapped in a scrap of oilcloth under her arm. Inside was the present for Leonie's fourth birthday, a wooden doll with jointed arms and legs and hair painted glossy black, like a raven's wing. For weeks, Bella had been saving the odd farthing or halfpenny by cutting short her omnibus ride and walking to the theatre. She was soaked to the skin by the time she boarded the omnibus in Cheapside, but she didn't care; this was a special day and she was determined to see Leonie.

The longing to see her child was a permanent ache in her heart; Leonie might even have forgotten her by now or, worse still, think that Mama had left her because she didn't love her. Bella bit her bottom lip to stop herself from crying, staring out of the grimy window with unfocused eyes.

The horse-drawn omnibus trundled through the City, stopping to put passengers down and pick up new ones. Bella had done this journey many times over the past few months, even though she was tired after late nights at the Palace of Varieties. She sighed and closed her eyes.

How many hours had she spent watching the house in Dover Street, waiting for the new nanny to take Leonie for a walk to the park just so that she could get a glimpse of her baby? Her whole life centred on her determination to get Leonie back, but first she had to provide her with a secure and stable home. The rough and tumble of Tanner's Passage was not for Leonie; she would be brought up in a decent house, in a respectable district, far away from the slums of the East End. Leonie's lungs would not be polluted with the stench of industrial waste and sewage that contaminated the river. She would not play in the street with lice-ridden, barefoot urchins who used the language of the gutter. Leonie's youth and innocence would not be taken away from her before she had reached womanhood. Bella wriggled her toes inside her wet boots and shivered. Her daughter would not be sold to a man old enough to be her father; Leonie would marry for love. Bella heaved another sigh as she stared out of the window at the city streets. She would claw her way back to top billing in the West End, or die in the attempt. And if that meant allowing lecherous old men like Bert to give her a quick fondle every now and again, then that was just the way things were.

She arrived in Dover Street just in time to see the nanny walking down the street holding Leonie by the hand. Bella's heart did a somersault and her eyes misted over at the sight of Leonie's sturdy little legs working hard to keep time with the nanny's brisk steps. Following at a discreet distance, Bella had to stop herself from running up to them and snatching Leonie up in her arms. She had toyed with the idea of abducting her own daughter, but Desmond had the law on his side and she didn't; it was as simple as that. If she could just let Leonie see her, speak to her now and then, reassure her that Mama loved her and wanted her, the waiting would be worthwhile. She would never give up, never.

The nanny, a big woman sailing along like a tea clipper under full canvas, whose corsets must be creaking like ropes stretched taut as the wind filled the sails, crossed Piccadilly, heading for Green Park. Closing the gap between them, Bella could hear Leonie's high-pitched voice complaining that her legs ached. The nanny ignored Leonie's pleas to be picked up and carried.

Callous bitch, Bella thought, I'd like to give her a piece of my mind. It was torture to have to walk behind them as though nothing mattered, but somehow she forced herself to do it.

When they reached the park, the walks were crowded with nannies pushing perambulators.

Leonie's nanny moored herself to a park bench near the bandstand and began chatting to another of her calling, as if they were old acquaintances. Set free from the iron hand, Leonie bounded off to play beneath the trees with a group of small children. The sun had fought its way through a featherbed of grey clouds and Bella stood watching with tears in her eyes as Leonie danced around on the grass beneath the candlestick blossoms of horse chestnut trees.

When she was certain that the women were too deeply engrossed in conversation to notice, Bella moved stealthily towards Leonie, as if she were stalking a wild woodland creature. When she was close enough, she knelt down on the damp grass and called softly. Leonie stopped gyrating and stared, plugging her thumb into her mouth.

'Leonie, darling! It's Mama. Don't you recognise me, sweetheart?'

Leonie hesitated for a moment and then shook her head, backing away.

'Don't be afraid, dear. I've brought you a birthday present.' Bella tore the oilcloth wrapping from the doll and held it out towards Leonie.

'My mama is in heaven with the angels,' Leonie said, eyeing the doll doubtfully.

Bella caught her breath on a muffled sob. How could Desmond be so cruel as to tell the child that she was dead? He had threatened he would but she hadn't thought him evil enough to carry it through. She edged a little closer, shuffling on her knees. 'No, Leonie! Mama had to go away for a while but I'm here now, just to wish you a happy birthday, darling.'

'Mama?' Leonie snatched the doll, keeping her wide-eyed gaze fixed on Bella's face.

'Yes, baby, it's Mama,' Bella cried with tears streaming down her face as Leonie ran into her arms. 'I didn't want to leave you, darling, but I had no choice. I couldn't let your birthday go by without seeing you.'

A scream from the park bench brought Bella abruptly to her senses, and she scrambled to her feet, clutching Leonie to her breast. The two nannies steamed towards her waving their umbrellas.

'Put that child down or I'll call for a constable.'

Hugging Leonie, who had started to cry with fright, Bella drew herself up to her full height and reverted to her role as Lady Mableton. 'Don't be ridiculous. I'm her mother. I have every right to see my daughter and give her a birthday present.'

Huffing and gasping for breath, the nanny stopped dead in her tracks, eyes popping out as she stared at Bella. 'I've been warned about you.'

'Nanny Briggs has been warned about you,' echoed her companion. 'You do like she says and hand the child back, or there'll be trouble.'

'I can handle this on me own thank you, Lizzie.' Nanny Briggs took a menacing step towards Bella. 'Sir Desmond told me you might try to snatch the child. If you don't put Miss Leonie down this minute, I'm going to shout for that constable over there.'

Following her gaze, Bella could see a constable patrolling not very far away – too near for comfort anyway – and she had no illusions about Desmond proffering charges against her. She kissed Leonie's wet cheek and gently set her on the ground. 'Happy birthday, my darling, and always remember that Mama loves you very much.'

As she hurried towards the nearest park gate, blinded by tears and stumbling, Bella could hear Leonie's screams. Weaving her way in and out between horse-drawn vehicles, motor cars and omnibuses that thronged Piccadilly, Bella barely heard the shouts from the cabbies and drivers as she lurched in front of them. Half Moon Street was directly opposite and, almost without realising it, she headed for Rackham's lodging house. She hammered on the lion's head door knocker and when no one came to answer it, she sank down on the doorstep, burying her face in her hands, her body racked with sobs.

'Bella! What the hell is going on?'

'Giles?' Raising her head at the familiar sound of his voice, Bella saw Rackham standing in front of her.

catch a husband. We meet in secret and she thinks it's *Romeo and Juliet* all over again.'

'My God, she must be desperate.'

Rackham grinned, exposing perfect white teeth. 'I think you underestimate the Rackham charm.'

'You are the most unprincipled, devious rogue that I have ever met,' Bella cried, stamping her foot. 'Make up to Iris and get yourself a rich wife, but don't pretend that you're doing it for me or my child. I can manage perfectly well without you.'

'Could it be that you are just a tiny bit jealous?'

With a snort of disgust Bella ran to the door, wrenched it open, and left, slamming it behind her.

When Bella arrived at the theatre that evening, Bert was waiting for her in her dressing room. Still furious with Rackham, and unable to erase the sound of Leonie's parting sobs from her memory, Bella wasn't in the mood for being nice. When he came at her, with his intentions written clearly in his lustful expression, she shoved him away with a contemptuous curl of her lips.

'Now then, girlie,' Bert said, scowling. 'That's no way to treat a man who was about to offer you top billing next week.'

'Top billing?'

'And the raise in wages that goes along with it. But if you're not interested . . .'

The thought of the extra money was almost too tempting to turn down, but the look in his eyes and the sour smell of his breath as he moved closer, pressing her against the dressing table, made her feel physically sick. Bella held him off with her hands pressed flat against his chest, her thoughts racing. She was painfully aware that refusal would mean losing her job, and acceptance would inevitably result in having to take him as a lover. She was going to be sick; she could taste the bile in her throat and her stomach heaved. Playing for time, she closed her eyes and pretended to swoon, leaning her cheek against his greasy lapels. 'I – I'm sorry, I feel a little f-faint.'

Bert pushed her down on the stool. 'Sit quiet for a moment. I'll send the call boy for some water.'

'I'll be all right. Give me a few minutes, Bert.'

He backed towards the door, his face crumpled in anxious lines. 'You're on in half an hour. Don't get yourself worked up, girlie. We'll talk about it after the final curtain.'

The familiar smell of the greasepaint, as she applied her stage make-up, helped to transform Bella into her *alter ego*. The red dots at the inner corner of her eyes, the blue eye shadow and the layers of spit-black on her eyelashes went some way to disguising her reddened and swollen eyelids. When she slipped her costume over her head, lacing it in as best she could without the aid of a dresser, and pinned the large flowery hat on top of her head, she was ready to go out onto the stage. She would think about what to say to Bert after the show.

As she took her final bow, the thunderous applause, whistles, cheers and cries of 'Encore!' rang in Bella's ears. She blew kisses to the gallery, curtseying and smiling until her face ached.

'Wait for me in your dressing room,' Bert said, as she left the stage. 'I'll be there in two ticks.'

Reality slicing through the euphoria, Bella ran to her dressing room. Tossing her hat and parasol into a corner and ripping off her gown, she struggled into her day clothes. She perched on the dressing table stool, pinning her hair back and slapping on cold cream. Her hands trembled as she jabbed at her face, streaking the grease-paint in her efforts to clean it off before Bert arrived. If she was quick she might be able to escape from the theatre and catch the last omnibus home. What she would do tomorrow was another matter.

A rap on the door made her drop the piece of flannel that she had used to wipe the last vestige of cream and make-up off her face. 'C-come in.'

A short, stockily built man, smartly clad in evening dress, stood in the doorway. 'Miss Lane?'

'Yes, I'm Bella Lane.'

'I'm Humphrey Chester.' He produced a card from his breast pocket with a flourish, like a conjurer pulling a rabbit out of a hat. 'Impresario and owner of the Vaudeville Theatre, Haymarket. I've seen your act, Miss Lane, and I'm impressed. I think we might be able to do business together.'

Bella's mind went hazy with shock. She opened her mouth and closed it again but, before she could make sense of his words, Bert came thundering along the passage and tried to push past Humphrey Chester.

'Excuse me, Sir,' Humphrey said, fixing a pince-nez on his nose and glaring at Bert. 'You are interrupting a private conversation.'

'I'm the manager here, I'll have you know.'

'And is Miss Lane contracted to you in any way?'

Bert choked and went red in the face. 'Not exactly, but we were about to arrange something more permanent, weren't we, Bella?'

Suddenly the mist cleared and Bella spotted a way of escape. She jumped to her feet. 'Actually, no! I have no contract with this theatre, Mr Chester. I'd be most interested to hear what you have to say.'

'Splendid.' Humphrey held out his arm. 'Then allow me to take you somewhere for a little light supper and we'll discuss terms.'

Bella slipped her hand through his arm and, as

he led her past Bert, she gave him a half-smile. 'Sorry, Bert, but I think this is goodbye.'

As they emerged from the theatre, Humphrey's chauffeur leapt out of his seat to open the door of the shiny, black motor car.

Bella paused, her curiosity getting the better of her. 'Tell me, Mr Chester, do you often visit East End music halls?'

'No, my dear, only when I'm given the tip that someone of unusual talent is performing.'

'And may I ask who gave you this information?'

'My good friend Giles Rackham; I believe you know him?'

Chapter Twelve

Setting off for home, Kitty was swept out through the iron gates by the mass exodus of workers from the blacking factory. Men, women and children, barely recognisable as human beings beneath a thick layer of black dust, stumbled out onto the road, exhausted after a twelve-hour shift. To Kitty, each day was hell on earth, but without references, and with so many hungry mouths to feed at home, there had been no alternative but to take the job, even though the pay was poor and the conditions appalling. Her dream of working in a fashionable dress shop, surrounded by silks, satins, sequins and lace, was growing ever more distant. In her worst moments, it seemed to Kitty that she was stuck in the bottom of a black pit, gazing up into the sunshine, but with no way of getting there.

Numbed by weariness, she endured being hustled along with the crowd, but when it began to thin out and the workers went their separate ways, Kitty's nerves jangled with alarm bells, as they did every time she had to walk alone through the streets around Billingsgate.

Although she couldn't believe that Sid had survived that fall into the Thames, there was still the possibility that by some cruel miracle he might have been saved. As far as she knew, there had been no body washed up on the foreshore and no one, apart from Mr Harman, had even seemed to notice or to care that Sid was missing.

Harman had turned up on the doorstep of number seven Tanner's Passage the night after Sid's disappearance. Kitty had run to answer the door with her knees shaking and her heart beating so fast that it made her dizzy with fright. She had been certain that it would be the police coming to arrest her – or, even worse, Sid, who had managed to clamber to safety and was now coming to get his revenge. Although she was terrified, she had to face the fear head on. On this occasion, she had opened the door just a crack to see Harman's mongrel terrier face peering back at her. He had demanded to speak with Maggie, and Kitty had had no choice but to show him to the kitchen. At the sight of Harman, Maggie's face had paled to ashen and she had sat down heavily on the nearest chair, her mouth working soundlessly.

Harman had taken his cap off and had stood there, spinning it round between his stubby fingers, a dull red flush creeping up the back of his neck. He had told them that Sid had not turned up for work that day, nor was he to be found in his usual drinking haunts. He had not been seen in Sugar Yard, or anywhere else for that matter, and Harman had said, clearing his throat, that the missus had insisted that Maggie ought to know. Maggie had thanked him for his trouble but had said that it was no longer any concern of hers. She had left that brutal bastard and hell could freeze over before she would ever want to see Sid Cable again. Harman had left hurriedly, and Maggie had washed her hands in the sink, attacking them with the scrubbing brush until her skin had turned bright red.

'Good riddance to bad rubbish,' she had said.

But was it good riddance? Kitty, hurrying homeward behind a group of chattering factory girls, wondered if she would ever be free from the fear that Sid would turn up. Dead or alive – either way it would be bad news, particularly if the police started asking questions. She hadn't pushed him, it had been an accident, but then neither had she raised the alarm nor made any effort to save him. Would that amount to a charge of manslaughter or even murder? She didn't know, but the very thought of it kept her awake at night, terrified of going to sleep, in case the nightmare should return. She could still see his evil face, smell the disgusting mix of stale sweat and beer, and relive the agonising rape of her innocent body. She hoped that he was dead; floating bloated and swollen like a dead cow that she had once seen carried out to sea on a flood tide. But she couldn't shake off the gnawing anxiety, and neither could she confide in anyone.

How could she admit that she was in all probability a murderess and could be hanged for her crime? She couldn't burden Maggie with the truth, even though it meant she was possibly a widow now and free of Sid forever. She couldn't tell Betty, who was still struggling to come to terms with Polly's death. Maria would probably tell her to stop whining and put it behind her, and Bella had enough troubles of her own. No, Kitty thought, wearily as she plodded along the quay wall towards home, she was on her own and would have to live with the guilt and fear. There was only one person whom she might possibly tell and Jem was not due home for at least another fortnight.

As she neared Tanner's Passage, Kitty was aware of a crowd of people milling around a newsboy. Then someone threw his cap up into the air with a great whoop and everyone began cheering and slapping each other on the back. Forgetting her own problems for a moment, Kitty hurried closer but she couldn't get near enough to see anything. Recognising one of the older women who worked in the blacking factory, Kitty tapped her on the shoulder. 'What's up?'

'It's Mafeking,' the woman said with a gap-toothed grin. 'Been relieved at last. My boy's out there somewhere. Thank the Lord, we're beating the bloody Boers.'

It was truly wonderful news for those with husbands and sons serving in the army, and Kitty couldn't wait to tell Bella. Quickening her step, she hurried home, but as she let herself into the house, she stopped and stood still for a moment listening. Something was different; something had changed the female-dominated atmosphere of the house. There was the faint scent of tobacco and spice and the sound of excited chatter coming from the kitchen. She could hear Betty's voice lightened by happiness followed by the deep baritone laugh of a man. Kitty hesitated, her heart throbbing, painful as a boil; it couldn't be Sid or there would be no laughter. It might be Rackham, but then Bella had sworn he would never enter the house. Kitty curled her fingers around the brass doorknob and opened the kitchen door.

Jem sprang to his feet and came towards her, his arms outstretched. 'Kitty!'

'Jem!' Kitty cried, unable to believe her eyes. 'It really is you.'

Betty clapped her hands in delight. 'Isn't this a grand surprise, Kitty? He just turned up at the front door. Seeing him standing there, large as life, gave me such a turn I thought I was going to drop down dead on the spot.'

Jem grabbed hold of Kitty in a great bear hug and kissed her on the forehead and the tip of her nose, just as he had done when they parted on the quay wall. 'I've waited a long time to do that.'

Kitty held him at arm's length, studying his face. A happy bubble welled up inside her and she found herself laughing for the first time in months. 'I didn't think you'd be home for ages yet.'

'Ah, that's the wonder of having huge steam engines to drive the ship as well as sail. We made good time this trip and I wanted to give you all a surprise.'

'And you did, son. It's the best surprise in the world,' Betty said, smiling proudly. 'Isn't he just the most handsome young man you've ever seen, Kitty?'

Jem struck a pose, hitching his thumbs in the top of his waistcoat. 'Isn't that the truth, though? What d'you think, Kitty?'

'He looks just the same as ever he did to me,' Kitty said, giggling as Jem lunged at her. She dodged his outstretched hands, putting the length of the kitchen table between them. She wasn't going to admit it, but he was maturing into a fine-looking young man. The hard life on board ship had broadened his shoulders and chest, giving him a powerful, finely honed look of an athlete. His hair was streaked flaxen by the sun and his skin tanned, so that his eyes were more startlingly blue by contrast. It was so good to see him that she had to hold herself back from showing it too much; she had seen the warm gleam in his eyes when he looked at her but she was not ready. Maybe she would never be ready to have a proper relationship with a man. Sid's shadow hung over her still.

Picking up a wet cloth, Kitty threw it at Jem.

Peeling the cloth off his face, Jem grinned. 'I ought to shove this down your neck, but I know you'd get me back.' Reaching for his ditty bag, he delved inside and pulled out a scrap of tissue paper. 'I should give these to one of the sweethearts who are pining for me in every port, but seeing as how I bought them for you, I suppose you'd better have them.'

Holding out her hand, Kitty took the package and, teasing the paper apart, she gave a gasp of delight at the sight of a pair of emerald green earrings. 'They're beautiful, Jem. I don't know what to say.'

'Ta would be a start,' Jem said, sprawling on the nearest chair. 'They're New Zealand greenstone. I took a good deal of time and trouble picking them specially for you, although I don't know why when you're such a torment to me.'

Kitty held them to her ears, squinting at her reflection in the cracked wall mirror. 'I'll have to get my ears pierced before I can wear them.'

'Better wash your face too,' Jem said, eyeing

her critically. 'You look as if you've been shovelling coal in a ship's boiler room, or is that the latest fashion?'

'What would you know about getting your hands dirty? I been grafting twelve hours a day to put food on the table, not strutting about on deck with me nose in the air.'

'Here, that ain't fair. You've got no idea what life at sea is like.'

'And you don't know what we've been through here.'

'Now, now,' Betty said, pouring tea. 'You're both behaving like five-year-olds. And you're being unkind to Kitty, Jem. She's been working all hours in the blacking factory and sewing seams for me at night when she should be resting.'

Jem's grin faded to a frown. 'If only I'd known you were all in such a state I'd have sent more money home. You should have told me, Ma, just like you should have let me know about poor Poll.'

Tears welled up in Betty's eyes but she dashed them away on her sleeve. 'Our Polly's gone to a better place where there's no pain and suffering, but I do miss her so very much.'

'She never complained about her lot and was always ready for a laugh,' Jem said, reaching across the table to clasp Betty's hand. 'But to wish her back in that poor body wouldn't be a kindness. I'm only sorry I wasn't here to say goodbye to her.'

'She loved you, Jem,' Betty said, sniffing. 'She loved us all.'

'Ma, don't take on,' Jem said, patting her hand. 'I'm here now, for a bit anyway. I'll see that things get easier for you.'

Betty fished in her pocket for a scrap of a hanky and blew her nose. 'Don't you worry about me, son. I know our Polly wouldn't want me to mope about, and I've taken comfort from having Maggie's nippers raging around the house. Made it seem like the old days when you were young.'

'Maggie's nippers?'

'Kitty will tell you all about it later. They'll be back soon, starving hungry as usual and yelling for their tea.'

'What's been going on?' Jem demanded, turning to Kitty. 'I seem to have missed a whole lot.'

'And there's Lady Mableton and Maria too,' Kitty said, chuckling at his bemused expression. 'You've come home to a big family, Jem.'

'I'm afraid I gave your bedroom to Bella and her ma,' Betty said, frowning. 'Kitty gets up first so she's in the attic and Maggie and the children are in my best letting room.'

'Ma, stop fretting,' Jem said, throwing up his hands. 'If you'd seen where I sleep on board then you wouldn't worry about putting me in the cupboard under the stairs. I can sleep on a spar, and that's the truth.'

Later that evening Kitty and Jem strolled along the quay wall. The Thames flowed molten gold in the rays of the setting sun and the dockside buildings were fading into a misty sepia tint. The turn of the tide had taken with it the worst of the city smells and there was a warm hint of approaching summer in the air. With her hand clasped firmly in Jem's big paw, Kitty felt safe for the first time in ages. It was so good to have him home, she thought, stealing a surreptitious glance at his craggy profile. The boyish lines of his face had all but disappeared, and the rounded cheeks had tautened to reveal a strong, stubborn jaw line.

As if sensing her glance, Jem turned his head and grinned. 'Penny for 'em.'

'I was just thinking that it's good to have you home. I've missed you, Jem.'

Jem stopped and sat down on the edge of a stone horse trough, pulling Kitty down beside him. 'Not half as much as I've missed you, Kitty.'

Kitty stared down at his slim, work-hardened fingers that so effortlessly covered her whole hand. 'Don't go running away with the wrong ideas now. We're pals, that's all.'

'Is that so? We'll see about that.'

'It is so and I mean it, Jem.' Kitty snatched her hand away and folded her arms across her chest, kicking at small pebbles with the toe of her boot.

'Go on then,' Jem said, after a long moment of silence. 'Spit it out, girl.'

Startled, Kitty shot him an anxious glance. 'What?'

'I'm not daft, Kitty. I know there's been something going on round here or else why would Maggie have moved into Tanner's Passage with the kids? What's happened to Sid Cable? And you keep looking over your shoulder as if you expect Jack the Ripper to pop up round every corner.'

'Don't joke about things like that – they never did catch the villain.'

'No, sorry, that was a stupid thing to say, but I've got all night. I ain't budging from this spot until you tell me exactly what's been going on while I've been away at sea.'

Chewing her lip, Kitty met his eyes reluctantly and, with a long-drawn-out sigh, she told him everything. It all came tumbling out in muddled half-sentences, punctuated by broken sobs, as she relived the horrors of the rape that had been committed not too far from where they were sitting. Jem said nothing but she felt his body stiffen and his arm crept around her shoulders, his fingers digging into her flesh. When she had finished, he leapt to his feet, striding up and down and running his fingers through his cropped hair.

'It wasn't my fault, Jem,' she whispered, her voice breaking. 'I never led him on and I didn't mean to kill him.'

'Hell's bells, Kitty, of course you bloody didn't,' Jem said, throwing himself down on his knees in front of her. His eyes flashed with anger and he gripped her hands so hard that her knuckles cracked. 'And if you had killed him it was what he deserved. If he wasn't dead now, then I'd go and kill him myself.'

'No one else knows. I daren't mention it to a soul but they haven't found his body yet.'

Getting up, Jem pulled her to her feet, wrapping his arms around her. 'And probably never will. The tide will have taken him way out to sea and the chances are he'll never be found. I've seen men fall overboard and be swallowed up in an instant, never to be seen again.'

Resting her cheek against the rough cloth of his reefer jacket, Kitty closed her eyes and felt a faint flutter of hope. 'D'you really think so?'

'I know so,' Jem said, lifting her chin and looking deep into her eyes. 'You're safe with me, Kitty, love. I'll never let anyone hurt you again.'

'Oh, Jem!' His arms holding her so tightly felt strong and warm and for the first time in her life she felt safe and at home. 'I – I've missed you so,' she whispered.

'Kitty, you don't know how many times I've imagined you saying those words to me.' Jem's eyes darkened as he drew her closer, slipping his hand behind her head so that their lips were almost touching.

Kitty pushed him away. 'No. Jem, I – I can't.'

'Don't pull away from me, Kitty. You can't think I'd mean to hurt you? I think the world of you, you know that.'

Kitty knew she had hurt him – she could see it in his eyes, she could feel it in her heart. It was her own turbulent emotions that baffled and confused her. She stared down at her feet, shaking her head. 'I just want things to be like they used to be between us. You know, when we was younger. You could always make me laugh and we had good times together.'

'Of course we did and we will again. You've been through a terrible time and I wasn't there for you – how do you think that makes me feel?'

Searching his eyes for an answer, Kitty shook her head. 'I dunno.'

'It makes me bloody angry and it makes me want to cry.'

'Cry? You?' Kitty giggled. 'I've never seen you cry. Snivel a bit maybe, but not have a good bawl.'

Jem's eyes lit with a smile. 'At least I've made you laugh again, Kitty. I haven't seen you laugh for a long time.'

'What happened to us, Jem?'

'We grew up,' Jem said, clasping her hands and holding them to his chest. 'We grew up, that's all.'

'I want us to still be friends.' Kitty raised her eyes to his face. 'We are, aren't we, Jem?'

'We'll always be friends,' Jem said, tracing the contour of her cheek with his finger, running it so softly down the column of her neck that it was like the touch of a cobweb. 'Nothing can change that.' He broke off abruptly as he reached the hollow at the base of her throat and the hurt crept back into his voice. 'I thought as how you'd be wearing my keepsake.'

'I was. I mean, I did –' Kitty broke off, not wanting to admit the truth.

Tugging at a thin gold chain around his neck, Jem drew out his half of the coin. 'I've worn mine night and day. It kept me close to you no matter where I was, and I thought you would do the same.'

The reproach in his eyes was too much for Kitty. It wasn't fair that he arrived home without warning, upsetting her world and confusing her emotions. What did he know about the life they had been forced to lead? A wave of irrational anger welled up inside her. 'We were starving, Jem. Can't you get that into your wooden skull? I didn't want to let it go, but you can't eat a bit of metal.'

'You pawned it? You took it to old Sparky's pop shop?'

'I didn't want to and I ain't apologising, but I had no choice.'

Next day when Kitty left work, she found Jem waiting for her outside the factory gates.

One of the girls jabbed Kitty in the ribs. 'Kitty's got a fella.'

'Forget her, sailor. She's a bag of skin and bone.' A flame-haired woman, who had been one of Kitty's worst tormentors from the start, sidled up to Jem. 'I could show you a good time, ducks.'

Kitty pushed past them, embarrassed by their lewd remarks and catcalls. 'You shouldn't have come,' she scolded, as Jem fell in step beside her.

'That's a nice way to greet a fellow who's gone out of his way to see you safely home.'

'I don't need anyone to walk me home. You're making a show of me, Jem. I'll never live it down.'

Jem scowled back at her, shoving his hands deep in his pockets. 'I don't like you lowering yourself to work in that place anyway. You're better than a common factory girl.'

Coming to an abrupt halt, Kitty spun around to face him. 'Shut up! You don't know what you're talking about.'

Jem grabbed her by the arm as she went to

walk away. 'Don't you tell me to shut up! And I do know what I'm saying. I want you away from the docks and the East End. What's happened to your fine ambitions to work up West, I'd like to know?'

'You'd like to know?' Kitty wrenched her arm free. 'You don't know nothing about how we've had to grub around just to get enough to eat. You've been gone for a year, Jem. A lot has changed in a year and you've got no right to come home telling me what to do. D'you hear me?'

'Aye, I hear you and so does the whole of Billingsgate and probably Southwark too.'

'Bah!' shouted Kitty, and stalked off with a toss of her head.

'It's all that woman's fault,' Jem grumbled, catching up with her and matching his long stride to hers. 'Bella Lane or Lady Mableton, whatever she likes to call herself, is no better than she should be. If you ask me a woman who leaves her husband and child should be ashamed of herself.'

'Don't you dare criticise Bella. It wasn't her fault. She fell in love with Mr Edward and he with her. Sir Desmond is a beastly man.'

Jem's generous mouth set in a hard line. 'You should have left her to get on with her own life. But no, you go and get yourself a job in that filthy factory just to keep her ladyship in comfort.'

'That's so unfair,' Kitty cried, staring at him in disbelief. 'I can't believe you just said that.'

'I said it because it's true. You've worked yourself to the bone for that woman. You're worth a hundred of her sort.'

'You – you pompous twerp!' Kitty shouted, punching him on the shoulder. 'Go back to your stupid ship, cabin boy!'

'I'll have you know that I've got my third mate's ticket,' roared Jem. 'And I'm studying for the second. By the time I'm twenty I'll have my first mate's ticket and then you'll see what I'm made of.'

Kitty snorted in disgust and walked away.

'And you haven't worn the earrings I bought you,' Jem shouted after her. 'I expect I'll find them in old Sparky's shop, along with the half-sovereign.'

For the first time in her life, Kitty had fallen out with Jem and it upset her deeply. She knew he was hurt that she had pawned her half of the gold sovereign, but there had been no need for him to be so unreasonable about it. He had got her all shaken up inside. He had no right to come back and start demanding the impossible from her, nor had he any right to criticise Bella, when he knew nothing about her or the dreadful treatment she had received from Sir Desmond. She waited for him to apologise, but he remained stubbornly silent.

Not being on speaking terms with Jem proved almost impossible in the narrow confines of the house in Tanner's Passage. Kitty took to getting up extra early and leaving for work before anyone else had woken up. One evening, after more than a week of silent feuding, Jem made a point of packing up his textbooks and took them upstairs to the sitting room, stating loudly that he was going to study. Bella and Maria had already left for the theatre, seemingly oblivious to the strained atmosphere. Betty and Maggie exchanged meaningful glances and Kitty bowed her head over the particular piece of sewing that she was working on.

Kept awake by the niggling cough that had only come on since she started working with the choking fumes and dust in the blacking factory, Kitty lay on her narrow bed, looking up at the stars. She thought about the times when she had imagined that they looked down on Jem, sailing far away on his ship, and gradually her anger faded. She wished with all her heart that they could be friends again, but some stubborn little core inside her would not allow her to apologise. She would not permit Jem, or any other man, to tell her what to do, even if he happened to be right on occasions. She would not admit that her dearest wish was to get away from the filthy, back-breaking and tedious work in the factory. She couldn't tell him that her lungs were becoming congested, or that the black stains wouldn't scrub off her skin and made cracks appear on her hands, which rapidly turned into infected sores.

No one knew how she suffered daily from the taunts and jibes of the other girls. They had picked on her from the start, mimicking the way of speaking that she had learnt in Dover Street, and that now came naturally to her. Although she sometimes found herself slipping back into the rich cockney tones of the people working around her, they took it to be a mocking impersonation and punished her for her quick ear. Sometimes she found a lump of boot black in the bottom of her mug of tea; her slice of bread and dripping would mysteriously disappear, so that she had nothing to eat at dinner break. Unspeakable things were scrawled about her, in big black letters, on the walls of the outside lavvy. The girls tormented her, the younger men tried to get off with her, and the older ones either turned a blind eye or fancied their chances along with their younger workmates and, of these, the foreman was the worst. Altogether, the blacking factory was a place of torment and Kitty knew she had to escape, but she would do it when she was ready, when she had found a suitable alternative, and not because Jem Scully said so.

As the end of the week drew nearer, Kitty knew she had to do something. There was no show on Sundays and Bella and Maria would be around for the best part of the day. Maria's sharp eyes would spot that there was something wrong, and Bella would be upset if she discovered that she was in some way to blame for the row, although these days she was so preoccupied with her stage career that she seemed to be living in another world. Apart from all that, Kitty was heartily sick of avoiding Jem. Sometimes, she could feel his eyes boring into the back of her head, but when she turned around, he would look away. Jem was as stubborn as the proverbial mule and he would not be the first to give in; Kitty racked her brains to think of a way that would save face for both of them.

It was Saturday evening and Kitty was feeling particularly low. The children had been sent to bed early, after an exciting day trip. They had come home grubby, tired and sick from stuffing themselves with ice cream and gobstoppers, babbling incoherently about the sights they had seen. Jem and Maggie had taken them to the Royal Victoria Gardens on the riverbank in Silvertown, but Kitty had not been included in the invitation. As she had to work every Saturday, it had not really been an option, but that didn't prevent her from feeling left out and miserable. Betty hadn't said anything, but Kitty had seen the 'well, it's your own fault' look on her face.

Maggie's happy smile faded as she came into the kitchen and found Kitty, on her own for once, standing at the sink, peeling potatoes.

Kitty dropped the last potato into the big black saucepan full of water. She gave Maggie a sheepish grin. 'It's all right, Maggie. I know I brought it on myself. You obviously had a lovely day.'

'Make it up with him, Kitty,' Maggie said, yanking the hatpin from her battered straw hat. 'He's planning to go back to sea next week because he feels so bad.'

'I'll not apologise,' Kitty said, hefting the pan onto the range. 'He's got to learn that I won't be pushed around.'

'Takes two to quarrel, ducks, and you're upsetting Betty.'

'I know it,' Kitty said, picking up the long, slightly rusty hatpin and staring at it thoughtfully. 'You're right, Maggie, but I'll need your help.'

Kitty eyed the blackened tip of the hatpin nervously; beneath the layer of soot it was hot from being held in the fire. She handed it to Maggie, who stood poised for action, holding the cork from a vinegar bottle.

'Make it quick then,' Kitty said, closing her eyes and holding her breath.

'This might hurt a bit,' Maggie said, jabbing the

pin right through Kitty's earlobe until it stuck in the cork.

Kitty let out a squeal of pain, her eyes watering. 'Bloody hell!'

'Don't swear, it ain't ladylike,' Maggie said, tugging at the hatpin and drawing it out through the blackened hole. 'Hold on while I slip the earring in. Oh, and better hold that cloth to your ear, it's bleeding a bit.'

'That really hurt,' Kitty said, dabbing at her ear and examining the bright scarlet stain on the material.

'Don't be a baby,' Maggie said, stabbing at the other ear. 'There, it's all over.'

Tears of pain ran unchecked down Kitty's cheeks as Maggie hooked the last earring into her raw flesh. She was staunching the trickles of blood when Jem walked into the kitchen.

'What's going on? It sounded like someone stuck a pig.'

Kitty shook her head making the earrings jiggle painfully. 'I love the greenstone earrings, Jem,' she said, with a wobbly smile. 'I don't want us to fight.'

Jem opened his arms and Kitty walked into them.

In spite of Kitty's pleas and Betty's tears, Jem had made his mind up to go back to sea and nothing would budge him.

'It's not too late to change your mind,' Kitty said, trotting along beside him as he strode towards the docks.

'You'll get into trouble at the works if you're late,' Jem said, quickening his pace.

'I don't care, Jem. I'm not giving up so easily.'

Jem slid his sea chest off his shoulders and dumped it on the pavement, mopping his brow on his sleeve. 'I can't stay in that house full of women; it's driving me barmy. The *Mairangi* is sailing again tonight and I've got to go with her if I want to stay with Captain Madison. It's a rough old life at sea, Kitty, and I think I might have given up at times if it hadn't been for him.'

'I know, I know,' Kitty said, hopping from one foot to the other. 'He's a grand chap, so you keep saying, but think about your ma – she needs you more than ever now.'

Jem hefted the chest onto his shoulders and picked up his ditty bag. 'Don't go making me feel guilty. I've told you my reasons and, anyway, it's best that I go now since you made it plain you don't want me around.'

Breaking into a run in order to keep up with him, Kitty tugged at his sleeve. 'That's not true. I care for you, Jem, and I'll miss you something awful when you're gone.'

Jem stopped walking. 'D'you mean that, Kitty?'

'I do, but not in a lover-like way – not yet, anyway.'

'You mean you might, later on?'

'I just don't know. Later on is a long time away.'

Jem strode on, saying nothing. He kept up a smart pace until they reached the jetty. Horse-drawn carts, laden with provisions, were ranged alongside the *Mairangi*, while stevedores finished loading the casks, sacks and crates into the ship's hold. There was bustle and noise all around them as people milled about, bustling like ants up and down the gangplanks, going about their business. Huge cranes lifted heavy items off the quay wall, swinging them precariously overhead and then unloading them expertly onto the deck. Kitty covered her ears to shut out the thunderous sound of the metal hatch covers closing over the refrigerated holds. She gazed around in awe, feeling small and insignificant in the shadow of the huge ship.

Jem, for his part, seemed totally at home and Kitty recognised a gleam of excitement in his eyes. Pushing his cap to the back of his head, he bent down and kissed Kitty on the cheek. 'This is it then.'

'I suppose it is. You're the most stubborn person I've ever met, Jem Scully.'

'You're a stubborn little monster yourself, but I love you all the same.'

'Here we go again. Don't you ever give up?'

'You do care for me, Kitty. Don't deny it.'

'I will miss you, Jem, and I'll pray every night for your safe return.'

Pulling something out of his pocket Jem held his clenched hand out, palm downwards. 'Give me your hand.'

Eyeing him doubtfully, Kitty shook her head. 'It's not a spider, is it?'

Chuckling, Jem took her hand and he pressed the half-sovereign, now fixed to a fine gold chain, into her palm. 'Luckily old Sparks hadn't found a customer for it.'

'Oh, Jem, you shouldn't have. Now I feel really mean.'

'Take it as a friendship token,' Jem said, taking the chain and fastening it around her neck.

'I'll wear it always,' Kitty said, touched beyond anything and attempting to smile.

A toot on the ship's horn made them both jump.

'Got to go.'

'Take care of yourself, Jem. Have wonderful adventures and come back and tell me about them.'

'I'm going to catch a falling star,' Jem said, caressing Kitty's cheek with the tip of his finger, 'and hear mermaids singing.'

Kitty stared at him in alarm. 'Have you gone barmy?'

'It's a poem by a geezer called John Donne, a chap who died centuries ago.'

'You reading poetry.' Kitty giggled. 'Whatever next, Jem Scully?'

'Captain Madison has a sea chest full of books and he lets me read any that I've a mind to. I'm educating myself.'

'Blimey!'

'One day I'll be a rich man and make you proud of me.'

'I'm proud of you now, but from what I've seen of rich men it don't make them any better than the poor ones.'

'We ain't all bad, Kitty. If only I could make you believe that.' Holding her face between his hands, Jem looked deeply into Kitty's eyes. 'If only I could rub away those bad memories, I know I could make you love me.'

Swallowing hard, Kitty blinked away tears. 'Oh, Jem, please don't. I do love you, of course I do.'

'But not in the way I love you.'

'I don't know. Just give me time.'

'I'll give you all the time in the world and more, sweetheart, and I'll catch that falling star and bring it back for you to wear in your hair. You see if I don't.' Picking up his gear, Jem headed off towards the gangplank, whistling cheerfully.

That's how I'll always remember him, Kitty thought, smiling through a veil of tears. 'Go and catch your falling star, Jem,' she whispered. 'I hope you hear your mermaids singing, but more than that, I want you to come back, safe and sound.'

The factory gates were locked. Kitty shook them, shouting for the gatekeeper to let her in. He came out of his hut, eyeing her suspiciously.

'Let me in,' Kitty gasped, trying to catch her breath, having run all the way from the dock. 'I'm late as it is.'

He shook his head and spat into the dust at her feet. 'Gates is locked. No one in and no one out till the hooter blows. You've had it for today.'

'Oh, please. I can't afford to lose a day's pay.'

Glancing over his shoulder, the gatekeeper produced a bunch of iron mortice keys and unlocked the side gate. 'Slip in quick and you might be lucky but don't let on it was me what let you in.'

'Ta ever so,' Kitty said, scuttling past him and hurrying to the shed where she worked. She opened the door just wide enough to slip through the gap, and was making her way to her end of the workbench, when she saw the foreman bearing down on her.

'You're late, Miss Cox.'

'I – I'm sorry, Sir. I was taken poorly in the night but I feel a bit better now.'

'This could be a sacking offence, you know.'

'But that's not fair. This is the first time I've been late and I work hard.'

'We could discuss this in my office.'

He was leaning so close to her that Kitty could smell onion breath and stale sweat; he was smiling and his yellowed teeth reminded her of fangs. Old memories came flooding back, she felt sick, and when he trailed his fingers over her breast she could stand it no longer.

'Get your hands off me. You can keep your bloody job. I wouldn't work here another day if you paid me in gold.'

Kitty let herself into the house and went to the kitchen to get a glass of water. She found Betty sitting at the kitchen table, holding her head in her hands, her shoulders heaving.

'Betty, what's wrong?'

Betty raised a tear-stained face and thrust a sheet of paper in Kitty's hands. 'We're ruined, Kitty. The lease on the house has expired and the land agent wants sixty pounds to renew it. He might as well have asked for six hundred, because there's no way I can raise that sort of money.'

Kitty dropped onto the chair next to her. 'But I thought Captain Scully had bought the house.'

'He did but it was leasehold. I never thought to check the deeds when Herbert passed away. I assumed it had years to run but it hasn't. Kitty if we can't find sixty pounds by the end of the month we'll all be out on the street.'

Chapter Thirteen

Battling with first-night nerves, Bella stood in the wings of the Vaudeville Theatre in the Haymarket. Fighting down the nauseous feeling in her stomach, and the almost overwhelming desire to run back to her dressing room and hide, she swallowed hard and braced her shoulders. The stage stretched before her like an endless floodlit plain. She couldn't see the audience in the dark void beyond the footlights, but she sensed them as a living, breathing entity that, in just a few seconds, would judge whether or not she still had the power to handle a West End crowd. She breathed in as deeply as possible, allowing for the vicious grip of her whalebone corsets. Maria had cinched her waist into a hand's span, lacing the stays to a suffocating tightness. Making a supreme effort to put everything else out of her mind, Bella wiped her damp palms on her skirt and waited for the orchestra to play her intro.

She was on – no time now for stage fright. She swept onto the apron of the stage, painting a smile on her lips, and holding her arms out in a gesture of supplication to her audience. There was a faint murmur of appreciation and Bella relaxed. Thank God, they were friendly. This was her big break and she was not going to fluff it! She broke into her first song, moving sinuously across the stage and addressing herself to every part of the theatre, from the front stalls to the gallery.

As usual, she began her act with an upbeat, saucy, cockney song that never failed to warm up even the toughest audience. Bella had learned long ago to play on the purity of her soprano voice and her fragile blonde beauty. She had discovered that she could sing the most risqué words, tempering their vulgarity with a studied air of innocence, which usually brought the house down. Her early days, singing in her father's East End pub, had taught her how to use her sexuality to dazzle and enthral the male members of the audience. For them she would adopt the guileless manner of a little girl singing a naughty grown-up song. Having captured the hearts of the men, she would then launch into a heart-rending, sentimental ballad that would win over even the toughest of the East End fishwives, and have them weeping into their gin or port and lemon.

She was well into her second number when, as she swept her gaze around the boxes that flanked the stage, she spotted Rackham. He was watching her with an appreciative smile on his lips. Seated next to him was Iris; this time the catch in Bella's voice, and the way her hands flew to clutch her heaving bosom, was entirely spontaneous. She had not believed him when he said that he intended to see Iris again, and she had certainly not thought that Iris would be so stupid as to take him back. They could both go to hell for all she cared . . . But she did care, that was the biggest shock of all. Somehow Bella managed to falter her way through a fog of barely controlled emotion, ending the ballad with a genuine sob that rippled, in a sympathetic echo, throughout the auditorium.

She left the stage to the sound of tumultuous applause and calls of 'Encore!' Blinded by angry tears, she collided with top-of-the-bill comedian, Sam Lennard.

'Hey, look where you're going, ducks,' he growled, breathing whisky fumes into her face. Then, as if by some magic metamorphosis, his furious expression changed into a smile, and he cantered onto the stage.

'What's wrong?' demanded Maria, as Bella burst into the dressing room and threw herself down on the stool in front of her make-up table.

'What's wrong? Giles Rackham, that's what's wrong. He's out there watching the show.'

Maria whipped off Bella's ostrich feather headdress and began to undo the tiny pearl buttons at the back of her gown. 'Pardon me for being stupid, but didn't Rackham get you this job in the first place? Stand up, I can't reach the bottom buttons.'

Dragging herself to her feet, Bella leaned her hands on the dressing table, making a huge effort to control her ragged breathing. She must calm down or the tight lacing of her corsets would cause her to swoon. 'He's a lying, cheating, swindling cad.'

'That's not news,' Maria said, slipping the gown to the floor. 'Lift your feet up.'

'He's with Iris. He's actually courting that bitch Iris! He's brought her here so that she can crow over my situation and run straight back to Desmond telling tales.'

Maria shook the creases out of the gown and slipped it over a hanger. 'What if she does? You've got second billing and you're back up West. You're not starving in the gutter, which was what your old man wanted.'

'No, but it won't make it easier for me to get Leonie back if Desmond tells the Court that I'm singing lewd songs in a music hall. He could convince any judge that I'm an unfit mother and I'll never see my baby again.' Bella beat her fists on the table, sending up a flurry of face powder. 'How could Rackham make up to that hateful bitch, when he knows how I've suffered at the hands of the Mableton family? How could he?'

Maria stared hard at Bella's reflection in the mirror. 'Why would you care what Rackham does? Serve him right if he marries Iris, she'll make his life hell. Isn't that what you've always wanted?'

Bella seized a stick of greasepaint and scrubbed it onto her pale lips. 'He can rot in hellfire for all I care.'

'On stage, please.' The call boy rapped on the door. 'Grand finale, Miss Lane.'

'Pull yourself together,' Maria said, slipping Bella's finale costume over her head. 'And get out on that stage.'

At any other time, Bella would have been thrilled by the standing ovation she received, and delighted by the fact that she was even more popular than Sam Lennard.

'Well done, ducky,' he hissed in her ear, holding her hand and bowing as the curtain fell for the third time. 'I'll have to watch my back or you'll be taking over the number one spot.'

'No chance of that,' Bella said, as the curtain went up again.

The call boy ran on and presented Bella with a huge bouquet of red roses. She didn't have to read the gilt-edged card to know that they were from Rackham, but a quick glance in his direction confirmed her suspicions. He rose to his feet, clapping enthusiastically, and he blew her a kiss. Iris was not applauding. She tugged at Rackham's sleeve, her expression laced with venom.

A cold fist of anger balled in Bella's stomach and she ripped out a long-stemmed rose, tossing it into the front stalls, following it with another and another until the whole bouquet had been thrown to a wildly appreciative audience.

'You completely upstaged me, you bitch,' Sam said, through clenched teeth, as the final curtain fell, even though the audience was still calling for another encore.

Humphrey Chester was waiting in the wings, his arms outstretched. 'Well done, my little angel. I knew you could do it,' he said, kissing Bella on both cheeks.

'Seems to me you only need a fine pair of titties to get on in this game.' Sam lurched against Bella, pushing her into Humphrey's arms.

'You've been drinking, Lennard,' Humphrey said, sniffing suspiciously. 'I warned you what would happen if you didn't keep off the booze.'

'So I had a drop or two to steady me nerves, guvner. You can't blame a fella for that.' Sam's aggressive manner vanished, replaced by an ingratiating grin and he winked at Bella. 'Just joking, girlie!'

'Another joke like that and you'll be busking outside the theatre,' Humphrey said, slipping his arm around Bella's shoulders.

'It's all right, Humphrey,' Bella said, twisting free of his grasp. 'I can take a joke and if I upstaged you, Sam, it wasn't intentional.'

Sam glared at her from beneath his bushy eyebrows.

'A handsome apology from a real lady,' Humphrey said, his scowl turning into a grin. 'By George, that's it. We'll bill you as Lady Bella, the *crème de la crème* of songbirds. The lady with the face and voice of an angel.'

'I don't think so,' Bella said, backing away. 'If you'll excuse me, I must go and change.'

'You don't fool me so easy,' Sam whispered in her ear. 'You're no bloody lady.' He pushed past her and lumbered off.

Bella hurried towards her dressing room but she could hear Humphrey's footsteps following her.

'Bella, stop. You must at least allow me to escort you home in my motor car.'

Pausing outside her dressing room door, Bella turning her head, forcing a smile. 'Thank you, but I wouldn't dream of imposing on you. We'll take a hackney carriage.'

'This isn't good enough, my dear. We really must find you more suitable accommodation.' Humphrey smiled into her eyes, caressing her cheek with his fingertips. 'I can't have my new star living so far away from the theatre and in such a dismal place.'

'You're very kind, Humphrey, but I don't mind the journey and I'm quite happy where I am.' Bella pushed the door open and hit something hard.

'Ouch!' Maria moved away quickly, nursing her elbow.

'Have you been listening at the keyhole?' Bella demanded, closing the door behind her.

'It's the only way to find out what's going on. What *is* going on with you and old Humpty Dumpty?'

'Shhh,' Bella said, her nerves twanging like piano wire. 'He might hear you. And there's nothing going on, at least not on my part.'

'He's got his eye on you, Bella. Play your cards right and you'll be top of the bill by the end of the week.'

'I'm not selling myself to any man again. I made a mistake marrying Desmond and I'm not in the market to be any man's mistress. Not without love.'

'If you're still hankering after that Edward, you'd better think again. He's never going to go against Sir Desmond and marry you.'

'I love Edward. I love him and he loves me.'

'Well, he's not here and may never come back from fighting the Boers so you'd best forget him, my girl. We've got more pressing things to think about at the moment. Humpty Dumpty was right about one thing: we ought to leave Tanner's Passage and get rooms nearer the theatre.'

'I can't just walk out on Betty. It wouldn't be fair to desert her now after she took us in.'

'She'll understand.'

'I can't do it, not yet, anyway. She's been upset enough and there's Kitty to consider too, and Maggie and the children.'

'Don't forget your own child. You won't get Leonie back unless you can provide a proper home for her. And I thought you wanted to get back at Rackham. What better way than to set up your own establishment in a well-to-do area, and prove you don't need him, nor any man to help you get on.'

Bella put her hands over her ears. 'Stop, stop. You're making my head spin.'

'Someone's got to talk sense, my girl,' Maria said, grabbing Bella by the shoulders and shaking her. 'You tell Humpty Dumpty that he can help you find some nice digs. Put your own family first.'

'You mean yourself, Mother, don't you?' Bella cried, pushing Maria away. 'You didn't put me first when you ran away with your fancy man and left me with my pig of a father. You weren't there to stop him . . .' Bella stuffed her fist in her mouth, shaking her head, unable to put the terrible deed into words.

Maria's stern face cracked into a maze of fine lines and her mouth drooped at the corners. 'I had to get away before he killed me in one of his drunken rages, and then Ernie came along, promising me the world, but only if I left you behind. I didn't want to leave you but I thought I'd never get another chance like that. I knew your dad was a beast, but I never thought he'd lay a finger on you, Bella, not in that way, I swear it.'

Bella sank down on her dressing stool and buried her face in her hands. It was all too much! Everything that had happened that day had built up into a fogbank of disaster. Something had been terribly wrong at home in Tanner's Passage. Betty had obviously been crying and Kitty had seemed upset, but they refused to tell her what was wrong. As if all that hadn't been bad enough, Rackham had brought Iris to watch her performance. That was an unspeakable act, even for someone as low as Giles. Sam Lennard's jealousy had been slightly less disturbing than Humphrey Chester's thinly veiled motive behind his offers of help.

Having rubbed her closed eyes with her knuckles, Bella opened them again to see that her face was streaked with greasepaint and spit-black.

'You look a sight,' Maria said, throwing her a scrap of cloth. 'Best clean yourself up.'

A sharp rapping on the door made them both jump.

'May I come in, Bella?'

Maria thrust a pot of cold cream in Bella's hands. 'It's Humpty Dumpty, you don't want him to see you looking like a clown.'

Bella wiped her face and Maria opened the door slowly, blocking the entrance so that Humphrey could not enter without lifting her bodily aside. 'Miss Lane is tired.'

Peeping over Maria's head, Humphrey spoke directly to Bella. 'My dear, I apologise if I upset you in any way. I've instructed my chauffeur to take you and your maid home and then return for me. I've got some paperwork that needs attending to anyway.'

Wiping the last of her stage make-up off her face, Bella turned to him and smiled. 'That's very kind of you, Humphrey.'

'And you'll reconsider my suggestion about moving closer to the theatre?'

'Maybe.'

Bella slept badly that night and woke up early next morning to the sound of Kitty's footsteps pattering along the landing. She did not get up straight away, but lay in bed, listening to the familiar morning sounds of the household: the children's feet as they pounded down the staircase, with Maggie shushing them loudly and telling them that other people were trying to sleep. When she heard the front door close behind Maggie, who took the children to school every morning, still fearful that Sid might suddenly appear from nowhere, Bella slipped out of bed, pulled a cotton wrap over her nightie and went downstairs to the kitchen.

Kitty stood at the sink, washing cups and plates, and Betty was slumped in a chair at the table, holding a piece of paper in her hands that she quickly folded in half as Bella came into the room.

'I know there's something terribly wrong,' Bella said, taking a seat opposite Betty. 'What is it? You've been so good to us, Betty, I want to help in any way I can.'

Betty's face crumpled and tears ran unchecked down her cheeks. 'I just don't know what to do. We're ruined and I can't see any way out.' Dropping the letter, she buried her face in her hands, sobbing.

Bella reached across the table and picked up the letter. When she had read it, she shot a questioning look at Kitty. 'I don't understand. I thought Betty owned this house.'

'She does, but the land is leasehold. She went and saw the land agent yesterday and he said, unless she can find the sixty pounds, the landlord will take the house in lieu of the money.'

'He can't do that.'

'The agent says he can.'

Bella stared at the address in Lincoln's Inn

Fields and folded the letter, slipping it into her pocket. 'We'll see about that. Is there any tea left in the pot?'

Bella sat in the dingy office of Feeney, Feeney and Rumbelow tapping her foot as she waited for Mr Feeney, Junior to see her. The clerk had done his best to put her off, but she had seated herself on a hard wooden settle and informed him that she would sit here all day and all night if necessary. Glancing up at the white-faced clock on the wall, she saw that she had been waiting for one hour and thirteen minutes. She cleared her throat, staring pointedly at the clerk. He dropped his gaze, looking slightly uncomfortable and went back to writing in his ledger. Every time there was the sound of movement from behind the closed door bearing Mr Feeney, Junior's name, inscribed in neat gilt letters, Bella looked up hopefully. She had just decided that she was going to barge in unannounced, when the door opened and a short, balding man stuck his head into the room, peering at her with pale, sheep-like eyes.

'Is this the young person, Potter?'

'Yes, Mr Feeney.'

'Show her in.'

Bella leapt to her feet, pushing past Potter before he had time to clamber off his stool. 'About time, too! Do you know how long you've kept me waiting Mr Feeney? Did you really think I'd give up and go away?'

Mr Feeney scuttled behind his desk and sat down, steepling his fingers. 'Take a seat, young lady.'

'Thank you, I prefer to stand,' Bella said, thrusting the letter under his nose. 'You wrote this, I believe.'

'It came from this office, yes.'

'You can't treat Mrs Scully like this. It's quite preposterous. I demand to see the landlord. Let him tell me, face to face, that he's going to turn a poor widow out of her own home.'

Blinking and flushing brick red from the top of his starched white collar to the tips of his ears, Mr Feeney blew out his cheeks and made a huffing noise. 'Quite out of the question! Out of the question.'

Bella slammed her hand down on the desk, causing the silver inkstand to jiggle. 'You will tell me who this man is or I will go to the press. Fleet Street is only round the corner and I know they would be more than interested in my story.'

Mr Feeney's pale eyes rolled in their sockets, looking as though they might pop out at any moment. 'Don't you threaten me, Miss, er – to whom am I speaking?'

'Lady Arabella Mableton.'

Mr Feeney jumped to his feet, knocking his chair over in his haste. 'You are Lady Mableton?'

'I am indeed.'

'You must leave this office at once. I can't speak to you, Madam, it would be a conflict of interest.'

Bella shook off his hand as he tried to take her by the arm. 'Don't you lay a hand on me or I'll add common assault to the charge. You'd better tell me who this person is, Mr Feeney, before I lose patience altogether.'

Feeney's face went from red to ashen. 'My God, Ma'am, you put me in an impossible position.'

Bella took a step towards the door. 'Tell me now or I'm going to the newspapers.'

'Your husband is the landowner. Sir Desmond Mableton owns all the properties in Tanner's Passage and I'm just following his instructions.'

Outside the office, Bella clutched the iron railings, taking deep breaths as her stomach roiled in fury. So Desmond was at the bottom of this cruel stroke! It was typical of his vindictive way of dealing with anyone who dared to cross him, but how on earth had he found out where she was staying? She didn't have to stretch her imagination far to realise that there was only one person who could have passed on the information – Rackham! What sort of double-dealing game was he playing? She paced up and down outside the building until she realised that Potter, and

Mr Feeney himself, were staring out of the window, watching her every movement.

Be calm, she told herself, stopping in her tracks and counting slowly to ten. Think, Bella, think logically what is to be done. There was no use in appealing to Rackham for help, he had made it clear that he had gone over to the enemy, as usual playing the hand that was likely to bring him the best return. Well, good luck to him with that skinny old maid whose veins ran with sour milk instead of blood. Rackham was an unspeakable cad, a louse, a despicable creeping insect who should be trodden into the ground. Best forget him and leave it to Iris to make the rest of his life as miserable as he truly deserved. Bella put her head down and strode onwards; there were more important things to consider than the abominable Giles Rackham.

Thanks to Desmond's callous actions she was now responsible for Betty and everyone who lived in number seven Tanner's Passage. Their lives were inextricably linked and it was up to her, not only to find them a new home, but also to think of a way they could earn enough money to support themselves.

Bella continued walking, not really considering where she was going, until she realised that she was halfway down the Strand and heading in the direction of the theatre. Humphrey Chester had offered her his help. All right, she thought, so it would not come without strings, but a plan was already forming in her head. If things worked out as she hoped, then she would be able to pay Humphrey off with money, rather than the only other marketable commodity at her disposal. She would not think about that now; this was an emergency and the lives of everyone in Tanner's Passage depended on her making the right decision.

The faint smell of a Havana cigar wafted down the narrow corridor that led to Humphrey Chester's office. Bella squared her shoulders, knocked on the door and entered without waiting for an answer.

Humphrey was seated behind a large mahogany desk littered with theatre posters, handbills and piles of correspondence. He glanced up and smiled. 'My dear Bella, what a pleasant surprise.'

Bella sat down on the edge of the chair in front of his desk, folding her hands on her lap and looking him straight in the eye. 'I've been thinking about what you said last night, Humphrey.'

'Excellent. And what was your decision?' Humphrey leaned back in his chair, eyeing Bella with a calculating gleam in his eyes.

'You were right, I do need to move to a better neighbourhood closer to the theatre but at the moment it's a question of money.'

Humphrey made an expansive gesture with his hands. 'Not a problem, my dear.'

'I want to keep this on a strictly business level.'

His lips twitched but he held her gaze without blinking. 'Name your terms, Bella.'

'I want a house in a good address, large enough for my family, preferably with a small garden. I want a guaranteed tenancy agreement for at least one year, with the option to renew it then, and no restrictions as to use.'

'And what kind of use would that be?'

'Not the kind you're thinking,' Bella said, smiling. 'I intend to set up a perfectly respectable business as a modiste to ladies of fashion.'

Humphrey pursed his lips as if considering this idea. 'And you intend to pay me back out of the profits of this venture?'

'Precisely! But it will take a bit of time to establish the business. I will pay you back with a reasonable percentage of interest, beginning at the end of the first year.'

'And if you can't pay?'

A trickle of sweat ran down between Bella's shoulder blades and her heart began to race but she forced her lips into a smile. 'We'll renegotiate then.'

'That doesn't appeal to me, my love.' Humphrey leaned forward, his eyes clouding with desire. 'We're both adults, Bella, so let us stop pretending. You know what I want and I'm prepared to wait for just so long and no longer. If you can't repay my investment, with interest at ten percent at the end of the first year, you will become my mistress.'

Shuddering inwardly, Bella nodded. 'You have my word.'

'I don't usually wait so long for a woman,' Humphrey said, taking out a gold cigar case and extracting a cigar. 'But you have an exceptional talent and a degree of notoriety that adds a bit of spice as far as the audiences are concerned. They'll turn up in droves to see a titled lady discarded by her rich husband and forced to sing for her supper.' He snipped the end off his cigar with a silver cutter, pierced the tip and lit it with a match.

Alarm bells jangled in Bella's head. 'I don't want that sort of publicity, Humphrey. Can't we keep my married name out of this?'

'If we do this deal we do it on my terms.' Humphrey chewed on the end of his cigar, his smile fading and his eyes narrowed. 'You put yourself professionally in my hands or we don't do business.'

'I have a child,' Bella said, her voice breaking. 'Desmond won't let me have access to her and above all things I want her back.'

'That's your problem, Bella. Not mine. Now do we have an agreement or not?'

When she arrived back in Tanner's Passage, Bella

gathered everyone together around the kitchen table. Having told them everything, from Desmond's vicious plan to put them out on the street, to her bargain with Humphrey Chester, she faltered and stopped, glancing anxiously at their faces as they struggled with the enormity of what had happened.

Kitty jumped to her feet. 'You mustn't blame yourself, Bella. You've suffered as much as any of us. It's that rotten, stinking Sir Desmond who's done this.'

'You're the best friend anyone could have,' Bella said, smiling mistily, 'but I brought trouble on this house simply by coming here. Can you ever forgive me, Betty?'

White-faced and with her eyes brimful of tears, Betty shook her head. 'I don't blame you, Bella, but it's all come so sudden. I don't know what to say.'

'I can't tell you how terribly sorry I am for what Desmond has done,' Bella said, clasping her hands together to stop them from trembling. 'I feel so guilty that you are suffering on my account, but I'm trying to make amends in the only way I know how.'

'And there's no alternative but to leave my house?' Betty's voice broke on a suppressed sob.

'Not unless we can find sixty pounds, and even if we did I think Desmond would find another way to evict us.'

'Bella is taking an awful risk if we fail, Betty,' Kitty said earnestly. 'But with Mr Chester's money we can buy sewing machines and material. I think we've just got to stick together and make a success of what we do.'

'I say we're wasting our time sewing gowns for city folk,' Maria said, glaring at everyone as if daring them to argue. 'We can charge ten times as much if we get a rich clientele up West. I say we take a chance.'

'And where do me and the nippers fit in with this grand plan?' Maggie demanded.

'We're all in this together,' Kitty said, casting an appealing glance at Bella. 'You wouldn't leave Maggie and the nippers behind, now would you, Bella?'

'I might have answered differently once, but like Kitty says, we're in this together. The children will go to a better school, and have more of a chance to get on in the world. Maggie, it's up to you, but just stop and think. Do you want to send them to work in a factory at thirteen, or in the fish market? Haven't you said dozens of times that you're afraid to walk out round here just in case your Sid turns up?'

'I should say so,' agreed Maggie, turning pale and shuddering. 'It scares me to death just walking to the school or to the corner shop in case I bump into him.'

'You won't see him again,' Maria said. 'He's

333

either dead from the drink or found himself a totty hardbake.'

'No woman in her right mind would have him,' Maggie said, with a wry smile. 'But what if it don't work out? What happens to us then?'

'You'd be no worse off than you are now, ducks.' Reaching across the table, Betty clasped her hand. 'But Kitty is right, all working together we've got a chance. And, for myself, having the children around has helped me cope a bit better with losing our Polly.'

Wiping her eyes on her sleeve, Maggie's voice cracked with emotion. 'You've been so good to us, Betty. You know I'll do anything I can to help. I'll work me fingers to the bone, I promise you.'

Betty squeezed her hand. 'Good for you, Maggie!'

Glancing at the clock on the wall, Bella realised that she would soon have to leave for the theatre. Unsteadily, she rose to her feet. 'I'm not saying it's going to be easy and we might fail dismally, so we all need to be agreed that it's the right thing to do. Are you absolutely certain you want me to go ahead with this, Betty?'

Betty thought a minute and then her tired face creased into a smile. 'I've got to think of Jem as well as myself. He needs somewhere to come home to, and now I know there's no chance of saving this house, I say yes.'

'I know just how difficult this must be for you,'

Bella said, with a catch in her voice. 'I'll do my best not to let you down again.'

'You've not let us down,' Kitty cried, rushing round the table to hug her. 'It wasn't none of your fault, Bella, just that beast Sir Desmond. I hate him.'

'Don't we all!' Maria said, grimly.

Bella laid her hand over Kitty's as it rested on her shoulder. 'What about you, Kitty? You always wanted to work in a dress shop up West? What would you say if I put you in charge of selling gowns to fashionable ladies? Maybe you could design them, like the one you did for my first show? What do you say?'

Chapter Fourteen

As the last customer of the day left, followed by her maid carrying the finished ball gown, carefully wrapped in white butter muslin, Kitty closed the front door of the tall, narrow house in St James's. It had been a long and tiring day, beginning at six o'clock in the morning. A quick glance at the long-case clock in the hallway told her that it was almost seven thirty in the evening, and there was still work to do. Kitty went into the salon, humming a popular tune, as she set the spindly gilt chairs back in a regimented line against the wall, taking care not to bruise the fashionable William Morris wallpaper.

If she lived to be a hundred, she thought, she would never cease to wonder at, and wallow in, the luxury of their new surroundings. Her feet sank into the thick pile of the wine red carpet, sending a warm glow of satisfaction through her whole body. She couldn't resist switching on the recently installed electric light that made the chandeliers sparkle like diamonds, reflecting in rainbow prisms on the cream paintwork. Bella had insisted that no expense should be spared when it came to the salon, as wealthy clients would expect high standards. What Mr Chester thought of this, she did not say, but Kitty suspected that Bella had had to use a great deal of charm to wheedle the money out of him.

The evening sun slanted in through the windows and, although she didn't need the light to write up the day's business, it was a thrill to conjure up the miracle of electricity at the flick of a switch. Kitty sat down at the gilt console table and began to write out the worksheets ready to hand over to Betty, who was in charge of the cutting and sewing room behind the salon. Two more ball gowns, and an entire trousseau for a well-known actress, would keep them busy for several weeks. The work would be made easier now they had two spanking new treadle machines that Bella had purchased with some of the money loaned by Mr Chester.

Kitty chewed the end of her pencil and frowned. It was almost a year since Bella had found the house in Sackville Street. Because of its run-down state, she had managed to negotiate a reasonable rent, considering its situation in the fashionable area on the edge of Mayfair and St James's. They had hired workmen to paint and decorate the front of the four-storey terraced house, and to turn the parlour into a smart little salon. There were now two dressing rooms, tented in pink silk, reminding Kitty of the inside of a chocolate box, just like the one that Mr Chester had given them at Christmas time.

He had tried to offer advice about starting up the business, but Bella would have none of it, tossing her head and telling him that she knew very well what she was doing. This had puzzled Kitty. She could not understand why Bella seemed to dislike him, when Mr Chester was the one who had set them up in business in the first place. He was all right, Kitty thought, when you got to know him, and he wasn't a bounder like Giles Rackham. Although, of course, Mr Chester was not nearly as good-looking as Mr Rackham. He didn't have the wicked twinkle in his eye, or the charming smile that made you shiver inside, like eating ice cream on a hot day.

Realising that she had just written the same thing twice, Kitty picked up a piece of India rubber and scrubbed at the worksheet. Recalling the one and only time Mr Rackham had visited them in Sackville Street had made her mind wander. It had been last February just weeks after the dear Queen had died. There had been an outpouring of grief and the whole country had gone into mourning. The only good to come of it was that they had been inundated with orders for black gowns and they had all worked night and day to complete them by the second of February, the date of Her Majesty's funeral. Rackham had simply turned up, walking into the house as though he had never been absent, and Kitty had been caught up in the blazing row that had erupted between him and Bella. He had said he hadn't come for a fight, and he had brought a huge bouquet of flowers for Bella, a small photograph of Leonie in a silver frame, a basket of fruit from Covent Garden for the 'other ladies', and a pound of bullseyes for the children.

Bella had stormed into the room and come right out with the accusation that he had been responsible for Sir Desmond knowing about the house in Tanner's Passage. When Mr Rackham had denied it, she had thrown the flowers at his head and, as if she was a clockwork toy wound up until her spring was nearly busting, Bella had told him exactly what she thought of him. She had used swear words that had made Kitty gasp in surprise. It was as if one of the carved stone cherubs in the graveyard, where Ma and Pa and her little brothers rested, had opened its rosebud lips and come out with language that would have done justice to a Billingsgate porter. Bella had finished up by listing all Miss Iris's many faults, and she had accused Mr Rackham of making up to her for her money. That, she had said, made him the lowest sort of creature that crawled on the earth's surface.

Kitty scratched her head, puzzled. So what if he was engaged to Miss Iris? That was his business although, as far as she could see, he must be either mad or desperate to hitch himself to such a mean, nasty woman. Bella seemed to have forgotten that it was Mr Rackham who had journeyed through snow and ice, in a borrowed motor car, to rescue her from Mableton Manor, and that he had gone to prison for biffing Sir Desmond on the nose.

Kitty pressed so hard on the paper that she broke the point on her pencil, and had to search the drawer for a penknife. She rubbed her eyes and yawned. Perhaps she would finish the orders early in the morning. She didn't want to risk making a mistake and catching the rough edge of Maria's tongue. Now there was a woman you didn't want to cross if you could avoid it! Maggie might moan a bit and have a grumble; she could be blooming grumpy, if pushed too far, but her tempers were all flare and soon fizzled out. Maria was another kettle of fish altogether, and when she lost her temper, you'd better watch out. Kitty had never seen a volcano erupt, but she had a vague idea that it must be something like Maria when she let fly.

Getting to her feet, Kitty set everything straight on the desk and, as she went to leave the room, she caught sight of her reflection in one of the long mirrors. The girl who stared back at her with a hint of a smile was a far different person from skinny little Kitty Cox, the scullery maid. She had grown at least a couple of inches in height and, although she was still reed slim, she now had soft curves above and below her tiny waist. Kitty did a little twirl, casting a critical eye over her appearance. She had made herself a white cotton lawn blouse, with a high neck and pintucks down the front, and a navy-blue, serge skirt that was both neat and practical. With her hair put up in the fashionable cottage-loaf style, she was confident that she could pass for eighteen, even though her eighteenth birthday was not until July. At least that was her aim, and it had seemed to work as far as the clients were concerned.

'Miss Kitty Cox,' Kitty said, addressing her reflection, and giggling. 'You're barmy!' Her stomach rumbled in answer and Kitty suddenly realised that she was starving hungry and had not eaten since dinner time. 'No,' she said, shaking a finger at herself. 'You've got to remember that it's lunch at dinner time and dinner at tea time.'

Still chuckling at her own silliness, Kitty left the salon with one last, loving look around, closing the door behind her. Still, she thought, as she made her way down the back stairs to the kitchen, it wasn't so easy moving up in society; leaving Tanner's Passage and starting up the business had taken its toll on everyone. Whereas before they had been united in the common struggle to survive, things were not quite so rosy now.

For the first time, they were squabbling amongst themselves. Maggie grumbled that she was getting fed up with doing all the cooking and washing, as well as looking after her children and, on top of that, having to spend long hours at the treadle machine. Betty did the cutting and, although her rheumaticky fingers wouldn't allow her to use a needle, she was able to use the sewing machine and probably worked hardest of them all. Although Betty never moaned, and was always ready to step in as a peacemaker, Kitty sensed that Polly's death had ripped a great hole in Betty's heart, and that she was sad at having left her memories locked up in the old house.

Betty missed Jem terribly, Kitty knew that, and she missed him too, much more than she would ever have thought possible. His letters were infrequent and disappointingly short, packed with anecdotes about his travels but with little reference to his feelings or emotions. Kitty sighed and fingered her half of the gold sovereign that never left her neck; she had told him not to bother with the lovey-dovey stuff, but a few affectionate words would have been a great comfort. Confused by the turbulent emotions that woke her in the middle of the night, Kitty couldn't help wondering if Jem had taken her at her word and given up hope of ever winning her love. If he had, then she had only herself to blame and, after all, just being friends was what she had always wanted. Wasn't it? She didn't need a man to tell her what to do; she was well on her way to fulfilling her ambition to become a fashionable modiste. Shrugging her shoulders, Kitty opened the kitchen door.

Maggie had left a pan of vegetable soup simmering on the hob and Kitty's mouth watered as she sniffed the delicious aroma. Taking a bowl from the dresser, she helped herself to a generous portion. Setting it down on the table she cut a thick slice of bread and spread it with butter. The soup was good and filling and, although they still had to watch the pennies, living frugally, no one went hungry now. The food they ate was plain, but it was wholesome, and there was more than enough to go round.

Sitting back in her chair, Kitty was aware of the sounds coming from the street above the basement window: the carriages and hanson cabs rattling past with the clip-clop of horses' feet and the sound of the newsvendor's cries on the corner of Sackville Street and Piccadilly. Indoors the house was drowsing in evening silence. The children would have been tucked up in their beds in the attic room for a good hour. Maggie and Betty would be relaxing in the sitting room on the first floor, although, Kitty thought, Maggie was probably darning socks or mending the children's clothes. If Betty was not writing a long letter to Jem, she was more than

343

likely having a quiet snooze. Bella and Maria would be at the theatre by now and preparing for the evening show.

A feeling of sadness crept into Kitty's heart as she thought of Bella who, despite her continuing success on the stage, and the fact that Humphrey Chester obviously adored her, seemed deeply unhappy. Cupping her hands on her chin, Kitty thought hard. She knew that Bella was miserable because she was separated from Leonie – that was only natural – but was she also still pining for Mr Edward? Kitty shook her head, not knowing the answer, but was suddenly aware that she must do something to help. She couldn't make the war in South Africa finish, or bring Mr Edward home safely, but if she could discover the new nanny's daily routine, she could tell Bella when Leonie might be out for a walk in the park. If she saw that Leonie was well and happy, then it might ease the pain of separation.

Kitty jumped up from the table and, piling her dishes in the stone sink, she seized her shawl from the back of the chair and let herself out of the tradesmen's entrance.

It was a balmy May evening, and the sun had gone down in a fiery blaze, leaving crimson streaks slashed across the sky and deep purple shadows between the rows of tall houses. Wrapping her shawl around her shoulders, Kitty quickened her pace. At the end of the street she turned right into Piccadilly, heading in the direction of Dover Street. She had only a vague plan of what she would do once she got there, but she wasn't afraid to face any of those who had tormented her in the past. She could even face Mr Warner or Mrs Brewster, if she had to, and as for Olive and Dora . . .! Kitty squared her shoulders and ran lightly down the area steps to rap on the door.

Luckily it was Florrie who opened it and her face crumpled into a grin. 'Why Kitty Cox, just look at you.'

'Hello, Florrie. Can I come in for a minute or two?'

Florrie glanced nervously over her shoulders. 'I dunno about that, Kitty. Mrs Dixon wouldn't like it.'

'Who is it, Florrie?'

Kitty peered over Florrie's broad shoulder as she recognised George's voice. 'George, it's me, Kitty.'

Pushing Florrie aside, George came to the door, grinning broadly. 'Kitty, you're a sight for sore eyes, my girl.'

Kitty took a step backwards, looking George up and down as she took in the details of his footman's uniform. 'Why, George, I didn't know you'd got yourself promoted.'

George puffed his chest out so that the brass buttons on his uniform looked in danger of flying off in all directions. 'I should say so. I'm second footman now and I daresay I'll be first footman before long, that is if James and Dora get hitched.'

'James and Dora? I thought he was sweet on Jane?'

'That was yesterday,' George said, grinning. 'Jane ran off with the baker's boy. We got a new girl now.'

Kitty shivered as a cool breeze whipped down the stone steps, bringing with it a flurry of bits of straw and paper from the street above. 'Can I come in?'

George stepped back into the house with an expansive wave of his hands. 'Of course you can, and Florrie will make you a cup of tea.'

'Hold on, George,' Florrie said, backing into the scullery. 'What if Mrs Dixon sees Kitty?'

George frowned. 'She's got a point, Kitty. Better stay here and say what you've got to say.' He turned to Florrie. 'You go and keep the old girl busy, while I have a chin-wag with Kitty.'

'You always were soft on her,' Florrie said, sniffing. 'It's not fair. I wanted to hear what Kitty has to say.'

'And I'm your superior,' George said, bridling. 'Be a good girl, Flo, and do as you're told.'

Florrie snorted and flounced off into the kitchen.

'Well then,' George said, leaning his shoulders against the doorjamb. 'What's up?'

Looking him up and down, Kitty could hardly believe how much George had changed. He seemed to have grown at least four inches, and his mop of wild, carroty hair was sleeked down with Macassar oil. The dark green footman's uniform suited and flattered him, and his new-found air of assurance was oddly comical and yet endearing. She smiled. 'Nothing, George! I just thought I'd look you up for old time's sake.'

George blushed to the roots of his hair. 'I say, Kitty. Really?'

She couldn't lie. 'Well, that's half the truth and I am pleased to see you, but mostly I wanted to find out about Miss Leonie so that I could tell her poor ma, who is still fretting something awful for her little girl.'

George seemed to think about this, frowning a bit at first and then his freckled face broke into a grin. 'So you are pleased to see me just a bit?'

'Of course I am, George. We were mates and that hasn't changed.'

'You have, Kitty. You've changed a lot. I think you're really – pretty.'

Kitty felt a hot blush flooding her own cheeks now and the appreciative look in George's eyes was both flattering and confusing. 'I – er, thank you, but can we talk about Leonie for a bit?'

'She's all right, I suppose. I don't think much of her nanny, but then she keeps herself to herself, so we don't really know about what goes on in the nursery.'

Impulsively Kitty reached out and grasped him by the arm. 'George, I really need your help.'

George stared at Kitty's hand on his sleeve and swallowed hard. 'I'd do anything for you, you know that.'

'I just want to know when the nanny takes Miss Leonie to the park so that Bella, I mean Lady Mableton, can see her. That's all.'

Covering her hand with his, George cleared his throat a couple of times before he could speak. 'And if I do, will you do something for me, Kitty?'

'Name it and I'll try.'

A drop of perspiration ran down George's forehead, trickling down his cheek and disappearing into his starched collar. 'Will you step out with me on my next day off?'

Kitty stared at him in surprise; she hadn't ever thought of George in that way before. But where was the harm? George was a friend and she trusted him. It might be nice to get away from the house and work for an hour or two. 'If you like.'

Before George could speak Florrie came flying out of the scullery and tugged at his coat-tails. 'The master's bell is jangling like fury, George. Best get up there quick or you'll be for it.'

Kitty took a piece of paper from her skirt

pocket, and a pencil; she scribbled down the address in Sackville Street, handing it to George.

'I'll be in touch then, Kitty.'

Kitty stayed up late, long after Betty and Maggie had gone to bed, sitting in the window upstairs, waiting for Bella to come home so that she could give her the good news. She was half asleep when, sometime after midnight, a cab drew up outside the house. Dragging herself out of the chair, Kitty raced down the stairs, arriving in the hall just as Maria came through the front door. She was alone.

Maria took off her bonnet, glaring at Kitty. 'What are you doing up this late?'

'Where's Bella?'

'Gone to supper with Mr Chester. Not that it's any business of yours, Miss,' Maria snapped, tossing her bonnet onto the hallstand. 'Shouldn't you be in bed?'

Kitty hesitated, eyeing Maria and backing away. She was best avoided when she was in a mood, and she was obviously in a mood now. 'Yes, I'm going.'

'Not so fast. You'd better tell me what's so important that it kept you from your bed.'

'It's nothing to do with you. I've got some news for Bella.'

'Anything that affects Bella has something to do with me. I'm her mother and just you remember that.'

'I've got news about Leonie.'

'What? She's not ill or anything?'

Seeing Maria's sallow skin turn the colour of lemon icing, Kitty shook her head. 'No, nothing like that. I went to Dover Street and I spoke to George. I thought maybe we could arrange for Bella to see Leonie.'

Maria grabbed Kitty by the shoulders, shaking her until her teeth rattled. 'Don't be a fool, girl. Bella is just getting back on her feet – do you want to ruin things?'

'But that's not fair.'

Maria struck Kitty across the cheek with the flat of her hand. 'That's what you get for nothing; see what you get for something.'

Kitty broke free, holding her hand to her cheek. 'Why are you being so cruel to Bella? She loves Leonie.'

'And Mr Chester is besotted with my Bella. I don't want anything to spoil her chances there.'

'But he's married. He told me so last Christmas when he brought us those presents. He said he had been out buying gifts for his family.'

'Yes, he's married but he'll set Bella up with a nice little house of her own and treat her right. You'd better do some growing up, my girl, and then you'll realise that no respectable man is going to offer my Bella anything other than being his mistress. That's the way life goes for people like us. Get that into your pretty little head and maybe you'll do all right for yourself, but don't you dare go encouraging Bella with a lot of romantic nonsense or you'll have me to answer to.'

Maria hung her coat on the hallstand and stomped up the stairs, leaving Kitty standing in the hall staring after her. She wasn't going to have a fight with Maria, but neither was she going to pay any attention to such bitter words. Just because Maria had had an unhappy time with Bella's father, and seemed to hate all men, it didn't mean that Bella had to suffer.

Kitty crept into the salon and pulled up a chair by the window, determined to wait until Bella came home, no matter if she had to stay up all night.

Waking up with a start, Kitty uncurled her cold, cramped limbs and peeped out of the window. In the guttering light of the gas lamps she saw Mr Chester handing Bella out of the back seat of his shiny, black motor car. Kitty dodged back behind the curtain as they mounted the steps together and, waiting until she heard Bella's key turn in the lock, she ran to the door and slipped out into the hall.

'Thank you for supper and for seeing me home,' Bella said, stepping inside.

Kitty couldn't quite make out his reply but Humphrey's voice sounded soft and persuasive.

'I shall probably sleep all day tomorrow, my dear,' Bella said. 'And then I have fittings for my new stage costume. I'll see you at the theatre on Monday.'

Kitty edged forward as Bella shut the door. 'Bella, it's me, Kitty.'

Bella spun round, clasping her hand to her chest. 'Kitty! You frightened the life out of me. What's wrong?'

Kitty grabbed Bella's hand and led her into the salon. 'I didn't mean to scare you but I had to wait up and give you the good news.'

'Good news?'

'George is going to let me know when Leonie is being taken for a walk in the park.'

Bella sank down on one of the gilt chairs. 'Kitty dear, I appreciate your efforts but I've been going to the park for months to catch a glimpse of Leonie. She doesn't know I'm there, bless her, but at least I've seen her.'

'But you never said!'

'No, I thought it was best to keep it to myself. Maria doesn't approve. She thinks I should let Leonie go, but I can't. I simply can't.' Bella's voice thickened with tears and broke on a sob.

Kitty threw her arms around Bella and hugged her. 'Don't cry, Bella.'

'I'm all right, dear, just exhausted. It's been a long day and I need my bed.' Raising herself from the chair, Bella moved towards the door.

She paused, turning to Kitty with a tremulous smile. 'But I appreciate what you did for me. Thank you, Kitty.'

Next morning, it being Sunday, Kitty was using the quiet time while the salon was closed to work on some designs for a costume for one of Bella's theatrical ladies.

Bella and Maria were still in their rooms, presumably sleeping. Betty had gone to morning service and Maggie had taken the children for a walk in Hyde Park. The silence was shattered as the front door opened and the children burst into the hall, chattering and giggling, with Maggie telling them to hush. She popped her head round the door, smiling.

'We're back, Kitty.'

'I'd never have guessed.'

'Go to the kitchen and you can have a glass of milk and a rock cake,' Maggie called to the children. 'One each, mind, and no more or you'll spoil your dinner.' She came in, taking off her bonnet and shawl. 'It's lovely in the park, just like being in the country.'

Looking up, Kitty raised her eyebrows in surprise. 'You've never been to the country.'

'I did go once, a long time ago before you was born. Mum and Dad took me and Lennie to Southend on the train. We saw green fields, trees and flowers; cows and sheep, pigs and chickens;

farm houses with weatherboard fronts and thatched roofs. It were like a dream. Lennie died of the typhoid just weeks later but at least he'd seen the country.'

Kitty leaned back in her chair, chewing the tip of her pencil. 'Why Maggie Cable, I never knew you were so taken with country things.'

'Like I said, it's just a dream, Kitty. Living where the air is fresh and clean in a house all of me own.'

'And I never knew you were so ambitious.'

'Not for myself, I'm not, but I want things for my kids. One day I want a nice little house out Romford way with a proper garden where the kids can play. Somewhere safe where Sid won't find us – if he ever decides to start looking, that is.'

Kitty stared in surprise at Maggie's animated face. She had changed so much since they'd left Tanner's Passage. Now that her fear of Sid turning up again had diminished, and freed from the grinding poverty of Sugar Yard, Maggie looked more like the pretty young girl she had been before her marriage. An involuntary shudder shook Kitty as the memories of that terrible night came flooding back. She could hear the scrape of Sid's boots on the quay wall followed by the muffled splash of his body hitting the water. She couldn't tell Maggie that, if she hadn't actually killed Sid, she had done nothing to save his miserable life. She hadn't screamed for help or run to find a constable, she had just lain there panting, gasping for breath and her only feeling at the time had been relief that Sid couldn't get to her. Her hands were shaking and she dropped the pencil. 'Whoops-a-daisy,' she said, bending down to pick it up.

'Look at you, Kitty. You're all fingers and thumbs,' Maggie said, chuckling. A commotion from the hallway distracted her and Maggie ran to the door. 'Less noise out there, boys! Bella and Maria are trying to sleep. If you've had your milk you can go out in the back yard and play until I call you for dinner.'

Five-year-old Violet ran into the room dragging Harry behind her; his short legs only just keeping up with her long strides. Running to Maggie, he clutched her hand, reverting to his baby habit of sucking his thumb.

'There now, Harry love,' Maggie said in a softer tone, patting his head. 'What's up?'

'They've been teasing us, Mum,' Violet said, pouting. 'They said Harry was a baby and made him cry.'

'You tell those bad boys that they'll feel the wooden spoon across their knuckles if they tease Harry.' Ruffling Violet's curls, Maggie gave Harry a quick cuddle. 'Go along with Violet, poppet. And, Vi, you tell the boys that if anyone so much as nibbles the crust of that apple pie they'll be in for it.'

Shooing the children from the room, Maggie returned, shaking her head. 'They'll be the death of me, them boys.'

'Don't be hard on them, Maggie,' Kitty said. 'They're good lads.'

Maggie slipped off her cape and laid it neatly across one of the chairs. 'I know it, but I want them to grow up proper, and have some respect for other people, not like their dad.' Maggie's face darkened for a moment and then she smiled. 'Anyway, it's not likely that he'll dare show his face again and I'm saving every penny I gets in wages. You never know when all this is going to come to an end.'

'But, Maggie, we're doing well at the moment. We've got everything we could possibly want.'

'In my experience, things don't last forever and I got to think of the future. It's a rum setup between Mr Chester and Bella. I never seen a man prepared to wait for so long for what he wants.'

'What do you mean by that?'

'If you can't see it, then I ain't going to be the one to tell you, ducks. Anyway, it's time I went downstairs and sorted them kids out.' Patting Kitty on the cheek, Maggie hurried from the room, leaving Kitty staring after her.

Heaving a sigh, Kitty picked up her pencil, chewing it thoughtfully. She knew that Mr Chester was sweet on Bella, but that was hardly surprising; what was shocking was Maggie's inference that he might expect more than just ten percent as a return on his investment. And he seemed to be such a gentleman.

Then there was Maggie herself, whose words had made Kitty think of her sister in a new light. Tongues of guilt licked at her conscience. She had dragged Maggie away from the squalor and deprivation of Sugar Yard, settled her in Tanner's Passage and then transplanted the family to Sackville Street, without ever considering that Maggie might have ambitions and aspirations of her own. Everything that she had done had been with the best of intentions, but still Maggie was not completely happy. Kitty rubbed her hand wearily across her eyes. Why was life never simple?

The sound of the brass door knocker being energetically used brought her back to the present with a jolt. Kitty jumped up and ran to open the door.

George stood on the top step, dressed in his Sunday best and grinning broadly. 'Hello there, Kitty. You haven't forgotten have you?'

Kitty stared at him, trying to reassemble her scrambled thoughts. 'Forgotten?'

'You promised to walk out with me this fine Sunday.'

'Oh, George, I had completely forgotten. I'm so sorry but I've got a lot of work to do.'

Taking off his straw boater, George stepped across the threshold. 'You promised, Kitty. I'm not moving from this spot without you.'

Kitty opened her mouth to argue but George laid his finger across her lips. 'It's just a stroll in the park. You needn't worry about me, Kitty. I'm a perfect gent.'

'Don't be daft, George. I never thought anything else.'

'Good,' George said, grinning. 'Then get your coat and hat, Miss Cox. We're stepping out.'

She hadn't wanted to go with him but, to Kitty's surprise, she found herself having fun for the first time in years. They walked to Hyde Park, took a boat out on the Serpentine and ate ice cream sitting near the bandstand and listening to a band playing military marches. At Speaker's Corner there was a man ranting against the continuing war in South Africa and the infamous concentration camps, where Boer women and children were dying in horrifying numbers; an Irishman demanding self-rule for Ireland; a woman calling for her sisters to unite in women's suffrage and a preacher to whom no one was paying any attention but who was shouting the loudest of all, promising hellfire and damnation for more or less everyone.

Late in the afternoon, they were strolling back along Piccadilly and Kitty was laughing at a silly joke that George had just made, when she saw Giles Rackham standing on the corner of Half Moon Street.

'What's up?' demanded George as Kitty stopped suddenly, tugging on his arm.

'Over there on the other side of the road. It's Mr Rackham.'

'What if it is? We've done nothing wrong.'

'Oh, bother! He's seen us.' Kitty glanced around for some means of escape but Rackham was already halfway across the road.

'Well, then,' Rackham said, tipping his hat to Kitty. 'This is a pleasant surprise. I didn't realise that you two were so friendly.'

'It's my afternoon off, Sir,' George said, jumping to attention.

'We just went for a walk,' Kitty said, eyeing him warily. 'We're old friends.'

Rackham put his head on one side with an alert expression in his eyes. 'So, are you now? That might be very useful.'

'I'm sure I don't know what you mean, Sir. Please let us pass, George has to be back on duty by five o'clock.'

'I've just come from Dover Street. Sir Desmond has taken to his bed with a touch of gout and Miss Iris is too busy telephoning her friends to tell them her news to notice that the second footman's late for duty.'

'I'd best get back quickly.' George ran a finger

around the inside of his collar, sending Kitty an anxious look. 'I bet Mrs Dixon is on the warpath.'

'That's not what I meant, young man.'

'What did you mean, Mr Rackham?' Kitty demanded, wondering if Mr Rackham had gone completely mad. 'What news?'

'Miss Iris is engaged to be married, Kitty.'

'Not to you, Sir!' exclaimed Kitty, outraged. 'You're not going to marry Miss Iris?'

Rackham tapped the side of his nose and laughed. 'Perhaps. Who knows?'

'And you pretended to be Bella's friend,' Kitty cried, brushing off George's restraining hand. 'How could you?'

Rackham's smile faded. 'I am Bella's friend and I want you both to remember that. I'm doing this for Bella and for Leonie, but I'll need your help. Can I count on you?'

'What are you saying?' demanded Kitty.

'I'm asking you to trust me,' Rackham said, his expression serious for once. 'I can't reveal my plans at this moment in time, but can I count on you both to help me?'

Chapter Fifteen

It had been the night of all nights in the theatre. The audience had been even more appreciative than usual and Bella had taken curtain call after curtain call. She could still hear the cheering and applause echoing in her head as she slapped cold cream on her face, scrubbing at the thick coating of greasepaint with a flannel.

'You look like a circus clown,' Maria said, staring critically at Bella's reflection in the mirror. 'I hope you're not going to get all temperamental now that you're top of the bill, my girl.'

Bella snorted with laughter. 'Not much chance of that with you around, Mother dear.'

'When you call me Mother, I know you've really got the hump.' Maria pursed her lips. 'What's up?'

'You haven't heard the news then?'

'Mafeking and Ladysmith have been relieved. No, that was last year. Um, let me guess . . . I know, the King has sent you a personal invitation to his Coronation next year along with Lillie Langtry and the rest.'

'Very funny, Mother. I might die laughing.'

'Then what is it? Stop playing games, for God's sake, Bella, and tell me.'

'Rackham is engaged to Iris.'

'So what? Why does that nark you? They should suit each other down to the ground.'

'Because,' Bella said, wiping off the last of her make-up, 'Giles was supposed to be on my side. I never believed him when he said he was seeing Iris in order to help me get Leonie back. He's a cheat and a liar and he makes me sick.'

'You're well rid of him and the Mableton family. You should concentrate on Humphrey. He's mad about you and he's rich. If you play your cards right he might get his lawyers to take your case.'

'He wouldn't do that; he's not interested in my child. Humphrey just wants me to be his mistress but I don't want him.'

'Bah!' Maria snorted. 'You're not still pining for Edward, are you?'

Shaking her head, Bella opened her mouth to deny it, but the sound of someone knocking on the door drowned her reply.

Maria went to answer it. 'Mr Chester, I thought it was you, Sir.'

'Is Bella ready?'

'Humphrey, I'm really tired,' Bella said, rising slowly to her feet. 'Would you mind if I went straight home tonight?'

Humphrey stepped into the tiny room, his

face creased with concern. 'Are you unwell, my darling?'

'No, but it's been a long day.'

Slipping his arm around Bella's waist, Humphrey smiled into her eyes. 'A glass or two of champagne will work wonders. Get dressed, my love, and I'll wait for you in my office.'

'I'd really like to go home,' Bella said firmly. 'Maybe tomorrow night?'

Humphrey brushed her lips with a kiss. 'Nonsense, sweetheart! I've got an old friend of yours waiting to see you. You wouldn't want to disappoint him, now would you?'

'An old friend?' Bella's heart began to race.

'The friend who brought us together in the first place, my dove. Giles Rackham.'

Sparks of anger ignited in Bella's brain. 'Give me five minutes, Humphrey,' she said, pushing him towards the door.

As he left the room, Humphrey blew her a kiss. 'I knew you'd change your mind.'

Snatching up the pot of cold cream Bella flung it at the opposite wall with all her might. It shattered in a starburst of broken glass and white cream. 'Rackham! I might have known he'd come to gloat.'

'Don't get yourself in a state,' Maria said, snatching Bella's evening gown off its hanger. 'Forget Rackham and be thankful that you've got a man who thinks the sun shines out of your backside.'

'Not likely,' Bella cried. 'Not blooming likely! I want to see Giles face to face and I'll give him what for.'

Without knocking, Bella marched into Humphrey's office.

Rackham had his back to the door but he turned as she burst into the room, smiling and holding his arms outstretched. 'Bella, your performance was spiffing, as usual.'

'And you are despicable, Giles, as usual!'

'Bella, that's not like you.' Humphrey leapt to his feet and, moving swiftly for such a large man, he came from behind his desk to place his arm around Bella's shoulders. 'You poor darling, you really must be exhausted after that sparkling performance tonight.'

'Humphrey, would you mind if I had a word with Giles? Alone!'

'Not at all, if it will help to straighten things out,' Humphrey said, kissing her on the cheek. 'Don't upset, my brightest star, Giles, or you'll have me to answer to.'

As he left the room, Bella turned on Rackham. 'You despicable cad! How could you stoop so low as to make up to Iris?'

Rackham seized her hands. 'Bella, listen to me,' he said, urgently. 'Everything I've done is to help you, you must believe me.'

'I don't believe anything you say.' Struggling,

Bella attempted to break free but his grip was pure steel.

'All right, but just hear me out if you want your daughter back.'

'What are you saying?'

'Make any excuse you like, but refuse Humphrey's supper invitation. I've arranged everything. Kitty is waiting outside in a hackney carriage and George will let us into the house in Dover Street.'

'I – I don't understand. What wild scheme have you dreamed up?'

'Do exactly what I tell you, and by midnight you'll have Leonie safely back with you, where she belongs.'

Mableton House was eerily silent as Bella followed Rackham and Kitty up the servants' staircase. The only sound that Bella could hear, apart from the soft pitter-patter of their feet on the stone steps, was the drumming of her own heart. George had let them in, and now led the way through the sleeping house. When they reached the nursery suite, he slipped away to stand guard at the top of the main staircase.

Rackham turned to Kitty. 'Go and get Leonie.'

'Let me go in first,' Bella whispered. 'Leonie will be frightened at being woken in the middle of the night.'

Rackham shook his head. 'Kitty knows her way round the nursery, even in the dark.'

'Leonie will remember me, Bella,' Kitty whispered. 'Best do as he says.'

Rackham put his arm around Bella's shoulders. 'Trust me, Bella.'

She could feel his muscles tense, ready to spring into action, and the firm pressure of his fingers on her upper arm was oddly comforting. This time, to her own surprise, she didn't flinch or pull away.

'Keep calm,' he said softly. 'It won't be long now.'

A loud crash from inside the nursery was followed by screams. Pushing Bella aside, Rackham wrenched the door open and switched on the light. In the middle of the room, Nanny Briggs, with her nightcap askew and her eyes bleary with sleep, was clutching Leonie's arm in an attempt to wrest her from Kitty. Nanny's screams and Kitty's cries of protest were all but drowned by Leonie's angry howls. Rackham seized Nanny, pinning her arms behind her back. 'Get Leonie out of here,' he told Kitty, as Nanny kicked out at him. 'Stop struggling, woman.'

Sweeping Leonie off her feet, Kitty hefted the hysterical child over her shoulder.

Beside herself with joy mingled with fear, Bella tried to take Leonie from Kitty's arms. 'Mama is here, baby. Give her to me, Kitty.'

'Don't, Bella,' Kitty said, struggling to keep hold of Leonie. 'She's terrified and she's heavy.'

'For God's sake, just get her to the carriage,' Rackham gasped, as he struggled to restrain Nanny Briggs, who was trying to bite his hand. 'That's enough from you, madam.' Hefting her off her feet, he dumped her in the bedroom, turning the key in the lock. 'Run for it, both of you. Someone's coming.'

'Stop that noise,' Kitty commanded Leonie in a stern voice that silenced her for a minute. 'We're going on a big adventure. Hold my hand and don't let go.'

Wide-eyed and trembling, Leonie clutched Kitty's hand, casting an anxious glance at Bella.

'Do as Kitty says, my darling.' Giving Leonie a gentle push, Bella followed them out of the room, only to find Iris on the landing, barring their escape. With her hair wound up in rags and her nightgown billowing around her skinny body, she looked wild to the point of madness.

'Help,' Iris shrieked. 'Father, help! They're kidnapping Leonie.'

'Run, Kitty!' cried Bella, grabbing Iris by the sleeve. 'Run!'

'Let me go, bitch,' screamed Iris, giving Bella a hefty shove that sent her staggering backwards into Rackham's arms. Bundling her skirts above her knees, Iris tore after Kitty as she headed for the main staircase.

George stood at the top of the staircase, seemingly stunned and unable to move, as Kitty hurtled past him, clutching Leonie, closely followed by Iris with Bella and Rackham making grabs at her flailing arms. They all came to a sudden halt on the landing below, confronted by Sir Desmond, breathing heavily and purple in the face as he leaned on his cane for support.

'What the bloody hell is going on?'

'Father, Father, they're trying to take Leonie,' Iris wailed.

Sir Desmond advanced on Kitty, who dodged him and started to run down the next flight of stairs. She almost bumped into Warner, who appeared round the bend in the stairs, struggling into his dressing gown.

'I heard the commotion, Sir,' he said breathlessly. 'What's happening?'

'Kidnap, that's what's happening, Warner,' Sir Desmond said, wheezing and waving his stick wildly above his head. 'You there, George! Don't gawp like an idiot. Fetch the constable.'

Rackham lunged forward, seizing Sir Desmond by the throat. 'Let Bella have her child, you miserable bastard. Haven't you caused her enough misery?'

'Take your hands off me.' Sir Desmond's florid complexion darkened a few shades. 'This time you'll go to prison and I'll make sure that it's for life.'

'And you said you loved me.' Iris flew at Rackham, beating her fists against his back. 'You're a cad and a liar. Hanging is too good for you.'

Keeping his hold on Sir Desmond, Rackham turned his head to look at Iris with a flash of his old humour. 'Does that mean our engagement is off, my love?'

Iris leapt backwards with a scream of rage, tugging at the ring on her finger and hurling it at Rackham, catching him on the cheek. 'You swine, I hate the sight of you. How could I ever have imagined I loved you?'

A trickle of blood ran down his cheek where the diamond had cut him. 'I'm broken-hearted, my dear,' Rackham said, wiping his cheek on the back of his hand.

'You, George,' roared Sir Desmond. 'I told you to fetch the constable.'

Kitty sent him a pleading look. 'Don't do it, George.'

George hesitated, glancing nervously from Sir Desmond to Warner, who had reached the top of the stairs and was eyeing Rackham uncertainly.

'Kitty, take Leonie to the carriage,' Bella whispered. 'If we're not out in five minutes tell the cabby to take you home.'

'I'll not leave you like this,' Kitty said, attempting to pacify Leonie, who was sobbing against her shoulder.

'We're leaving, Mableton,' Rackham said, relaxing his grip so that Sir Desmond toppled against the banister. 'The child belongs with her mother and I'd advise you not to try and stop us.'

'You'll go to jail for this, Rackham,' Sir Desmond spluttered, as Warner helped him to his feet.

Iris rounded on Bella. 'You bitch. This is all your doing. You were never good enough for my father and you tried to seduce my brother. I'll make it my business to see that no one in polite society will have anything to do with you, or your ridiculous shop.'

'They'll be too busy laughing at you, Iris,' Bella retorted. 'You'll be the object of society gossipmongers, not me.'

Iris drew back her head, eyes-narrowed, hissing and poisonous. 'Do you really sell gowns or your own personal services? I always thought you were just a common whore.'

Bella leapt at Iris, her hands balled into fists. 'Take that back.'

'That's enough!' Rackham stepped between them, his face pale with fury. 'Iris, if you so much as breathe a word against Bella, I'll see to it that the name of Mableton is smeared all over the newspapers. I'm sure that everyone would love to know that Sir Desmond is a wife beater and his daughter was prepared to buy herself a husband.'

Iris threw up her hands and screamed. Sir Desmond lifted his cane and struck out at Rackham, who dodged the blow. Losing his balance, Sir Desmond stumbled, tried to save himself by clutching the handrail, and toppled headlong down the staircase. The dull thuds of his heavy body bouncing down the stairs were followed by stunned silence as everyone froze to the spot.

Iris's screams brought them back to life. Rackham was the first to move, running down the stairs to examine the crumpled body, sprawled like an ungainly puppet whose strings had been cut. Kitty and Bella followed him more slowly and Iris collapsed in hysterics at the top of the stairs.

'Fetch the doctor, George,' Rackham said, kneeling down and feeling for a heartbeat.

With an anxious glance at Mr Warner, who seemed momentarily dumbstruck, George scurried off, his footsteps echoing through the silent house.

Warner leaned against the newel post and, taking a large, cotton hankie from his pocket, he mopped his brow. 'Is he breathing, Sir?'

Shaking his head, Rackham got to his feet. 'I don't think there's anything to be done. We'll wait for the doctor.'

Wrapping her arms around Leonie, Bella cuddled the sobbing child to her breast. 'There,

there, my darling. Mama is here and I'll never, never leave you again.'

Warner cleared his throat. 'Perhaps it would be better in the circumstances if you took Miss Leonie down to the drawing room, my lady.'

Bella nodded silently, not trusting herself to speak. Her knees were shaking, and it was all she could do to stop herself from burying her face in Leonie's blonde curls and sobbing, as shock and relief surged over her in huge, drenching waves.

'Let me have her, Bella. Best to get her away from this,' Kitty said, holding her arms out to Leonie. 'Come to Kitty, darling.'

Sobbing, Leonie wrapped her arms around Kitty's neck and reluctantly, Bella let her go.

'I'll wait in the cab,' Kitty whispered, taking Leonie by the hand. 'Be brave, Bella.'

Bella made to follow Kitty as she hurried down the staircase, pushing past Warner, but a cry from the upper landing made everyone look up. Pointing an accusing finger at Bella, Iris came down the stairs, white-faced and shaking with fury. 'You murderess! You killed my father.'

Rackham moved swiftly, placing himself between Bella and Iris. 'It was an accident.'

'She killed him. Send someone for the constable, Warner.'

Warner cleared his throat with a nervous little cough. 'Begging your pardon, Miss Iris, but Sir Desmond slipped and fell. We all saw it.'

'I don't care what you say you saw.' Iris's voice rose to a screech. 'She was responsible. And she's not going to take Leonie away from her home.'

'Pull yourself together,' Rackham said, his voice cold as chipped ice. 'Warner is right. It was an accident and I think you're forgetting that Lady Mableton is Leonie's mother and legal guardian. This is still her home and I'd be careful what I said if I were you, Iris.'

'My father is dead and it's all your fault.' Iris drew herself up to her full height. 'At least show him some respect.'

'This is very distressing for you, Ma'am,' Warner said. 'Might I suggest you adjourn to the drawing room until the doctor arrives?'

'You're quite right, Warner,' Rackham said, taking Bella by the hand. 'We'll wait in the drawing room.'

Bella stared at the inert body of her husband and she was shocked to realise that she felt nothing but relief. Glancing up into Rackham's face, Bella read sympathy and understanding in his eyes and she looked away quickly.

'I'm staying with Papa,' Iris said, through clenched teeth. 'Make the most of your freedom, Giles. I promise you it won't be for long.'

Back in the safety of the house in Sackville Street, Bella went to take the sleeping Leonie from

Kitty's arms. 'Let me take her, Kitty. I want to put her down in her own little bed next to mine.'

Kitty shook her head. 'Best not waken her, poor little moppet. I'll put her to bed, but it's you she'll see when she wakes.'

Bella knew this was good sense but her arms ached to hold Leonie once again. She longed to breathe in the sweet scent of her child, who was no longer a baby but had grown, during their enforced separation, into a beautiful little girl.

Rackham laid his hand on her arm. 'Kitty is right, don't disturb the poor child.'

Bella swallowed the lump in her throat, wiping her hand across her eyes. 'I've waited so long for this moment.' She watched Kitty as she carried Leonie up the staircase, and suddenly the enormity of what had happened that evening flooded over her in a tidal wave of shock and pent-up emotion. She did not resist when Rackham put his arms around her. 'It all seems like a bad dream, Giles,' she said, resting her head against his shoulder.

'It's all over now, my pet,' Rackham said, speaking in a tone he might have used to comfort Leonie. 'You are a free woman.'

'And I have you to thank for it, Giles. I've been a bitch to you recently, and I'm truly sorry.'

Rackham lifted her chin with his finger and laid it gently across her lips to silence her. 'I've deserved most of it, my love, but at least now I've managed to make amends.'

There was something so final in his tone that Bella searched his face, trying to read his carefully guarded expression. 'What are you trying to tell me?'

His smile didn't quite reach his eyes. 'I'm going away, Bella. You don't need me any longer.'

'You're leaving?' Bella clutched his arm, fighting down an inexplicable feeling of panic. 'But you can't just go like this. Not when I've so much to thank you for.'

Rackham patted her hand, smiling ruefully. 'You don't have to thank me. I had a lot to make up for and now it's done.'

Icicles of cold fear spiked in Bella's blood. 'What are you saying?'

'It's time for us to say goodbye, my dear.'

'No, Giles. This is silly. You don't have to go.'

'Bella, my darling, you've made it plain enough over and over again that you don't want me, and I've never pressed my suit on any woman. But the sad truth is that I love you, Bella. I've always been in love with you, right from the start when you were little more than a child. I was wrong to take you as I did, but for myself I've never regretted one moment of our time together. Now I hope I've made up just a little for everything that happened in the past.'

'You love me?'

'I do love you.'

'No, you don't. You've said that to hundreds of women, including Iris. I don't believe you, Giles.'

'That's your prerogative, my dear, but I've never lied to you,' Giles said, kissing her lightly on the lips. Prising her fingers gently off his sleeve, he turned to go.

'Giles, stop! You can't go now.' Bella's lips burned from the brief caress and she clutched her hand to her mouth.

Rackham paused, shaking his head. 'There's bound to be gossip even though we've got witnesses to prove that Mableton's death was an accident. It's best for all of us if I leave the country for a while.'

'That is so stupid,' Bella cried, stamping her foot. 'You're running away, as usual, Giles, and it's not fair.'

'I don't play fair, Bella, you ought to know that. I'm a bounder, a cad, a rotter, anything you like to call me, and you are better off without me. I'm leaving for Monte Carlo first thing in the morning.'

Forcing her frozen limbs to move, Bella ran and caught him by the hand as he opened the door. 'You are none of those things, Giles. You've done all this for me and I've been hateful to you. Please, please, stay.'

Rackham's eyes were sombre. 'Do you still

love Edward Mableton? Give me an honest answer, Bella.'

Pain constricted her throat, tears burned the back of her eyes, but she couldn't lie to him; couldn't speak; couldn't even shake her head even though it might make him change his mind about leaving.

'I thought as much. Goodbye, Bella.'

The door closed and he was gone. 'No, Giles, no,' Bella cried, tears pouring down her cheeks. She wrenched the door open and ran down the steps into the quiet street. His tall figure was striding away towards Piccadilly, his opera cloak billowing out behind him. She opened her mouth to call him back, but no words came and, clutching at the iron railings, she sank down onto the steps watching until he was swallowed up by the night. Suddenly she was afraid. Afraid like the fourteen-year-old girl violated by her own father, waiting in the filthy back parlour of the pub in the Commercial Road: waiting for the man to whom she had been sold for a few golden guineas. It had never crossed her mind until this moment that she had been lucky that the man was Giles Rackham. She had not realised, until he had gone, that in some unexplainable way she had relied on the knowledge that, when she needed him most, he would be there for her. She had told him she hated him so often that she had convinced herself that it was true; but now she realised she did not hate him at all. She had wasted so much time rebelling against their relationship. She had deliberately chosen to forget that it was Giles who had taught her the delights and sensual pleasures of physical love. He had been patient and gentle with her, until she had learned to respond to his lovemaking and then, it was true, he had taken her to the heights of ecstasy and beyond. But, she thought miserably, he had never told her he loved her. She had felt lonely and abandoned when he went off on his gambling trips; the fact that he had made her stay in England for her own welfare and safety had not occurred to her then, but the truth flooded over her now in a painful revelation.

Rackham had left her financially well provided for in the hotel in Dover and, if Maria had not been down on her luck and come searching for her, Bella had to admit to herself that she would have waited for him to return. He always came back, sooner or later. Maria had encouraged her to think the worst of Rackham and the best of Sir Desmond. Still, Bella thought miserably, she could have refused to have anything to do with Maria's plans for her, but instead she had listened to her mother and followed her instructions to the letter.

Bella sighed, shaking her head. It had been the lure of financial security that had made her sell herself to a much older man. She could have said no at any time, but she did not. She could not blame Maria or Rackham; the choice had been hers and hers alone. Dragging herself to her feet, Bella wiped her eyes on her sleeve. Giles had been a part of her life for so long that she could not imagine going on forever without him. He would be back. Rackham always came back, didn't he?

There was surprisingly little furore over Desmond's death. Of course it was in the newspapers the next day, and the funeral was reported, with Miss Iris Mableton being named as the chief mourner; Captain Sir Edward Mableton, Bt. not having returned as yet from the war in South Africa. The fact that Lady Arabella Mableton, widow of Sir Desmond, was absent from her husband's funeral was not mentioned in any of the reports, and for that Bella was grateful. She wanted nothing to do with the house in Dover Street; at least not until Edward returned, and then things would be different. Now that she was widowed there was nothing to stand in their way. She was certain that he still loved her and she settled down to wait for his return.

Bella received weekly postcards from Giles – not that he wrote much by way of a message, but using the same old code they had developed years ago, he sent her a card from every town and city that he visited. She kept them, tied with a blue satin ribbon and tucked behind a teacup, on the kitchen dresser. Giles was, she had realised, her *alter ego*; his failings were her own failings, his strengths were her strengths; they were bound by invisible cords and, without a doubt, he would return one day to annoy and torment her. She had been devastated when he left but she would get over it. After all, it was Edward whom she really loved and the war could not go on forever.

In the meantime, it was pure joy to have Leonie back. At first the little girl was a bit uncertain and shy, overawed by the number of people living in the same house and a bit nervous of the other children. But, as the days went by Leonie grew in confidence and she had taken a liking to Violet, who was immediately her devoted slave. Leonie now bossed Harry around and had a fit of the sulks when it didn't work with the older boys. Maggie had really taken to Leonie and, like a mother hen, cared for her along with her own brood, relieving Bella of the dreary tasks of motherhood that, with a houseful of servants, had never been her lot.

There was only one problem brought about by her sudden state of widowhood, and that was due to the fact that Humphrey now thought of her as being his own personal property. He was becoming more and more persistent in his attentions, and his veiled suggestions that he might set her up as his mistress in an establishment of her own had become daily demands. Bella had so far managed to fend him off with smiles and vague promises but she knew that, sooner or later, she would have to refuse outright and that would not go down well with Mr Chester. She could not afford to lose her job, and possibly her home, especially now that she had Leonie's future to consider.

The letter from Feeney, Feeney and Rumbelow requesting her attendance at their Lincoln's Inn Fields offices came as a complete surprise. Maria said sarcastically that Sir Desmond had probably bequeathed her a fortune in his will, but Bella was instantly alert and terrified that the legal matter might have something to do with Leonie. What would she do if Desmond had made her a ward of court or, even worse, made Iris her legal guardian? She had no knowledge of the law and no one to consult. If only Giles were here, she thought, as she sat in the hansom cab on her way to Holborn. If there were any doubts about her right to bring up her child, she would have to take Leonie and flee the country.

The clerk did not keep her waiting this time. He showed her into Mr Feeney's office and left immediately. Mr Feeney rose from behind his desk and came round to offer her a chair.

'Please get to the point, Mr Feeney,' Bella said, nerves making her voice sharp.

'Of course, my lady. It's good of you to come to my office.' Mr Feeney cleared his throat nervously and picked up a document with a big red seal on the front. Unfolding it he cleared his throat again. 'This is your late husband's will. He altered it just a few weeks before the tragic accident. I won't read the part that doesn't concern you but –'

'Just tell me the important bits,' Bella said, praying that he couldn't see that her hands were trembling. She just wanted to know the worst and get it over with.

'I'm afraid, my lady, that you are not mentioned in the document except for the fact that you are named as the sole legal guardian of your daughter, Leonie Eugenie Mableton.'

Closing her eyes Bella was unable to prevent a sigh of relief escaping from her lips. 'Thank God.'

Mr Feeney made a sympathetic noise in his throat. 'Sir Desmond has left your daughter a considerable sum of money, the capital to be put in trust until she is twenty-five or until she marries, whichever occurs the soonest, and the interest to be used for her maintenance and education. He has also bequeathed to her Mableton Manor in Essex, although I believe the said property is in a sorry state of repair and needs a great deal doing to it to make it habitable.' He stopped and peered at Bella over the top of the document. 'Are you feeling faint, my lady? Would you like a glass of water?'

Walking towards the cabstand on Waterloo Bridge, Bella was too preoccupied with her thoughts to notice the bustling crowds around her; nor did she hear the blare of motor car horns, the clatter of horses' hooves or the cries of the street vendors. Sitting in the cab, she struggled to think of a reason why Desmond would have changed his mind and been so generous to Leonie. She knew that it was not because he had a particular fondness for their child, he had made it plain that she was just another possession. He might well have taken a sadistic delight in making Iris her guardian, so why the change of heart? Bella opened her eyes with a gasp, as the obvious truth washed over her like the 'alleluia chorus'. Edward! He was the only person, apart from Iris, whose opinion carried any sway with Desmond. Edward must have received at least one of her letters begging for his help. Dear, dear, Edward, he had quite obviously communicated in some way with his father, pleading with him to be generous and fair. Bella clasped her hands and stuffed them into her mouth to stop herself from crying out with sheer joy. It had to be Edward's way of letting her know that he still loved her.

It was just a matter of time now until Edward returned home, and then Humphrey could find himself another star. She was free to marry Edward and she would delight in telling Humphrey what to do with his offer to set her up as his mistress. She would leave London forever and take Leonie to her rightful home. Once they were set up in Mableton Manor, away from the gossip and tittle-tattle of London society, Edward could join them, and they would live together in perfect bliss. Bella wanted to shout it out at the silly sheep-like people who thronged the Strand, scream it to the lions that crouched protectively around Nelson's column in Trafalgar Square. She had the mad desire to climb up and hug the statue of Eros, the God of love, poised on his plinth in Piccadilly Circus. She was so happy that it hurt.

In the months that followed, Bella lived in a blissful world of her own; dreaming dreams of Edward's return and their own private happy ending. She had Leonie to pet and fuss over and she was top of the bill, keeping Humphrey happy with gratifying front-of-house receipts. Kitty was rapidly earning a reputation as a designer and modiste to Society's darlings and, for once, everyone in the house seemed to be getting along quite happily.

During a brief Christmas leave, Bella had even

managed to get on the right side of Jem and, when he had returned to sea, they had parted as friends. Poor Jem, she couldn't help feeling a bit sorry for him. It was obvious that he doted on Kitty, who continued to treat him like her best friend; Bella did not need a crystal ball to tell her that this was the last thing Jem wanted. Then there was George; a frequent visitor to the house in Sackville Street, who larked around with Kitty and the children and was charming to Betty and Maria, but Bella had been quick to see the devoted spaniel look in his eyes every time they rested on Kitty. Well, she had always known that Kitty would be a stunner one day. She sensed that there would be trouble before the New Year was out.

Bella had just arrived at the theatre on Sunday morning, the first day of June, for a dress rehearsal of her new act, when the call boy came rushing up to her brandishing a morning newspaper.

'Miss Lane, Miss Lane, the war is over. We've beaten them Boers. They've signed a peace treaty at a place with some foreign name what I can't say. Miss Lane, are you all right? You've gone a funny colour?'

Suddenly the ground came up to hit her.

Chapter Sixteen

'Give us a kiss, Kitty.'

'Stop it, George,' Kitty said, giving George a playful slap on the wrists. 'Not in front of the children.'

George grinned, holding his hands up in a gesture of submission. 'You can't blame a chap for trying. We have been stepping out for a while now.'

'George and Kitty are spooning,' crowed Frankie.

'Don't be vulgar, Frankie Cable,' Kitty said, attempting a frown. 'You're supposed to be helping the young 'uns with their packing. You'll be the first to complain when you get to Mableton Manor and find you've left half your things behind.'

Frankie grinned at her. 'I'd rather stay here and watch George make sheep's-eyes at you, Kitty.'

'Cheeky boy.' Kitty caught him a clout on the ear, but it was not a hard one. 'George and me are just friends.'

'Anyway, who wants to go and live in the blooming country?' Frankie mumbled, kneeling down on the attic floor, and tossing things into a tea chest. 'I don't know why Ma took it into her head to move us all to blooming Essex.'

'Mind your language, young man,' George said, sliding his hands around Kitty's waist.

'Thank you, George, but I can handle this,' Kitty said, pushing him away. 'And, Frankie, you mind your manners. You'll be the man of the house when you're living in Mableton Manor. I expect you to help your ma and not bother her with your complaining.'

Frankie rolled his eyes, but he did as he was told.

George sat down on the bed and patted the coverlet. 'Come and join me, Kitty.'

Shaking her head, Kitty began packing neatly folded piles of clothes into a cardboard suitcase. 'Haven't you got anything better to do than bother me?'

'I can wait,' George said, taking out his tobacco pouch and starting to roll a cigarette.

'No smoking up here, if you please. I don't want the house set on fire,' Kitty said, tempering the severity of her words with a wink and a smile.

'Aw, Kitty!' George protested, putting his pouch back in his pocket.

On the floor, Violet and Harry were playing with Leonie, rolling about tickling, giggling and yelping. Charlie sat cross-legged reading a book, while Billy slithered under the bed and began throwing out long-forgotten items – a lead soldier, a doll's wooden arm and some fluff-covered bullseyes.

'Nearly done,' Kitty said, struggling to close the lid. 'Give us a hand, George.'

Obligingly, George leaned across and pressed the lid down so that the locks snapped shut. 'When are they for the off?'

'Bella is taking the nippers to Liverpool Street tomorrow morning, to catch the eight thirty train for Colchester. The carter is coming for the heavy stuff this afternoon.'

'You'll miss them,' George said. 'But at least you'll have more time for me.'

'Don't you ever give up, George Jones?'

'Not until you promise to be my girl, Kitty.'

'Don't start all that again. I've got enough to do keeping things going here since Maggie and Betty went off to Essex to get the house ready. I never saw it myself, but Bella said it was in a right old state, and the housekeeper and her old man were two nasty pieces of work.'

'You can't dodge the issue forever, Kitty. I'm dead serious about you. I ain't playing the fool this time.'

Frankie glanced up and opened his mouth as if ready to jump in with a saucy remark, but he subsided beneath a fierce look from Kitty.

'This isn't the time or place.'

'It never is. I just want you to take me seriously.'

'Kitty, Kitty,' Violet said, tugging at her skirt. 'I can hear the doorbell. Maybe it's the carter.'

'Oh, heavens, there's no one downstairs to answer it.' Kitty made for the door. 'Keep an eye on the little ones, please, George.'

The knocking grew more impatient and Kitty ran down the four flights of stairs, arriving breathless and panting at the front door. Wrenching it open, she let out a shriek of delight. 'Jem!'

'Ho there, Kitty!' Jem said, his lazy grin revealing teeth that flashed white against his deeply bronzed skin. 'What took you so long? I was beginning to think you'd gone and moved house again.'

Kitty flung her arms around his neck and hugged him, laughing and crying at the same time. 'Jem, I can't believe it's you! Why didn't you let us know you were coming?'

'Hello, what's all this?' demanded George, who had come up behind them unnoticed.

Frankie pushed him aside with a whoop of glee. 'It's Jem, come home from the sea. Jem, Jem, d'you remember me?' He surged forward, followed by Billy and Charlie hurling themselves at Jem and sticking to him like burrs.

'What a welcome,' Jem chuckled. 'But it would be nice if you'd let me inside, all of you, instead of keeping me standing on the doorstep.'

'Come in do,' Kitty said, dragging Jem inside with the children still clinging to him. 'Jem, you remember George. You met him at Christmas.'

'Pleased to see you, mate,' Jem said, smiling. 'I'd shake hands if I had one free.'

Hackles raised, George remained unsmiling. 'So you're on leave again. How long before you go back to sea?'

'George!' Kitty said, nudging him in the ribs. 'What a thing to say when Jem's hardly over the threshold.'

George went red in the face. 'I was just asking.'

'Not to worry,' Jem said, equably. 'It's the same question everyone asks when you come home on leave, and the answer is, I don't know. Not as yet, anyway.' Disentangling himself from the boys, Jem swept Kitty off her feet and gave her a loud, smacking kiss on both cheeks and a more lingering one on the lips. 'You look good enough to eat, my girl.'

Making a noise something between a cough and a growl, George slipped between them, putting his arm around Kitty's shoulders. 'Hold on, there fella. Kitty is my girl now and I don't appreciate your familiarity.'

'Don't you dare speak to him like that,' Kitty said, wriggling free. 'And, anyway, I'm not your girl. I'll thank you to mind your tongue, George.'

Before George could argue or Jem get a word in, a loud cough followed by a sharp rap on the brass door knocker, made them all spin around to see the carter standing on the doorstep.

'I come to collect some boxes to go to Mableton Manor,' he said, tugging off his cap.

'What's going on, Kitty? You're not really on the move again, are you?' Jem said, plucking Billy and Charlie off his back and setting them down on the floor.

'I'll explain later,' Kitty said, beckoning to the carter.

'Is this to go, Miss?' he asked, pointing to the sea chest and ditty bag that Jem had abandoned on the front step.

'I should say not,' Jem said. 'I'll shift it out of your way, mate. Give us a hand, you lads, and you can show me up to my room.'

'It's all ready for you,' Kitty said, standing aside as the boys rushed forward, jostling each other and squabbling over which one of them would carry the most. 'Betty and me did it up special, so it would be ready for you whenever you came home.'

'It's easy to see who's favourite here,' George said, scowling. 'You've made a real fool of me today, Kitty.'

'You made a fool of yourself, acting all stupid and jealous and embarrassing me in front of Jem.'

George's colour deepened from dull red to purple. 'You and me have been stepping out for months. I thought you liked me.'

Regretting her sharp tone, Kitty slipped her hand through his arm. 'Oh, George! Of course I like you.'

'You got a funny way of showing it.'

'I'll leave you to it then,' Jem said, hoisting his ditty bag over his shoulder. 'Nice to meet you again, George. Any friend of Kitty's is a friend of mine.' He started up the staircase, holding Charlie by the hand, and grinning up at Violet, Leonie and Harry, who were peering at him through the banisters.

'You see, George,' Kitty said, with an apologetic smile. 'Jem's more like a brother to me, so naturally I'm pleased to see him.'

The carter cleared his throat and shuffled his booted feet. 'Er – Miss?'

Turning to the carter, Kitty started towards the sewing room. 'If you'd come this way, please.'

'I suppose I'd better go then?' George said, in a sulky voice.

'Just hang about a bit, George, I'll be with you in a tick,' Kitty said, opening the door to the sewing room and ushering the carter inside. 'Most of the boxes are in here and there are a couple of tea chests on the top floor.'

'Righty-ho, Miss.'

'Stay and have a cup of tea,' Kitty said, turning to George, but he had gone. 'Bother,' she said. 'Oh, bother!'

'What's up?' demanded Jem from the staircase.

'I was a bit hard on him,' Kitty said, frowning. 'He's a good sort and I'm fond of him, but George gets too serious.'

'I'll put him right for you, Kitty. Just say the word.'

'Just say the word, Kitty,' called Frankie, grinning at her through the banisters. 'I'd like to see Jem take on old ginger George.'

'You watch your tongue, young man,' Kitty said, trying not to laugh.

Behind her, the carter gave a polite cough. 'Excuse me, Miss.'

His arms were full of boxes and Kitty stepped aside to let him pass.

Jem bounded down the last few steps. 'Here, mate, let's give you a hand and we'll get it done in half the time.' He beckoned to Frankie and Billy. 'Come on, lads, make yourselves useful.'

The carter having filled his wagon and departed, Kitty settled down to make a plate of sandwiches for Jem and the children. While they were all munching, she told Jem everything that had happened during his absence. But once the food was eaten, it was impossible to have a sensible conversation. The children were bubbling over with excitement about the move and Frankie and Billy bombarded Jem with questions about his voyages. In the end, Jem solved the problem by taking them for a walk in the park with the promise of ice creams all round if they behaved themselves.

'We'll have plenty of time to chin-wag when they're in bed,' he said, winking at Kitty. 'Right then, troops. Line up, two by two, holding hands and don't break ranks. All except you, young Harry, you get the special sailor's hoist.' Hefting four-year-old Harry onto his shoulders, Jem opened the front door. 'Quick march.'

'Good Gawd, what's happened?' Maria exclaimed, yanking the long hatpin from her straw hat. 'Have you locked them dratted nippers in the cellar?'

Kitty raised her eyes from the afternoon gown that she had been finishing off. 'Jem took them to Hyde Park.'

Maria curled her lip. 'So the sailor boy has turned up again, has he? Nice of him to let us know he was coming home.'

'He could hardly send us a telegram from the ship,' Kitty said, folding the soft silk and setting it carefully aside. 'And Betty will have a lovely surprise when she comes back from Mableton Manor.'

Maria threw her hat and gloves onto the hall table. 'I dunno, we get rid of the kids and then we have a man to feed. I'm fed up with it all.'

Kitty recoiled, upset. 'That's not fair, Maria. I didn't hear you complaining about the crush in

Betty's house. You were glad enough of a roof over your head then.'

'That was then. Humpty Dumpty has made Bella an offer that she'd be mad to refuse and she won't even consider it now she knows that bloody, toffee-nosed Captain Edward is coming home. Selfish cow! We could have had our own house in Hampstead or Swiss Cottage with a couple of servants and no snotty kids messing up the place and leading Leonie astray.' Maria stomped off in the direction of the back stairs.

Incensed, Kitty followed her to the bottom of the staircase. 'Our kids are good kids and they're not snotty. Leonie loves them and they love her.'

'Leonie was born to be a lady. I don't want her brought up with a lot of street urchins.'

'Don't you dare call our kids street urchins.'

'I'm not going to argue about it,' Maria said, mounting the stairs. 'I'm going for a lie-down before we have to go back to the theatre.'

Kitty bit her lip; there was no talking to Maria when she was in one of her moods. She went back to the salon and slammed the door, leaning against it with her arms folded across her chest until the angry pumping of her heart calmed to normal. Maria was just a selfish old woman who didn't know the meaning of love and loyalty. How dare she say things about Maggie's kids?

Shaking her head, Kitty went to pick up her sewing and sat down by the window, where she had a good view of the street. She kept looking up from her work, keeping an eye open for Jem and the children, but it was Humphrey Chester's motor car that arrived first. Kitty watched as the chauffeur leapt out and opened the door for Bella. Brushing his offer of help aside, Bella sprang from the vehicle and ran up the steps. Jumping to her feet, Kitty hurried to open the front door.

One look at Bella's face told her that something was wrong.

'Bella? What is it?'

Bella pushed past Kitty, throwing her weight against the door, but with one push Humphrey sent her skittering across the tiled floor as he barged his way into the hall.

'Bella. You're behaving like a hysterical school-girl.'

Bella turned on him, her eyes flashing and two bright spots of colour staining her cheeks. 'Hasn't any woman ever said no to you before, Humphrey?'

Humphrey's expression changed subtly and he raised an eyebrow. 'Quite often, my dear, but they didn't mean it.'

'Well, I do,' Bella said, stamping her foot. 'And you should treat me with more respect. I've made a fortune for you in the past year.'

'Undoubtedly, but without me you'd still be living in that rat-infested slum.'

'I sang for the Prince and Princess of Wales when they attended one of the free dinners that the King gave for the poor to celebrate his accession,' Bella said, her voice breaking with emotion. 'I'd have sung to the King himself if he hadn't been confined to his bed after having his appendix out. If he hadn't been ill, I'm sure he'd have clapped my performance just as enthusiastically as everyone else did. They all loved me, Humphrey. They loved me.'

'So I made you a star!' Humphrey said, showing his teeth in a wolfish smile. 'I made you and I can break you too, my pet.'

'And I've made you even richer than you were before. I've turned down offers from other theatre managers, but I chose to stay with you. You can't bully me into becoming your mistress, Humphrey. I have my daughter to think about.'

Humphrey struck his silver-headed cane against his gloved hand. 'For God's sake, Bella! You know I can't marry you but I can offer you my protection.'

'And I'm supposed to be grateful for that?'

'With your reputation, my love, I think you ought to be grateful for any offer.'

Bella leapt forward, slapping him hard across the cheek. 'No man speaks to me like that. If Edward was here you wouldn't dare say such things to me.'

'This has gone far enough,' Kitty said, unable

to keep quiet a moment longer. 'You can't talk to Bella like that.'

Holding his hand to his cheek, Humphrey shook his cane in Bella's face. 'Do you really believe that Edward Mableton would have anything to do with you now? You poor stupid bitch, he'd never marry you. No respectable man will ever touch you.'

Kitty made a move towards Humphrey but Bella, now icy calm, held her back. 'I'm asking you to leave, Humphrey. Please go.'

'You are used goods, my dear Bella. Beautiful and talented but tarnished. Without me you are nothing.'

'That's not true!' Bella's voice shook, but she drew herself up to her full height.

'And you owe me money,' Humphrey said, his eyes narrowing so that they almost disappeared in the fleshy folds of his cheeks. 'Don't forget we made a bargain, Bella. You haven't repaid my capital and I'm not prepared to wait any longer.'

'You'll get your money, you dreadful man,' Kitty said, placing herself squarely in front of Bella. 'We'll pay you back every last farthing.'

'You don't care about me.' Bella's voice cracked with suppressed passion. 'If you cared about me at all you wouldn't hold me to that foolish bargain.'

'I care enough to offer you a good home,

comfort and security. What more do you want, woman?'

'I want love,' Bella cried, clasping her hands to her bosom. 'You don't know the meaning of the word.'

'Romantic rubbish. Your pretty little head is stuffed with dreams and cotton wool, but it's your body I want, my pet, not your brain.' With a half-turn towards the door, Humphrey hesitated, glaring at Bella. 'If I leave here alone your career in my theatre is finished.'

'You can't do that. I have a contract for the new show.'

'And I can cancel it just like that,' Humphrey said, snapping his fingers. 'There wouldn't be a theatre manager in the whole of London who would take you on. You'd end up singing on street corners, my pet, or running back to that scoundrel Rackham.'

'At least Giles was always honest with me.'

Humphrey threw back his head and let out a shout of laughter. 'Honest? Rackham? He used you just as the honourable Captain Mableton used you. Face up to it, my dear. You are a high-class whore.'

'You bastard.' Kitty flew at Humphrey, catching him off guard so that he stumbled and fell against the door. 'You are a disgusting, evil man. Get out of here.' Knocking his straw boater off his head, Kitty stamped on it.

For a moment she thought he was going to strike her, but Humphrey righted himself and, picking up the ruined hat, he opened the front door. 'I expect that sort of behaviour from a common little slut like you. Two sluts together – you should deal famously. I suggest you turn this establishment into a bordello. It's the only way either of you will make a living now.'

But before the last words left his mouth, Humphrey was hoisted off his feet and thrown bodily down the steps. Jem stood in the doorway, slapping his hands one against the other as if brushing off dirt. 'I don't know who you are, but you could do with a few lessons in good manners, mate.'

Kitty peered over Jem's shoulder to see Humphrey sprawling on the pavement with his chauffeur trying to help him to his feet.

'I'll have you in court for assault, you hooligan,' Humphrey shouted, shaking his fist at Jem.

'You do that,' Jem said, hitching his thumbs in his belt. 'The newspapermen would enjoy telling the public about a rich bloke who bullies helpless women.'

'I'd enjoy it too,' Kitty said, linking her arm through Jem's.

Brushing off his chauffeur's helping hands, Humphrey picked up his crushed boater, his face dark with rage. 'You'd better watch out for yourself, son. I haven't finished with you. And as for you, Madam,' he added glaring at Bella, 'your career is over.'

He climbed stiffly into his car and they watched it glide away.

'Where are the children?' Kitty said, panicking. 'You never left them all alone in the park, Jem?'

'I saw the motor car outside the house and I took 'em in the back way. They're all safe and sound eating their ice creams in the kitchen.' Shooing them inside, Jem closed the front door. 'Now, are you ladies going to tell me what the devil has been going on?'

Sitting around the kitchen table for the second time that day, drinking tea laced with generous quantities of sugar, Kitty told Jem everything, while Bella sat pale-faced and silent. Outside the children played noisily in the back yard.

Jem listened without comment until Kitty had finished. He was quiet for a moment, considering, then he turned to Bella. 'I think you did right refusing him, but can he really stop you getting work?'

Bella's hand shook and the teacup rattled as she put it back on its saucer. 'I thought he was my friend.'

'Leave her alone, Jem,' Kitty said, jumping up and flinging her arms around Bella. 'Can't you see she's had enough for one day?'

'Someone has to be practical. Can you keep this house going with what you earn from your dressmaking?'

'I can try.'

'I really wish that Giles was here,' Bella said. 'He can always see a way out of any situation.'

'He'd tell you to fight back.' Getting up from the table, Kitty went to the oak dresser, picked up the bundle of postcards and flung it on the table in front of Bella.

'What's that got to do with anything?' Jem asked, frowning.

'Mr Rackham has been sending Bella a postcard every week from wherever he travels in France and Italy.'

'Every casino and every racecourse,' Bella said, smiling as she untied the ribbon and spreading the cards out on the table. 'Giles is a hopeless gambler and he'll never change, but at least he hasn't completely forgotten me.'

Jem stared at her, running his fingers through his hair. 'Giles Rackham? But I thought you were in love with this Captain Edward, chap?'

'I am, of course I am,' Bella said, shuffling the postcards into a deck as if she were about to deal a hand. 'And he should be home any day now. After all, Lord Kitchener returned in triumph only last week.'

'He did, Jem. It's a pity you missed all the excitement,' Kitty added, momentarily forgetting their troubles and smiling at the memory. 'You should have been here to see the celebrations and the people lining the streets to cheer him on. Me and the children went to watch and wave our Union Jacks and join in the shouting. What with that, and the Coronation coming up next month, I've never seen London so festive.'

'Even so,' Bella said, her eyes lighting up, 'it can't be long before Edward comes home. That's why I wanted Leonie to be at Mableton Manor, for I'm certain he meant us to live there. At least now I'm free to go and wait for him.'

A cold hand of anxiety clutched at Kitty's stomach. 'Bella, he's been gone a long time.' She wanted to say that Captain Edward's actions were hardly those of a man deeply in love, but it would be cruel to dash poor Bella's hopes when she had been through so much.

'But everything has changed now,' Bella said, jumping to her feet. 'I'm going round to Dover Street this minute and make Iris tell me exactly when he is due home.'

Despite Kitty and Jem's combined efforts to make her change her mind, Bella refused to listen and only reluctantly allowed Kitty to accompany her to Dover Street. Waiting outside the front door and listening to approaching footsteps echoing around the vast entrance hall, Kitty felt a strange sense of foreboding. Warner opened the door and a momentary flicker of astonishment crossed his set features.

Bella sailed past him, dragging Kitty by the hand. 'Good afternoon, Warner. Is Miss Mableton at home?'

Seeing George standing to attention in the background, Kitty smiled at him, but he looked away. Kitty suppressed a sigh. She was fond of George and she had enjoyed his company; they had been friends for a long time, but he had wanted more than she could give. A pang of guilt shafted through her heart; she had not deliberately led him on, but his hurt expression made her feel terrible. She would have to make things right with him.

'I'll see if Miss Mableton is receiving visitors, my lady,' Warner said, looking down his nose.

'I'll ask her myself.' Without waiting for his reply, Bella made for the drawing room, followed by Kitty.

'Please, my lady.' Warner came hurrying after them, an anxious note creeping into his voice. 'Allow me to speak to the mistress first.'

But Bella had already flung the double doors open and marched into the room. If Kitty had not been so anxious, she might have laughed at the comical expression of horror on Iris's face as she leapt up from the sofa, scattering fashion magazines onto the Persian carpet.

'What is the meaning of this?' Iris cried.

'Warner, how dare you allow this person into my house?'

'Don't blame Warner,' Bella said, ice cold. 'And it isn't your house, Iris. It belongs to Edward.'

'Get out of here.' Iris's voice rose to a screech. 'Leave immediately or I'll have Warner call for a constable.'

Glancing over her shoulder, Kitty could see George peering into the room, with Dora and Olive hovering behind him. She went to the door, closing it and shutting them out.

'Sit down, Iris and stop being melodramatic,' Bella said, maintaining her calm. 'I only want a moment of your time, and then I'll leave, and I'll never set foot in this accursed house again.'

Iris sat down suddenly, her flat chest heaving above her tightly laced corsets. 'What do you want?'

'I want to know when Edward is expected home. Just that and then I'll go.'

Warner gave a small cough and made a move towards the door. 'Shall I go for the constable, Miss Mableton?'

Kitty leaned against the door folding her arms. He would have to lift her bodily out of the way if he wanted to call for help. But strangely, a slow smile had spread across Iris's face and she began to laugh.

'You poor, stupid bitch. I heard that Rackham had deserted you again.'

Kitty wasn't going to stand for that. 'He had to leave the country because of you, Miss Iris.'

'Just answer my question, Iris.' Bella's voice shook but she did not move a muscle.

Iris's smile widened and her eyes flashed with malicious pleasure. 'All right, I'll tell you. Edward will be arriving home next Tuesday and bringing with him his new wife. A beautiful and virtuous young lady, by all accounts, and extremely wealthy too. I believe they are idyllically happy together – why, Bella, aren't you feeling quite well?'

The colour had drained from Bella's face and, seeing her swaying on her feet, Kitty leapt forward to support her. 'She's lying, Bella.'

'Not so high and mighty now, are you?' With a disdainful snort, Iris turned to Warner. 'Get them out of here. Throw them out on the street, where they belong.'

Warner strode to the door and, as he flung it open, George and the maids almost fell into the room. Choosing to ignore their misdemeanour, Warner stood aside. 'Show Lady Mableton to the door, George.'

Between them, Kitty and George helped Bella through the entrance hall to the vestibule. 'Thank you, George,' Kitty said, softly so that Warner could not hear. 'And I'm truly sorry if I hurt your feelings.'

'It felt like you've been stringing me along.'

'No, no, I'm really fond of you, George. I just can't –'

'Get back to your duties, George.' Warner's voice echoed around the marble columns.

George jumped to attention. 'Yes, Mr Warner.'

The door closed and they were alone in the street.

'Oh, Kitty,' sobbed Bella. 'What shall I do? What shall I do?'

Chapter Seventeen

Kitty sat at the table in the salon, with a blank sheet of paper in front of her, making a huge effort to focus her efforts on a design for a ball gown for the coming out of Mrs Harrison-Cholmondley's plump, and painfully plain daughter. Picturing the unfortunate Mabel in her mind only made matters worse; it would have been easier to design a gown for a pig. She sighed heavily. Ideas simply wouldn't come and, throwing the pencil down, Kitty rose to her feet and went to smooth the folds of the blue silk ball gown that lay draped across a chair, ready for collection. It had taken hours of intensive labour to finish off the complicated design, with yards of lace-trimmed frills and intricate embroidery. Kitty frowned as she laid the garment back on the chair; there were two more ball gowns waiting to be finished off, that had to be ready before the first week in August and the King's Coronation but, without Maria's nimble fingers, it was going to be nigh on impossible to complete them on time, if at all. It seemed that the whole of London was in a festive mood, celebrating the great event, and yet the house in Sackville Street lay beneath its own dark cloud.

Filled with restless energy, Kitty paced over to the window, pressing her forehead against the cool glass. The silence of the house seemed to close in on her. She had not realised, until they had gone, how much she would miss the noisy presence of the children. At this moment she would even have welcomed the sound of Maggie and Maria bickering in the kitchen or Betty's constant, cheery chatter, as she worked away on the treadle machine in the sewing room. Dear, brave Betty, who missed Jem and still mourned for Polly, but never complained or made others feel uncomfortable with her grieving.

Then there was Bella who, after days of moping and indecision, had decided to join Leonie at Mableton Manor. Kitty sighed, thinking of the sleepless nights she had spent, lying in her bed and listening to Bella's muffled sobs from the room above her own. Poor Bella, she thought sadly, so beautiful and talented and yet so unlucky in love.

There had been a fierce argument during breakfast with Maria and Bella screaming at each other. Maria had wanted Bella to stay in London and make it up with Mr Chester but Bella had refused, saying she would rather die. In the end, Maria had come round a bit and had packed her bags, insisting that she would not let Bella travel to the wilds of Essex on her own. Although, Kitty thought, Maria was probably only going so that she could have another try at persuading Bella to take up Mr Chester's offer of protection. Maria quite definitely had her sights set on a quiet life in a cosy suburban villa. Kitty hoped fervently that, this time, Bella would have the strength to stand up to her mother.

Jem had left the house before breakfast, without saying where he was going. Kitty chewed the end of her finger and frowned. Although he had seemed to be his usual, cheery self, there had been a certain reserve between them since he came home on leave. He had seemed preoccupied and, with so much going on in the house, there had not been an opportunity for a proper talk. For the first time in her life, Kitty didn't know what was going on in his head and this scared her, but she couldn't blame him for wanting to get out of a house full of arguing women.

Jem had sent his mother a telegram announcing his arrival and Betty had replied by return, promising to come home as soon as she could leave Mableton Manor, but the old house had been in such a filthy state that it was taking much longer to make it habitable than she had anticipated. Although it would be lovely to have Betty back home, Kitty dreaded telling her that, without Bella's financial help, they would be unable to afford the rent on the house in

Sackville Street. They would have to move to a less salubrious area, maybe Highgate, Bloomsbury or even Islington, and begin all over again.

With a determined lift of her chin, Kitty walked out of the salon, closing the door behind her. This was just a hiccup, a temporary setback; she would not give in to despair. After all, she was young, she was fit and strong, not afraid of hard work, and she must look after Betty, who had taken her in and cared for her when she had fled from Sugar Yard. Her stomach rumbled, reminding her that she had not eaten anything since the previous evening and now it was past midday. No wonder she felt weak and weepy. All she needed was some food and a cup of tea and then everything would look a lot brighter. She was just about to go down to the kitchen when the front door opened and Bella walked in.

'Bella! I thought you were going to Mableton Manor.'

'I couldn't do it,' Bella said, stooping to pick up the morning post that lay strewn all over the doormat. 'When it came to it I just couldn't face going back to that awful house.'

'But why? I thought you wanted to go for Leonie's sake.'

'I do – I mean I did. I stood on the platform with Mother and then, as the steam engine came chugging towards us, I knew that I couldn't do it. I couldn't bury myself in that hateful house, with all the ghastly memories, and I'd die of boredom if I had to live in the country.'

'But, Bella, you've waited all this time to be with Leonie. You can't mean to throw that away just because you have bad memories of Mableton Manor?'

'Of course I want to be with Leonie and I will, when the time is right.'

'I don't understand what's going on. Where is Maria?'

Bella waved her hands vaguely. 'She caught the train. She said she would look after Leonie until I was settled.'

'So you've decided to make it up with Mr Chester?'

'Never! Not in a million years.'

'But, Bella, he'll see to it that you can't get work in London, he said so.'

'Leave me alone. I know what I'm doing.' Bella stalked past Kitty and ran up the stairs, still clutching the bundle of letters.

Kitty stood watching her, too shocked to move, until a hot wave of anger washed over her. Selfish, she thought bitterly, selfish Bella, acting as usual out of self-interest, without a thought of how they were going to live, or for Leonie's welfare. Kitty raced up the stairs, following Bella into the sitting room and slamming the door behind her.

'Just what do you think you're doing?'

Standing in front of the wall mirror, Bella yanked the pin from her hat, turning her head with a look of blank surprise. 'What's the matter, Kitty? I thought you'd be pleased to see me.'

'Pleased? For goodness' sake, stop and think what you're doing for once.'

Bella's lovely mouth drooped and trembled like a sad baby. 'Don't talk to me like that, it's not fair after everything I've been through.'

Kitty threw up her hands. 'You, you, you! It's all you, isn't it? You never stop to think that there are other people in the world.'

'That's so cruel,' Bella said, her blue eyes swimming in tears. 'I'm always doing things for other people and now I'm going to do something for myself.'

Glaring at her, Kitty felt her rage evaporating. Bella was impossibly selfish, but there was not an ounce of malice in her whole body. 'Please don't cry.'

Bella sniffed and swallowed. 'I'm not crying and I do think about other people.'

'All right, forget what I said.'

'I've made up my mind, Kitty. I know what I have to do now and no one is going to stop me.'

Kitty sank down on the sofa. 'I'm listening.'

Bella gave her a brilliant smile, blinking away the tears that trembled on her long eyelashes. 'I lay awake all night thinking things over and I realise now that I was just living a dream thinking that Edward still loved me. I think I always knew, deep down in my heart, that he wouldn't have gone away if he'd truly cared for me.'

'I expect you're right,' Kitty said, watching Bella riffling through the post, tossing letter and circulars on the floor as she searched for something.

'I knew it would have arrived.' With an exultant cry, Bella held up a postcard. 'There's always a card from Giles on a Wednesday. Do you see what's on it?'

Squinting at the sepia tint, Kitty nodded. 'It's a windmill.'

'It's the Moulin Rouge, a famous nightclub in Paris. Giles told me all about it and he made it sound so exciting that I've always longed to see it for myself. He promised me that one day I would sing and dance there in the cabaret.'

'Sorry,' Kitty said, shaking her head. 'I don't understand.'

'This postcard, it's his way of telling me that he's in Paris. Giles doesn't waste time with words.'

'Surely you're not . . .' Kitty stared at Bella, shocked. 'You wouldn't?'

Clasping the postcard to her bosom, Bella perched on the arm of the sofa, her eyes shining. 'Giles is the only man who has never let me down. I know he's a gambler and a rogue, but he's always loved me, Kitty. He loves me.'

'Are you sure of that? You're not just upset because of Edward Mableton marrying some heiress?'

'Giles rescued me from a life of poverty and debauchery. He was good to me, only I was too young to realise it at the time. I'd never have left him if it hadn't been for Maria.'

'But Bella, she is your mother, maybe she had your best interests at heart.'

'She left me with my brute of a father when I was only twelve. She only came back when her fancy man deserted her, and by that time, I was living with Giles. Well, to be more exact, I was alone in the hotel in Dover waiting for him to come back from Paris. I'd never have left if she hadn't persuaded me that it was the right thing to do.'

'But you said he abandoned you.'

'Not quite, I may have exaggerated a bit.' Bella rose to her feet, pacing the room. 'He went to Paris for a special card game, leaving me in a hotel in Dover. He said it wasn't the proper place to take a young woman.' Bella sighed, clasping her hands to her breast. 'But I wanted to go to Paris and I hated being left on my own. I was really, really furious with him for leaving me behind.'

'It sounds as though he did it for the best,' Kitty said, grudgingly.

'I didn't think of that at the time. Anyway, Maria arrived at the hotel. She'd been searching for me for weeks, or so she said. She had no money and I was sorry for her, so I got her a room next to mine.'

'And then?' prompted Kitty, as Bella seemed to go off into some sort of daydream.

'It was there that I met Desmond. He courted me with champagne, flowers and expensive gifts. Maria persuaded me that Giles had deserted me and wouldn't be coming back.'

'But you'd promised to wait for Rackham. Didn't that matter to you?'

'My head was turned by Desmond's attentions and Maria insisted that I would never do better. It was her idea that she pretended to be my maid, making out that I was a respectable young woman abandoned by a feckless fiancé. When Desmond proposed, she said I would be mad and wicked not to accept him. I was young and foolish, Kitty, but I'm neither young nor foolish now. If I'm to be any man's mistress then it's going to be the man I truly love.'

'You love Rackham? But you always said you hated him.'

'Love and hate – they're not much different, Kitty. Sometimes I do hate Giles, but at other times he's the most exciting man I've ever met. He's never intentionally cruel and he's never dull.' Bella's eyes shone and a pink blush tinted her pale cheeks. 'I do love him and I'm going to find him and tell him so.'

Kitty angled her head, her mind racing. 'You can't intend to go to Paris on your own?'

'Indeed I can and I will.'

'And abandon Leonie? I can't believe you would do that.'

'I'm not abandoning her. Don't say that. Leonie is with people who love her and will look after her. Maybe I'm a bad mother, but I need to be loved. I need Giles.'

'He might have changed his mind.'

'For all his faults, and I admit they are many, Giles is loyal and I trust him.' Bella swooped on Kitty and seized her by both hands, holding her gaze with a piercing look. 'Loyalty and trust are the two most important things in a relationship. I have that with Giles and I believe you have that with your Jem. Don't throw it all away as I almost did, Kitty. Don't throw it away.'

Bella went to her room to pack her belongings and Kitty couldn't wait for Jem to come home to confide her anxieties in him.

It was late in the evening and Bella, who said she was completely exhausted, but more than ever determined to travel to Paris next day, had gone to bed. When she heard Jem's key in the lock, Kitty flew out of the sitting room, running down the stairs to meet him, pouring out half of the

417

story before he had even had time to hang up his hat.

Finishing the telling over mugs of cocoa in the kitchen, Kitty waited for Jem to agree with her but he merely shook his head.

'It's her life, she must do what she thinks best.'

'Jem, you can't let her travel abroad on her own.'

Cocking his head on one side, Jem raised his eyebrows and grinned. 'I think she's perfectly capable of looking after herself.'

'Something awful could happen to her.'

'Not much worse than being forced to live as a kept woman with old Chester, I shouldn't think.'

'How can you be so heartless?'

Reaching across the table, Jem grasped her hand in his. 'There's only one girl I care about Kitty, and you know who that is.'

Kitty snatched her hand away, unable to control the blush rising to her cheeks as she met his intense gaze. 'Don't start all that again. I can't think about that now.'

'Say you don't care about me and I'll shut up and not mention it again.'

Fingering the chain around her neck, Kitty dropped her gaze. This wasn't how she had imagined the scene when she finally admitted her deep feelings for Jem and she was suddenly nervous and shy. 'I don't want to talk about it.'

Gently, Jem hooked his finger around the chain, revealing the half-sovereign, and held it in the palm of his hand. 'You still wear this, though.'

The warmth of his hand so close to her skin made Kitty's heart beat just a bit faster and her cheeks stung with the heat. 'Of course I do,' she said, attempting to pass it off with a laugh that sounded false even to her own ears.

'You needn't be scared of me.'

Kitty couldn't meet his gaze. She knew what he said was true, and she did trust him, but the thought of being intimate with any man brought back memories of Sid and his vicious assaults. Her feelings for Jem were a puzzle in her head that never quite fitted together; he was the other piece of the gold sovereign that, with her half, made one. He had been part of her life for as long as she could remember and Jem had his special place in her heart, but that might all be destroyed and lost forever if she could not get the grisly phantom of Sid out of her mind. Jumping to her feet, she turned away, covering her hot cheeks with her hands, shaking her head. 'I know that, and I'm not scared of you. I do care about you, Jem.'

'Enough to tell me what's really bothering you?'

'I don't know what you're talking about.'

'Yes you do,' Jem insisted, jumping up and taking hold of Kitty by the shoulders. 'And it don't take a genius to work it out. You can't afford to keep this place on without Bella's money, now can you?'

'Oh! That!' Fearing that he had read her thoughts, Kitty could have cried with relief. 'It's my problem, not yours.'

'If it concerns you and my old lady, then it's my problem as well.' Jem shook her gently. 'Look at me, Kitty.'

Reluctantly, Kitty looked up into his candid blue eyes.

'Now I'll tell you what I've had in mind ever since I found out that Ma lost her home. I'm coming ashore for good and I'm going to take care of you both.'

Kitty gasped as the full force of what he had said hit her like a slap in the face. 'But, Jem, you can't do that. The sea is your life.'

'I want you to be my life, Kitty. I've seen the way George looks at you and, even if you don't care for him, there'll be other men who'll make a try for you. I won't leave you to struggle on your own. I love you, Kitty.'

Her thoughts reeling, Kitty stared at Jem, seeing for the first time, the man and not the boy. 'I don't want anyone else. I never promised George anything. I do care about you, Jem.'

'I want more than that, and I'm not going away again and risk losing you,' Jem said, holding her so tightly that she could scarcely catch her breath. 'I know you love me, deep down; I just want you to face up to it and we can work the rest out together.'

'You'd give up your dreams for me?'

'And what about your dreams? You've spent all your time looking after everyone else and I'm not going to stand by and see you lose everything you've worked so damned hard to get.'

Looking deeply into her eyes, Jem took her in his arms, claiming her mouth with a kiss that sent Kitty's senses soaring out of control. For a moment, she tried to push him away, but his embrace was steel, softly padded with velvet, his lips demanding and yet tender. Giving way to the firestorm of sweet sensation flowing through her veins, Kitty closed her eyes and the taste of him was sweet as pineapple; the scent of him was musk and Christmas spice. Jem's lean body was hard, as hers was soft and pliable.

Then panic set in and she struggled, pushing him away. 'I – I can't, Jem. I'm sorry.'

'It's all right, Kitty. I understand.'

Hardly able to look him in the eyes, Kitty shook her head. 'You deserve more than I can give you, Jem.'

Stroking her hair back from her forehead, Jem's generous mouth curved into a smile. 'Don't fret, Kitty. I know what you been through and I swear that when the time comes for me to love you properly, as a man should, you'll not be afraid and you'll not be disappointed.'

'I don't know what to say.'

'I know, girl.' With his arm around her shoulders, Jem gave her a hug. 'We'll be all right you and me, Kitty. We'll face it all together and we'll come through because I love you.'

Next morning Bella was up before Kitty, and had somehow managed to drag her portmanteau and travelling trunk down three flights of stairs to the hall. She was standing by the mirror, fixing her bonnet, when Kitty came down the stairs.

'So you're going then?'

Bella flashed her a smile. 'I'll be in Paris this evening.'

'What will I tell Leonie? She's six years old, she's not a baby any more.'

'Tell her I love her and I will come back for her one day.'

'Won't you reconsider? Oughtn't you to send Rackham a telegram or something to make sure he's still there?'

'I've often stayed in Paris with Giles and he always uses the same hotel. I know he'll be there.'

Kitty glanced up as Jem came down the stairs behind her. 'Jem, make her see sense.'

'I think Bella knows what she's doing.'

'You could help me find a cab,' Bella said, pulling on her gloves.

'I'll do better than that,' Jem said. 'Kitty and me

will come to Victoria with you and see you off on the boat train.'

'We will?' Kitty folded her arms across her chest. 'You ought to be stopping her, not encouraging her in this wild goose chase.'

Jem brushed her cheek with the tip of his finger, smiling into her eyes. 'You and me have a bit of business to do after we've seen Bella off.'

'What are you talking about?'

'Wait and see.'

Kitty had to bite back tears as the train pulled out of Victoria Station. If anything happened to Bella she knew she would never forgive herself, and she prayed silently that Giles Rackham would prove to be as true as Bella believed him to be. Although she was appalled by Bella's selfishness and her callous indifference to Leonie's feelings, Kitty could not entirely blame Bella, who had been abandoned by all those she loved and trusted: first Maria, then Rackham, Desmond and now Edward. Beautiful, kind and selfish Bella. Kitty saw her suddenly as a child yearning to be loved. They had been through so much together that they had become as close as any sisters, and saying goodbye hurt.

She gripped Jem's hand and he gave it a comforting squeeze, silently passing her his handkerchief. Wiping her eyes, Kitty allowed Jem to steer her out of the station to the hackney carriage stand. Having settled her inside, Jem gave instructions to the driver and leapt in beside her. The cabbie urged his horse out into the street, which was choked almost to a standstill with horse-drawn vehicles, motor cars and omnibuses.

'Where are we going?' demanded Kitty. 'Why all the mystery?'

Jem sat back against the squabs and grinned. 'There's someone I want you to meet, Kitty.'

The streets of Knightsbridge were unfamiliar to Kitty, but in the end she gave up trying to get Jem to tell her where they were headed, and sat back to enjoy the view. The cab went at a spanking pace along Buckingham Palace Road, turning onto the Embankment, heading west towards Chelsea. Finally the cab drew to a halt outside a terraced Georgian townhouse.

Jem leapt out, paid the cabbie, and held up his hand to help Kitty onto the pavement. 'You're going to meet the man who's been the making of me,' Jem said, rapping on the brass lion's-head door knocker. 'Captain Madison, who's been like a second father to me.'

Moments later, the door was opened by a plump, pleasant-faced woman, dressed in mourning black.

'We're not too early, I hope, Mrs Weston,' Jem said, dragging off his cap.

'No, indeed. Come inside.' Nodding and smiling at Kitty, Mrs Weston held the door open.

They were shown into the front parlour that was simply, but comfortably, furnished with dark furniture and heavy green velvet curtains at the tall windows. It was, Kitty thought, looking around, a distinctly masculine room. The walls were covered with pictures of sailing ships and, jostling together on every available surface, there were curios from foreign parts. On the mantelshelf there was a startling array of clocks, all telling different times. Before she could ask Jem the reason for such an apparently mad display of time telling, the door opened and a thin, slightly built man with grey hair and whiskers entered. He clapped his hands on Jem's shoulders in a rough mannish form of embrace and turned to Kitty with a beaming smile. His shrewd, grey eyes crinkled at the corners and Kitty found herself smiling back.

'So this is the young lady you've told me so much about, Jem.'

'Yes, Sir,' Jem said, proudly. 'This here is Kitty Cox. The prettiest girl in London.'

Jem hooked his arm around Kitty's shoulders. 'And this, Kitty, is Captain Jasper Madison.'

Instinctively, Kitty bobbed a curtsey, but the captain took her by the hand and gave it a squeeze that made her bones creak. 'I'm delighted to meet you at last, Kitty.'

'Me, too,' Kitty said. 'I'm pleased to meet you, Sir.'

Captain Madison took a seat in a big leather chair by the fire. 'Well, sit down! Sit down, both of you. Make yourselves at home. Mrs Weston will be bringing us some tea and, if we're very lucky, some of her delicious seed cake.'

Kitty settled herself on the edge of the sofa, folding her hands in her lap. 'Has the poor lady lost someone close to her, Sir?'

Captain Madison looked puzzled for a moment and then he slapped his hands on his knees, chuckling. 'My good Sophia has worn black ever since the accident at sea that took the life of her husband more than twenty years ago. D'you know, Kitty, I don't think I've ever seen her wearing anything else, not in all those years.'

Encouraged by his twinkling smile, Kitty pointed to the clocks. 'They're all wrong, Sir, except one.'

'They show the time in New York, Tokyo, Auckland, Hong Kong and Bombay,' Jem said, standing with his back to the fire. 'For instance, if you think about Auckland, it's the middle of the night there.'

'Well, I never did!' Kitty stared at the clocks in amazement.

'I've heard so much about you, Kitty,' Captain Madison said, smiling. 'And Jem didn't exaggerate a bit.'

Kitty was saved from answering by Mrs Weston bustling in with a tray loaded with tea and cake. 'There,' she said, smiling at Kitty. 'You can be mother, dear. Just ring the bell if you need any more hot water.' She whisked herself out of the room, closing the door behind her.

'I've explained everything to the cap'n,' Jem said, taking the cup of tea from Kitty and passing it to Captain Madison. 'I'm not going back to the ship.'

'Tell him he's making a big mistake,' Kitty said, casting an appealing look at the captain. 'Tell him, Sir.'

Captain Madison shook his head, sipped his tea and then replaced the cup firmly on its saucer. 'Jem came to see me yesterday and we had a long talk. I've been thinking about it all night.'

'I knew you'd come up with some good advice,' Jem said, flinging himself down on the sofa beside Kitty. He snatched her hand and held it in a vice-like grip. 'You just listen to what the captain has to say, Kitty.'

Captain Madison's eyes twinkled but his lips curled in a rueful smile. 'I'm not the oracle, Jem. Tell me one thing. How do you propose to earn a living if you leave the shipping company?'

Jem's grip on Kitty's fingers tightened. 'There's plenty of work down at the docks, Cap'n. I started as apprentice lighterman when I left school. I can always go back to that.'

'No, Jem.' Kitty pulled her hand free. 'You've

got a future in the merchant navy. I'll not let you throw it away.'

'But, Kitty –'

'Just a minute.' Captain Madison rose to his feet, took a tobacco jar from the mantelshelf and a pipe from a wooden rack, before settling himself back in his chair. 'There are some men who are born to the sea; salt water runs in their veins and the moment they feel the swell of the ocean beneath the keel they can put life ashore out of their heads. But for others, being separated from their loved ones and being far from the sight of land is a constant misery. Jem's father and I were men of the first sort. Jem is the latter.'

'That's true, Sir,' Jem said, nodding. 'I thought as how I could follow in my father's footsteps, but I've done all the adventuring I want to. Now I want a home and a family and I'm prepared to work hard for it.'

Captain Madison lit his pipe, puffing clouds of blue smoke up the chimney. 'Then listen to what I have to say.'

'I'm listening, Sir.'

'My next trip is to be my last. I'm an old man and I don't mind admitting it. My seafaring days are behind me, but the thought of endless landlocked days have made me carry on at sea longer than I'd intended. I've no family of my own and no wife to share my sunset days.'

Jem jumped to his feet. 'Don't talk like that, Sir.'

Captain Madison smiled, gripping his pipe between his teeth. 'Don't worry, lad. I hope I've got a few more years before I die and I don't intend to waste them. I've got a tidy nest egg put aside and, with my bonus for this last trip to New Zealand, I plan to buy a craft that can be converted into a pleasure boat. There's money to be made taking day-trippers up and down the river, but I can't do it on my own. That's where you come in, Jem.'

'Me, Sir?'

'We'll need to search out a suitable vessel, have it made ready and then I'll need a man I can trust to skipper it. I'll handle the business side of things but I'll teach you how to take over and run it on your own, for when the day comes that I can't do it any longer.'

Jem ran his fingers through his cropped hair. 'I don't know what to say, Sir.'

'There's one condition.' Captain Madison took the pipe from his mouth. 'That is that you sail with me, as second mate, on my final voyage.'

'But, Sir . . .' protested Jem.

'It's part of the bargain,' Captain Madison said, tapping the contents of his pipe into the fire and refilling it from the tobacco jar. 'You'll earn a bonus and you'll study for your skipper's certificate while you're at sea. We'll do this thing properly, or not at all.'

'My mother and Kitty need me at home,

Cap'n,' Jem said, pacing the floor. 'I can't go away and leave them homeless.'

Kitty jumped to her feet. 'What a lot of nonsense you talk, Jem Scully. Here's the captain offering you the chance of a lifetime and you're worrying about details. Betty and me will be fine. Don't you worry about us.'

'You're a remarkable young woman, Kitty,' Captain Madison said, getting up and holding out his hand. 'Jem is a lucky young fellow to have a girl like you.'

Jem and Kitty argued all the way home in the hackney carriage. Jem insisted that he was not going back to sea unless he saw Kitty and his mother settled and secure. Kitty told him that he would be a fool to pass up such an offer from a man whom he admitted had been a second father to him, and didn't he owe the captain something for the way he had looked after him during his years at sea? They were still squabbling like a pair of starlings when they entered the house in Sackville Street.

The salon door opened and Betty rushed into the hall. 'Jem! Kitty! I could hear your raised voices outside in the street. What will the neighbours think?'

Jem and Kitty looked at each other and burst out laughing.

'What's so funny?' demanded Betty, offended.

Jem flung his arms around her. 'It's so good to see you, Ma. I've missed you.'

'And I've missed you too, son,' Betty said, smiling and returning his embrace. 'But I don't understand what was so funny.'

'Just us being silly,' Kitty said, suppressing a grin as the tension leached from her body. Worrying about what the neighbours might think seemed so trivial compared to the huge decisions that they had to make, with their future hanging in the balance, but sharing the humour of it with Jem had eased the situation between them. There would be plenty of time to explain everything to Betty later, when they were on their own. In the meantime, she had something to do that simply couldn't wait another day.

'Where are you going?' demanded Jem, as Kitty made for the door.

'There's something I must put right. Someone who was a good friend to me and whose feelings I hurt, though I never intended it that way. You enjoy a quiet time with your ma. I won't be long.'

Florrie opened the door to the servants' entrance. 'Kitty!'

'I must see George,' Kitty said, putting her foot over the threshold. 'Is he about?'

'I daresn't let you in. Miss Iris has given orders that none of us is to have anything to do with

Lady Mableton's household and that includes you.' Florrie glanced nervously over her shoulder.

'Please, Florrie. I must see George. I promise I won't stay more than a minute or two.'

Florrie bit her lip, frowning and shaking her head. 'I can't.'

'All right then, just close your eyes, count to ten and then forget you ever saw me.'

Florrie pulled a face, but she closed her eyes and stood aside.

'Ta, Florrie,' Kitty said, brushing past her. 'You're a brick.'

Avoiding the kitchen and running up the back stairs, Kitty made her way to the entrance hall. She came to an abrupt halt, hiding behind a pillar as she heard Mr Warner's voice giving instructions and George's monosyllabic replies. Then Mr Warner's brisk footsteps crossed the marble floor and she heard the faint sigh of the hinges on the green baize door leading down to the servants' quarters and kitchens. Peeping round the corner, she saw George on his own, polishing the brass door furniture.

'George.'

He spun around, dropping the polishing rag, his face crumpled in shock. 'Kitty! What the bleeding hell are you doing here?'

Kitty stooped to pick up the rag and handed it to George with an apologetic smile. 'I had to see you, George. I couldn't let things end between us in a bad sort of way.'

George grabbed the rag, scrunching it up in a ball. 'You made a proper fool out of me.'

'No, George. I didn't. We were just friends, I told you, and told you that it couldn't be any more than that, you just didn't believe me.'

'Well,' George said, rubbing hard at the brass door handle. 'I believe you now.'

Kitty watched him for a moment, desperately trying to find the words that would comfort him, salve his hurt pride; for hurt pride was all it was, she was certain of that. 'You're a fine, honest man, George. You deserve someone better than me.'

George stopped what he was doing and straightened up, facing Kitty and looking her in the eye. 'I deserve better than the way you treated me, Kitty. You should have told me that there was someone else, right from the start.'

Kitty laid her hand on his arm. 'I didn't know it myself until now. I'm so sorry, George.'

George opened his mouth but, before he could speak, the sound of horses' hooves and carriage wheels made him open the door and look outside. 'My God. It's Captain Edward and his new bride. We weren't expecting them until tomorrow. Get out quick, before they see you.'

Chapter Eighteen

Kitty started towards the back staircase, hesitating as Mr Warner came striding towards her from the direction of the servants' quarters. The expression on his face was enough to make her dash for the front entrance, where George stood, stiff-necked and red in the face, holding the door open for the new arrivals. Darting past him, Kitty caught her heel in the hem of her skirt, stumbling over the top step. She regained her balance but landed awkwardly on her right ankle, which gave way beneath her, sending her tumbling down the remaining steps straight into the arms of Captain Sir Edward Mableton.

Warner strode down the steps, his face blank with outrage. 'Begging your pardon, Sir Edward. This young person has no right to be here.'

Edward set Kitty back on her feet. 'It's all right, Warner. It was an accident.'

'I'm sorry, Sir,' Kitty gasped, momentarily winded. 'Please, Captain Edward, don't blame George. It was all my fault, Sir.'

Edward stared at her for a moment, and then

his handsome features melted into a charming smile. 'Why, it's Kitty Cox, isn't it?'

Kitty bobbed a curtsey.

'Edward, I'm waiting.' A stern voice emanating from the carriage made everyone turn to look at Edward's new wife, whose expression showed that she did not appreciate being kept waiting.

'Don't run away, Kitty,' Edward said, in a low voice. 'Just coming, Adeline, my sweet.'

Kitty hesitated, eyeing Mr Warner; she could see that he was inwardly seething with indignation, but he would not question an order from the master of the house and he stood to attention, staring straight ahead of him.

'Warner will show you into the drawing room, my dear,' Edward said, handing Adeline from the carriage. 'I'll be with you in a moment.'

Adeline paused, giving Kitty an appraising look. 'Don't be long, Edward.' She picked up her skirts and followed Warner up the steps.

'Why have you come here, Kitty?' demanded Edward, when his wife was out of earshot. 'Did Bella send you?'

'No, Sir. It was all my idea.'

'But she is all right, isn't she?'

'I hope so, Sir.'

'What do you mean?' Edward seized Kitty by the shoulders, staring intently into her face. 'Don't you know?'

'Bella left for France this morning, Captain Edward. She's gone to find Mr Rackham.'

'Oh my God, no!' Edward paled alarmingly beneath his suntan. 'I can't believe that she's turned to that libertine.'

'Begging your pardon, Sir,' Kitty said, stung by his attitude. 'But what did you expect? She was really cast down when she heard you'd gone and got yourself married.'

'I thought she would go to Mableton Manor with Leonie.' Edward brushed his hand across his eyes and his voice shook with emotion. 'I wrote to my father entreating him show a little compassion for a mother's heart and to allow Bella to have custody of Leonie. I wanted to look after Bella and her child in the only way I knew how and I begged him not to deprive Leonie of her rightful inheritance.'

Warner reappeared at the top of the steps, coughing discreetly. 'Excuse me, Sir Edward. My lady sends her compliments and wonders when you will be joining her in the drawing room.'

'Tell my wife I'll be there directly.' Edward's voice crackled with irritation and he waved Warner away. 'Kitty,' he said urgently, 'if Bella returns to England, if she needs help in any way, I want you to come straight to me. Do you understand?'

Kitty met his anxious gaze steadily. Captain Edward might be rich and powerful but he was just a man, after all, and it was obvious that he still cared for Bella; all the more shame on him then for treating her so badly. 'It's a pity you weren't here to stop Sir Desmond having us thrown out of the house in Tanner's Passage. If we hadn't lost our home things might have turned out different.' Noting the stunned look in Edward's eyes, Kitty was satisfied that she had at least given him something to think about. Turning on her heel, she was about to walk off when he caught her by the wrist.

'I knew nothing of that. What house are you talking about?'

'You ought to know it, Sir. You own it now, I believe.'

'Kitty, for God's sake stop. Tell me in simple plain words what the hell has been going on in my absence.'

Kitty arrived home with hope in her heart for the first time in months. Captain Edward had denied all knowledge of his father's draconian action in having them thrown out on the street. He had been even more shocked when Kitty had told him about Bella's unhappy relationship with Humphrey Chester but, best of all, he had dashed off a letter to Mr Feeney, instructing him to look urgently into the matter of the lease on Betty's house. As she walked home, Kitty decided against telling Betty, or even Jem, that in her pocket she had the address of Captain Edward's solicitor. It would be wrong to raise their hopes if it turned out that there was nothing to be done to remedy the situation.

Opening the door to the house in Sackville Street, Kitty felt a pang of sadness at the thought of having to leave her home. She would start all over again, of course, but it was going to be a wrench to leave this elegantly set-up house and go back to the mean streets of the East End with the smell of poverty hanging over them. Taking off her straw hat and shawl, she hung them neatly on the hallstand. This was just a temporary setback, nothing that couldn't be overcome by willpower and sheer hard work.

Pausing at the top of the staircase, Kitty could hear the clatter of pots and pans and the sound of voices coming from the basement kitchen; she braced her shoulders and went down the stairs to face Jem and Betty.

Next morning, Jem left the house early to make his way over to Chelsea. After much discussion over supper the previous night, they had all come to the conclusion that Captain Madison's offer was too good to refuse. Jem had been reluctant to go back to sea, even for one trip, but Betty and Kitty together had persuaded him that they could manage very well on their own for a few months. They had enough orders for gowns to keep them busy, and money to come in from rich ladies, who only paid up after persistent dunning. Maria had always undertaken this task and she was rather good at it, Betty said. If all else failed, they could always get Maria up from the country for a few days to collect the debts. The idea of sending gunboat Maria out after the debtors, armed not with rifles and grenades but her own fierce attitude, had made them all laugh and, it had seemed to Kitty, that a weight had lifted off them. She had gone to bed after an affectionate hug from Betty but when Jem had tried to kiss her, she had turned her cheek, avoiding the intimacy of his lips.

Next morning, having secured her best hat with a gilt hatpin and fastened the buttons on her jacket with the new and fashionable leg-of-mutton sleeves, Kitty told Betty that she was going to Liberty in Regent Street where they had advertised a clearance sale of cretonnes at an unbeatable price. Picking up her purse, Kitty was about to open the front door when someone pounded on the knocker as if they meant to beat the door down. Turning the key in the lock, Kitty opened it a fraction and was almost knocked down as Humphrey Chester barged past her, red in the face and breathing heavily.

'Where is she?'

Kitty didn't pretend to misunderstand. 'Bella has gone.'

'Gone? She can't have gone. She's under contract to me.'

'Mr Chester, please keep your voice down.' Kitty glanced towards the basement staircase, hoping that Betty had not heard the commotion. 'Bella has left the country.'

'The bitch!' Humphrey spat the words out like a bad taste. 'The conniving, cheating little bitch! I'll see she never works on the London stage again.'

'She's gone and she's not coming back,' Kitty said, going to the door and holding it open. 'Please leave, Mr Chester.'

Pacing up and down, Humphrey struck out at the walls with his silver-topped cane. 'She's duped me, taken me for a complete fool. I want you out of this house, young lady. Pack your bags and get out.'

Trembling, Kitty drew herself up to her full height. 'This house is in the hands of the letting agent, Sir. We have two more weeks of the lease to run. You can't turn us out.'

Humphrey scowled at her and, for a moment, Kitty thought he was going to hit her, but he vented his spleen by kicking the door.

'That may be so, but everything in this house belongs to me. It was bought with my money.'

440

'And we've been repaying you month by month.'

'Bella still owes me,' Humphrey said, through clenched teeth. He pushed his face close to Kitty's. 'I'll be sending a carter to collect every stick of furniture in this house. I want everything that that little bitch bought with my money, from the chandeliers to the carpets. D'you hear me?'

'The whole street can hear you shouting, Mr Chester.' Betty hobbled towards them, puffing and panting with the exertion of taking the stairs too quickly on rheumaticky knees. 'What's going on, Kitty?'

'It's all right,' Kitty said hastily. 'Mr Chester is just leaving.'

'Yes, I'm going,' snarled Humphrey. 'But you can expect a visit from the bailiffs.'

Pushing past Kitty, Betty shook her fist in Humphrey's face. 'Don't you speak to Kitty like that, or I'll fetch my son and he'll sort you out.'

Humphrey's mouth twisted in rage. 'And you, Madam, you tell that oaf to keep out of my way. I haven't forgotten our last meeting and if he tries to stop me reclaiming my property, I'll have the law on him.' Storming off down the steps, Humphrey climbed into his motor car, shouting instructions to the chauffeur.

Betty clutched at Kitty's arm. 'He can't do this to us, can he?'

'I don't know. But he's rich and we're poor. I expect the law is on his side all right.'

Betty began to cry. 'What shall we do? What'll happen to us now, Kitty?'

'Don't worry, Betty dear.' Kitty wrapped her arms around Betty in a comforting hug. 'We'll talk about it when I come back.'

Sniffing, Betty wiped her eyes on her apron. 'Surely you're not going to the sale now? I don't see how spending money on material is going to help get us out of this mess.'

'I'm not going to the sale. I'll tell you all about it when I get back.'

'Where are you going? Don't leave me all alone in the house. What do I do if the bailiffs come while you're out?'

Pausing on the threshold, Kitty forced a confident smile. 'They won't, and I'll not be long. Don't answer the door to anyone while I'm out, not even if Lord Kitchener himself comes knocking.'

'Mr Feeney will see you now, Miss.'

Kitty jumped up from the hard wooden chair in the outer office, hurrying past the clerk as he held the door for her. Mr Feeney sat behind his cluttered desk, polishing the lenses of his spectacles on a blue silk handkerchief. He peered at Kitty with pale, myopic eyes that only came into focus when he restored his specs to the bridge of his bulbous nose. 'Miss Cox?'

'That's me, Sir,' Kitty said, standing with her hands clasped in front of her. 'Captain Edward, I mean Sir Edward said you'd sort this business out for me.'

Mr Feeney glanced down at the letter. 'Ah yes! The property in Tanner's Passage.' Picking up a scroll of parchment, he untied the red tape and laid the document out in front of him, smoothing it flat with his hand that was white and smooth as a lady's.

He's never done a stroke of hard work in his life, Kitty thought inconsequentially as she moved from one foot to the other, clasping and unclasping her hands, waiting while he read slowly, his lips silently forming the words. After what felt like hours instead of merely minutes, he looked up.

'And you represent the said Mrs Elizabeth Scully?'

'I do, Sir.'

'You realise, young lady, that Feeney, Feeney and Rumbelow merely act as ciphers for their clients?'

'I might, Sir. If I understood what you meant.'

'It means that we, the firm, undertake to carry out our client's instructions, within the law, of course.'

Kitty shrugged her shoulders. Perhaps he

would come to the point sooner rather than later.

'Carrying out the instructions from the late Sir Desmond Mableton, Baronet, we, the firm, withdrew the lease on number seven Tanner's Passage.'

'Withdrew? Do you mean that the lease had not run out?'

Keeping his head bent over the document, Mr Feeney rolled it up, concentrating all his attention on retying the tape. 'I see from the deeds that the lease was, in actual fact, for ninety-nine years. It seems there was a slight misunderstanding . . .'

'Misunderstanding!' Kitty leaned across the desk, snatching the scroll from his hand. 'Sir Desmond had us thrown out on the street for nothing other than sheer badness. How could you stand by and let that happen?'

Mr Feeney's neck seemed to disappear into his high starched collar as he blinked up at Kitty. 'I can assure you that nothing improper has taken place, Miss Cox. Sir Desmond owned the land and –'

Kitty waved the parchment at him. 'But the lease had over seventy years to run. The house belongs to Mrs Scully right and proper, as it has all the time. I'd be ashamed of myself if I was you, Sir.'

Mr Feeney jumped to his feet, making as if to

snatch back the document. 'Don't take that tone with me, Miss.'

'I'm keeping this to show Mrs Scully and Sir Edward.' Kitty tucked the scroll beneath her arm. 'Hand over the keys, Mr Feeney.'

Number seven Tanner's Passage felt cold and damp. The air was stale and musty and a thick film of dust covered the surfaces with a grey bloom. Absently, Kitty wrote her name in the dust on the kitchen table, while Betty darted around the room, opening cupboards and exclaiming in delight on finding everything precisely as she had left it. Jem turned on the cold water tap and grimaced as a stream of brown, rusty water spluttered into the clay sink.

'This water's got legs,' he said, grinning.

'Let it run,' cried Betty. 'Let it run a bit. I'll soon have everything shipshape and Bristol fashion and just as it used to be.' She opened the larder door, snorting with disgust. 'Mice! I can smell mice. We'll have to get a trap, Jem. Or, better still, we'll get ourselves a cat. I've always wanted a little cat, but I couldn't have one with our Polly so weak and fragile and needing so much attention, bless her little heart.' Betty's lips quivered and unshed tears sparkled on her pale lashes.

'Bless her,' Jem said, hooking his arm around Betty's shoulders and giving her a sympathetic hug, but Kitty could see that his eyes had misted and reddened; his lips trembled but he forced them into a smile. 'God rest her brave little soul.'

'Amen to that,' Betty said, patting his hand. 'It's good to be home at last.'

The afternoon sun slanted through the small windowpanes, frosted with dirt, and Kitty suppressed a sigh. Betty was so obviously overjoyed to be back in her old home and Jem would be leaving in a few days, going back to his ship for his last voyage.

Try as she might, Kitty simply couldn't muster any enthusiasm for returning to the East End. She had attempted to keep her true feelings from Jem and Betty, but leaving Sackville Street had seemed like the end of a beautiful dream. She had had to stand by while the house was stripped of its elegant furniture and fittings down to the last china ornament. Humphrey Chester had made sure that everything of any value, however small, was snatched under the eagle-eyed supervision of the bailiffs. She had managed to save one treadle sewing machine, two dressmaker's dummies, cutting shears, material and spools of thread, by claiming them as tools of their trade, but that was all. Kitty knew that she could and would begin again, but the heady days of being a modiste in the West End were over – for the time being, anyway. Returning to Tanner's Passage was coming home to Betty; to Kitty it was returning to the nightmare of her past. She could not even confide in Jem, for fear that he might refuse to do this last trip with Captain Madison. This was a purely personal battle and she knew she had to fight it alone.

Betty rolled up her sleeves with a businesslike air. 'Right then! I'm going to get the fire going in the range and we'll have our first cup of tea at home. Jem, you go and see if there's any coke in the cellar, while I clean out the ashes.'

Jem picked up the hod and shovel and went off whistling.

Betty reached for her purse. 'Here's some money, Kitty. Why don't you go to the corner shop and get us a poke of tea and some milk?' Dropping some coins in Kitty's outstretched hand, Betty gave her a shrewd look. 'I know this ain't what you wanted, ducks. Just give it time.'

In the days that followed, Kitty was kept so busy that she had little time to fret or feel sorry for herself. Betty's abundant good spirits carried them all through the sheer hard work of restoring the damp, neglected house into a place where they could comfortably live. Jem helped when he could, shifting the heavy furniture and then putting it back in place after Betty had scrubbed the floors, bleaching the wood to the colour of bone. Curtains were taken down and

447

boiled in the copper out of doors in the back yard, and the faded squares of carpet were hung on the washing line and given a beating that sent showers of grit and dust onto the cobblestones.

Every morning, Jem went off to join Captain Madison in the search for a suitable craft with which to start their business, but so far without success, although they had combed the boatyards and jetties from Chelsea Reach to Limehouse. When their searches brought them close to home, Jem brought Captain Madison to the house and he became a regular visitor. Having known him since the early days of her marriage to Herbert, Betty welcomed a chance to talk about old times. Sophia Weston sometimes accompanied Captain Jasper on these visits, having struck up an instant rapport with Betty; as widows of seafarers, they had much in common and spent many pleasant afternoons drinking tea and chatting. Despite a heavy heart, Kitty was glad to see Betty happy again in her old home and she tried her utmost to make the best of things.

On the last day before Jem and the Captain were due to return to the *Mairangi*, they were all sitting in the kitchen at Tanner's Passage, with the exception of Sophia, who suffered from headaches brought on by the summer heat and had remained at home. Betty and Jasper Madison sat on opposite sides of the range, where the kettle bubbled and hissed out steam and the big brown teapot sat on a trivet, beneath its knitted cosy. Jem and Kitty sat at the kitchen table in companionable silence, drinking tea and eating slices of a cake that Sophia had sent from Chelsea, while they listened to the older couple reminiscing. Seeing Betty with someone near enough to her own age, a friend from years ago, Kitty realised for the first time how much Betty must miss her late husband. While talking over past times with Captain Madison, Kitty could see traces of her youth in Betty's animated countenance before widowhood and poverty had etched their harsh lines on her face. It was good to hear Betty laugh at Captain Madison's wry humour, and Kitty was beginning to understand why Jem was so devoted to this unassuming, and rather reserved, man who had never taken a wife of his own and who had spent virtually all of his adult life married to the sea.

'So you had no luck again today then, Jasper?' Betty reached for the teapot. 'More tea?'

Jasper raised his hand, shaking his head. 'Thank you, no. I really must be getting along. Sophia will have supper ready in spite of the fact that I told her to rest.'

Jem jumped to his feet. 'But we're not giving up on the boat, are we, Sir? Even though we sail tomorrow.'

'No, indeed!' Captain Madison rose stiffly,

flexing one knee and then the other. 'My joints aren't what they used to be. I'll be glad to swallow the anchor, and that's the truth. I've left instructions with my agent, Jem, and if he finds anything suitable while we're away, he can act for me. I've told him we want a craft big enough to navigate the river as far as Southend. That's where the future lies. Taking Londoners for a day out that they'll never forget.'

'My Herbert would be so proud of you both,' Betty said, rummaging in her pinafore pocket for her hankie. 'So proud.'

'Herbert was a fine man.' Jasper made a harrumphing noise deep in his throat. 'I'll see you on board ship tomorrow, Jem.'

'I'll be there, Sir.'

Jasper turned to Kitty, holding out his hand, a smile crinkling the corner of his eyes. 'Goodbye, Kitty. I'll bring him back safe and sound, don't you worry.'

'We'll walk you to the cabstand, Cap'n,' Jem said. 'Coming, Kitty?'

Jem and Kitty walked back slowly, arm in arm, along the wharf. A cool, easterly breeze brought a bit of relief from the sizzling July heat, but the city smells hung in a miasma over the slinking, brown water.

'I don't want to go,' Jem said. 'I'll miss you every moment of every day, Kitty.'

'I'll miss you too, Jem.' Kitty squeezed his arm. 'It's not for long. You'll be back before you know it.'

Jem stopped, slipping his arms around her waist. 'Everything I do is for you – you know that, don't you?'

Kitty angled her head, avoiding the intensity of his gaze. 'Of course I do, silly.'

'I love you, Kitty. More than you'll ever know.'

'I know that too.' Kitty smiled up at him and wriggled free. 'Come on, we'd best get home to Betty. She's going to miss you too.'

'You just can't say it, can you?' Jem stuck his hands in his pockets, falling in step beside Kitty as she turned towards Tanner's Passage. 'Why won't you say it, Kitty?'

'It's just words. You know I care for you.'

'Then prove it.' Catching hold of Kitty's hand, Jem stopped, pulling her round to face him.

'Prove it?'

'Say you'll marry me, Kitty. Give me your promise and I'll live on it until you're good and ready.'

Looking into his eyes, Kitty longed to say yes, but a mist blurred her vision and a feeling of panic constricted her throat. 'I – I can't, not yet. It's too soon.'

'Too soon?' Jem's voice deepened with anger. 'We've known each other all our lives. I want to spend the rest of mine with you.'

Shaking her head, Kitty couldn't meet his fierce gaze. 'I'm not saying no. I just need time to get used to the idea. Getting wed changes people for the worst and I don't want to spoil things.'

'It won't be like that with us, I swear it.'

'Give me time, Jem.'

'I can wait, as long as you promise not to get tied up with anyone else.'

Raising her eyes to his, Kitty managed a wobbly smile. 'That's a promise I can give you, no trouble at all, Jem. Cross my heart and hope to die.'

Standing side by side, Kitty and Betty waved a tearful farewell to Jem as he boarded his ship. They stood on the quay wall; silently watching until the ship was out of sight, before turning away and walking slowly back to Tanner's Passage. Betty was snuffling into her hankie and Kitty had to steel herself not to join in; she had felt sad when Jem had gone away in the past, but this time was subtly different, as if part of her soul was being wrenched from her body, leaving her feeling desperately alone. They walked home slowly and in silence. As they turned into Tanner's Passage, Kitty saw a carriage waiting outside the house. A pair of perfectly matched bays moved restlessly, flicking their ears and tails as clouds of flies buzzed around their heads. Kitty recognised the coachman before she realised that the lady seated in the open carriage was the new Lady Mableton.

'My goodness,' Betty whispered. 'That's the Mableton crest on the carriage door. Who's that, Kitty?'

'Go and open the front door, Betty,' Kitty said, giving her a gentle push. 'I'm almost certain that it's Captain Edward's wife, though what she wants with us I can't think.'

Allowing the footman to help her from the carriage, Lady Mableton turned to the coachman. 'Walk the horses, Tompkins. Come back in half an hour.' Picking up her skirts, she strolled into the house as though she visited the East End every day.

'This is an unexpected honour, Ma'am,' Betty said, dropping a curtsey.

'I've come to see Kitty. Could we speak somewhere in private?'

'Take her ladyship up to my sitting room,' Betty said, nodding her head to Kitty. 'Can I offer you a cup of tea, Ma'am?'

'No, thank you.' Lady Mableton followed Kitty up to Betty's sitting room. She sat down on the sofa, arranging her skirts as she glanced around the room; if she was surprised to see a large bed taking up half the space in the sitting room, she did not show it. 'I expect you're wondering why I've come, Kitty? Please sit down, don't hover.'

Fascinated by Lady Mableton's unfamiliar accent and her eye-catching crimson gown, Kitty perched on the edge of the window seat. 'What can I do for you, my lady?'

'I'll come straight to the point. I've heard that you are not only an excellent dressmaker but that you design gowns for fashionable ladies. Am I right?'

'I did – I mean I do – but how did you know, Ma'am?'

Lady Mableton peeled off her silk gloves. 'You knew my husband's stepmother, I believe?'

'Yes, Ma'am.' Kitty clasped her hands in her lap, an uneasy feeling making the skin on her neck crawl. Where was this all leading?

'Kitty, I'm a plain woman. My family made their fortune farming in the Cape Colony and I've no patience with people who put on airs and graces. Since I arrived in London I've had to listen daily to gossip and innuendo involving that woman and my husband. Do you understand what I'm saying?'

Kitty had a vision of Miss Iris and her pinched, acidic face. It did not take much imagination to picture the forthright, handsome Lady Mableton crossing verbal swords with her new sister-in-law. Kitty nodded her head.

'I've been subjected to scandalous tales about my husband's stepmother until I could scream with frustration. I know you were close to her and I want to know the truth. But that can wait. More importantly, my husband and I have invitations to the Abbey to attend the King's Coronation and I need a very special gown. Iris has told me that it's impossible to have such a gown designed and made in just over a week. Could you do that for me?'

'I – I think I could, Ma'am.' Kitty took a deep breath. 'No, I'm certain I could, Lady Mableton.'

'I thought so. I summed you up perfectly the first moment I laid eyes on you. I'm never wrong about people.'

'I would need to take your measurements right away, my lady.'

'Exactly so. Do this thing for me, Kitty, and I will pay you well. If I am satisfied with your work, then I will order more gowns.' Lady Mableton patted her swelling stomach. 'As you can see, I am in an interesting condition and will need a whole new wardrobe, especially as I understand an English winter can be very unpleasant. Well, what are you waiting for? Fetch your tape measure and let us begin.'

Kitty took detailed measurements, noting them down in her workbook. They discussed shape and style and she did a few rough sketches that met with instant approval from Lady Mableton.

'You have talent, Kitty.'

'Thank you, my lady.' Kitty chewed the end of

her pencil, wondering how to broach the subject of the money she would need to purchase the costly material for such an important gown.

'And no doubt you are in need of funds.' Adeline reached for an embroidered purse, handing it to Kitty. 'As I told you, I'm a practical woman, not one of your effete English aristocracy. I know the value and the power of money and I'm not afraid to use it.'

The purse felt reassuringly heavy in Kitty's hand. The thought crossed her mind that perhaps it was a little too heavy for the task in hand, but she wasn't about to refuse such a generous gesture. 'Thank you, my lady, but we still need to discuss material and colour.'

'That won't be necessary; I have a bolt of Chinese silk that my brother, an inveterate traveller, brought back from China just before those wretched Boxers rebelled, causing all that trouble in Peking. I'll send my coachman round with it this afternoon and you can begin at once.'

'I could come to Dover Street, my lady,' Kitty suggested. 'Perhaps, in view of your delicate condition . . .'

'Nonsense. I'm as strong as an ox and I hate fuss. Also, I don't want Iris to know what I'm doing. This is strictly between ourselves, Kitty. Is that clear?'

'Yes, my lady. Perfectly clear.'

'And now,' Adeline said, her dark eyes

blackbird bright, 'now you are going to tell me everything you know about the scandalous Bella Lane.'

Kitty worked night and day on the gown for Lady Mableton. She got by on two or three hours' sleep every night, working until her fingers bled and her eyes blurred into double vision. Betty did what she could to help, having recovered from the initial shock of seeing the bolt of emerald green silk, interwoven with gold thread making patterns of exotic, oriental flowers and mythical beasts. Kitty had tried, tactfully, to suggest that perhaps ivory satin or plain cream silk would be more suitable for the occasion, but Adeline had proved to be as stubborn as she was handsome.

'White or cream is for pale, insipid English-women,' she had said, with a disdainful toss of her head. 'I know what suits me and I don't give a damn for convention. I want the stuffy English nobility to notice me and I intend to become the most fashionable hostess in London. With my fortune behind him and with my social skills, Edward will go far in politics. Our son will inherit a dukedom, if I have anything to do with it.'

Adeline came in person to collect her gown late in the afternoon of Friday, the day before the actual Coronation. Trying on the gown for the final time, Adeline gasped with despair as Kitty struggled ineffectually to fasten the last of the tiny back buttons.

'I simply can't have grown bigger since yesterday,' Adeline said, sucking in her breath. 'Try again, Kitty.'

Kitty exchanged worried glances with Betty. 'It's no use, my lady. Whatever the cause, I can't do it up. I'll have to let out some seams.'

'It's probably a touch of wind,' Betty said. 'Begging your pardon, Ma'am, for mentioning such a thing, but I had wind something terrible when I was carrying our Polly.'

'Nonsense.' Adeline jerked the material from Kitty's hands. 'Stop fiddling with the buttons, girl. There isn't time to let out seams. Lace me up a bit tighter, Kitty.'

'Are you sure that's wise, my lady?'

'Just do it.'

Betty folded her arms across her chest, shaking her head. 'Think about your delicate condition, my lady.'

Adeline whipped around to face Betty. 'When I want your opinion, I'll ask for it. Go away.'

Betty's cheeks flamed scarlet and, bobbing a curtsey, she hurried from the room.

Without further comment, Kitty loosened the laces of the whalebone stays.

Adeline let out a gasp of what might have been

relief. 'Now pull them tight as you can,' she said, taking a deep breath.

Eventually, after much tugging and pulling, Kitty was able to do up the last of the tiny gold buttons. Adeline's satisfied smile was wiped off her face by a spasm of pain that made her gasp, holding her hand to her side.

'My lady, are you all right?' Kitty asked anxiously.

'Of course, I am, don't fuss.' Adeline grasped the back of a chair, leaning forward and panting. Beads of perspiration stood out on her forehead and her face was deathly pale, but she pulled her lips back in an effort to smile. 'I'm perfectly fine. It's just a touch of dyspepsia. I'll be at Westminster Abbey in time for the Coronation tomorrow, if it kills me.'

Chapter Nineteen

Next day, on the morning of the Coronation, Betty and Kitty walked all the way to Westminster, leaving at the crack of dawn in order to secure a position close to the Abbey. The day was bright and sunny and the streets heaved with flag-waving, cheering Londoners, lining the route of the procession. With a bit of pushing and jostling and the judicious use of elbows, Kitty and Betty managed to edge their way to the front of the crowd, watching eagerly as the dignitaries arrived, walking along the red carpet to take up their seats in the Abbey.

'There she is,' Betty cried, nudging Kitty, and pointing.

It was impossible to miss Lady Adeline Mableton, who was half a head taller than most of the other ladies, and her emerald green and gold gown stood out amongst them, exotic as an orchid in a field of white daisies. Kitty craned her neck to get a better view and couldn't help feeling just a bit proud of her own handiwork, and it seemed that Lady Mableton had got her wish, all eyes were upon her. She paused in the entrance to the Abbey, raising her white-gloved hand in a wave of acknowledgement to the crowd and receiving a cheer of appreciation in return. Sir Edward looked slightly uncomfortable as he led his wife out of the sunshine into the cool, dark interior of the Abbey.

'Oh, well,' Betty said. 'She's got what she wanted, but I don't think it'll do her much good with the rest of the toffs.'

'Who is that?' Kitty asked, as loud cheers rippled through the tightly packed crowds.

'Why, don't you recognise him?' Betty said, chuckling. 'It's Lord Kitchener and there's Mr Balfour, the Prime Minister. Listen to the crowd cheering; it must be the King and Queen Alexandra arriving. Oh, Kitty, if only Jem and Polly were here to see this day . . .'

At the end of the ceremony, after the newly crowned King and his Queen had left the Abbey, followed by the illustrious guests, Kitty and Betty waited until the last.

'They haven't come out yet,' Kitty said, standing on tiptoe. 'We can't have missed them.'

The crowds had already begun to disperse and Betty was tugging at Kitty's arm, urging her to begin the long walk home.

'No,' Kitty said. 'I've waited this long. I want to see them leave the Abbey.'

At that moment, Sir Edward appeared in the

doorway, supporting Adeline on his arm.

'She's been taken poorly,' Kitty said, pushing through the crowd only to be stopped by a burly policeman, just as Adeline crumpled to the ground.

'I'm a nurse,' Kitty told the policeman. 'Let me by.'

'And I'm Lady Mableton's maid,' Betty said, assuming Maria's arrogant stance. 'Let us pass, Constable, if you please.'

The policeman hesitated for a moment, but a small crowd of curious onlookers had gathered round, diverting his attention and giving Kitty and Betty the opportunity to slip past him.

By the time they reached him, Edward had managed to get Adeline back on her feet. He stared blankly at Kitty for a moment. 'Kitty?'

'Can we help, Sir Edward?' Kitty bobbed a curtsey.

Adeline raised her head from his shoulder. 'It's just a fainting spell. I'll be all right in a minute.'

The Mableton carriage drew up in the road outside the Abbey and the footman leapt off to open the door and pull the steps down.

'You're unwell, my dear,' Edward said, lifting Adeline up in his arms with a considerable effort. 'I'm taking you home.'

'Put me down!' Adeline's dark eyebrows shot together over the bridge of her patrician nose.

'Put me down, at once! You're making a spectacle of us.'

Edward set her back on her feet. 'Really, Adeline. You're unwell, my dear. You must allow me to take you home.'

'I will go home, but Kitty and Mrs Scully will accompany me and you will go to the reception. You shan't miss this opportunity because of me.'

Edward's brow puckered into furrows. 'I don't understand, Adeline. How do you know these women?'

'Don't ask foolish questions, Edward. Kitty was recommended to me as a dressmaker. How else do you think I had this lovely gown made in less than a week?'

'Er, yes. Well done, Kitty. But, Adeline –'

'No, my dear, you mustn't worry about me and I'd rather have sensible women with me at the moment than your fussing.'

Holding her breath, Kitty saw that Sir Edward was still puzzled and she wondered how Lady Mableton was going to explain her reasons for choosing her out of all the dressmakers and modistes in London. Would she admit that it was Iris's spiteful tittle-tattle that had sown the seeds of jealousy in her mind, leading her to believe that her handsome husband was still in love with his stepmother? But Adeline brushed aside Edward's questions, insisting that she merely needed to rest and, as most of the servants had

463

been given the day off to watch the Coronation procession, she wanted to be sure of having female company. Edward dithered but in the end Adeline won by sheer force of will, sending him off to the reception. Holding herself very straight, Adeline stood by the carriage, watching until he was out of sight and then she seemed to crumple at the knees. Kitty and Betty rushed to support her.

'Get me home,' Adeline said, grimacing with pain. 'I'm afraid I am not very well.'

Warner let them into the house and, if he felt hostile towards Kitty, he kept his feelings well under control. Having sent the new hall boy for the doctor, Warner went in person to the kitchen to ask Mrs Dixon to make tea for her ladyship. Slowly, and with many stops along the way, Kitty and Betty managed to help Adeline up the stairs to her bedroom. It took both their efforts to get her undressed and into her white lawn nightgown and, by the time they helped her into bed, it was obvious that she was very poorly indeed. Her cries and moans echoed round the room as she clutched Kitty's hands, squeezing them until Kitty felt that her bones would snap.

By the time the doctor arrived, it was all over. With tears running down her cheeks, Betty wrapped the tiny body in a clean towel and took it from the room. Kitty sat at the head of the bed, bathing Adeline's face with cool water, while the doctor did what was necessary to make her comfortable. When Adeline was asleep, sedated by a generous dose of laudanum, Kitty went to look for Betty and found her in the kitchen, drinking tea with Mrs Dixon and Mrs Brewster. George had just returned from watching the Coronation procession and he stood listening to the sad news, with a Union Jack still clutched in his hand.

'And it was a baby boy too,' Mrs Dixon said, all her chins wobbling in unison. 'A son and heir. The master will be so upset.'

'It's very sad, but then I lost three myself before I had Jem,' Betty said, sipping her tea. 'There'll be other babies. She's a big, strong lady.'

'That's very true,' agreed Mrs Brewster. 'Thank God you was here to help, Mrs Scully, for I don't think I could have managed, given the circumstances.'

George drew Kitty aside. 'Are you all right, Kitty. You look very pale.'

Kitty managed a smile even though she didn't feel in the least like smiling, but it was good to know that George had forgiven her at last. 'I'm fine, thank you, George.'

He hooked his arm around her shoulders, giving her a friendly squeeze. 'That's the ticket. You always was a spunky little thing. Sit down

465

and have a cup of tea and then I'll call a cab to take you and Mrs Scully home.'

Thinking of the cost, Kitty shook her head. 'We can get an omnibus.'

'Not much hope of that,' George said, taking a leather purse from his pocket. 'London's gone mad with celebrating. I'm sure Sir Edward would insist on paying for a hansom cab to take you both safely home. It's the least he could do in the circumstances.'

Whether Sir Edward was grateful or not remained a mystery. A month passed by and then another – Christmas came and went without a word from Dover Street. Kitty worked hard finishing off the orders for gowns that she had begun in Sackville Street and even managed to deliver them on time. She used some of their hard-earned money to place advertisements in the *Lady's Pictorial* magazine and also in the *Lady*, and was agreeably surprised to receive a steady trickle of enquiries. Some of these came from her old clients, the wives of wealthy City merchants and bankers, but the majority now came from ladies of quality. Kitty couldn't help wondering if Lady Mableton had something to do with this, whether by recommendation, or simply because her gown at the Coronation had caused something of a stir. However, what really mattered was the fact that Kitty was slowly but surely becoming recognised once again as a modiste to the rich and fashionable. She was pleased, but too exhausted by hard work to realise the full implications of her success.

In her rare moments of free time, Kitty wrote to Jem, telling him all the positive things that happened and taking care never to complain about living back in Tanner's Passage. His replies came in the form of postcards and the occasional letter, including one, dated just a few weeks before Christmas, telling them that Captain Madison's agent had come across a vessel, beached in Chelsea Creek, that needed a bit of reconstruction but was ideal for their requirements, and he had secured it at a good price. Kitty and Betty read and reread the letter, chuckling over Jem's enthusiasm that leapt off ink-blotted pages, scrawled with misspelt words; but then, as Betty said, Jem had never been much of a scholar, he was more a practical man, just like his father. They would, Jem wrote, be home in early spring, this time for good.

'You'll have to make up your mind then, Kitty,' Betty said, having just reread the letter, as they were finishing breakfast.

Kitty took the letter, folding it carefully and tucking it back in her writing case, keeping her head down to avoid Betty's candid gaze. 'Make up my mind?'

'You know very well what I mean. My Jem loves you and I don't want to see him hurt.'

'I'd never do such a thing. I'm too fond of Jem for that.'

'Too fond isn't the same thing as being in love, Kitty. If you can't love him like a woman then don't keep him dangling after you, like you did to poor George.'

Kitty jumped to her feet. 'That's unfair. I never led George on. I told him often enough that I didn't want that sort of thing.'

Betty's face creased into anxious lines. 'I know what you went through, ducks – we all do – but you can't let it ruin your whole life.'

'I've got work to do,' Kitty said, scooping up her writing case and pencils. 'I'll be in the sewing room, if you need me.'

Upset and unable to get Betty's words out of her head, Kitty was just settling down to finish some sketches for one of her new clients when the loud noise of someone knocking on the front door made her jump up to look out of the window. Tweaking back the net curtain, she saw the Mableton carriage drawn up alongside the kerb. She spun around as the door opened and Betty ushered Adeline into the sewing room.

'My dear Kitty, how well you look.' Adeline glanced at the half-finished gowns pinned to dressmaker's dummies. 'And you are busy too. That's all to the good.'

Kitty bobbed a curtsey. 'Are you completely recovered now, my lady?'

Adeline didn't answer immediately. She peeled off her kid gloves slowly, finger by finger. 'You helped me when I was taken ill,' she said, sitting down on the nearest chair and arranging her skirts, plucking at the material with long, white fingers. 'I need you to help me now.'

'My lady?'

Adeline raised her head, her eyes dark pools in a pale face. 'My physician tells me that I will never be able to bear another child. No, don't say anything. I've had enough platitudes to last me a lifetime.' Adeline rose to her feet, nervously wringing her hands as she began to pace the floor. 'I'll come straight to the point. My infectious disease of a sister-in-law has finally persuaded some fool to marry her. If she should breed, heaven help us, then her child would inherit the Mableton estates. I won't have that happen. I simply won't.'

'I don't understand,' Kitty said, appalled by this sudden outburst. 'What has all this got to do with me?'

'It was you who told me about the child Leonie. *Her* child – the woman that my husband still loves in spite of everything.'

'Oh, no, my lady,' Kitty cried, clasping her hands together. 'I never said any such thing.'

Adeline spun around to face Kitty. 'My

husband married me for my fortune and to produce an heir to the Mableton estates. I can't give him that heir but my money can buy one. I want the child Leonie. Do you understand, Kitty? I want to adopt her and bring her up as my own.'

'But my lady, Leonie has a mother. Bella would never agree to such a thing and Maria would never let you take Leonie.'

'I visited Mableton Manor and I've seen Leonie. She's running wild, learning bad habits from those unruly urchins that belong to your sister. All her potential will be lost if she isn't rescued, given a decent upbringing and an education suitable for a young lady. I want you to go to Mableton Manor and persuade Maria to give Leonie into my care.'

Kitty covered her ears, shaking her head; she would not listen to such wild ranting.

Adeline sprang at her, wrenching Kitty's hands away so that she was forced to listen. 'I'm a desperate woman but I'm neither unfair nor unkind. I'm offering Leonie a better life. You must see that.'

'You can't take her away from the people she knows and loves. I won't help you in such wickedness.'

'You would do best to reconsider.' Adeline's lips tightened into a straight line. 'If you don't help me, I will tell my husband to evict your sister and her brats from Mableton Manor. I will have the Lane woman thrown out on the streets and I will bring Leonie to London with or without your help.'

'You wouldn't be so cruel.'

'Cruel? Wasn't it cruel enough that Leonie's mother abandoned her and went chasing off to France after her worthless lover? With me, Leonie will have everything she could ever want in life and more. I can give her all this, but I would rather have her willingly and with her grandmother's consent. Maria and that sister of yours will listen to you. Bribe them with money, say anything you like, but don't come back without Leonie.' Adeline emptied her purse onto Kitty's worktable, spilling out a heap of golden guineas. 'That will cover your expenses.'

'It's not right, my lady. And even if I did go, Maria would never agree to such a thing.'

'Everyone has a price. I believe that Maria sold her own daughter to Sir Desmond. Do you really think she can't be bought again?'

'I know that Maria loves Leonie and that she is sorry for everything that happened to Bella. She's had a hard life, my lady, but she's not a bad person.'

'Bah! She's as selfish as her daughter. They're a useless pair of nobodies who will drag the child up in their own self-centred mould.'

Shaking her head, Kitty held out her hands,

pleading. 'Please, my lady, don't do this thing. I know Bella is sometimes selfish, but she adores Leonie and she fought so hard for her.'

'You're a good friend to that woman, better than she deserves.' Adeline's expression changed subtly and her voice softened. 'Help me, Kitty. I promise you that Leonie will be loved just as I would have loved my poor, dead child. After all, she is Edward's half-sister. She belongs with the Mableton family.'

Fighting back tears of desperation, Kitty struggled to find the words that might change Lady Mableton's mind, even though she had to admit that some of her accusations against Bella and Maria were true.

Adeline closed her purse with a snap. 'I'll allow you a fortnight. If I haven't heard from you by then, you know what will happen.'

The poor lady had gone mad with grief, having lost her one chance at motherhood; that was Betty's opinion but, like Kitty, she was equally horrified at the thought of Leonie being used as a pawn in Adeline's master plan to keep control of the Mableton estate. The heap of gold coins lay untouched on the sewing room table as Kitty and Betty racked their brains to think of a way to contact Bella. She had sent a hastily scrawled postcard from Paris, shortly after her arrival, announcing that she had found Rackham and that everything was absolutely wonderful. There had been a Christmas card with a scribbled note inside announcing that Bella had found instant success, singing and dancing in a famous nightclub, but characteristically she had not thought to include a forwarding address. Unfortunately the original postcard seemed to be lost, even though they searched the house from top to bottom. The only detail that Kitty could remember was the photograph of a windmill. Although, for the life of her, Kitty could not think what a windmill would be doing in the centre of Paris.

In the middle of the night, waking from a fitful sleep, it came to her in a flash of inspiration: the one person who might possibly have gleaned bits and pieces of worldly knowledge from her employer lived not a million miles away.

Sophia Weston led Kitty into her private parlour at the rear of the house in Chelsea and then, despite Kitty's protests that she was neither hungry nor thirsty, Sophia hurried off to fetch tea and cake. Unlike Captain Madison's starkly masculine sitting room, Mrs Weston's parlour was cosily crowded with clutter. A coal fire roared up the chimney beneath a mantelshelf swagged with moss green velvet that matched the curtains and portières. China figurines jostled for position with silver-framed photographs on every available surface, and it would have been difficult, Kitty thought, looking around the room, to stick a pin between the plaques and watercolour paintings that covered the walls.

Sophia returned carrying a laden tea tray, settling it down on a table covered with a crimson chenille cloth. 'Now then, Kitty,' she said, pouring the tea. 'I can see that something is troubling you. Would you like to tell me about it?'

With her tea untouched and rapidly cooling, Kitty plunged into the story, leaving nothing out and ending with a description of the postcard from Paris.

'Well, that's the easy part,' Sophia said, smiling. 'The windmill is a famous nightclub in Paris, called the Moulin Rouge. Although from what you've told me about her, your friend could well have moved on by now.'

'But she might still be there.' Kitty jumped to her feet. 'I'll send a telegram. The only trouble is I don't know how.'

'There I can help,' Sophia said, heaving herself out of her comfortable chair by the fire. 'Captain Jasper is very fond of newfangled inventions, particularly the telegram. We'll go to the telegraph office straight away.'

A week passed and Kitty's worst fears were realised when there was no reply to the telegram.

Betty urged her to go to Mableton Manor to warn Maria, but Kitty knew that would not solve the problem. Maria would become angry and defensive but she would be helpless against the wealth and power of the Mableton family. With time running out, Kitty decided to go to Dover Street and speak to Sir Edward himself. After all, he was a reasonable man and he had shown her small kindnesses in the past. Maybe, if she put it very tactfully, he would try to dissuade his headstrong wife from pursuing this disastrous course. Betty was frankly sceptical, but Kitty insisted that anything was worth a try and she set off for Dover Street early the following morning.

Walking part of the way, Kitty caught an omnibus from Ludgate Hill and, as she left the uniform greyness of the docks and the City behind her, the rain clouds parted and the sun shone from a clear blue sky. Alighting in Piccadilly, Kitty felt a surge of optimism as she walked briskly towards Dover Street with the soft spring breeze fanning her cheeks and, for the first time that year, there was real warmth in the sun's rays.

George opened the door and, although he listened sympathetically, he said it was more than his life was worth to let her over the threshold. Glancing anxiously over his shoulder he advised Kitty to leave before she got herself into trouble. At that moment, Warner appeared, his face as dark as the clouds that had rolled suddenly across the sky, bringing with them a sharp, April shower. Sir Edward, he said was not at home to the likes of her and then he slammed the door in her face.

Kitty couldn't go home to Tanner's Passage and face Betty's 'I told you so' expression, even if she said nothing. She began walking and without quite knowing why, she found herself knocking on the door of Captain Madison's house.

Sophia did not seem surprised to see her and, having ushered Kitty into her parlour, she listened intently while Kitty told her everything.

'Have you thought,' Sophia said, angling her head, 'that with a mother who puts herself before her own child, Leonie might just be better off living in London with her half-brother and his wife?'

Kitty stared at her aghast. 'But Bella loves Leonie.'

'You'll excuse me, Kitty, for I don't know the lady, but it seems to me she loves herself the more.' Sophia picked up her knitting. 'After all, Leonie was born a lady and maybe she should be educated and brought up in the society that one day she'll be expected to marry into. She won't be a sweet little child forever.'

Kitty shook her head. 'But Lady Mableton only

wants her so that if Miss Iris should have children they won't inherit the estate.'

'They're not like us, dear. We're ordinary people, we don't think the same as they do.'

Kitty flicked angry tears from her eyes with the back of her hand. 'If it was my child I wouldn't let anyone, not anyone, take her from me.'

Sophia dropped her knitting in her lap and she reached out to clasp Kitty's hands. 'But that's how you feel, my dear. One day you and Jem will have children of your own and you'll be a wonderful mother.'

Kitty snatched her hands away. 'I never said I'd marry Jem. And I didn't come here to talk about him and me.'

'He loves you, Kitty.'

'He's just a boy.'

'He's a man and he's giving up his life at sea because of you, Kitty.'

'He'll soon get fed up with being ashore and be off again before you know it.'

Sophia jumped to her feet. 'I'm going to show you something. Get your coat on, Kitty.'

Walking briskly along Cheyne Walk, they were caught in yet another shower, but Sophia refused to stop until they reached Chelsea Creek and a small boatyard that had obviously seen better days. Negotiating a concrete ramp and holding up her skirts, Sophia picked her way across the mud to where a large, dilapidated craft that was little more than a hulk lay beached.

'This is the boat that Captain Jasper's agent has found for them,' Sophia said, laying her gloved hand on the flaking paintwork. 'This will be their pride and joy when it's made shipshape. This will be their very own *Mermaid Singing*.'

'But it's a hulk,' Kitty exclaimed, dismayed. 'It's a mess.'

'No,' Sophia said, smiling. 'The *Mermaid* is part of a dream, like the poem they're both so fond of. Captain Jasper and Jem are both dreamers. Their feelings run deep, only they aren't very good at expressing them.'

'I don't understand,' Kitty said, pulling up her collar as another shower spilled from the clouds.

Sophia smiled, in spite of the raindrops trickling down her cheeks. 'You may think the captain is a dried-up old bachelor but I can tell you that once, a long time ago, he was very much in love.'

'So why didn't he marry her?'

'He was ambitious and he wouldn't marry Norah until he was in a position to support a wife. Her family were wealthy and they didn't approve of their only daughter marrying a mere first mate, but she loved him and she promised to wait.'

Kitty forgot the cold east wind and the rain

that had turned to sleet. 'What happened?'

'She died of consumption just weeks before he arrived home and it broke his heart.'

'That's very sad. But what has that got to do with Jem and me?'

'Jem's like the son he never had. That's why Captain Jasper is willing to invest his life savings into this business venture. He knows what's in Jem's heart, and he wants to see you both get the chance of happiness that was denied him.'

Kitty laid her hand on the flaking paintwork of the clinker-built hull and, as a strong breeze from upriver caused the boat to rock gently on its cradle of mud, she felt a small vibration through the timbers, a faint heartbeat as though there was still a flicker of life in the craft. The clouds parted and Kitty felt the sun on her face and the wind in her hair. She closed her eyes and thought of Jem and a sudden longing surged through her veins. The loneliness of the long, cold winter melted in the warmth of the spring sunshine and with it came the realisation that she did not want to go on alone. She might strive for fame and fortune and yet still end up like Adeline who, with all her money and position, could not buy love or happiness.

'You do love that boy, I can tell,' Sophia said softly. 'Don't throw away your chance of happiness with a good man.'

'You're right,' Kitty said, shaking her head.

'And if I have to make a choice then I would put Jem first. But, Sophia, I hate the thought of spending the rest of my life in Tanner's Passage.'

'I know, my dear,' Sophia said, linking her arm through Kitty's. 'Betty and I understand more than you think. You must go home now and speak to Betty. She should be the one to tell you.'

Stunned by Betty's news, Kitty couldn't speak for a moment. Wavering between tears and laughter she clasped Betty's gnarled, rheumaticky fingers until Betty drew them away with a protest.

'It's true, ducks,' Betty said, laughing and crying at the same time. 'Sophia and me have been mulling it over for weeks, ever since we first heard about the *Mermaid*. We knew it wouldn't work with Jem and the captain practically living on board the ship and us stuck here miles away. We knew you was pining for the house in Sackville Street and we couldn't get that back for you, but we come up with something sort of in between.'

'But you can't sell this house. It's your home, Betty. You and Jem love it.'

'We love you more, ducks.' Betty fumbled in her pocket for a hanky and blew her nose. 'It's done. This house is up for sale, and me and Sophia paid a month's rent on the house in Flood Street. It ain't Mayfair but it ain't too far to Kensington, and if them rich ladies can shop at

Harrods, then they can go the distance down the King's Road to our establishment in Flood Street.'

'But this is your home. Your memories are all here. I can't let you do this.'

'My memories are all in me head and in me heart, Kitty, love. We got this far together and I ain't going to let you down now just because I'm a selfish old woman.'

'You're never selfish,' Kitty cried, flinging her arms around Betty and hugging her. 'You've been like a mother to me and I love you.'

'And I love you and so does my Jem. Whatever happens between you two, or not as the case may be, we're a family, Kitty. We stick together.' Disentangling herself from Kitty's embrace, Betty reached on top of the mantelshelf and picked up a key. She pressed it into Kitty's hand. 'This is yours, Kitty, love. The key to the future.'

The house in Flood Street was perfect. Kitty loved it from the moment she turned the key in the lock and entered the hallway. It was neither as big nor as grand as the house in Sackville Street; it needed a lick of paint and a bit of imagination to make it the elegant establishment of her dreams, but the building seemed to wrap itself around her in welcome; she felt at home the moment she set foot inside its walls. Having explored every room from the basement kitchen to the top floor, Kitty found Betty and Sophia waiting for her in the front parlour, their faces positively shining with delight at her happiness. She hugged them both in turn.

'Thank you both, thank you so much. It's perfect and I love it.' Kitty twirled around the room, touching the marble fireplace, running her fingers along the dado and coming to stand by one of the tall windows. She experimented opening and closing the wooden shutters. 'This room is just right for the salon,' she said, smiling ecstatically. 'I can see it all in my mind's eye. We'll be famous, Betty, you and I; modistes to fashionable London Society. It's just wonderful. When can we move in?'

'Whenever you like,' Betty said, exchanging satisfied smiles with Sophia. 'The sooner the better.'

'Oh, no!' Kitty cried, clapping her hand to her forehead. 'I'd forgotten Bella. How awful of me. If we leave Tanner's Passage she won't know where to find us. We can't let that woman take Leonie away from those who love her most, we just can't.'

Two weeks later, with everything in Tanner's Passage packed and Betty having sent word of their new address to Jem, by way of the New Zealand Shipping Company Offices in Whitechapel, they were ready for the move to Flood Street. But all the while, Kitty waited for news of Bella, growing more anxious as the days passed and Lady Mableton's threatened deadline approached. Finally, when it seemed that Bella could not have received her frantic messages, Kitty took the only course of action left open to her. She caught the train from Liverpool Street, getting off at Maldon, and then paid a man with a dogcart to take her to Mableton Manor.

If her visit had been for any other purpose, she would have been overjoyed to see Maggie looking so fit, well and, above all, happy. The children had grown almost out of all recognition even in such a short time. They gambolled about her: a flock of spring lambs, healthy, noisy and so full of life that it made Kitty dizzy just to watch them. She sent them off with the bags of sweets that she had brought with her and, when she was certain that they were out of earshot, she took Maggie and Maria aside to tell them the bad news.

Their reactions were much as she had expected. Maggie burst into tears at the thought of losing Leonie, who had become so much a part of her family, and Maria's temper flared into a white heat. She stamped about the room raging against Bella for abandoning Leonie while she chased her lover halfway across Europe to God knows where. Then she vented her anger on Lady Adeline and Sir Edward. She was a jumped-up farmer's daughter and he was a lily-livered, spineless, milksop. Leonie was his half-sister and Maria doubted very much whether, under such circumstances, adoption would be legal. In any event, it would be done over her dead body. Maria stomped out of the room, leaving Maggie and Kitty staring at each other.

'I never thought she cared quite so much,' Kitty said, shaking her head.

'She's a funny one, all right. But I think she feels bad about the way she treated Bella and if she gives Leonie up to the Mabletons, then she's doing the same thing all over again.'

'And Bella would be heartbroken. I know she's silly sometimes and puts herself first, but she does love Leonie and she trusts us to look after her.'

'You're right,' Maggie said, nodding vehemently. 'We was trusted to care for the nipper and this is her home, she's happy here and we all love her. She might have everything what money can buy with the toffs in Mayfair but that don't necessarily bring happiness. You can tell her ladyship from us that Leonie ain't leaving Mableton Manor. Whatever her faults, Bella is Leonie's mum, and we ain't letting her go.'

Kitty laid a hand on Maggie's arm. 'You're a brick, Maggie, and I love you. But the Mabletons are rich and powerful – what if they was to throw you out on the street?'

'It wouldn't be the first time now, would it?'

Maggie said, chuckling. She gave Kitty's hand a squeeze. 'Lord love us, don't worry about me, girl. I'm not afraid of nothing now I'm certain that Sid won't come back and spoil things.'

'But you love this place, I can tell.'

'Aye, I do, but bricks and mortar is just that. If I has to, then I'll make a home for me and the nippers somewhere else. But Leonie owns Mableton Manor, all legal and above board and I don't think even Sir Edward could argue with that.'

'I had to warn you all the same.'

'I knows you did, love, and you done right. We're happy here and Maria and me have cleaned the house up lovely.' Maggie hooked her arm around Kitty's shoulders. 'Come with me and I'll show you what we done, though there's still a lot more to do.'

'It's wonderful to see you all settled and looking so well,' Kitty said, smiling.

'And it's going to stay that way. Bugger the Mabletons and their money. We'll let Maria calm down a bit and then we'll have a nice family supper, all of us together. We got fresh eggs from our very own chickens and vegetables from the garden. Our Frankie has turned into a proper little green fingers.'

Next day, Kitty said a reluctant goodbye, kissing everyone, even Frankie, who now considered that at ten he was the man of the house and had wanted to shake hands, but gave in after a bit of persuasion, even if afterwards he ostentatiously wiped his cheek on his sleeve. Kitty kissed Billy and Charlie, although they pretended that kissing was sloppy and copied Frankie by wiping their cheeks on their shirtsleeves, hooting with laughter. Violet and Leonie clung to her, hugging her and begging her to come again soon and Harry, at five, didn't mind being kissed and cuddled in the slightest.

Maria held out a dry, weathered cheek and allowed Kitty to give her a peck. 'Goodbye, Kitty. Tell that woman if she sets foot in this place I'll let the dogs loose on her.'

Kitty nodded, choking back a lump in her throat as she kissed Maggie and gave her an extra special hug. 'I'll come again soon, I promise.'

'You bring Jem with you next time,' Maggie said, smiling and crying at the same time. 'And Betty too. Come again soon.'

Steam from the engine blew past the train windows in great, cotton wool clouds and the wheels made a rhythmic clackety-clack sound as they sped over the iron rails. Kitty closed her eyes and let her mind drift to a peaceful dreamlike state. Maggie and the children were well and happy and, if the Mabletons caused